HE WAS FREE!

The smell of men surrounded him, acrid with fear. He leaped at the throat of one who backed away from him.

A loud crack, a sharp sting on his flank, an unpleasant stink, then his teeth sank into flesh and the hot, salty tang of blood flooded his tongue. But something wasn't right about the taste. He turned from the kill and ran down a fleeing man who stabbed at him with something sharp. As he broke the man's back he remembered its name. A knife. He turned, snarling, to the only man left on his feet.

"Jesus!" the man shouted, backing away. "A goddamn beast!" The man turned, sprang through an opening, and jumped to the ground.

He followed and the man died. But the taste of the man's blood was wrong and he spat it out. He craved blood, but not this kind. He'd leave the men and run under the moon, hunting.

Then he heard her calling his name, even as clouds covered the moon. Keeping to the deepest shadows, he loped toward the wall. But before he reached it, he felt a twisting, a terrible wrenching and then—he changed. . . .

Moonrunner #1:

UNDER THE SHADOW

Jane Toombs

A ROC BOOK

With special thanks to Jacqueline Lichtenburg.

ROC
Published by the Penguin Group
Penguin Books USA Inc., 375 Hudson Street,
New York, New York 10014, U.S.A.
Penguin Books Ltd, 27 Wrights Lane,
London W8 5TZ, England
Penguin Books Australia Ltd, Ringwood,
Victoria, Australia
Penguin Books Canada Ltd, 10 Alcorn Avenue,
Toronto, Ontario, Canada M4V 3B2
Penguin Books (N.Z.) Ltd, 182–190 Wairau Road,
Auckland 10, New Zealand

Penguin Books Ltd, Registered Offices:
Harmondsworth, Middlesex, England

First published by Roc, an imprint of New American Library,
a division of Penguin Books USA Inc.

First Printing, July, 1992
10 9 8 7 6 5 4 3 2 1

Printed in the United States of America

Chapter 1

He floated alone in darkness, the tiny flame of his awareness the only light in the stygian gloom. The flame flickered, fading; he had no will to keep it aglow. As he drifted closer to the dark shore of no return, a beam of blue energy seared across the blackness and, drawn to the power, his life force flared anew, growing as it fed on the surging fountain of energy.

Before he came to full awareness, the source he fed from cut off abruptly. He mouthed a soundless cry and opened his eyes. Pain speared through his head.

He lay naked, sprawled on his back on damp sand, just beyond the sea's reach. Overhead, fog blanketed the sun. Though the sand chilled the bare flesh of his back, he was covered with cloth that snagged on his roughened hands as he fingered its smoothness. Silk?

A midnight blue silken cape.

"I was right!" a woman's voice cried in triumph. "You see, *Tía* Dolores, he lives."

His mind automatically translated her words into his own language. Making a major effort, he tried to turn his head toward the speaker. A woman's pale face appeared in his vision as she bent over him. Dark eyes gazed worriedly into his. Her black hair, partially covered by a shawl, framed an attractive oval face whose soft pink lips looked more accustomed to smiling than being tightened in distress.

He'd never seen her before. Where was he?

His heart leaped in panic as he reached for memories and found a gray blankness. Pain tightened pincers against his skull as his mind roiled desperately, searching for a clue. Somewhere in the grayness a spool unwound a tiny thread of recollection—a man naked on a beach, a beautiful woman coming to his rescue with her servants; a princess rescuing a half-drowned adventurer.

"Nausicaa," he whispered, identifying the princess.

"I can't hear you," she said. "Is that your name?"

His name. He closed his eyes in despair. A man was no one with his name gone.

What was his name?

"I tell you he is of the dark one," warned a second woman's voice, this one cracked with age. "*Diablo's* servant."

"He's no more of the devil than you are, *Tía* Dolores," Nausicaa said tartly. Her fingers brushed his forehead, light as alder down.

He opened his eyes again, searching for the second speaker. She stood to one side of Nausicaa, an ancient crone in black glaring malevolently at him. A glimmer of blue energy crackled around her and he drew in his breath as he recognized the life source he'd fed on. The old woman possessed power.

Nausicaa's energy aura was normal, no more than a faint reddish glow.

How did he know these things and not his name?

"Who are you?" Nausicaa asked softly.

She wasn't Nausicaa, he realized confusedly. What he'd remembered was a tale—a Greek tale of a shipwrecked sailor cursed by the sea god who was washing onto the Phoenician shore, where he was befriended by the king's daughter. The name of the god-cursed sailor Nausicaa had rescued slid into his mind.

"Ulysses." He had difficulty pushing the word past his bruised throat.

"Les?" she echoed.

"*Diablo,*" the old woman muttered. "His name is *El Diablo.*"

He caught sight of a small black animal at the corner of his vision, an animal edging around a boulder to pad toward Nausicaa. A dog?

It stopped suddenly, turning its head to stare at him, then spat, tail erect, fur bristling.

"*Koshka!*" he exclaimed hoarsely, naming the cat in his own language. The black cat flew to the old crone and hid behind her skirts.

A witch, he thought. She's a witch and the cat is her ally.

"You see," the witch hissed. "Sombrito knows him for what he is."

Sombrito, the man repeated to himself, translating. The cat's name is Little Shadow. They're speaking Spanish and I understand the language though it's not mine. What am I if not Spanish?

"Señor Koshka?" Nausicaa said.

Mr. Cat. Why not? His true name was beyond his reach and Señor Koshka was as good as any other.

"Where am I?" he asked, trying to ease himself to a sitting position.

Nausicaa reached to help him sit, her hands white and soft as they grasped his arm. His head whirled dizzily and he stifled a groan as his bruised body protested the shift in position. The blue silk cape fell to his waist and he adjusted it hastily around him, noting an already healing gash on his chest. He lifted a hand to his aching head, finding sticky, matted hair over a painful lump.

"You are on the Alvarado rancho, my father's land," she said.

"Don Alfonso won't like this," the witch muttered.

He stared at Nausicaa. Alvarado land. Spain? He looked around at the boulder-littered beach, at the golden hills rolling away from the water.

"Señorita Alvarado," he said. "Where is your father's land located?"

"To the south of San Francisco," she told him.

A word slithered free of the grayness clouding his mind. California. He was on a California beach.

The old woman ventured close enough to tug at Nausicaa's arm. "Come away," she urged. "Your soul is in peril."

"*Tía* Dolores, you're making me impatient," Nausicaa declared. "Señor Koshka is injured. He needs our help, and all you can do is mutter about the devil."

"What will Don Alfonso say when you arrive at the casa with a naked stranger wrapped in your cape?" the old woman demanded.

Nausicaa flushed. He could see she was embarrassed and upset by the witch's words. The black cat leaped atop a rock and glared down at him balefully. His head throbbed with pain and confusion.

"Señor Koshka, I mean to help you, but there is a problem,'' Nausicaa said finally, clasping her hands together tightly. ''If you were to come with us now, my father might not . . . understand. But if someone brought clothes to you . . .'' She paused, her eyes traveling over him shyly but with determination as she estimated his size. ''You are tall,'' she added. ''What clothes we have may not be a good fit. *Tía* Dolores will—''

''No,'' the witch muttered. ''I won't bring him clothes. Such as he deserves nothing.''

''You'll see that it's done or I'll never forgive you, in this world or the next.'' Nausicaa's voice rose angrily. ''Mind what I say.''

The old woman glowered at her in silence.

''I'm sorry to make you wait.'' Nausicaa bit her lip as she looked at him. ''I can see you're in pain. A man will soon come with clothes and help you to our hacienda.''

''You've already saved my life, señorita. You and your companion.'' He glanced at the old woman as he finished speaking, wondering if she knew he lived because of her energy transfer.

Her malevolent gaze told him she did and regretted it. Why? What made her so certain he was allied to the devil?

Who was he? What was he doing in California? How had he been hurt so badly he'd almost died?

His mind provided no answers to any of the questions.

Why couldn't he remember?

''I must go,'' Nausicaa—no, Señorita Alvarado—said, leaving him with a farewell smile.

He watched her walk away, carrying herself with the proud confidence of a princess. Neither she nor the old crone looked back. The cat had disappeared. A snippet of memory teased him. Something about cats. Cats were dangerous.

Dangerous? He blinked. Cats were a source of danger only to small rodents and birds. Why to him? He seized his head in both hands, squeezing, trying to force his mind to disgorge what lay hidden from him in its depths. A dizzying jab through his skull was the only result. He dropped his hands, defeated.

Forcing himself to his feet, he noted that moving hurt less than it had at first. To be expected. His kind recovered quickly.

His kind? What in the name of God did that mean?

His mind refused to answer.

Gathering the silk cape, he wrapped it around his hips and thighs, tucking it in tightly at the waist. The smooth material stroked his bare flesh as he limped into the surf. He looked to the north, seeing smoke beyond the hills that lay between him and what Señorita Alvarado had called San Francisco. He knew the name. And more.

Gold. San Francisco and gold. California and gold.

Nothing else surfaced. He gave up the effort to remember and gazed southward. Not even smoke—nothing but hills and the sea. The Pacific Ocean. With the scent of brine in his nostrils, he stared westward over the waves, seeing the black smudge of islands; but what their names were, he didn't know.

Far out on the water a three-master sailed northeast. Had he been in a shipwreck? He stared around him. No telltale debris from a wreck littered the sands. Possibly he'd been a sailor who'd fallen overboard.

Then why the bruises? He glanced at his chest. The wound there—a knife slash, by its looks—had all but closed over. Gingerly, he felt his head. The lump was smaller. He healed fast.

They meant to kill me. He didn't understand how he knew this, but he did. He had no idea who "they" were or what he'd done to invite slaying.

Alone and naked, no possessions, not even a name. He wouldn't know an enemy from a friend. He could trust no one, with the possible exception of Señorita Alvarado. She promised to be a friend. He desperately needed a friend, but *Tía* Dolores was already an enemy. He'd have to watch her carefully since she'd set herself so determinedly against him.

He searched for the Spanish word to describe her. *Curandera,* a healer? More than that. *Bruja,* witch, was a better name for her. He'd do well to steer clear of her entirely.

He paced back and forth along the waterline, his legs strengthening as he walked so that his limp grew less and less pronounced, finally disappearing. The bruises changed from ugly blue-black to an equally unappetizing yellow-green, the knife cut closed over, the lump on his head vanished. Should he stay or leave?

Señorita Alvarado had promised clothes; he needed them. Unfortunately she'd left it up to the *bruja* to order them sent.

Obviously, the old woman would prefer to give quite another command to whoever came. And might well do so.

If he did leave, where would he go? Whatever he decided, he had to regain his strength fast. Since he had no weapons, there was nothing else to depend on. Once he was back to normal, he'd be difficult to kill.

How did he know that? Damn his memory for teasing him with bits and pieces and refusing to yield the whole.

He windmilled his arms, then twisted his torso one way and another, exercising, keeping a wary eye and ear out. Time passed. The sun's rays splintered the fog into wisps that the sea breeze scattered into nothingness. Warmth caressed his bare shoulders. He squinted at the sky. Near noon. Hunger gripped his stomach.

He forgot the pangs when he heard hoofbeats. One horseman. Had *Tía* Dolores sent friend or foe? Or was the rider someone else, someone who knew him? Assume the worst. He chose a fist-sized rock from those scattered on the sand and, holding it, concealed the rock among the folds of the cape. Feet apart, his back to the ocean, he faced the rise, waiting.

A mustached vaquero dressed in working clothes rode onto the beach. He was a big man, in his thirties, hard-faced and unsmiling. The man reined in the horse and stared down at him.

This man was no friend.

He met the vaquero's hostile gaze. "You bring me clothes. Where are they?"

The horseman hesitated an instant too long. In one smooth motion, the man on foot flung the rock. It struck the vaquero's temple and a half-drawn pistol fell from his suddenly limp grasp. He swayed, sagged, and slipped off the horse's left side, slumping unconscious onto the sand.

"Easy, boy, you're with a friend," the man on foot crooned to the sidling horse, grasping the reins. When he had the stallion calmed and tethered, he bent over the vaquero.

"How kind of you to bring clothes for me," he said, his face twisting into a grimace as he caught the rancid odor. "I could wish you were taller and that you washed oftener."

Otherwise, the horseman's clothes, including his excellent boots, weren't a bad fit.

"Ulysses Koshka," he muttered to himself as he rode

with the still limp, but now naked, vaquero draped across the horse in front of him. He allowed the stallion to choose the direction, certain it would head for the rancho.

He'd face more danger there, of that he was sure, but he knew its source and confronting the *bruja* was preferable to being chased as a horse thief. He didn't care much for the name he'd concocted. Still, it *was* a name, and so better than the blank in his mind. It was all he could offer to Don Alfonso and he was aware it might not be enough when the rancho's owner asked who he was and where he came from.

Neither he nor the name were Spanish, though he spoke the language with little effort. The don would certainly recognize this, despite the fact he was as dark as most Spaniards. He had to have a story ready: it was perilous to tell the truth, to admit he had no memory of how he came to be lying more than half dead on Don Alfonso's beach. A man with no memories was, in a sense, defenseless.

Ulysses was sure the vaquero had meant to kill him, but he also knew there'd been no recognition in the man's eyes. The horseman, he had no doubt, had been sent on *Tía* Dolores's orders to get rid of a dangerous stranger. She might hate and fear him, but she'd made it clear she'd never seen him before. Nor had the señorita. This didn't mean it was safe to bet that the don didn't know him, but he had a hunch it was the truth.

Ulysses Koshka, flotsam from the sea. He nodded. He'd make his a story of betrayal, one he vowed to avenge someday. For all he knew, that might even be what had happened. Pray God he'd soon remember. Meanwhile, he'd keep the pistol handy.

He rode over hills golden with long grass. Here and there clumps of trees clustered along watercourses. In the distance, long-horned cattle foraged. Higher hills humped to the east. Had he ever seen California before? Nothing looked familiar, but Ulysses felt a tug of belonging. The land appealed to him.

He topped a rise and the hacienda spread out before him, adobe walls sealing in the red-tiled casa. Could he reach the gate without challenge? A *compadre* of the vaquero would certainly recognize this spirited stallion. If the man also recognized the clothes Ulysses wore, there'd be trouble.

Ulysses slowed, removed the folded blue cape from a

saddlebag, and wrapped the silken folds around him to conceal as much of the clothes as possible. He'd have to trust to luck that no one would recognize the cape as Señorita Alvarado's.

As he neared the walls, an armed horseman rode to intercept him, commanding him to halt.

Ulysses slowed the chestnut stallion but continued to ride toward the rancho. "I bring an injured man to the hacienda," he shouted. "He needs care. Let me pass!"

"El Duro!" the vaquero cried, his eyes on the horse Ulysses rode.

Ulysses knew he couldn't give the man time to think. "*Tía* Dolores will know what to do for El Duro's master," he said, pushing the stallion on toward the wooden gate set in the adobe walls, hoping he was right about the old woman's status in the Alvarado household.

The vaquero hesitated, eyes flicking from the chestnut to Ulysses. Finally he wheeled his horse to ride alongside them, just as the naked man draped across El Duro groaned and twitched. The chestnut danced sideways. Putting what he hoped was a quieting hand on the still limp figure sprawled in front of him, Ulysses leaned forward to murmur into the stallion's ear. The horse calmed.

Ulysses looked up to find his escort staring at him with his mouth open. He tensed, but the man made no move. Then they were at the gate and the Alvarado horseman dismounted to open it. He waved Ulysses inside the gate and closed it behind horse and man, remaining on the other side.

The injured vaquero groaned again.

Ulysses slid off the chestnut. "Not just yet, amigo," he said under his breath. "My story gets told before yours."

He yanked off the silk cape and crammed it back into a saddlebag. Leaving horse and man, he strode up the white path, bootheels crunching shells. The red-tiled adobe was two-story, with a balcony, a rambling casa built around a courtyard. Red and pink flowering shrubs sweetened the air and a brilliant magenta vine clung to the house wall.

Ulysses reached the massive oak door and lifted his hand to the iron knocker, shaped like a double eagle. He froze, a revelation flickering evil as a corpse light, something from the depths of his soul that chilled his blood. Before he could grasp its import, the memory winked out.

Shaking his head, he grasped the knocker firmly, raised the black eagles, and let them fall against the iron plate.

A woman, old and dressed in black like *Tía* Dolores, opened the door, frowned at him, then gaped past him at the horse and the naked man on El Duro's back.

"Find *Tía* Dolores and bring her to care for the man," Ulysses ordered, "but first take me to Don Alfonso, Pronto!"

Without speaking, she led him through the house to the courtyard. As he passed the rooms, Ulysses noted that the furnishings, though not cheap, seemed slightly shabby.

In the courtyard, Don Alfonso stood beside a flower-girdled pool where fish glinted gold in the still water. He stood a head shorter than Ulysses, but his erect carriage made him appear taller than he was. The gray in his hair and the lines in his thin, tanned face marked him as old, at least fifty. Cold dark eyes measured Ulysses as he crossed the bricks toward the don.

Ulysses bent his head briefly in greeting. "I am Ulysses Koshka," he said. "I brought one of your men back unconscious. Your housekeeper is tending to him. I regret the necessity of having to borrow his clothes and his horse."

Don Alfonso's eyes widened momentarily as he reexamined Ulysses, taking special note of the boots he wore. "You speak of Don Rafael?"

Ulysses shrugged. "Your vaquero produced a pistol rather than his name."

"You wear Don Rafael's clothes. Are you telling me you rode El Duro?"

"I rode a chestnut stallion with a white blaze. He now stands before the casa with his master lying across his back."

The don kept his gaze on Ulysses for long moments. Ulysses stared back, doing his best to ignore the pistol that rested atop a blue-tiled rustic table, within easy reach of the Spaniard. He had time to wonder why Don Alfonso would need a pistol so close to hand in the safety of his own casa, before the don finally spoke.

"I will listen to your story."

"Your man accosted me on the beach. No doubt on your property, although I did not realize I was trespassing. He was mounted and armed. I was afoot, naked, I had no weapon. He drew his pistol and, believing he meant to shoot me, I threw a stone that hit his head. I am not a violent man, nor a thief. I chose not to remain naked while I returned the man and his horse to where they belonged, so I borrowed his clothes. The horse guided me here."

"Don Rafael is not my hired man," the don said. "He is a neighbor who kindly helps me with the cattle. You have made a lifelong enemy."

"He set himself to be my enemy before he knew me. I was dangerous to no one, naked and unarmed. Don Rafael's possible vengeance is not my concern. I have revenge of my own to tend to, vengeance against those aboard ship who conspired to rob me of all I possessed, who tried to kill me and then dropped me overboard to drown. God's favor alone brought me to shore."

Ulysses watched Don Alfonso carefully as he told the tale he'd concocted. Had the Spaniard relaxed ever so slightly?

"I must throw myself on your mercy," he continued. "I have been left with nothing."

Don Alfonso's lips twitched slightly, as though he might be repressing a smile. "You have Don Rafael's horse and his clothes," he pointed out. "Also, I suspect, his pistol."

"Borrowed only," Ulysses said.

The don nodded once, then again, as though he'd made up his mind. "If you rode El Duro and lived to tell of it, you are good with horses."

"I am." Although his mind released no memories of horsemanship, deep within himself Ulysses felt he spoke the truth.

"You are not a Spaniard, though you speak the language well. I can tell you're not one of those bastard Americanos, either. Your name is Greek?"

"I am not Americano," Ulysses agreed. "My name is Greek."

Again the don's lips twitched. "You are a man of few words, Señor Koshko, but I don't hold that against you. I happen to need vaqueros. In this way I can offer you assistance."

Ulysses took a deep breath, unsure of how he'd convinced the don to help him, but relieved that he had. He bowed. "I'd be honored to work for you."

"I will see to clothes for you. You may return Rafael's."

"*Gracias.*" Ulysses eyed the don. "I doubt he'll be happy to have me working here."

"That is as certain as sunrise tomorrow. But Don Rafael is my friend and he knows how it is with me. While you ride as my vaquero he will keep his peace. I expect the same from you."

"You have my word I have no quarrel with anyone except the men aboard the ship."

Don Alfonso held out his right hand. Ulysses, starting to reach his to meet it, suddenly held, staring in startled disbelief at the Spaniard's palm. A reddish glow discolored the skin as a five-pointed symbol enclosed in a circle formed. Even as he gaped, the star faded and was gone. Ulysses swallowed, forcing himself to grip the don's hand and shake it while ice formed along his spine.

Danger!

What from, he didn't know. But he knew he'd seen the star within a circle before. To his kind, the symbol meant death. Shaken to the depths of his being, he did his best to show nothing of what he felt.

Death stalked him here, too, it seemed. Desperately, he struggled to unblock his mind, but grayness covered everything except the few shards he'd already grasped.

What *was* his kind? Had he walked into a trap that even now clamped iron jaws about him?

Yet where else could he go?

Chapter 2

"They don't know what to make of me, Palo," Ulysses told his bay stallion as they rode out alone on the last day of February. "Who can blame them? I'm a mystery even to myself. Would you believe I don't know how old I am? I told the don eighteen because that number occurred to me. But am I? I'm never sure what I'll have to lie about next."

Palo flicked his ears and continued his steady lope toward the twenty or more long-horned steers grazing in one of the small valleys north of the Alvarado hacienda.

It was a fine, clear day, the only clouds high and wispy. Tonight, Ulysses thought, would be clear as well, unless the fog rolled in from the ocean as it sometimes did. He relished the mild and pleasant climate of these shores he'd been cast upon. All in all, he'd been fortunate where he'd washed ashore.

He was one of the three vaqueros working what remained of the don's cattle, but he always rode alone. Don Rafael spoke to him only if absolutely necessary and Juan took his cues from Don Rafael. As long as Don Alfonso remained cordial, Ulysses could shrug off the unfriendliness of the others—but it rankled.

Horses took to him, and so did the cows, the rancho dogs, and other livestock—even Esperanza's pet parrot. The only animal that mistrusted him was *Tía* Dolores's cat.

To hell with the cat and its glowering mistress—he'd much rather think of pretty Esperanza. At least the don's daughter smiled at him when they met. Not that they met often enough to suit him. He'd like to get better acquainted with her, but the old witch was always hovering about, a malevolent and formidable chaperone.

A formidable enemy, for that matter. The *bruja* had already tried to have him killed once. At the moment she was the dangerous one, not Don Rafael. In the three weeks he'd been working here, he'd learned enough about Spanish—or Californio—pride and honor to understand that the don had been right when he insisted Don Rafael would never exact revenge for his humiliation as long as Don Alfonso stood behind Ulysses.

If only he could remember some small part of his past, enough to furnish a clue to who he was, what he was. All he could be certain of was that he wasn't of Spanish descent, nor Americano, because neither of those languages was the one he used when he thought or spoke to himself.

He trusted the don and, because the Spaniard hated and mistrusted the Americanos, Ulysses was inclined to view them suspiciously even though he'd discovered that he knew a fair amount of their language—how or why, he had no idea.

Perhaps he really had been a sailor on a ship with men from many lands. That was the story he'd given the don yesterday after he'd translated for the Spaniard when an Americano visitor arrived unannounced.

The stranger, Henry Penfield, blustering and red-faced, had offered to buy the rancho. "Tell the don he might as well sell to me," Penfield had said, "because I'll get the land one way or the other anyway. California's a territory of the United States now and soon she'll be a state. When that happens, you Mexicans might as well skedaddle back to your own country."

There'd been no tactful way to translate Penfield's words.

"*¡Vamos!*" Don Alfonso had shouted. "Get out and never set foot on my land again."

After Penfield left and the don calmed down a bit, Ulysses cautiously asked a question. "What did he mean by Mexicans, sir? I thought you were Spanish."

The don stared at him for a long moment. "Surely you've heard that twenty-eight years ago Mexico fought for and won the right to be free of the Spanish yoke."

Ulysses covered as best he could. "I am not of these shores, sir, and it appears my education has been sadly remiss."

"I'm not certain what shores you *are* from."

Determined to keep his faulty memory hidden, Ulysses said, "I would gladly tell you, if I was at liberty to do so."

Giving him a stern, not altogether satisfied look, the don finally nodded. "I'll let it pass for the moment. If you weren't aware of Mexico's freedom from Spain, then you undoubtedly know nothing of what's happened to us Californios since the bedamned Americanos defeated our great General Santa Anna.

"California was a part of Mexico until exactly one year ago this month. As a result of losing the war with the United States, Alta California was ceded to them, leaving us Californios abandoned by our own country. If that wasn't misfortune enough, some fool had to stumble on gold nuggets."

The don had slammed his fist on the table. "Gold! This cursed California gold lures more of those damned Americanos here every month. This is my land and I will kill any man who tries to take it from me."

Ulysses believed him. He also had an uneasy premonition it might come to that. He'd noticed how arrogantly the Americanos behaved, as though they had a divine right to California land, no matter who it belonged to. And he'd heard talk of a hacienda south of the Alvarado rancho that had been sacked and burned, supposedly by bandits. The family—two sons, a mother, and a father—had been murdered.

Since he was neither Spanish, Mexican, nor Americano, California wasn't his country, but if fighting began, Ulysses knew he was squarely on the don's side.

"What and where *is* my country?" he asked Palo. "What is this tongue I speak to myself and to you?"

Palo raised his head, his ears pricked forward, and Ulysses came alert, his right hand reaching for the stock of the rifle in his saddle scabbard, his gaze searching for approaching riders. Because he had no past, all men were strangers and all strangers were potential enemies.

He sensed them before they crested the rise—two men, neither with dangerous energy levels. He reined in Palo, resting the rifle across his thighs. As he waited for the two riders to appear, he tried to understand how he sensed the men before he could see or hear them. He'd learned in the last three weeks that no one else at the Alvarado rancho had his ability. Except for the *bruja.* And that scared the hell out of him.

As soon as he saw the men, he knew by their clothes they were Americanos. He didn't quite aim the rifle at them, but he made sure they knew he was armed. They halted just over the crest, some sixty paces away. One was stocky, running to fat, the other black-bearded, lean, and rangy. Both wore holstered pistols.

"*¡Hola!*" Blackbeard called in Spanish.

"You're on Alvarado land," Ulysses called in return, speaking their Americano tongue. "What's your business here?"

"We've come to buy beef."

Aware Don Alfonso would starve before selling anything to an Americano, Ulysses replied, "We have none to spare."

Blackbeard gestured toward the steers below. "I see twenty head right there."

Ulysses repeated, "We have none to spare. And you're trespassing." He shifted the rifle.

Stocky's hand went to the butt of his pistol and Ulysses raised the rifle. Blackbeard spoke to his companion, his voice too low for Ulysses to hear, and Stocky took his hand away.

The two men wheeled their horses. At the crest of the hill, Stocky turned. "We'll be back, you Mexican bastard," he shouted.

And I'll be waiting for you, Ulysses told them silently, his lips drawing back over his teeth.

When Don Alfonso first gave him the rifle, the gun felt familiar in his hands, though he couldn't be sure what kind of a shot he was until he fired a few for practice. The first two were way off target, the third close, and the fourth smashed the empty bottle he'd balanced on a rock. Either he was a quick study or he'd fired a rifle many times before. Stocky didn't know how close he'd come to death.

When he was sure the men were gone, Ulysses shoved the rifle back into the scabbard. He urged Palo toward the cattle, intending to move them to a different location in case Shorty and Blackbeard came back that night. He wasn't certain they were after the steers, but it was best to take no chances. If the fog held off, the full moon would—

A shudder ran through him as something devil-dark slithered from behind the gray curtain shrouding his past. For a moment he shook like an alder leaf in an autumn gale, and then the sinister half-recollection faded and was gone before he could grasp its import.

A warning sprang into his mind.

The full moon brings death.

Unnerved, Ulysses rounded up the cattle. By the time he'd driven them from the little valley to new grazing closer to the hacienda, he'd recovered his equilibrium. He was damned if he'd let a full moon—or anything else—stop him.

When he rode in that evening, he reported the trespass to Don Alfonso but didn't mention his own plans for the night.

As usual, he ate with Juan in the vaquero quarters outside the fenced courtyard—the food brought to them by Paquita, the old cook. Ulysses was glad that Don Rafael never waited to eat, returning to his own casa when the day's work was finished. He suspected, though, if Don Rafael did stay, he'd eat inside with Don Alfonso and Esperanza, since he was not a hired worker but a neighbor.

Ulysses had pried from a reluctant Juan that Don Rafael had no cattle of his own—they'd either all been sold or run off by Americanos. Nor did Don Rafael have relatives in his casa.

"Like me, like Don Alfonso, Don Rafael has cousins in Mexico," Juan had said. "But no one here."

As they sat eating their *puchero,* a spicy stew, and tortillas, Ulysses made his plans. Not wishing to reveal his intentions to anyone, he'd wait until the other man slept before saddling Palo and riding.

It lacked an hour of midnight before Ulysses was finally ready to leave. The moon had risen just after sunset, but patchy clouds had alternately hidden and revealed it. At the moment the moon was cloud-covered. Feeling strangely restless, he swung into the saddle and rode from the corral, only to rein in abruptly when a figure in white crossed his path.

"Esperanza!" he exclaimed, dismounting.

She drifted toward him, stopping only a few feet away. "Señor Koshka," she said softly.

In her filmy white robe, she was a fairy-tale creature, a beautiful and desirable princess. He stared at her hungrily, wishing he had the right to claim her for his own.

"How your eyes gleam," she whispered, shivering, yet making no effort to flee from him.

"You shouldn't be outside the gate so late at night and alone," he warned.

"I feel restless tonight."

"The courtyard is safer."

"Would I have met you inside the gates?"

His heart pounded at the implication. Did she have any idea how he'd dreamed of finding her alone? Unable to help himself, he held out his arms to her. She hesitated, then reached to him until he clasped her hands. But when he tried to draw her close, she resisted. He forced himself to stop, fighting his arousal.

"Why are you riding Palo so late?" she asked.

Unsettled by her sweet and provocative woman's scent and the feel of her soft hands in his, he told her he meant to spend the night guarding her father's cattle against Americano thieves.

"But you may be hurt," she protested.

"Not me." Aware he wouldn't be able to control himself much longer, he released her hands, strode to the gate, and opened it. "I mean to see you safely inside before I leave."

By the time the gate had closed behind her and he was back in the saddle, the clouds had dissipated and the moon rode the sky, pale and luminous. Ulysses' insides churned. He dug his heels in, urging the bay into a lope, heedless of the perils of night riding. The quicker he left and the farther away he got from Esperanza, the better.

He was halfway to the valley when his inner churning turned to wrenching pains. Palo whinnied shrilly and reared. Ulysses, taken by surprise, lost his seat and sprawled onto the ground. He lay there for a moment, half stunned, listening to the frightened horse pounding back toward the hacienda.

What in hell had spooked Palo?

As he dragged himself upright to look around, something twisted hard inside his gut. *Free!* a voice inside his head demanded. *Free!* He found himself yanking off his boots, then tearing at his clothes in a wild desire to have nothing between him and the moon, full and bright above him.

Its silver rays bathed him, seeping inside to quicken his blood. To change him.

"No!" he shouted, terrified. "No!"

In vain. He had no more control over what was happening to him than he had over the moon. As he felt himself wrenching out of shape, exhilaration eroded his panic and sang through him.

Free! The night was his, the moon was his. He'd been set free to run.

His senses were overwhelmed by a multitude of odors and sounds—a rabbit, frozen with fright, crouched nearby to his left; a hunting owl, almost overhead, veered suddenly to avoid flying over him; and, some yards to his right, an alarmed steer caught his scent.

A craving gripped him, a need to hunt, to kill, to feast on his prey. The owl was beyond his reach, the rabbit beneath his notice. The steer, then. As he dropped to all fours, another smell drifted to him on the night wind, the intriguing and dangerous scent of man. He lifted his muzzle to better ascertain the direction.

The man rode a horse, the two of them upwind from him. The horse would scent him before the man saw him but not until they rode closer. Still, he dared not take a chance on giving way to the bloodlust, because then he'd be oblivious to all else. He fought his ever-increasing desire to run down the steer—now fleeing toward the man. Men could never be trusted. Men tracked his kind, tracked to kill.

Yet he'd marked the steer as his prey and refused to give it up. Once the steer no longer scented him, it would slow and stop somewhere beyond the man and horse. Stealth, not speed, would allow him to circle and remain safely upwind of his prey without being sighted by the man.

The bright moonlight made concealment difficult, so he detoured to take advantage of the shadows under a string of sycamores bordering a nearby stream. As he trotted swiftly along the bank of the stream, the damp smell of leaf mold mingled with odor traces of birds and mice and, once, the fear-rank scent of fox. The animals feared him, one and all. Men did, too, but men were craftier than any other animal. Except him—unless he was consumed by bloodlust and lost all sense of his surroundings.

Far away a wolf sang to the moon, his cries thinner and higher than remembered wolf songs from long ago. Soon a dozen or more joined the first. Their name flashed into his mind. Coyotes. Brother to the wolf.

Their cries thrilled through him. How glorious to be free, to feel the brush of the wind through his fur and to test each scent the wind carried. The moon, climbing the sky, filled him with its silver radiance. The moon was his; he belonged to the moon.

Soon the prey would be his as well, its hot blood salt-sweet on his tongue. Nothing else could satisfy the craving within him, a craving growing stronger and wilder with every passing moment.

The scent of horse and man and steer mingled. He scanned the silvered darkness with night-adapted eyes. There, ahead and to the left. The man shouted, seeing the steer, then yanked the horse sharply about and rode in pursuit. The steer increased its pace and veered toward the stream.

The man had no right to prey marked by him! For him! Rage overcame caution and he sprang from the concealing shadows to intercept horse and rider. Before he reached them, a loud crack assaulted his ears, an offensive stink filled his nostrils, and the steer stumbled, falling into the water of the stream.

He raced on. The horse shied from him, rearing, while the rider fought for control. He sprang, tumbling the man from the horse as it screamed and died, its neck broken. With the first taste of blood, his world turned red. With the bloodlust mastering him, he scarcely heard the second crack or felt the sting searing his temple. . . .

Ulysses opened his eyes to the grayness of predawn, his head aching and the remnants of a nightmare clouding his mind. He immediately took alarm. Where in hell was he and why was he naked and shivering? He sprang to his feet and staggered with weakness as he warily scanned his surroundings. He stood on the bank of a creek with not a living soul in sight—but death lay upstream.

Cautiously, he made his way along the bank until he gazed with horror on what and who had died so bloodily. A half-eaten steer lay in the water. Close beside the steer was a man's body so badly mangled Ulysses couldn't be sure whether or not it was the stocky man he'd seen the previous day. Farther from the stream, the torn remains of a horse mingled unpleasantly with riding gear and a rifle. A pistol lay between the man and the horse.

Ulysses couldn't bring himself to touch the gore-besmeared rifle, but he reached for the pistol and, as he did, saw his hand was encrusted with dark blood. He recoiled, fragments of his nightmare flitting like bats across his appalled mind. He'd dreamed of death and killing, dreamed of running on all fours under the moon, dreamed of the taste of blood.

His head throbbed so painfully that, without thought, he raised his bloodstained hand to his temple. To his surprise, his fingers encountered a healing but still aching wound running across the side of his head. He closed his eyes in momentary thankfulness—that must be where the blood on his hand had come from. His nightmare had been no more than a terrible dream, though it had left him weak and shaken.

But he was no closer to understanding what he was doing here. What had brought him to this spot? What horror had happened here? Striding to the creek, he rinsed his hands in the cold water and splashed cold water over his face, shivering in the cool breeze.

Where in hell were his clothes?

Putting aside the problem of what had happened during the night, he backtracked to where he'd awakened and then walked farther downstream, searching for his clothes. When he finally found them twenty paces away from the bank, he was more confused than ever.

Dressing hastily, he went over what he remembered of the night before. He'd planned to camp in the little valley in case the Americanos returned, so he'd ridden from the hacienda on Palo. He vaguely recalled feeling sick and being thrown by the normally obedient bay. Tracks showed a horse had been near the clothes but had galloped back toward the corral. Obviously something had spooked Palo.

Possibly whatever had killed the two animals and the man. A grizzly? He'd never seen one, but Juan had told him about the Californio bull and bear fights, a bull and a grizzly either chained together or put into a pit and aggravated until they turned on one another. He moved his shoulders uneasily. Why had he been spared? He touched the scab on his head. A wound from a grizzly's claws?

His troubled mind and aching head distracted him so that he almost missed the approach of two riders from the direction of the hacienda. He whirled to look, cursing himself because he hadn't picked up the pistol. Chances were the riders would be Juan and Don Rafael, but even so he'd feel safer with a gun. He relaxed slightly when he saw one of the men had a riderless horse on lead. They must be from the hacienda, searching for him and bringing Palo.

As they neared, he realized he was right about Juan but not the other—Don Alfonso himself accompanied the vaquero. If he had his choice, he preferred the don to Rafael. He walked to meet them.

When they came up to him, he took Palo's reins from Juan and swung into the saddle, saying, "I'm sorry to inconvenience you, Don Alfonso."

The don looked him over. "Knowing your way with horses, I was concerned when I discovered Palo had returned without you."

Ulysses explained why he'd ridden off at night, and the don nodded. "Apparently you met my daughter on your way. When we learned you were missing, she confessed that you scolded her for being outside the gates and she told me what you'd said to her about expecting Americanos to raid our cattle." His eyes narrowed. "What caused that gash on your head?"

"I'm not certain." Ulysses gestured upriver. "Something killed one of our steers last night—also a man and a horse."

Don Alfonso's eyebrows rose. "Some*thing?*"

Ulysses prodded Palo into a walk. "I'll show you."

Juan turned away gray-faced after one look at flies buzzing over the carnage, glutting themselves, but the don dismounted and knelt to examine the steer at closer range. His horse stomped nervously.

"I thought maybe a grizzly mauled them," Ulysses offered as he slid off Palo, willing himself not to be sick. He noticed a condor circling above them, waiting to feed on the carrion.

"An animal of some sort, certainly," Don Alfonso agreed, turning away from the mauled steer. "A wild and vicious beast." He strode to the man's body, crouched to study it, then went on to the horse.

"Whatever it was prefers beef and horse meat to human," the don said as he returned to his horse, retrieving the pistol on the way. "It killed the man but didn't eat any part of him."

"I'm not positive, but he could be one of the Americanos I saw yesterday," Ulysses said, trying to ignore the uneasy roiling of his stomach.

The don turned the gun in his hand. ''This is an Americano Colt revolving pistol.'' He glanced at the body and grimaced. ''Much as I detest Americanos, I'd wish such a death as this on no man. You were lucky to escape.''

Juan, still mounted, his face averted, crossed himself furtively.

The don came up to Ulysses, who stood almost a head taller than he. ''Bend down so I can look at that gash.''

Ulysses obeyed.

''You heal unusually fast, but that looks to me like a bullet crease. What do you think, Juan?''

Juan glanced down at Ulysses. ''I think as you do, Don Alfonso.''

The don nodded. ''In my opinion the man shot at you, Ulysses, and the bullet creased your head, stunning you. Then the animal attacked, sparing you because you lay motionless on the ground. I've been told grizzlies often don't harm men who play dead.''

''I agree that could be the way it happened,'' Ulysses said, ''but I don't recall being shot at.'' It didn't explain why he'd been naked, but he had no intention of mentioning he'd been without clothes when he woke.

Don Alfonso shrugged. ''It's possible you might not remember.''

Juan crossed himself again and muttered *''Diablo,''* catching the don's attention.

''Don't be a fool, Juan,'' he snapped. ''No devil's involved. Clearly an animal did the killing. Look for yourself.''

Juan swallowed. ''I take your word, as always, Don Alfonso.''

''Good. Then we won't need to waste time. I want you to get the rifle that's lying on the ground near the horse and then we'll be on our way.''

Ulysses, knowing the rifle was fouled with clotted blood and other death debris, saw the unhappy expression on Juan's face and decided he was better fit to retrieve the gun than the vaquero. But before he could take a step toward the horse, the don touched his chest, holding him back. Then he understood Juan was being punished, perhaps for not dismounting earlier, and Ulysses was not to interfere.

Very reluctantly Juan did as he was ordered, being noisily

sick into the creek afterward. Ulysses sympathized—he was queasy himself.

On the ride to the hacienda, Don Alfonso ordered Ulysses to rest for the remainder of the day. Ulysses didn't argue. Seldom had he felt so exhausted.

Once he pulled off his boots and flung himself onto his cot, he fell asleep instantly. When he came alert, sensing someone had entered the vaquero quarters, he had no idea how much time had passed. He didn't move or open his eyes more than a slit. He knew the intruder wasn't *Tía* Dolores, the *bruja*—he'd recognize the crackle of her energy anywhere. The intruder showed no more than ordinary energy as he slowly advanced toward the cot.

Ulysses tensed, preparing to spring up and defend himself. But before it came to that, the faint scent of violets came to him and he relaxed. The intruder wasn't a man.

She drifted to the side of his cot. A moment later he felt her soft palm on his forehead. Swiftly he reached, captured her hand with his, brought it to his lips, and opened his eyes.

"Oh!" Esperanza's cheeks burned crimson as she stared down at him. "You slept so long I came to see if you were feverish."

He sat up, her hand still firmly clasped in his. Muted light slanted in through the open door. "One touch of your hand would cure any illness," he told her.

Belatedly she tugged at her hand and he reluctantly let her go. "I can't stay," she said breathlessly. "Paquita asks if you wish food."

He was far from hungry—at the moment he didn't feel like he ever wanted to eat again. "Thanks, no." He took a deep breath and added, "What I do wish is that we could meet again sometime—alone."

Her eyes widened and he thought she meant to refuse indignantly. Instead a faint smile curved her mouth. "Perhaps I wish it, too," she said softly, then turned and walked quickly from the room.

He rose and crossed to stand in the doorway, watching, bemused, until she disappeared from view. If he'd ever made love to a woman in the past, he couldn't remember, but if he had, he was sure he hadn't wanted that woman half as much as he wanted Esperanza.

Staring into the gray light, wondering how soon she'd be

able to arrange their meeting and how long he could bear to wait, he realized fog had rolled in from the ocean to hide the sun. To hide tonight's moon.

It was then he recalled the warning from his hidden past that had come to him as he rode out last night.

A full moon brings death.

A premonition? He grimaced. A bloody accurate one.

He eased through the door and stretched to loosen stiff muscles. What other unpleasant secrets were concealed behind his curtain of forgetfulness?

Unease crawled along his spine and he whirled. The *bruja* was near; he could almost see the blue sparks of her energy. Uneasy as she made him, he refused to retreat. He'd face her.

The gate opened and her black-garbed figure slipped through. *Tía* Dolores stopped, one hand on the gate, and looked at him. "I've known from the first, you spawn of the devil." Her words dripped with venom. "The rest are blind, but soon enough all will see that you wear the mark of the beast."

Chapter 3

"Here comes the beggar again," Juan muttered as they finished supper. "The only thanks you get for feeding that damn parrot is to have him shit on you."

Ulysses paid no attention to Juan's grumbling, holding out his arm to offer Esperanza's parrot, Gayo, a perch as it flew through the open window. Gayo landed, sidled up Ulysses' arm to his shoulder, and rubbed his head against Ulysses' cheek. Ulysses offered the brightly colored bird the rest of his tortilla. Holding it in one claw, Gayo crunched the crisp corn pancake in his curved beak.

Juan pushed away from the pine table and eased himself flat on his bunk, hands behind his head, staring morosely at the ceiling. "When I close my eyes," he said, "even yet I can see him."

Ulysses knew he didn't mean the parrot but the bloody remains of the dead man he'd found by the stream two weeks before.

"It takes away a man's appetite," Juan complained.

Ulysses only half heard him, for as he caressed the parrot, he discovered a tiny tube of paper tied with thread to one of Gayo's tailfeathers. Heart pounding in expectation, he turned his back to Juan, removed the paper, and unrolled it.

One word was written inside—*Encina.*

Live oak. Ulysses knew Esperanza must mean the huge, ancient tree growing in the courtyard of the casa near the outer wall. He rolled the paper into a tube again and slipped it into his pocket. Tonight, when he met her there, he'd pass the paper back to her to use the next time.

He smiled at his assumption that she'd want to meet him

more than once. But he had tonight to look forward to, and he could at least hope for more.

"With your narrow escape from *el diablo,*" Juan said, "I can't think how you sleep at night."

Juan had said much the same to him every evening since that bloody night. Ulysses repeated his same answer. "I can't remember what happened."

"Who has to remember? Seeing what he left behind is enough. No animal kills like that—it was a devil-beast."

Ulysses much preferred anticipating what might lie ahead with Esperanza to Juan's devil-beasts. Though he'd accepted the don's explanation for the now completely healed wound on his head—a bullet crease—he couldn't imagine any reason why he'd been naked when he came to his senses. Unless he'd meant to bathe in the stream. If he *had* planned to, he didn't remember and he didn't think he'd have tried anything so foolish on a moonlit night when he expected to encounter armed trespassers.

Was it something from his past that had made him strip off his clothes in the moonlight? An involuntary shudder ran through him before he could thrust the thought away.

"A cat walked over your grave, no?" Juan observed.

Realizing Juan had seen him shiver, Ulysses forced a smile. "Maybe. Cats don't take to me. At least Sombrito doesn't."

Juan scowled. "Everyone knows black cats, they are bad luck. But *Tía* Dolores—" He paused and crossed himself. "She does what she will," he finished.

Juan suspected she was a *bruja,* just as Ulysses did.

To hell with this talk of witches and devil-beasts and bad luck. Tonight he'd be with pretty Esperanza, whose very name meant hope. Would she let him kiss her?

He was still wondering hours later when he scaled the wall and climbed into the branches of the giant oak. It crossed his mind that Don Alfonso wouldn't take kindly to this secret rendezvous, but he flicked the worry aside. Imagining how she'd feel in his arms was preferable to imagining what her father might do if he discovered them together.

The night was clear; the moon, less than a waning quarter, was just rising. The darkness was perfumed by the heavy, sweet scent of tiny white star-shaped flowers blooming among the glossy green leaves of the vines climbing the adobe wall. He must remember to ask Esperanza what they were called. Since he had no past, like a curious child, he was obsessed by a need to know the name of everything.

He glanced up through the oak leaves at the sky, brilliant with stars, and suddenly a memory drifted within reach, a remembrance of a time he'd watched the night skies with another, the two of them learning the constellations as though for a tutor, the two of them laughing together, close, sharing.

Grief overwhelmed him, burdening his heart, cutting off the memory. Gone, the other was gone. Forever. . . .

A rustle of clothing warned Ulysses someone approached and he came alert, the sadness wafting away like alder down blown by the wind. A vision in white drifted toward the oak and he slid downward until he perched on the lowest branch.

Why could he recall tales of beautiful princesses when he couldn't remember his own name? Esperanza, though her hair was dark instead of golden, reminded him of those fairy tales. Perhaps she was Nastas'ya—but no, though a princess, Nastas'ya was a warrior maiden while Esperanza was a soft and gentle girl.

When she stepped under the branches of the oak, he whispered her name. "Esperanza."

She glanced about her. "Where are you?"

He broke off a twig and let it fall onto the filmy scarf covering her hair.

"Oh!" Startled, she looked up and saw him.

Ulysses straddled the thick branch and reached down for her. She hesitated only a moment before placing her hands in his. He gripped her wrists and lifted her up and onto the thick branch where he sat, easing her down next to him.

"I've never been in a tree," she said breathlessly. "*Tía* Dolores taught me girls don't climb trees."

"Ah, but you didn't climb one."

"I won't fall, will I?"

He put his arm around her waist. "Not with me here to hold you."

She leaned against him, soft and warm and smelling of violets. "I can't stay long," she whispered. "I shouldn't be with you at all."

"I won't harm you." It was the truth. He'd never do anything she didn't want him to.

"I don't believe what *Tía* Dolores says about you."

He didn't want to hear what that was. "Is she really your aunt?"

"Papa says she's a distant cousin who came to be with my mother before I was born. She stayed on when my mother died. *Tía* Dolores has been very good to me." She pulled away to look at him. "But she's wrong about you."

He touched her cheek with the back of his hand. "When I came to myself on the beach and saw you bending over me, I thought at first you were Princess Nausicaa rescuing me, poor castaway that I was."

Her lips were temptingly close. "And now?"

"I still believe you're a princess." No longer wondering what might happen between them, no longer thinking at all, he bent his head and touched her lips with his. Though obviously inexperienced, she responded eagerly to his kiss, her arms going around his neck to hold him to her.

His hands followed the curves of her body, finding that tonight she wore no corset, only a thin nightgown and night-robe, both with ribbons in the front that tempted him to untie them. When her gown fell open revealingly, how could he be expected not to touch her round white breasts?

Her sighs at his caresses excited him as much as the feel of her softness under his fingers. He struggled to keep his head. A tree branch, no matter how solid and wide, was a precarious place for lovemaking.

He ached to possess her, but at the same time he feared he'd hurt her. "I want you very much," he whispered hoarsely. "I wish—" He stopped. He couldn't tell her that he wished he knew who he was, couldn't say he was a man without a past.

"What do you wish?" she murmured.

He answered with another question. "What do you think I'm wishing?"

She didn't reply directly. "I don't care if you aren't wealthy," she assured him. "It doesn't matter that you're not a don. Not to me."

"It would to your papa," he said, nuzzling her throat.

"Then you do mean to ask for my hand! Oh, Ulysses!" She kissed him fervently, clinging to him, almost making him forget his surprise at her words. The feel of her softness against him played havoc with his good intentions.

He forced himself to stop while he still could, lifting her arms from around his neck and holding her away from him.

"You'd better go in. We don't want *Tía* Dolores to wake and come looking for you."

"Saints, no!" She bit her lip. "I can't be sure when we'll be able to meet again."

He slipped the tube of paper into her hand. "Send Gayo with this when you can get away." He started to lift her down from the tree, but she stopped him.

"You *do* wish to marry me?" Her voice was uncertain, plaintive.

"With all my heart." Whether that was the absolute truth or not, Ulysses wasn't sure. He did know there wasn't a chance in hell of the don agreeing. Still, he wanted to reassure her. "The time's not right for me to ask your father. We must wait until I've proven myself to him."

And just how did he mean to accomplish that? Ulysses wondered.

Esperanza didn't ask him. Accepting his words, she allowed him to ease her down to the ground, blew him a kiss, and hurried toward the casa.

Ulysses sat on the branch a long time after she'd disappeared. Though he couldn't ask for a more beautiful bride, the mention of marriage had shaken him and the more he considered the problems, the more impossible a marriage between him and Esperanza seemed. He was not only a nobody, he had no past. He didn't even know how old he was.

Was he eighteen? That was surely too young to have left a wife behind somewhere, wasn't it? Though it was possible the someone he'd shared the night sky with at another time and in another land had been a wife. He had no way to be certain.

He eyed the waning moon through the oak branches and sighed. Damn, but he wanted Esperanza, wanted her at any and all costs.

On Wednesday of the following week, the don rode out with his vaqueros on his carved leather saddle ornamented with silver. When they split off to go their separate ways, Don Alfonso joined Don Rafael. On Thursday, he rode with Juan. On Friday, Don Alfonso's black stallion trotted alongside Palo as he and Ulysses checked cattle together.

"Every week we're missing two or three head," the don said. "I suspected Americanos of stealing them until I saw the beast's work. Now I'm not sure. But it must stop or soon I'll have no cattle left.''

''We haven't seen any more animal tracks like those by the kill,'' Ulysses pointed out.

''And those tracks led only to the creek.'' The don shrugged. ''Like a sly fox, he waded in the stream to throw off pursuit—he's a smart one. But I'm still not convinced all my losses are the work of an animal, no matter how clever and fierce. The Americanos are much more subtle and dangerous than any beast, *no es verdad*?''

Ulysses nodded. From what he'd seen of them, he agreed Americanos were certainly dangerous.

They tallied cattle all day. When they rode back to the hacienda as the sun disappeared behind the low hills to the west, the don's count showed four head were missing.

''In my father's time,'' he said, ''we possessed so many cattle they swarmed over the hills. It took fifteen vaqueros to round up the calves for branding in the spring and, in the summer and fall, the steers for slaughter. With more cattle than we could count, who cared if a hungry traveler—or a grizzly—occasionally killed a steer? Those were the true golden days, my young friend. Before the Americanos.''

Ulysses didn't have to ask how many cattle grazed on Don Alfonso's land now. Just under two hundred—he'd helped tally them.

''Never did my father ride among the cattle, as I sometimes must,'' Don Alfonso continued. ''Gentlemen had no need to work. And ah, the fandangos and the *meriendas*—dancing and food and drink and sport. The Californios came from miles around to celebrate with us. Now when do we gather together, those of us who are left? For a wedding, perhaps. Or worse—for a funeral.''

The don shook his head and fell silent.

Ulysses wondered what Don Alfonso would do if he asked for Esperanza's hand here and now. Kill him? Probably not. Ordering him off the property, never to return, was nearer the truth.

The hacienda was in sight before the don spoke again. ''We will set up a night watch, the four of us taking turns. The man on sentry duty will bring one of the dogs with him. Don Rafael has volunteered for the first night, you will take the second, then Juan, and, last, myself.''

''Yes, sir.''

"Next week the moon will be full again—*Tía* Dolores tells me this is when the beast is likely to appear. We must be on the alert."

A chill ran along Ulysses' spine at the don's words. He might have set aside the *bruja*'s threat to him, but he'd by no means forgotten it. If only he had some idea what she'd meant.

"You look as though you've swallowed vinegar," the don observed. "After your narrow escape, I can't blame you if you're afraid of that beast."

"It's not fear of the beast," Ulysses protested, stung. "I merely wondered how the *bru*—that is, Señora Dolores—could foretell an animal's movements."

"She has strange talents. I'm inclined to believe her."

"I volunteer to take the night of the full moon," Ulysses said, still smarting at the don's assumption he feared the beast.

"If the full moon arrives on your turn, certainly you shall." The don's tone brooked no argument.

By Ulysses' reckoning, Don Alfonso himself would be standing guard that night. He brooded about it for a week, finding no way to convince the don to change with him. If he followed the don, intent on protecting him, Juan was sure to know and to tell. Californios were touchy—the don would be furious, believing it a slur on his manhood that Ulysses should think he needed protection. He might well order Ulysses to leave the rancho.

Two days before what he'd come to think of as The Beast's Day, fog settled over the rancho, a damp gray blanket between earth and sky, a shroud that refused to lift. Ulysses' restlessness kept him from sleeping well, even after his all-night sentry duty. On the morning of The Beast's Day, he was already awake when Juan came in from his turn at sentry duty.

"Looks like rain," Juan said, yawning. "Fortune favors me—I'll sleep, you'll get wet. You can bet I didn't ride far last night in that fog. No man in his right mind would be out in it. Nor beast, either. Not even a devil-beast."

Ulysses had thought much the same the previous night. No doubt the don had decided they must take their regular sentry turns in case the fog lifted, as it sometimes did shortly after midnight.

The rain held off until noon, then a thin drizzle began.

By the time Ulysses rode home in the late afternoon, it was more mist than rain. Before he ate, he opened the window, ignoring Juan's grumbling. Esperanza's possible summons was more important than a bit of dampness.

He and Juan were digging into refried beans and enchiladas when Gayo flapped through the window and came to perch on his shoulder. As he fed the parrot, he surreptitiously felt along the tailfeathers as he did every time Gayo visited. He'd been disappointed until now. This evening his fingers found the tube of paper with *Encina* printed on it.

Excitement gripped him and he fought his impulse to leap up and shout. Where would he find the patience to pass the hours until they could meet?

What patience he mustered was worn as thin as the sole on a beggar's boot when Juan, refreshed by a day's rest, lifted down his old guitar and sang plaintive ballads slightly off-key for what seemed an eternity. He dared not leave until Juan slept.

Esperanza was already waiting by the oak when Ulysses finally scaled the wall. Eager to hold her, he dropped to the ground inside the courtyard, pulled her into his arms, and kissed her.

"Ah," she said with a sigh after a long, satisfying moment, "how I wish you would kiss me forever."

"I'm willing." He started to prove it, but she pulled back, covering his lips with her fingers.

"I asked you to meet me because *Tía* Dolores says the beast will appear tonight," she whispered, her voice shaking. "I'm afraid for Papa, afraid he'll be killed. Please, you must save him."

It was too late to stop Don Alfonso—he'd ridden off more than an hour ago. But go after him he would. He'd wanted to all along. Now he had the excuse. Esperanza's plea would go far to soften the don's wrath if he discovered Ulysses was on his trail.

"I'll do my best," Ulysses promised, and kissed her once more, quickly, before pulling himself up and over the wall.

As he coaxed Palo from the corral, he told himself it was easy to say he'd go after her father, but how was he to find the don on a night when the mist hid the moon? He couldn't sense the don's presence at any great distance and the rancho sprawled over more than a hundred acres. How was he

mist, his night vision was good enough to avoid stumbling head-on into trees, and he preferred being afoot.

Grulla quieted abruptly and Ulysses noted she was beside the lone man. Certain now he must be Don Alfonso, Ulysses focused his full attention on the other two.

They were moving. Not toward the injured man but toward two horses, their movements slow and cautious. Ulysses circled again, hurrying as fast as he could without crashing loudly through the bushes, to reach the horses before they did.

One of the animals snorted as he approached, but he laid a hand on its neck and the horse quieted. When he was certain neither was the don's black stallion, he untied them both and led them free of the trees, where he slapped one, then the other, hard on the rump. Both horses trotted away from the stream. Ulysses slipped back among the trees, intent on stalking his prey.

He blinked as the word crept into his mind. Not *prey.* Where had that idea come from? They were strangers, trespassers, enemies, but they were not prey; they were men. Yet he couldn't quite dislodge the word. It clung persistently to his thoughts, infusing his mind with a chilling lust to kill. He fought against it, appalled.

Kill, yes, but to protect himself, to protect the don. A man who killed for the sake of killing was no better than an animal. No, he was worse than an animal—animals killed to eat or because they feared an attacker or to protect their young or their mate. Not for the sake of killing—unless they were rogues. Outcasts.

He was no rogue.

Or was he? What did he know of his past?

Ulysses shook himself. Never mind a past he couldn't remember. He'd come to rescue the don. Gritting his teeth as though grinding unwelcome thoughts between them, he directed his full attention to the men, determined now not to kill them. No, he'd beat the hell out of them. Don Alfonso could make the final life-or-death decision.

He took the first one from behind, hooking his arm around the man's neck to strangle his shout. When the man almost immediately went limp in his grasp, he realized he'd exerted too much pressure. Had he killed him? He couldn't take the time to find out.

Dropping him on his face, Ulysses leaped at the other

man, who cursed and grappled with him, trying to knee him, to gouge his eyes. Parrying each attempt, Ulysses slammed his fists into the man's face and midsection until he, too, slumped to the ground, unconscious. He disarmed them both.

Somewhere in my past I learned how to fight, he thought absently as he hurried toward the flickering life force he believed was Don Alfonso. To his relief, he sensed him more strongly than before.

When Grulla ran to meet him, whimpering in her pleasure to see him, he was all but positive he approached the don. Still, it didn't do to take chances. He ducked behind a sycamore trunk and called softly, “It's Ulysses, Don Alfonso. I took care of the trespassers.”

“Ulysses!”

Definitely the don's voice. Ulysses hurried to his side.

“Took a bullet in my thigh,” the don said, obviously in pain. “Not too bad, leg's not broken. My horse is somewhere around—he'd never leave me. I should be able to ride.”

“I'll fetch the lantern and take a look at your leg first,” Ulysses told him.

Once he had the lantern in hand, Ulysses detoured to retrieve Palo and, with rope from the saddlebag, bound the two unmoving trespassers before returning to the don. He wasn't sure whether or not he was relieved to find them both alive.

He used Don Alfonso's neck scarf to bandage the oozing hole in his left thigh, recovered the black stallion grazing downstream, and hoisted the don into the saddle. The don swayed, grunting with pain, but stayed on the horse.

“You killed those damned Americanos?” he asked.

“No. Knocked them out.”

“Bring the lantern. I want to see the bastards who killed my dog and put a bullet in me.”

Grulla reached the men first and stood growling, hackles raised. Ulysses grabbed the rope and turned the first man, still limp, onto his back. He'd never seen him before. The second man was awake and cursed when Ulysses flipped him over. Blackbeard!

“This one I saw on your land a month ago,” he told the don.

"Dirty greasers," Blackbeard snarled. "You killed Pete."

"He's not dead," Ulysses said, ignoring the insult.

"Hell he isn't. I been looking for his grave. Found it tonight."

Then Ulysses understood who he meant. It *had* been Shorty the beast mauled.

"Kill them both," the don said through his teeth. "Now."

Ulysses thought of protesting, knew it would be useless. Wondering if he could possibly shoot a helpless man in cold blood, he reluctantly drew the Colt.

"On second thought, revenge is my right and my duty, not yours." Don Alfonso held out his hand for the gun.

Ulysses tried to conceal his relief as he gave up the Colt, but he couldn't prevent his involuntary flinch as the don fired once, twice.

Taking a deep breath, Ulysses gave thanks for the don's accuracy—the men had died instantly. He'd learned another lesson tonight. No matter how he hated a man, he'd never be able to do what the don had just done.

Shoot a man who meant to kill him or a friend, yes. In cold blood, no.

Chapter 4

"But I don't want you to stop!" Esperanza clung to Ulysses, the sweet pressure of her body against his further undermining his rapidly eroding resolve not to take advantage of her innocence.

The half-moon rode above the branches of the oak, but its pale light scarcely reached them, shadowed as they were by the leaves overhead. After he'd mentioned how her white nightclothes made her conspicuous in the darkness, Esperanza now came to him concealed in a black shawl.

As they lay on the shawl underneath the oak, wrapped in each other's arms, Ulysses made one last attempt to protect her from what they both desperately wanted. "There's something I have to tell you," he whispered.

She hugged him closer. "You don't know how long I've been waiting to hear you say you loved me!"

Ulysses was taken aback. He'd meant to confess to her that he was a man without a past, without even a name. What in God's name was he to do now?

Esperanza laughed, her warm breath teasing his ear. "Cat got your tongue?"

He tried to explain. "I wasn't—that is, you don't—"

She stiffened in his embrace. "You mean you don't love me?"

"I do, of course I do." He thought it was the truth. If his feeling for her wasn't love, he didn't know what else to call it.

She relaxed only slightly. "I won't believe you unless you say the words."

"I love you," he murmured.

She melted against him, her lips seeking and finding his,

her fingers tangling in his hair, her round, full breasts pressing against his chest. Aroused beyond endurance, he forgot everything but Esperanza and his need for her, retaining barely enough sanity to be gentle when at last they came together and he claimed her as his own.

Later, as she prepared to return to the casa, Esperanza said, "Tomorrow you must ask Papa."

Ulysses knew she was right and yet he dreaded the encounter. He wrapped the shawl around her and, with his hands on her shoulders, looked down at her face, pale in the moonlight. Now she was his wife in all but name. If it were up to him he wouldn't withhold that from her. False though his name might be, it was the only one he had. He'd wanted to tell her the truth, but now it was far too late.

"Tomorrow evening," he said at last. He'd make a formal request for her hand, though he knew very well he didn't have a chance in hell of marrying her. He could well imagine the don's rage when he asked.

The following day, Ulysses waited until after the evening meal to knock at the casa door. Rosa, the elderly houseservant, let him in without comment, motioning toward the room Ulysses thought of as the library because of the several shelves of books.

He tapped at the half-open door. "It's Ulysses, sir," he said.

Don Alfonso sat in a high-backed chair at a table with a green bottle of the brandy the Californios called *aguardiente* before him. His injured leg was propped on a stool.

"Enter, *mi amigo,*" he said to Ulysses. "Sit down and have a drink with me."

Ulysses thanked him, took the half-filled glass the don offered, and eased himself onto the edge of the straight-backed chair on the opposite side of the table. It wasn't the first glass of brandy he'd shared with the don since the night he'd rescued him from the Americanos, but it was the first time he'd come to the casa uninvited.

He took a swallow of the liquor, not rolling it on his tongue as the don always did. He needed the warm feel of the brandy in his stomach.

"How's the leg, sir?" he asked, putting off the fateful moment.

Don Alfonso grimaced. "Still keeps me hobbling. But it's healing, no doubt about that. *Tía* Dolores knows how to cure, even if she can't always predict the habits of beasts. Do you know her excuse?"

Ulysses shook his head.

"She claims with the full moon concealed, first by the fog, then by the rain clouds, the beast couldn't appear. It seems he only manifests himself under the light of a full moon." The don smiled wryly. "I hadn't realized she believes as Juan does, that the beast is more than an animal—a devil-beast, in fact. I'm afraid I insulted her when I told her the Americanos were devils enough for me."

Unease rippled through Ulysses and he took another sip of the brandy. Why was he so affected by the words of the *bruja*?

"Those particular Americanos will never bother you again," he told the don.

The morning after the shooting, he and Juan had been sent to bury the two men next to the stream near Shorty's grave. Badly injured as the don had been, he'd insisted on bringing Chico's body back to the hacienda when he and Ulysses had returned in the misty night. The dog was buried in the courtyard.

"I wish it were that easy to get rid of them all." Don Alfonso poured himself another brandy and held the bottle toward Ulysses, who declined.

"There's no end to those Americanos," the don went on. "They pour into California like ants from an endless anthill."

"Then you believe we'll have more trouble?"

"Of that I'm certain." The don sighed. "I sit here reliving the happy times of the old days. Once I thought there'd be no end to them—but I was wrong." He lapsed into silence, staring into the distance.

Ulysses was aware he must come to the point. He couldn't tell the don the truth about his past and he wouldn't mention that he had no money and no prospects because that was evident. There was really nothing to be said except a simple request for Esperanza's hand. Simple!

He set his glass on the table, took a deep breath, and blurted, "Sir, I've come to you to ask a very great favor."

Don Alfonso smiled at him. "I owe you my life, *mi amigo*. Anything you wish is yours."

Ulysses cleared his throat. Not this one. "My wish is to marry your daughter."

The don's smile faded as he stared at Ulysses in disbelief. "My Esperanza? You wish to marry her?"

"Yes, sir. We love one another."

Don Alfonso straightened in his chair, gathering himself, Ulysses was sure, for a furious refusal. Instead, he leaned on the table and examined Ulysses for a long time. Finally he shook his head and leaned back.

"First I'll say to you that I don't like the idea, not at all."

It was no more than Ulysses had expected. He steeled himself against fidgeting and watched the don warily.

"Are you of our faith?" the don asked.

Caught unawares by the question, Ulysses fumbled for an answer. How did he know what faith he was, if any? "I'm willing to be, sir," he said finally.

Don Alfonso grunted. "I'll speak to the priest. Mind you, I'm not certain he'll approve. As for me—" the don paused to finish his brandy, "what can I do? My daughter has always been stubborn; it runs in my family. If she wants you for her husband, as you say she does, then she won't accept another, no matter what I say or do. I'll never get the grandchildren I expect and deserve if she shuts herself into a convent, as she's very likely to do if I refuse to let her marry you."

"I—I'm very grateful," Ulysses stammered, stunned. Never in his wildest imaginings had he expected even a grudging approval.

"You should be. You will be marrying into an old and distinguished family." Don Alfonso reached across the table and poured more brandy into Ulysses' glass, then into his own. "We will drink to the betrothal. While you are not the husband I would have chosen for her, I'm not altogether displeased. At least my daughter will wed a strong, intelligent, courageous, and loyal young man. As I'm getting no younger, we'll plan for an early wedding. I'd like to see a few grandchildren before I die. Six weeks should be enough time to arrange the celebration, send the invitations, and allow the women to concoct suitable gowns."

The don seemed healthy enough; Ulysses didn't believe there was much danger of him dying soon. But why object to an early wedding? The sooner Esperanza was his wife, the better. He could hardly wait for the chance to make love to her every night.

He left the casa with his head whirling, not so much from the brandy as from the rapid and drastic way his life was changing. From a man who had nothing to being the prospective son-in-law of Don Alfonso Alvarado was not only unexpected but somewhat terrifying.

With no knowledge of his past, did he have the right to marry Esperanza? He didn't know the answer to that question. Would he ever know any more about himself than he did at this moment?

Standing alone in the night, he stared up at the moon. I'm alive, he thought, I'm in California, and I've named myself Ulysses Koshka. That's the extent of what I know. For me, there's only now. I'm young. I don't want my life darkened by fears of the unknown past. Whatever happened then is gone forever. Dead and gone.

In six weeks Esperanza would be his wife. Six weeks. That meant the moon would be full on their wedding night. A night for devil-beasts to roam, according to *Tía* Dolores. Would she accept him once he was Esperanza's husband? Somehow he didn't think so.

To hell with the *bruja* and her devil-beasts. She couldn't stop him from marrying Esperanza—he had Don Alfonso's approval. No one could stop him. He grinned, saluted the moon, and strolled through the gate, still bemused by his good fortune.

He fell asleep immediately, only to wake near dawn with unanswered questions coiling through his mind like rattlesnakes poised to strike. Why had he seen that strange symbol on the don's palm when they first met? And why had he known the sign meant danger? Why had he found himself naked when he roused that morning by the stream? And why had he dreamed of the taste of blood? Why had the *bruja* hated and feared him from the moment she set eyes on him? Did she know something he didn't, something he'd forgotten?

He sat up, the metallic tang of fear on his tongue. An impulse gripped him to grab his clothes and flee, to get away while there was still time. He leaped to his feet.

"*¿Que pasa?*" Juan's sleepy voice asked.

"*Nada.*" Ulysses stood motionless. He'd spoken the truth. It really was nothing, once he thought about it clearly.

He loved Esperanza—how could he leave her? Was he to allow a witch's prejudice and a nightmare to chase him away from his unexpected good fortune? As for danger, he was no coward; he'd face whatever perils he had to. He wasn't running, he was staying. And he'd marry Esperanza, no matter what.

When Ulysses returned to the hacienda the following evening, old Rosa was waiting for him. "You are to move into the casa, Señor Koshka," she informed him.

He wasn't so sure he wanted to, but he knew better than to object. It wasn't proper for Señorita Alvarado's future husband to sleep in the vaquero's quarters. Times being what they were, he might have to do a vaquero's work, but that was no disgrace—even the don must help with the cattle during the busy seasons.

Juan watched him gather his meager belongings. "Is it true?" he asked. "Are you to marry Don Alfonso's daughter?"

Ulysses nodded.

Juan whistled. "You are one lucky hombre."

"I know I am."

"Don Rafael, he won't be pleased."

Ulysses shrugged. Whether Don Rafael approved or not, there was nothing the Californio could do about it. He didn't give a damn what Don Rafael thought anyway—after their eventful first meeting they'd been sworn enemies forced to work together peacefully under the don's flag of truce.

"He once thought to marry the señorita," Juan said. "Others thought he might, too. All will be amazed."

No doubt. Ulysses smiled. Esperanza loved him—too bad about Don Rafael and all those others, whoever they were.

The next morning, as Ulysses and Juan left the hacienda, Don Rafael was waiting. He scowled at the two of them and jerked his head at Juan, who quickly rode past and kept going. Don Rafael then fell in beside Ulysses.

"If you ever harm Esperanza in any way," Don Rafael warned, his voice low and menacing, "as God is my witness, I swear I'll kill you. I'd kill you now with the greatest pleasure if I didn't know it would bring her grief."

Ulysses stared into the Californio's eyes, dark and glittering with hate. Angry, challenging words sprang to his tongue, but before he could speak, Don Rafael spurred El Duro and galloped away.

In the weeks that followed, Don Rafael didn't so much as

glance at Ulysses when they chanced to meet. Ulysses, when he'd cooled down, decided ignoring Don Rafael was the wisest course.

Every day he expected a belligerent encounter with *Tía* Dolores, but to his surprise and relief, she avoided him completely. When he was permitted to be with Esperanza for an hour in the evening, Rosa, rather than *Tía* Dolores, acted as chaperone. He and Esperanza were never left alone together for a moment and no more than a chaste good night kiss was allowed between them. He began to think the weeks until the wedding would never pass.

"*Tía* Dolores says I can't sit with you for the next three evenings," Esperanza told him at the end of two weeks.

"Why not?" he demanded. "God knows Rosa makes certain I can't even kiss you—not the way I want to."

"Hush, we have only a month more to wait."

"But if I'm not even to talk to you—"

"It's only three days. Because of the full moon, she says, I must stay in my room."

Ulysses frowned. "Are you telling me that *Tía* Dolores never lets you out of your room when the moon is full?"

Esperanza shook her head. "It's only since the beast came to the rancho. She insists I won't be safe when the moon is full unless I'm with her, locked in my room."

"She's loco!"

"I would never disagree with you," Esperanza said quietly, "but you misunderstand *Tía* Dolores. She's odd sometimes, but that's because she's a *curandera* and healers do not think and behave as you and I."

"She's a *bruja*!"

Esperanza's eyes widened. "Oh, no! Witches are evil. *Tía* Dolores would never harm anyone. When we are married you will get to know her better, and then you'll understand."

He sure as hell didn't want to know the old woman any better. After they were married, he damned well meant to do his best to send the *bruja* back to wherever she came from.

Later, still upset, Ulysses spoke to the don about what Esperanza had told him. "Does Señora Dolores actually believe the beast is going to force its way into the casa?" he asked angrily.

Don Alfonso shrugged. "Who knows what she believes?

It won't hurt Esperanza to humor her.'' He smiled and clapped Ulysses on the shoulder. ''I feel sure you'll survive being deprived of my daughter's company for an evening or two. In any case, if the nights remain clear, you'll be on sentry duty one of those evenings. Juan's taking tomorrow night, you the next, then Don Rafael.''

Ulysses eyed him thoughtfully. ''Then you do believe the full moon somehow attracts the beast.''

''Let's say I find the connection possible. If you recall, it attacked the first time during a full moon. Since there are too few of us to keep patrolling the rancho every night, doesn't it make sense to choose times when the beast is most likely to appear?''

Ulysses nodded. The don's argument was plausible—more so than any prediction of the *bruja*'s—but did nothing to relieve his uneasiness.

Before retiring, Ulysses walked into the courtyard and gazed up at the almost full moon, feeling a strange and disturbing ache as its silvery rays caressed him, filling him with strange longings. He didn't know how much time passed before he became aware the *bruja* was watching him. Though he couldn't see her, he sensed her blue energy crackling nearby.

''Damn you, witch!'' he shouted, turning toward where he sensed she was. ''Stop spying on me.''

''Beast!'' she spat from the shadows, and fled from him.

He started after her, then held. He knew with a sureness that permeated his very bones that no good came from any confrontation with a witch. A warning from his past? Wherever the knowledge came from, he decided to heed it.

Patience, he cautioned himself. You can do nothing now, but in a month you'll be Esperanza's husband, and then you'll have the right to send the *bruja* away.

Why did she call him a beast? She had no reason to. He cursed her again before leaving the courtyard on the way to his room. Once inside, he paced from one end of the small bedroom to the other, disturbed by his own restlessness as much as by the witch and her accusations. He yearned desperately for . . . what? He couldn't put a name to what he wanted and yet it churned within him, an urgent need impossible to fulfill. What seductive promise had he absorbed with the moonlight? What in God's name was the matter with him?

Though the moon wasn't shining on his side of the casa, he pulled the curtains over the window before hurling himself, fully dressed, on the bed, trying to ignore the mounting desire to fling off his clothes and run naked in the night. Frightened, he closed his eyes and searched his mind for a prayer.

He could find none.

Sitting up, he started to kick off his boots. Stopped. No. Whatever beckoned was unknown. Dangerous. *A full moon brings death.*

The moon wasn't quite full, but almost. He dared not undress, dared not give in to the frenzied need that throbbed through him. His desire for Esperanza, strong though it was, had never gripped him so violently. This urge had nothing to do with the coming together of man and woman or of any kind of mating. It was different. Wrong. Not human.

Ulysses covered his face with his hands. "No," he muttered. "No. I won't."

In his desperation, he drew in on himself, his otherwise constant awareness of the energy of others closed off by his inner struggle, a struggle he feared he was losing. Off came the boots, the shirt, the trousers. When the dogs began to bark, he hardly heard them.

The first he realized anything was amiss was the shout. *"¡Cuidado!"* Watch out! Alarm shrilled the man's voice.

A gun cracked in the night.

Ulysses came alert and found himself crouching by the the window, naked. Outside, men cursed in the Americano tongue, dogs barked. He sensed the presence of many men—eight or more.

Inside, Don Alfonso shouted. "Ulysses! Juan!"

There was no time to dress. Grabbing the dressing robe Esperanza had made for him, he shoved his arms in, wrapped the robe around him, and tied the sash as he flung his bedroom door open.

Colt in hand, he ran toward the courtyard door to make sure the heavy bar was in place. Before he reached the door, a woman screamed from upstairs. Esperanza!

Ulysses raced up the steps toward her bedroom. Below, a pistol cracked. The don's? He reached the door. Locked. Five people inside, one with a flickering life force. Esperanza screamed again. Ulysses stepped back and with all his strength slammed his shoulder into the door. The upper leather hinge gave, the door tilted into the room, and he crashed through, almost falling over *Tía* Dolores's limp body. Three Americanos were in the room, one forcing Esperanza onto the bed, one standing next to him, another near the balcony door.

Bringing the Colt up, he fired at the man near the balcony just as the Americano shot at him. The man staggered; Ulysses felt a sting along his upper arm. He turned the gun to the man beside the bed, fired again. The man fell. The third sprang up, holding the sobbing, half-naked Esperanza in front of him as he fumbled at his holster. Just as Ulysses sprang toward him, he sensed two men behind him.

A gun cracked as he dived for the legs of the man holding Esperanza, the bullet whistling over him. The man fell backward, losing his hold on Esperanza. For a moment Ulysses grappled with him, and then the other two leaped on him and he found himself fighting three men, one with a knife whose long, curved blade gleamed in the moonlight.

On the floor beside them, Esperanza whimpered. Aware of what would happen to her if he were killed, Ulysses snarled with rage. Something inside him twisted. He howled with pain and fury and then he knew no more.

Free! He was free! The smell of men surrounded him, acrid with fear. He paid no attention to those sprawled unmoving on the floor, leaping instead at the throat of one who backed away from him.

A loud crack, a sharp sting on his flank, an unpleasant stink, then his teeth sank into flesh and the hot, salty tang of blood flooded his tongue. But something wasn't right about the taste. He turned from the kill and ran down a fleeing man who stabbed at him with something shiny and sharp. As he broke the man's back, he remembered its name. A knife. He turned, snarling, to the only other man left on his feet.

"Jesus!" the man shouted, backing away. "A goddamn beast!" The loud crack came again—from metal in the man's hand.

Gun, he told himself, as a burning sting filled his gut. He leaped at the man. The Americano turned, sprang through an opening, climbed a metal barricade, and jumped to the ground, falling heavily. Ulysses followed, catching a glimpse of something large and hairy that he didn't recognize moving beside him. Since he could sense nothing there, he cleared the barricade in a running leap and landed lightly beside the man.

The man screamed, lurching to his feet in an attempt to flee. He died where he stood. The taste of the man's blood was wrong and he spat it out. He craved blood, but not this kind. Not the blood of men. Men weren't his proper prey.

With moonlight streaming over him, he felt the stinging from the knife and the gun ease, healing. He'd leave the men and run under the moon, hunting.

A high, quavering voice called from the room he'd left. "Ulysses! Oh, dear God, Ulysses! Where are you?"

Ulysses. He tensed. The call came not from a man but from a woman and she meant him, yet not him. She mustn't see him. He melted into the shadows, intending to clear the wall and flee. Clouds covered the moon.

A man crawled through a window onto the ground beside him, then saw him and screamed. The man didn't live to scream again.

With the moon hidden, the urge to hunt faded. But he couldn't stay here. Keeping to the deepest shadows, he loped toward the wall. Before he reached it, he felt a twisting, a terrible wrenching and then—nothing.

Ulysses stood in the courtyard by the oak, staring down at his naked body, a nasty taste in his mouth. Frightening thoughts of teeth tearing and of blood raked through his mind. What in God's name had happened? The last he remembered he'd been in Esperanza's bedroom trying to fight off three Americanos. How had he gotten here?

"Ulysses!" Esperanza's cry chilled him. Was she all right?

He raced to the door, found it barred, noticed an open window and stumbled over a dead body before he was able to climb through the window into the house. He grabbed a serape from a hook by the door and flung it over his nakedness as he plunged up the stairs. He caught up to Don Alfonso just as he reached Esperanza's door, half off its hinges. He remembered crashing through it.

In the room, Esperanza sat on the floor in a torn and bloody nightgown, *Tía* Dolores's head in her lap. "Thank God you're alive!" she cried when she saw the two of them. Then she burst into tears.

Since he sensed *Tía* Dolores still lived, Ulysses paid no more attention to her or to the four dead men on the floor. Gathering Esperanza into his arms, he sat her on the bed and wrapped a quilt around her. Her father eased down beside her.

"Have a look around, will you, to make certain we're safe?" the don asked. "I'll look after the women."

He couldn't assure the don he sensed no men nearby without revealing his unusual ability, so Ulysses nodded. As he started to leave the room, he saw his robe on the floor and bent to pick it up. Underneath was his Colt. As he rose, gun in hand, he caught a glimpse of himself in a large gilt-framed mirror hung on Esperanza's wall. He grimaced. His flesh not hidden by the serape was crusted dark with blood. He looked every bit as frightening as any beast.

Terror laced through him. One of the dead man had his throat torn out. By what? By the beast? It sure as hell looked that way. But how was that possible?

He turned abruptly and pushed past the broken door, his heart pounding in panic rhythm. As he searched the upstairs rooms, then those downstairs, he found two other dead Americanos near the library—both shot to death. In their room near the kitchen, Rosa and Paquita cowered in a corner, weeping.

"You're safe. The Americanos are all dead," he assured them before he unbarred the kitchen door to go outside.

He located one more dead man with a torn throat in the courtyard. Outside the gate, he found Juan's body. He lifted the dead vaquero and carried him into the quarters they'd shared, where he laid him gently on the bed. Juan had died trying to warn them.

"Adiós, mi amigo," he said softly.

Outside again, he scanned as far as he could sense. There were no human life forces near except for those in the casa—the three old women, the don, and Esperanza.

He stopped to wash the blood from himself at the bucket near the corral, then paused in his room to pull on his trousers, fighting off all thoughts of the beast. He must be mistaken. He *had* to be mistaken.

Don Alfonso was in his library, pouring brandy.

"Esperanza's unhurt," the don assured him. "*Tía* Dolores is coming around—they shoved her when she tried to protect my daughter and she hit her head on the corner of the wardrobe. She'll be all right—already she's consoling Esperanza." He handed a half-full glass to Ulysses.

Ulysses opened his mouth to tell him about Juan, but the don continued. "Esperanza tells a very strange story. She insists the beast was in her room."

Memories hammered into Ulysses' head like nails into his coffin. Waking naked on that morning by the stream. Naked an hour ago by the courtyard oak. The wrenching. The taste of blood. The truth burst through him with such force, he rocked back on his heels.

He knew what the beast was. Who the beast was.

Chapter 5

Stricken, Ulysses stared into his glass of brandy, not daring to look at Don Alfonso as he waited for the condemning accusation. If Esperanza had seen the beast, then she'd seen him change into the monster. She knew what Ulysses Koshka was and she must have told her father.

"Drink up," the don ordered. "We need more than the brandy to banish this night from our souls."

Numbly, Ulysses raised his glass and drained it, still not meeting the don's eye. The fiery liquor warmed his stomach but didn't touch the chill around his heart. Or maybe it was his soul. If he had one.

Oborot, a voice inside his head accused. Shapeshifter. He couldn't believe it was true, though at the same time he knew what he was.

I'm a man, he told himself desperately. A man.

Oborot. His own people's word for men who changed to beasts.

He was a man and yet he was not. And who in God's name were his own people?

"I drink to you," the don said, raising his glass. "You saved my daughter this night, and her life is dearer to me than my own."

Ulysses blinked and looked at him. To his surprise, the don was smiling.

"You've earned her hand ten times over, *mi amigo,*" Don Alfonso said. "Without you, we'd all be dead."

Was it possible Esperanza hadn't told her father everything?

"The beast?" Ulysses managed to ask.

The don shrugged. "Who knows? I don't doubt Esperanza believes she saw something strange, but at the time she was frightened nearly out of her wits.'' He scowled. ''The Americanos behaved like beasts, that was clear enough. How many men attacked us?''

''Eight. All dead.''

''I killed two. You and Juan accounted for the rest.''

Ulysses took a deep breath. ''Juan died fighting them.''

Don Alfonso sighed and crossed himself. ''He died nobly. May his soul rest in peace.'' He drained his glass and set it on the table. ''Dead or alive, the Americanos profane my casa. You and I, we must dispose of them.''

They hauled the two by the library into the courtyard before climbing the stairs to Esperanza's bedroom. Ulysses steeled himself to face her, but neither she nor *Tía* Dolores were in her room, only the three dead Americans.

''We will throw their bodies down from the balcony,'' the don said. ''They deserve no better.'' He paused by one of the bodies, studying it. ''No bullet killed this man. Observe how his throat is torn.''

''I noticed.'' Ulysses spoke tersely.

''Did *you* see a beast of any kind?''

''I—no, I didn't.'' The words sounded lame to Ulysses.

The don slanted him a look. ''Most likely the Americanos brought with them a vicious dog and, confused by the fighting, the animal turned on its master, *no es verdad*?''

Sweat broke out on Ulysses' forehead. Did the don suspect the truth? He swallowed, unable to speak, keeping his eyes from the mirror, half fearing he'd see the image of the beast instead of his own familiar face.

''Never mind,'' the don said. ''It matters little how these Americano pigs died. Between us, we routed them, you and I—if some animal assisted us, it was to our advantage. Come, *mi amigo,* we must dispose of these bodies. It's not proper for them to remain in my daughter's room.''

Ulysses had recovered most of his composure by the time they finished their grisly task. The don might not be completely satisfied about what had happened, but Ulysses felt confident he wasn't under suspicion.

Examining the thick trunk of the wisteria that wound around the balcony, he decided the Americanos had gained entrance to the casa by climbing the vine.

''Maybe Esperanza should take another room,'' he suggested as he showed Don Alfonso the gouges on the wisteria trunk. "Just in case."

The don nodded, his face grim. "I shall sleep here from now on. The bastards won't get past me! I'll have the servants make the change in the morning."

As they left the room, Ulysses glanced across the hall toward the closed door to the bedroom Esperanza occupied, and the don smiled.

"You wish to see my daughter once more before you sleep," he said. "I understand." Before Ulysses could say anything, he tapped at the door. "May we enter?" he called.

"Come in, Papa," Esperanza answered.

Ulysses noted she hadn't invited him in and he hung back, but the don propelled him forward. Ulysses braced himself. Would she accuse him the moment she set eyes on him?

Esperanza's gaze slid from her father to Ulysses. "Oh!" she said, bringing a hand to her breast, now covered with a soft pink robe.

He waited, holding his breath, while she stared at him, her eyes wide and dark.

"Thank God you're alive!" she said at last. "I feared the beast killed you, as it did the Americano." She dropped her face into her hands. "I've never seen such a horrible monster!"

Watching the don enfold his daughter in his arms, it filtered through to Ulysses that she made no connection between him and the beast. She'd missed seeing the change! He let his breath out. No one knew what he was. He was safe—if only for the time being.

From a cot at the foot of the bed, *Tía* Dolores raised her head and glared at him malevolently, telling him without words that she was well aware that he and the beast were one and the same. She'd been unconscious, she couldn't possibly have seen him change, and yet she knew. She'd known all along.

Spawn of the devil, she'd called him from the beginning. Apprehensively, he waited for her to spew forth her hatred, but she dropped back and closed her eyes. Not giving up, he was sure, but biding her time. Until she had proof.

Don Alfonso kissed his daughter and released her. "I think you might also offer a kiss to the brave man you are to marry," he said.

Esperanza smiled and stepped across to Ulysses, holding

up her face to him. He meant to merely brush her lips, but the realization that this would be the last time he'd dare touch her made him wrap his arms around her and kiss her deeply. He let her go reluctantly.

Everything he'd thought within his reach was not for him. He didn't dare remain at the rancho, much less marry Esperanza. He'd seen for himself how horribly those near him died when he became a beast. He must get away, far away from everything human. Even now, with the moon not quite full, he could barely control his longing to step into the courtyard and bathe in its silvery light.

And change.

With the moon at full, he'd be doomed, forced to shift into a beast. He grimaced, remembering that his wedding had been planned for the following full moon. Thank God he'd learned what he was in time to save Esperanza.

"I'll spend the rest of the night on the balcony, keeping watch," Don Alfonso said as they left Esperanza. "Sleep, if you can. In the morning you and Don Rafael will dig a pit for the Americanos' grave while I make arrangements for Juan to be buried from the church."

Ulysses nodded. He didn't dare try to leave until morning for fear of the moon. The least he could do is stay long enough to help bury the men he'd killed. He could slip away afterward and be far from the hacienda by moonrise.

Shut inside his room, he sat on the bed. Sleep? Would he ever sleep again? A yawn caught him by surprise. God, but he was tired. Was it because of the shifting? He hunched his shoulders, filled with desperation and disgust. A monster . . . he was a monster.

As those on the ship must have discovered. He still couldn't remember what had happened, but he no longer blamed the sailors who'd beaten him and thrown him overboard. He could almost see it happening—a ship, a full moon, no place for the shifted beast to hide and no place for prey to escape the beast. He covered his face with his hands, wishing they'd killed him.

Apparently he was hard to kill. In the darkness, Ulysses glanced toward the chest where his Colt lay, the pistol taken by the don from the first of the beast's victims. Or had that man been the first? He groaned. He ought to pick up the gun, put the barrel to his temple, and pull the trigger. But recalling how quickly he healed, he wondered if he might not survive even a bullet to his brain.

If he understood where he came from, if he remembered his past, maybe he'd have some idea of how to prevent the shifting. And maybe not. All he could do was get as far away from other people as possible and try to survive the best he could.

He groaned at the thought of leaving the Alvarado rancho. He'd respected and admired Don Alfonso from the first. The don needed him here, needed his help to run the rancho. He'd feel hurt and betrayed when Ulysses deserted him without so much as an *adiós*. Esperanza—Ulysses shook his head. He couldn't bear to think about her.

With him gone, at least they'd be safe from the beast—he'd have that thought to comfort him. But what would Esperanza have to comfort her?

Feeling trapped in his small, dark room, he fought the urge to rush into the moonlight. He flung himself backward onto the bed and closed his eyes, determined not to dwell on the agony of leaving in the morning. You have to live with the beast, he told himself, so you might as well start getting used to the idea.

A shudder of revulsion shook him. How could a man grow used to such an abomination?

He gritted his teeth. If he wished to go on living, he'd have to try.

He knew the moon was his enemy. Moonlight triggered the shifting, and it seemed that the nearer full the moon, the harder it was for him to control the change. Under a full moon, probably impossible. But if the moon was hidden by clouds or fog, he could resist successfully.

He sensed the life energies of others, that reddish glow surrounding each human and animal. In some, like the *bruja* and her cat, the energy flared and crackled blue. Why? Because they had unusual powers? Would his own life force show a similar difference from normal humans?

He'd do well to steer clear of humans with blue energy, lest, like the *bruja*, they knew what he was. He couldn't be certain if all cats had Sombrito's ability, but it didn't matter. Cats weren't the danger; humans were.

Except for cats, he could handle animals better than the humans he'd met. At least while he remained a man. Palo had thrown him and bolted for home when he started to shift, so even animals he knew well feared him in his beast form.

When he returned to himself, he'd found he couldn't recall what the beast had done. He had no way of discovering what knowledge the beast had of his memories, if any, but the beast was a dangerous and formidable killer. The last he remembered of the fight with the Americanos was three men pummeling him—one with a knife. Though he was strong and fit, he couldn't have vanquished all three. The beast had killed each and every one. He'd changed involuntarily because his life was in danger, so it was possible the necessity to survive would prompt a change. Did the moon have to be near full for danger to prompt a shift? He couldn't be sure.

So far, the beast hadn't killed anyone Ulysses knew, but he couldn't count on that. A shudder rippled through him as he pictured a newly married Esperanza waking up in the night to find a beast in bed with her.

He'd learn more the longer he lived with the beast, Ulysses thought grimly. He turned onto his side and a faint scent of violets drifted to him from his pillow. A lump rose into his throat. Esperanza. How could he bear to leave her? Tears stung his eyes and he fought to keep from sobbing.

When the time came, the original Ulysses had to leave Nausicaa, he reminded himself. Ulysses had to go home.

Ah, God, where was *his* home?

Ulysses drifted in darkness with danger pressing close on all sides. His only chance to survive was to remain a man. The first glint of silvery light tensed him. Not the moon!

With the moonlight came the scent of violets. No, he cried silently, not her. If he changed and died, what did it matter? But if he changed and killed her—

Ulysses sprang up, blinking in the sudden light. Sunlight. And Esperanza.

"How you startled me!" she scolded. "I almost dropped the tray."

He sat back on the bed, his heart pounding. He'd fallen asleep in his room at the casa. It was morning.

"I had a bad dream," he confessed.

Esperanza frowned. "I don't wonder. But last night is over and done with, the saints be praised, and we're still alive. See, I've brought you breakfast." She set the tray on a small table next to the bed. "I prepared everything myself."

Ulysses couldn't tear his gaze from her. Though paler than usual, she was so lovely, with her big dark eyes and shining black hair.

Esperanza blushed. "You're staring at me." She reached for a cup and handed it to him. "Here, drink this."

He took the cup and put it to his lips, still bemused. Sipping the sweet reddish liquid, he wondered vaguely what it was. Some kind of fruit juice, he supposed.

"Don't put the cup down until you drink it all," she insisted. "It will help you regain your strength."

He drained the cup, set it on the table, and reached for her hand, holding her palm to his lips. "I'd sooner taste you than anything else," he told her, desire simmering inside him, despite everything.

She smiled. "That's why I left the door open."

He hadn't noticed. Dropping her hand, he shook his head. He no longer had any right to touch her.

"Before Papa left the casa he told me to tell you Don Rafael has brought two men to help today, so you won't be needed."

Damn it, he'd wanted to dig the graves. It was his duty to bury those he'd killed. Ulysses started to rise, found his head swimming, and sat down abruptly. What was the matter with him? Even as he wondered, his vision blurred and his mind grew fuzzy. He struggled against the lethargy creeping over him, fear fueling him.

The *bruja*—she'd done this to him.

"Ulysses!" Esperanza cried, her voice coming from far away. "What's wrong?"

He heard no more.

Ulysses, naked, woke to night and cold. His eyes slitted open, he lay still, gathering his wits. The scent of pine and the chill breeze told him that, though he lay on wood, he was outdoors. Where? Without moving his head, he opened his eyes fully. It wasn't true night but the hours just before dawn. The moon, thank God, had set.

When he was certain he sensed no human near him, he sat up cautiously. His head ached slightly, his mouth tasted foul, but otherwise he was all right. He blinked as he looked at the bars crisscrossed in front of him, unsure of what he saw in the uncertain light.

He stood and his head brushed wood. His touch confirmed what he'd seen. Metal bars in front of him, solid wood on the other three sides, a wooden floor and ceiling. He was in a cage.

He was naked, as he always was after shifting. Had he shifted? He didn't know, but he didn't think so. The last he recalled was morning in his room in the casa and Esperanza giving him a cup of juice, urging him to drink it all. He'd passed out from a potion the *bruja* had put into the juice. He didn't blame Esperanza—she knew no better than to trust *Tía* Dolores.

Now it was nearly dawn. Who'd taken him from his room and locked him in this cage? Not *Tía* Dolores, at least not alone. Don Rafael? He nodded. Easy enough for the *bruja* to drug Esperanza as he'd been drugged, so she wouldn't know what was happening. Don Alfonso had been going to arrange for Juan's church burial—no doubt he'd ridden to the tiny church on the road to Monterey to talk to the priest.

But why lock him in a cage? Why hadn't they simply killed him when he was helpless? Remembering what tonight was, the hair prickled on his nape. Tonight a full moon rode the sky. And the *bruja* knew what happened to him then. He'd be a caged beast for whatever sinister purpose she intended.

With a yell of rage and frustration, he wrenched at the bars, struggling to free himself. He slammed into one side of the cage, then the other, but nothing gave. At last he was forced to pause for breath. Had they made this cage to hold him? Ulysses shook his head. No, his prison wasn't new. And when he took the time to notice, he smelled a definite stink of bear.

He was trapped in a grizzly cage.

He thought of Juan's stories of bull and bear baiting. Did they mean to pit the beast against a bull? Aware of the ferociousness of the beast, he thought it would be no contest. The bull would die in minutes. A grizzly would be another matter. He'd never seen one, but if Juan's description could be trusted, grizzlies were twice as large as black bears and ten times as dangerous.

Did his beast self stand a chance against a grizzly? All he knew was that the beast would be hard to kill. If, by chance, the beast overpowered the bear, would he be allowed to run free? Ulysses grimaced. Never!

The Californios would have their sport. Whatever happened, they'd kill him, one way or another. He was doomed. Who could save him? Not Don Alfonso. Though he doubted the don had been told what Ulysses was, once he knew, he'd regard the beast with loathing, regard Ulysses with loathing.

Once the full moon shone on him, all watchers would see the shapeshifting abomination for themselves.

Again he flung himself at the bars, yanking at them with all his strength. Some of the wooden cross-hatching gave way, but not the metal bars, nor the heavy oak they were set into. He couldn't reach the massive bolt securing the door and it wouldn't jar loose no matter how he rocked the cage.

Eventually he tired and stopped. He was also hungry and thirsty and he was well aware he wouldn't be fed or given water. If he exhausted his strength in a futile attempt to escape, wouldn't the beast's strength tonight be that much less?

Crouching in a corner of the cage, he rested.

A hell of a way to die, he told himself, wishing that Don Alfonso wouldn't be a witness to his shifting—but Don Rafael would make certain the don came. Juan had told him the señoras and señoritas didn't watch the bull and bear fights, so at least Esperanza would be spared the horror of knowing what he was—for whatever comfort that gave him.

When the sun rose, Ulysses saw exactly where on the rancho he was—in the small pine grove at the eastern edge of the Alvarado property. He wondered where the fight was to be—if that's what Don Rafael and the *bruja* had in mind. Perhaps they only meant to exhibit him like a zoo animal. Ulysses shook his head. He'd humiliated Don Rafael; exhibition wouldn't be enough revenge. Don Rafael would relish watching him torn to bits by a grizzly, would delight in killing him if the grizzly didn't.

Even if Don Rafael didn't hate him for personal reasons, he'd stand no chance. Men killed his kind whenever they could. He may have forgotten his past, but that was a truth bred in his bones.

He'd never had a day pass so slowly. Though he did his best to ignore his thirst, his need for water tormented him until it distracted him from his perilous predicament. He cursed the *bruja* and her evil potions that first stupefied a man and then drove him mad with thirst. He pictured water spilling from the high reaches, cool and delicious, splashing into the streams that fed the rivers flowing into the sea, water from the snowmelt on the cone-shaped mountains.

Ulysses blinked. Cone-shaped? He'd seen no mountains like that since he'd come to on the beach. Was this a memory from the past?

Cone-shaped meant volcanic. How well he remembered studying volcanos. He'd been smart enough but not as brilliant as the one he shared his studies with, not as smart as—

The thought winked out like a quenched ember and he couldn't bring it back, couldn't recall the name that, for a moment, had hovered on the edge of his mind—a name he was sure would uncover his shrouded past.

Bitterness overwhelmed him. Was he to die without knowing who that other had been? Die without his own real name? He slammed his fist on the solid floor of the cage. He could almost believe he'd been cursed with an evil *dolya* at the moment of his birth.

A *dolya* was man's fate personified, and her power had no limits. Nor could a man ever rid himself of her. A good *dolya* helped a man all his life, smoothing his path and bringing good fortune. His, obviously, was the wrong kind.

Ulysses pressed the heels of his hands to his temples. Why could he remember a *dolya* instead of what he so desperately longed to know?

The sun was lowering when he sensed the horses and their riders. Four. And another man, with oxen. He waited as calmly as he could, determined to show no fear. They reined in near the cage. Don Rafael, the only man he recognized, dismounted and swaggered close to the bars.

"What have we here?" Don Rafael taunted. "It looks like a man, don't you agree, *compadres*? The devil is clever at disguise."

"Let's get the cage on the cart and be done with it," one of the riders said, crossing himself.

They were all Californios, the four riders and the man driving the oxcart. Ulysses hadn't expected otherwise. Slowly and deliberately, he looked from one to the other. Nobody but Don Rafael met his gaze, and two more of the men crossed themselves. They feared him, even in human form. *Tía* Dolores must have assured Don Rafael that the beast wouldn't appear until the moon rose, but though Don Rafael glared his hatred, Ulysses thought he seemed uneasy.

"See the eyes," one of the men muttered. "Yellow, like a wolf's."

"Do you know what's in store for you, devil-beast?" Don Rafael asked.

Ulysses said nothing.

"For the love of God, Don Rafael," the oxcart driver pleaded, "the sun is almost gone. Do not delay."

"You will die tonight!" Don Rafael cried. "You will die most painfully, with all of us watching and cheering as you beg for your life."

Ulysses clenched his jaw to keep from replying to the taunt. He was damned if he'd ever beg for his life. Not that he'd be in control once he shifted. But the beast sure as hell wouldn't beg—the beast would fight to the finish, no matter what the odds. And far more adeptly and viciously than he, as a man, could.

Don Rafael glanced at the sun, half hidden behind the western hills, and nodded to the oxcart driver.

Ulysses braced himself as the cage dipped and swayed while the four men struggled to lift it into the cart. When he caught himself thinking he didn't look forward to the jolting ride to wherever the pit had been dug, he half smiled. At least he'd survive the ride.

"Mother of God, he smiles," a rider muttered. Without looking, Ulysses was certain the man had crossed himself again.

Dusk had settled over the land by the time the cart lurched to a halt. By torchlight the men again lifted the cage, this time fastening ropes around it. From close by an animal snarled menacingly. Ulysses, who'd sensed the grizzly for some time, now smelled the bear as well.

Using the ropes, they lowered his cage into one end of a large and deep trench. In a similar cage at the other end, a massive golden brown grizzly eyed him malevolently, fangs showing. Long, sharp claws rang against the metal as, growling, the bear sought to get at him.

Staring at the bear, its scent rank in his nostrils, Ulysses prayed he *would* shift when the moon rose. Otherwise he didn't stand a chance—a naked man against a grizzly.

At the lip of the pit, Don Rafael looked down and laughed. "A worthy opponent, devil-beast."

Ulysses fought to control his panic. If he didn't keep his head, he might find himself begging, after all. Crouching once more in the far corner of his cage, he did his best to ignore the bear as well as the men who came to peer into the pit.

There'd be quite a crowd tonight. As Juan had told him, the Californios enjoyed a good fight between animals. Too bad Juan would miss this one. At the moment he envied the dead man—for Juan, at least, it was all over.

The evening darkened into night and Ulysses welcomed his first tinge of restlessness, recognizing it now as the beginning of the urge to shift. Since he had no choice, he positioned himself at the bars, so the moon's light could reach him, and waited.

Above him men laughed and shouted in the flaring torchlight as more and more Californios arrived. A gathering, he thought, like those in what Don Alfonso referred to as the golden days. If only the don didn't have to see what Ulysses was.

A single ray of silver light pierced the gloom in the pit and Ulysses took a deep breath.

"No!" a woman's voice cried from above. "What have you done with him?"

Esperanza! He looked up and saw the *bruja* gripping Esperanza's arm, forcing her to look at him. No! he tried to shout as his insides twisted painfully. No, don't watch!

It was too late. He heard the grizzly roar as the terrible wrenching began. Then—nothing more.

Free! Yet not free. He crouched behind metal bars, the stink of bear strong, the sense of many men equally powerful. The bear roared in challenge. Above him a woman screamed in terror. He flung himself against the iron bars, but they held. So did the bars keeping back the enraged bear.

The bars didn't give on his second or third try, so though his only thought was escape, he stopped hurling himself against them and waited, his every sense alert. Grizzly, he remembered, this golden bear was called.

Two men, ripe with the acrid stink of fright, eased down into the pit on ropes. He heard the clink of metal once, twice, then the men were hastily yanked up and out. He shoved against the bars and they gave, swinging open like a door. He was free!

Before he could leap to the top of the cage and climb from the pit, the other cage door flew open and the fear-maddened grizzly rose on his hind legs and attacked.

Chapter 6

Moonlight touched the men lining the rim and slanted into the pit where, teeth gnashing, spittle foaming from its mouth, the grizzly bore down on the beast. With no room to duck aside in the narrow trench, the beast leaped into the air, twisted, and came down on the bear's head and shoulders, forcing the animal to drop to all fours while he tore at its neck with his fangs.

Roaring with pain and rage, the grizzly fought to shake his adversary, slamming him against the sides of the trench, but the beast remained on the bear's back. With the first taste of blood, the beast no longer heard the curses and shouts of the men above him, no longer even sensed their presence. Bloodlust shone redly in his eyes. His mind held only one command.

Kill.

From his perch on the back, he couldn't reach the throat. He dropped to the ground. Before the beast's long yellow teeth reached him, he slid underneath it and savaged its throat, hardly feeling the bear's claws rake down his back. Grizzly blood spurted over him; the bear coughed, staggered, then convulsed and collapsed. With its body half covering him, he drank his fill of the hot blood, still pulsing with life.

A loud crack from above brought him to awareness, the bloodlust fading. Another crack, another and another. Sharp stings in his shoulder and neck. Men. Guns. Escape or die.

He slid from under the dead bear and leaped to the top of the grizzly cage, then clawed his way to the rim of the pit. Men shouted; guns cracked. The wounds along his back from the bear claws and the pain from the bullets slowed him, but he pulled himself over the top and leaped to his feet. Snarling his defiance, he charged through the men, slashing with his fangs to right and left as he fought his way clear.

He raced past the flaring torches but knew any men who pursued could still see him in the moonlight. He could easily outrun men, but they had horses. His injuries sapped his strength; he must find cover or he was doomed.

Skirting the temporary safety of a thicket because he feared he might be surrounded and trapped inside, he made for the nearest stream, sensing riders behind him, following.

By the time he plunged among the trees along the stream, he realized he was flagging. He was in trouble. Never before had he been so badly hurt. If he could find a safe place to rest, he might recover, but he wasn't sure. He couldn't outrun the horses—to have any chance at all he must outwit their riders.

He waded into the water and partially eased his raging thirst before padding upstream, sometimes on all fours, sometimes on his back legs to ease the pain in his shoulders. When the stream widened and the water grew deeper, he scrambled onto the far bank and angled quickly between the trees toward dimly sensed hills. In the hills lay safety. If he could reach them.

His pursuers thinned, dwindling finally to one rider. In his weakened state he feared he wasn't a match for a man with a gun, so he staggered on through the night. Around him animals either froze in terror or fled. Far off in the hills a coyote wailed, the sound beckoning him on. This brother to the wolf wasn't an ally—the beast had no friends—but he felt a kinship to the coyote as well as the wolf, a kinship he might have extended to the grizzly under other circumstances.

He longed to find a hollow among the trees and curl into it. If he didn't rest soon, he'd collapse. But the rider, either by luck or instinct, still trailed him. He now traveled on all fours, lacking the strength to rise onto his hind legs. His muzzle dropped low and his senses began to blur. He didn't scent the bear until he was almost upon it. A female. With a cub.

Veering abruptly, he made a wide half circle around

mother and child. In his condition even the cub might prove too much for him.

When he was well past the bears, he stopped and searched for the rider, finding no trace of man and horse. Either the man had given up or he'd come on the bears and retreated. Females with cubs were dangerous.

Using the last of his strength, he searched for a safe den, rejecting a hole dug by an animal under tree roots. It was easy to be trapped inside a hole. Ordinarily he could climb trees, but the effort would be too much for him now. At last he located a hidden niche high in a rocky outcropping and settled into it. He'd done all he could. If he healed, he'd live; if not, he'd die. Closing his eyes, he slept.

Ulysses woke, naked and shivering, to gray light. Without moving, he surveyed his surroundings. Rocks. Where in hell was he? He sensed no men around, so he uncurled, groaning. Why did he ache all over? Examining himself, he saw numerous healing wounds beneath the crusted blood that covered him. Bits of flattened metal littered the rocks. It took him a moment to realize they were bullets. Thrust from his body by the rapid healing? He wasn't sure, but where else could the bullets have come from?

He'd shifted last night, he remembered that much. Shifted while he was caged in that foul pit with the grizzly. Evidently the beast had gotten away. Easing from the shallow cave, he pulled himself to his feet, swaying dizzily. He was damned weak. Whatever had happened had taken a lot out of him.

He saw nothing familiar, nothing that looked like any part of the Alvarado rancho. Scraggly pines and other conifers grew between the granite slabs that sprouted like rocky growths from the hills surrounding the outcropping where he stood. Treading warily, he made his way down to a stream and drank. Then, shuddering from the chill, he sluiced water over himself until his skin was free of bloodstains.

Grizzly blood, he supposed. How else could the beast escape except by killing the bear? He didn't want to think about last night's horrors. Not ever. Or at least not until after he decided what to do next.

He seemed to be some distance from Alvarado property—that gave him a chance. If a naked man, hungry and weak and alone in the wilderness, had any chance to speak of.

Not knowing what else to do, he walked slowly upstream, pausing often to rest. A bluejay, disturbed by his passing, followed him, warning everything within hearing of his coming. When he finally sat down on a rock, the jay perched above him for a time, squawking, then lost interest and flew off. Ulysses, hunched forward, didn't move, conserving what strength he had.

He sat so still that a snake slithered onto the rock beside him. Seeing it wasn't a rattler, Ulysses remained where he was, trying to decide if he was hungry enough to eat raw snake. He hadn't made up his mind when he suddenly sensed men and horses approaching. He tensed. The snake, startled by his movement, slithered away.

The riders weren't behind him or in front, but followed a course parallel to his. Californios? Ulysses tried to count the men but found the large number made it difficult. Twenty? He frowned. Though there'd been at least that many Californios at the pit last night, would Don Rafael be able to persuade them all to ride in search of him?

Since he was nearly helpless, his only defense was to remain hidden. He hadn't sensed dogs, so he needn't worry about being nosed out.

But what if the riders weren't Californios? Strangers wouldn't know what he was. Strangers might help him—even if they were Americanos. He'd called Americanos his enemies when he fought on the side of the Californios. What would he call them now that the Californios were his enemies?

God knows he needed help. He'd never know whether they were enemies or strangers unless he looked.

Choosing a course to intercept the riders while keeping to cover, Ulysses hurried as fast as he could. After several hundred paces he found a trail. Ducking into a stand of willow saplings, he crouched and waited.

Clinking metal and creaking leather announced the riders before they rounded the curve of the hill. The first, a tall red-haired man in a blue uniform, rode alone, while the rest, all in blue uniforms, followed.

Soldiers! They'd be Americanos. Ulysses hesitated momentarily, then stepped from concealment onto the trail and held up his hand. He had no quarrel with Americano soldiers.

"Column, halt!" the officer in the lead ordered. His men

obeyed and he walked his horse toward Ulysses, stopping just short of him.

"Please help me," Ulysses said as calmly as he could, his voice quivering despite his efforts.

"Good God, man, what happened to you?" the officer demanded, his dark eyes flicking over Ulysses.

"Bandits," Ulysses said, rapidly concocting a story. "They stole my horse, my clothes, everything I own and left me for dead."

The officer dismounted, untied a blanket from his saddle, and handed it to Ulysses. "I'm Lieutenant Sherman, United States Army. We'll do what we can for you."

Wrapping the blanket about his nakedness, Ulysses desperately sought a name to give the lieutenant, aware Ulysses Koshka must die, here and now. "Uh—my name's Sherman, too," he stammered. "Sherman Oso."

First he was Mr. Cat, now he was Señor Bear—not very imaginative.

The lieutenant nodded. "Think you can ride?"

The newly christened Sherman nodded. The way he felt, the prospect of riding, even naked, was preferable to walking.

The lieutenant snapped orders, supplies were transferred from a packhorse to other animals, and a spare saddle was found.

Sherman found himself riding at the head of the column with the red-haired officer. "Sorry to put you to this trouble, Lieutenant," he said.

The officer waved a dismissive hand. "We're patrolling for Indians. Been looking for two days—haven't seen a sign of one. Have you seen any?"

Sherman shook his head. "You and your men are the first to come along. Since the bandits."

"California's full of desperados. Didn't anyone warn you it's not safe for a man to travel alone in these parts?"

"I had to ride south to meet a friend in Los Angeles, so I took a chance," Sherman improvised. He remembered Los Angeles as the name of a southern hamlet the don had mentioned once or twice.

"We'll see what we can find to outfit you when we camp for the night," the lieutenant promised. "We're riding southeast for the rest of today—you can keep company with us until we turn back. I'd advise you to return with us, but if you feel you must continue south, I think the U.S. Army can spare that old swayback you're riding.''

Sherman stroked the horse's neck. ''Thanks. He's got a few good years left, swaybacked or not.'' He was careful not to commit himself to any plan.

He still had tonight to get through. Glancing at the sky, heavy with clouds, he prayed for rain, rain that would last through the night so the moon couldn't shed her deadly rays on him. Otherwise he'd have to slip away from the night camp before moonrise without a mount. No horse could survive the beast.

A drizzle began in midafternoon and the lieutenant ordered an early night's camp near a stand of pines. By the time the tents were up, the rain was coming down in earnest. To Sherman's surprise, he was invited to share the lieutenant's tent for the night. He could hardly refuse.

By then he'd gotten a pair of uniform trousers from one soldier—too short, but a tolerable fit otherwise—and a shirt from another. The lieutenant found a spare pair of his own socks for him. There were no extra boots to be had, but Sherman was grateful for the clothes and the blanket and, especially, the food.

''I haven't eaten for two days,'' he said as he took the second helping of salt pork and beans offered by the lieutenant's orderly. ''Lucky for me you came along when you did. I owe you my life.''

''A naked man afoot's at a disadvantage, all right,'' the lieutenant agreed. He eyed Sherman appraisingly. ''Still, I'll wager you would've survived. You strike me as the kind who doesn't give up.''

Give up? Never—in spite of what he was. He watched the orderly pour more of the thick black coffee into their cups. The lieutenant produced a metal flask and added a generous dollop of brownish liquid to each. Liquor, Sherman decided from its taste and by the way it warmed his stomach. He sipped the mixture with relish.

''A special brew from Captain Sutter's distillery,'' the lieutenant said.

Sutter. Sherman had heard the name mentioned before in connection with gold. ''Have you been in California long, sir?'' he asked the lieutenant.

''Hell, call me Cump—you're not one of my men, no

need to say sir. I've been stationed in California for a couple of years—was raised in Ohio."

Sherman had never heard of Ohio. Was it a city or one of the United States? Asking would reveal his ignorance, so he said instead, "I've never been to Ohio."

"You've missed some mighty pretty country." He gestured toward the open tent flap. "Nothing like this barren land. I hope to be transferred back east soon." He stroked his short reddish whiskers. "You're an Englishman, I take it."

"Why do you say that?" Sherman asked, both taken aback and relieved at finding a possible excuse for being unfamiliar with the United States. England, he recalled, was across the ocean from America. Perhaps he'd learned the Americano tongue from an Englishman somewhere in his unknown past.

Cump smiled. "You don't have much of an accent, but I have a good ear. Your name threw me off for a bit—Oso's Spanish. But it's obvious you're no Californio. You came here looking for gold, I'll wager."

Sherman hesitated, fearing being trapped in a web of lies. "No," he said finally, "I work with horses. And cattle."

Cump stared at him as if puzzled. "Most everyone's interested in grubbing for gold these days. Even my men would much rather be in the gold fields than hunting Indians. To tell you the truth, so would I."

The don had grumbled about Indians stealing an occasional steer, so Sherman knew they were around, though he'd never seen any.

"For that matter," Cump went on, "I can think of a hundred better things to do than chasing Diggers."

"Diggers?"

"That's what we call the tribes in these hills. The women dig for food. The men are a thieving lot." He sighed. "When I trained at West Point I didn't foresee a career of rounding up Diggers." Evidently recalling that an Englishman might not understand, he added, "The United States Military Academy is at West Point in New York. A fine establishment."

Cump offered him more of Sutter's liquor, but Sherman declined, aware he had to keep his wits about him. Who knew when the rain might stop and the sky clear? Cump took another drink himself and went on talking about his years at West Point, much as the don had reminisced about the golden time of the Californios.

What kind of a past did Sherman Oso have? Would he enjoy recalling those days if he could remember them—or were they better forgotten?

"Your first name being the same as my last is quite a coincidence," Cump said, focusing Sherman's attention on him once more. "I've always been interested in how people get their names. Take mine. The reason I'm called Cump is because my father named me Tecumseh Sherman after the Ohio Shawnee chief who fought with the English against the Americans back in 1812."

Cump smiled. "Tecumseh was one of your countrymen's allies, but my countrymen didn't let him live long enough to regret it. Even though the Shawnee fought on the enemy side, my father admired Tecumseh's courage. But when my foster mother had me baptized as a child, the priest added a saint's name, William. So I became William Tecumseh Sherman.

"I've sometimes wondered what my namesake—Tecumseh, not Saint William—would think about my military forays. So far they've all been against Indians. My first duty, nine years ago, was rounding up Florida Seminoles. I learned a lesson there I won't soon forget: Destroy the enemy's supplies and you break his morale."

"Do you enjoy Army life?" Sherman asked.

Cump frowned. "Not in California. If I don't get out of here, I may remain a lieutenant for life. A man can't get married on a lieutenant's pay."

A man like me can never get married, Sherman thought, even if he became as wealthy as King Midas.

When at last they rolled themselves in their blankets for the night, Sherman fought sleep as long as he could but eventually succumbed.

A high-pitched scream brought him abruptly awake, driving him to his feet, heart pounding. A horse whinnied, shrill and terrified. Sherman stared at his hands. Human. He was himself, thank God. Some other beast was after the horses.

The lieutenant plunged through the tent flap and Sherman hurried after him. Rain pelted them as they ran across the soggy ground toward the crude brush enclosure that corralled the horses. The god-awful cry came again, raising the hair on Sherman's nape.

" 'Tis a varmint!" one of the troopers shouted as three of them pounded up to join him and Cump.

Just as Sherman sensed the animal, perched on a pine limb, ready to launch itself onto the nearest horse, the lieutenant sprang toward the frightened, milling horses, bringing himself directly under the animal in the tree.

It was too late for a warning. Grabbing a rifle from the nearest trooper's hands, Sherman took aim and fired. The beast dropped from the limb, hitting Cump on the shoulder and knocking him to the ground. A chestnut horse screamed, rising on his hind legs to trample the dead animal. Cump tried to scramble out of the way of the sharp hooves.

Thrusting the rifle back at the trooper, Sherman lunged at the panicked horse, catching the tether rope and dragging him to one side. As Cump leaped to safety, Sherman vaulted onto the chestnut's back to keep from being crushed by the milling horses and, leaning forward, soothed his mount to calmness.

Touching those near him, he murmured words in his own tongue, soothing, quieting one after another until the horses were calm enough for the soldiers to handle.

Later, when the dead beast had been dragged away from the horses and into the lantern light, he stood with Cump staring down at an animal he'd never before seen—some kind of gigantic tawny cat.

"Puma, they calls 'em around these parts," a sergeant said. "Sort of a mountain lion, they be." He glanced at Sherman. "You got an eagle eye, I'll say that. Never saw the critter, myself."

"Me neither," another trooper said. "But he grabbed my gun and nailed the varmint with one shot."

Cump clapped Sherman on the shoulder. "You sure as hell saved my neck," he said. "We could use a man like you in the Army."

Sherman wished he dared join. He'd be handed food, clothes, a horse, and living quarters—everything he lacked. Even if he dared remain near the Californios, though, the Army wasn't for his kind. It was no safe haven for a man who shifted shape when the full moon rose.

"I have other obligations," he said regretfully.

"If you ever change your mind, look me up," Cump urged. "I owe you, and I don't forget obligations."

Before returning to the tent, Sherman took one last look

at the puma's limp body. Though he'd felt he had no choice except to kill the animal to save Cump, he wished he hadn't been forced to. He had a strange, uncomfortable feeling it was like killing the beast part of himself.

The rest of the night passed uneventfully. The soldiers broke camp at dawn to return to San Francisco.

"Without sighting a single damn Digger," Cump commented as he shook hands with Sherman. "I hope to see you again one day."

Earlier, without comment, he'd handed Sherman one of his pistols—a new Colt—and a pouch of bullets.

"Thanks to you, I may live to see that day," Sherman told him.

"Thanks to you, so may I," Cump countered.

Sherman mounted the swaybacked dun, Rawhide, then waved and set off southward without looking back.

He hated to ride away from Cump Sherman. He'd liked the tall, red-haired lieutenant from the beginning, and now he felt he was leaving a friend. He truly regretted it, but what choice did he have? He was a man who didn't dare make a friend. He was glad, though, that he'd chosen part of Cump's name for his new identity.

He owed Cump more than he could ever repay. Shooting the puma wasn't enough. Cump had given him not only a horse and clothes and supplies but also an acceptable reason for his ignorance about his country—being an Englishman in the strange country of the United States.

He'd regained his strength; the wounds from the grizzly were practically healed. Not that he remembered getting them—he'd been the beast then. All he recalled was the grizzly roaring as a slim finger of moonlight touched the caged Ulysses.

No, not quite all. Oh, God, why couldn't he wipe away the rest? He'd remember forever the cursed *bruja* forcing Esperanza to the edge of the pit to look down at him, to watch as the moonlight changed him.

He hated the *bruja* as much for what she'd done to Esperanza as for the evil she'd worked on him. Don Rafael, whether he liked him or not, he could understand—he'd bested the Californio and then stolen his woman. Don Rafael wanted him dead for good reason. But the witch had planned his death an hour after she and Esperanza had found him on the beach. When her scheme failed, she'd bided her time and tried again. For no reason other than suspecting what he was.

With nothing but unhappiness for company, he traveled along the trail until the sun was halfway up the sky, when to the west he sensed many horses. He halted Rawhide. What now? After a moment, he realized the horses had no riders. The don had told him of wild horse herds—is that what he sensed? Sherman decided it must be.

Ready to ride on, he held, thinking. He had nothing but what Cump had given him. If he took over the herd and drove it south with him, he'd have horses to train and then sell when he reached Los Angeles.

Nodding, he altered his course to intercept the horse herd, confident of his ability to control them. As long as he remained human. During a full moon he'd be more danger to them than a marauding puma.

Somehow he must learn to control his shifting. If such a thing was possible.

Nine months later, he hadn't found any way to avoid changing under the moon. Though he'd done well for himself with the horses, well enough to buy his first California land, he was still at the moon's mercy.

Living alone in the desert east of the village of Los Angeles kept him away from humans. His nearest neighbors, a small tribe of Havasupais, left him alone. After he learned enough of their language to talk to them, he'd arranged for a man called Bony Tail to guard his horses for three days of every month—the three days of the full moon—while he disappeared into the hills.

Oso, the Indians called him. Bear. He wondered if they suspected what he was. If so, they didn't let on. Nor did they go out of their way to avoid him. They were good neighbors, neither friendly nor unfriendly. He didn't intend to make friends. Not with Bony Tail of the Havasupais or any man, ever again.

He wasn't happy, but he didn't expect happiness. When he had enough land, he meant to build a fortress in the wilderness and live out his days in isolation, protected from men. As they'd be protected from him.

Meanwhile, he was safe—or at least as safe as any *oborot* could be.

How long would his precarious safety last?

Chapter 7

"Harder," *Tía* Dolores urged. "Push harder, my child."

Esperanza drew in a ragged breath and, tears streaming down her face, tried to obey. She'd never known such grinding pain—how could she push? Through blurred eyes, she stared in desperation at the familiar ceiling of her room. Her child fought against being born and she couldn't blame him.

Mother of God have mercy, she prayed silently.

The pain increased until she thought she'd faint. Instead, she found herself grunting, pushing, forcing the child from her body whether he wished it or not. *Tía* Dolores gave a cry of triumph, and suddenly Esperanza was free of the terrible pain.

But only briefly. Renewed pain gripped her. Though it wasn't as severe, Esperanza moaned. She'd hoped it was over.

"A boy," *Tía* Dolores said.

Esperanza had known all along it would be a boy. Despair wracked her. She was far too weak to protect her son, now that he was no longer safe inside her.

"Let me see him." Her voice quivered with fatigue.

"He never took a breath," *Tía* Dolores said. "You must thank the Lord he did not."

Dead? Her son was dead? "I don't believe you!" Esperanza cried.

Tía Dolores handed her the blanket-wrapped baby. "Look for yourself."

Gazing at her beautiful little son, his skin already mottling with death, Esperanza scarcely noticed the renewed pain in her grief. *Pobrecito,* she thought, he resembles his father.

She eased the initialed tin cross his father had given her from under her pillow and laid it on his breast. "Go with God," she whispered.

Tía Dolores took him from her and laid the little body out of her sight. "All is not over," she warned. "There's the afterbirth still to come. Drink this. It will ease the pain."

Esperanza choked down two swallows of a foul-tasting brew, but the pain persisted, going on and on into eternity. When at last it eased, the exhausted Esperanza collapsed into a drugged sleep in which she dreamed she heard a baby's cry. She struggled to rouse, fearing *Tía* Dolores had lied to her.

"He lives. I hear him," Esperanza gasped, too weak to raise her head.

"You saw his dead body for yourself."

"God will punish you for all eternity if you lie." Esperanza's voice was so faint the words were scarcely audible. "Harm my son and you risk your immortal soul."

"He is dead!" *Tía* Dolores insisted.

Unable to keep her eyes open no matter how hard she tried, Esperanza slipped into darkness.

Without so much as glancing at her, *Tía* Dolores crossed herself, picked up two bundles, and hurried from the room. She left one in the storeroom off the kitchen. Hastily pulling a cloak over her shoulders, she eased from the house with the other and walked rapidly into the night.

Don Rafael was in the courtyard waiting for *Tía* Dolores when she returned to the casa. "Well," he asked impatiently when she opened the gate, "is it over?"

Tía Dolores glanced quickly at him, then away, focusing her gaze on his polished boots. "It is over and done with," she muttered. "The boy was cursed in the womb and could not live. You will dig his grave and I will bury him, for it is not fit such as he should lie in hallowed ground. I've done what I can to prevent your next son from such contamination."

He turned away without a word, but not before she'd seen his thin smile of satisfaction. He might be Esperanza's husband, but he knew as well as she did the dead child was not his, but devil-spawn, conceived by another before he'd claimed his bride.

She hadn't lied to him. A child had died and they'd bury him. The one she hadn't mentioned wouldn't survive either. Esperanza's unexpected curse had prevented her from smothering him as she'd first intended, but abandoning him in the hills meant just as sure a death from animals or exposure—without endangering her soul and inviting the wrath of God. She'd rid them of every last remnant of the devil-beast by placing the tin cross in his son's blanket.

She'd done her part. One child dead at birth, the other as good as dead. It was up to Don Rafael to hunt down their father and rid the world of such a devil, once and for all.

Liwanu, the elder of the two Miwok men searching for a stray steer, heard the whimpering first and froze, holding up his hand for silence. Toloisi held, both men listening carefully. Their eyes met. Unshed tears shone in Toloisi's.

Liwanu sighed. Grief choked his son. One sun earlier, Toloisi's wife had birthed a babe before it was strong enough to live. If not for that, Liwanu would have gestured for them both to return the way they'd come. They were uncomfortably close to white men here, so it was no Miwok child they heard. Who knew what peril the crying baby might bring upon them?

Peril or not, the sight of his son's tears drove him to investigate.

When the men trotted back along their own trail, Toloisi hugged a blanket-wrapped baby to his chest.

As blue shadows lengthened over the rocky slopes of the desert, Sherman shifted his shoulders uneasily and Rawhide's ears flicked as though sensing his master's tension. For the best part of an hour Sherman had known a rider trailed him. Though he'd given no indication he realized he was being followed, he'd made certain to stay far enough ahead to be out of rifle range.

Since there was little cover in the desert, he'd ridden on until dusk cloaked his movements. Unless one of the Havasupais stalked him—and why should that be?—in darkness he had the advantage. Of all the men he'd met in California, only the Indians were as capable as he at night. They had the advantage of long practice in their home territory, but he had better night vision, as well as his extra ability to sense humans from a distance, making him their equal.

He didn't believe his pursuer was a Havasupai. Though he and the men of the tribe weren't friends, they appreciated one another's abilities. They knew his habits, so they had no reason to track him.

Women, of whatever race, he avoided altogether. In any case, no woman would be following him.

The rider was a man. Who? And why?

He rarely ventured into Los Angeles except to sell a horse or to return one he'd been hired to break and train. As far as he knew, he'd made no enemies in the hamlet. He doubted a bandit would bother with a horse trainer and trader—they looked for better pickings. Besides, bandits rode in packs and usually attacked from ambush.

A Californio from the north? Sherman drew in his breath. Would they search for him this far south? He'd changed his name and lived far from any town—they'd have trouble locating him if they did come looking.

The blue of evening shaded into night's darkness. He knew it was the dark of the moon; there'd be only starshine to guide him. Swerving Rawhide abruptly to the left, he began a wide circle toward his back trail. The Havasupais weren't the only desert dwellers who knew the country, for Sherman had memorized, for miles around, every hill and the location of each large desert plant, those strange spiked growths.

The rider stopped, apparently uncertain. Until nightfall, tracking had been easy because Sherman had deliberately stayed on the trail. Now, either the pursuer mistrusted the darkness or him. Or both. Sherman's lips drew back over his teeth. The man had cause for fear.

Sherman continued his circle until he reached his goal, a large spreading agave next to the trail and behind the man who followed him. He reined in Rawhide and laid his hand on the dun's neck. Swaybacked or not, Rawhide was his favorite mount—the horse had an unusual ability to sense what his rider wished. In this case, to keep quiet.

He waited. At the moment he was just behind his pursuer. If the man rode on, he'd follow. If the man turned back, he'd be ready.

At last the tracker wheeled his horse. Sherman urged Rawhide to the side of the agave farthest from the rider, eased his feet from the stirrups, and climbed onto the saddle, where he crouched. Rawhide remained rock still.

When the rider started past the agave, Sherman leaped, knocking the man from the saddle onto the ground and landing on top of him. Before the man regained his breath, Sherman disarmed him and yanked him to his feet, his arm crooked about the man's neck from behind. By then he didn't have to ask his name.

"Don Rafàel," Sherman said flatly. "We meet again."

"Lobombre!" Don Rafael gasped, choking as he fought to breathe, with Sherman's hold cutting off his wind.

Lobombre. Man-wolf. Whatever he was, Sherman thought, it wasn't a wolf. Easing his grip slightly, he asked, "What the hell do you mean by that?"

"Well, you know, devil-beast," Don Rafael sputtered. "You're a *lobombre,* a man who turns into a wolf when the moon is full. God has cursed you for your sins; you are forever damned. You will burn in hell for all eternity."

"Since I'm already damned, it makes little difference if I kill you, *no es verdad*?"

"Kill me, then! Another will come in my place. Kill him and another will come, and then another. We have vowed to rid the world of such as you. You cannot be permitted to live, to go on killing. Already Don Alfonso lies in his grave, his throat torn out."

Sherman was appalled. "No! Not by me!"

"By the wolf you became—what's the difference? You murdered him when you escaped from the pit. As you would have killed Esperanza one day if *Tía* Dolores hadn't drugged you."

"Never," Sherman protested. "I would never have harmed her."

"Esperanza is *my* wife, not yours, and she will bear my sons, not your devil-spawn. Yours was a monster; it died at birth, too malformed to live, an abomination to God and to man. As its father is."

Don Rafael raved on, but in his shock, Sherman hardly heard him. Esperanza had borne a son? His son? Just as well the child died rather than growing up to become what he was. *Lobombre. Oborot.* Shapeshifter.

Grief twisted in his chest for the bride he'd lost and the son he'd never see. And for Don Alfonso as well. Without willing it, his arm tightened around Don Rafael's neck.

Don Rafael gagged and choked, struggling. Before he went limp, Sherman realized what he was doing and loosened his grip. God help him, he didn't want to kill another man.

"How did you find me?" he demanded.

It took Don Rafael several moments to gather enough breath to gasp the answer. "Asked all Californios to watch for you. Heard from Los Angeles about a dark-haired man who charmed horses. Traced you here. Follow you wherever you go. If not me, another."

What was he to do with Don Rafael? Sherman asked himself. Even if he brought himself to kill him, another Californio would ride to hunt him. Must he kill them all to save his own life?

"Oso," a voice said from the darkness. "I am here."

Sherman started. In his agitation, he hadn't sensed the Havasupai's approach. He knew it was Bony Tail, the man who watched his horse herd three days a month.

"I saw the man follow you. I followed him," Bony Tail added.

"I need help," Sherman told him. "This man wishes to kill me. I don't wish to kill him."

"You want me to kill him for you." It wasn't a question.

"No. I wouldn't ask that of you. Or of anyone. What I ask is that you keep him your prisoner until I've traveled five suns from this place. Take him then to the trail north and let him go. See that he doesn't try to follow my trail."

"You leave forever." Again, it wasn't a question.

Sherman felt his heart constrict at the realization he couldn't return. He'd come to think of California as his home. Unlike Cump, he'd grown to love this land.

"Forever," he confirmed, sadness tinging the word.

"I will do as you ask," Bony Tail said.

"Choose what horses you like from my herd for your village," Sherman told him. "I will bring the rest with me."

Switching from Havasupai to Spanish, he spoke to Don Rafael. "I won't kill you. Neither will the Indians. Once I'm gone from here, they'll turn you loose. Don't try to follow me. If you do, Bony Tail will kill you."

Quickly binding Don Rafael's hands, he shoved him toward the Havasupai. "I will leave tonight," he told Bony Tail.

"My heart is heavy for you, man of darkness," the Indian said, "for you bear a great burden. May the Great Spirit light your pathway."

With the remnants of his horse herd, Sherman made camp in the desert a few hours before dawn. Before he'd left, Bony Tail had drawn a map in the dirt showing water holes as far into the desert as the tribe had ever ventured. There weren't many.

"White men follow a trail along what they call the Gila River," Bony Tail had said. "From there you will find much dry country until the river they call the Rio Grande. There is talk of a river as wide as a sea beyond the Rio Grande. I do not know the truth."

As he settled into his blanket beside Rawhide, Sherman wondered if he'd ever reach this river as wide as a sea. Much as he regretted leaving California, curiosity about the rest of the United States eased his sadness. Perhaps one day he might even see Cump's Ohio, wherever that might be. If he lived long enough.

Bony Tail had warned him of hostile Indians along the Gila and the Rio Grande. "Apache. Comanche. Hide from them or you'll die."

If he was successful in avoiding the hostiles, he had fourteen days to reach a place where he could safely corral his horses and then stay apart from them for the three days of the full moon. Otherwise what horses the beast didn't kill would scatter and be lost.

He'd discovered while living at the hacienda that he needed less sleep than Juan and the others—another difference between him and men who didn't shift shape under the moon. He planned to get by with as little sleep as possible while crossing what Bony Tail called the "no-good-to-live country." He didn't mind the barrenness of the desert, but he needed to find more hospitable land for himself and his horses.

Though he fought against reliving his meeting with Don Rafael, what the Californio had told him darkened his mind before sleep claimed him. Don Alfonso dead. Killed by the beast. By him. Sherman clenched his fists against the pain in his heart. If the *bruja* hadn't drugged him, he would have left of his own volition and the don would still be alive.

He hated Don Rafael for his part in the drugging, but he couldn't blame the Californio for hunting him down.

Don Alfonso had been a friend, a benefactor—he'd have given anything not to be responsible for the old man's death. It cut him to the heart to think of poor Esperanza, left alone to bear his child—a baby so malformed and monstrous it hadn't lived.

I'll never father another child, he vowed. Never.

How cruel to bring a child into such an existence as his. Who was his own father? *What* was his father? He might never learn, but he wouldn't be satisfied until he knew. Even if it meant spending the rest of his life trying to find the answers.

With St. Vrain beside him, Sherman stood at the rail of the sidewheeler that had brought him from Galveston in the state of Texas and was now approaching the dock in New Orleans, in the state of Louisiana. He'd gotten over his amazement at the broad waters of the Mississippi as they traveled upstream from the Gulf of Mexico, but the gracious plantation houses with their vast acreages on the riverbanks still bemused him.

"There she is, my beautiful city," St. Vrain said as the steamboat rounded a curve and buildings and church spires came into view. "*La belle* New Orleans."

Sherman felt a fleeting recognition as he stared at the spires, rounded rather than steeply pointed like those in Galveston. They were almost like the domes of the churches in—

The thought cut off before completion, and no amount of effort brought it back. Frustrated, he turned away from the city to look at St. Vrain.

Sherman admired anew the elaborately flowered brocaded vest the gambler wore. Otherwise St. Vrain dressed entirely in black except for a ruffled white shirt.

"She's all yours," St. Vrain continued, stroking his dark mustache. "All the temptations and the pleasures, all the pitfalls and perils. I'd wish I were your age again if I could be sure of remembering what I've learned in the twenty years since I was nineteen."

Sherman glanced again at St. Vrain's city. He saw at once it was larger than Galveston. The church with three rounded towers was flanked by two impressive buildings of at least three stories.

"Where you see the cannon, that's the Place d'Armes," St. Vrain said, "with St. Louis Cathedral behind the parade ground, the Cabildo to the left and the Presbytere to the right. Remarkable, *n'est-ce pas*? Unfortunately, farther to the right, along the docks, runs a street I urge you to keep away from, especially at night—Gallatin. In the day, few are about on Gallatin Street, but at night, the vampires appear to prey on the fools who venture into that pit of hell."

One word had startled Sherman. "Vampires?"

St. Vrain waved a hand. "So to speak—whores and thieves and murderers. No more than you do I believe that dead men rise at night to suck the blood of the living, but those who ply their trade on Gallatin Street are far worse than any tall tale of vampires. Stay away."

Sherman nodded, thinking back to his first meeting with the Creole. Shortly after the boat pulled away from Galveston, he'd wandered into the saloon, noticed men seated around a table playing cards, and sauntered over to watch. The game, he discovered, was vingt-et-un, French for twenty-one. Some of the Americans called it blackjack.

As soon as he understood the point of the game, he quickly realized the man wearing the flowery vest was by far the cleverest player and so watched him exclusively.

Later, on the deck, the annoyed St. Vrain had confronted him and asked why in hell Sherman kept breathing down his neck.

"I'm trying to learn to gamble before I reach New Orleans," Sherman admitted. "You're the best I've seen."

His frankness had disarmed St. Vrain, leading the gambler to further the acquaintance.

As the boat pulled into the dock, Sherman shifted his shoulders uneasily. New Orleans was much larger than he'd expected. Smells and noises assailed him—scents of tar and fish mingled with the sweetness of flowers growing everywhere in colorful profusion. Black dockworkers shouted to one another and carts clattered over the wooden planks of the wharf. Steamboat whistles hooted, and from St. Louis Cathedral a deep-toned bell tolled.

"Nervous?" St. Vrain asked.

"Yes."

St. Vrain smiled. "Good. That'll keep you on your toes. If you're going to be a gambler, you have to stay alert. Always."

He didn't know Sherman must be on his guard at all times, gambling or not.

"Just because you're a natural," St. Vrain said, "doesn't mean you won't run into trouble. Tell me, what will you do if you find someone at your table is cheating?"

Sherman repeated what St. Vrain had taught him. "Cash in and leave as soon as possible. No confrontations."

"Right. Accusations of cheating lead nowhere but to death." He adjusted the gold cuff links set with diamonds he wore on the sleeves of his shirt. "And what if you win big?"

"I'd expect to be followed and robbed, so I'd take precautions. No drinking, no women."

"See that you remember. And for the love of God don't rush out and buy a brocade vest with your first winnings."

Sherman blinked. "Why not? You wear one."

"Son, I'm a gambler. It's in my blood; it's how I make my living year after year. If you're telling me the truth, you only want to make enough money to buy wilderness land—God knows why. But it's none of my business."

He scanned Sherman quickly, head to toe. "Your clothes mark you as country and that's in your favor. No one expects a rough lad to know beans about cards. I dress the way I do so people realize I'm a gambler, so they'll come and play with me, trying to beat me. I dress like what I am—and so must you. No fancy vests. If you must buy new clothes, get working clothes."

Sherman nodded. He meant to buy the vest in spite of what St. Vrain said, but he wouldn't wear it when he gambled.

"I wish I didn't have to go upriver to St. Louis," St. Vrain said. "I'd like to be with you at least once to make sure you know what you're doing. New Orleans is fancy and slick on the surface but rough and tough underneath."

"I'll be careful."

"If you hadn't latched on to me, you wouldn't last a minute in this town. Even with all I've told you—" St. Vrain paused and sighed, putting a hand on Sherman's shoulder. "You're a likable lad—I wish you well."

"Meeting you was the best thing that's happened to me for a long time," Sherman told him. "If ever I can do anything for you, I will."

"Remember, son, there are no old gamblers. Win your stake and buy your land. And never cheat. Sooner or later, you get caught." He gripped Sherman's shoulder hard for a moment, turned away, and disappeared into the crowd on deck.

Is what I do cheating? Sherman wondered as the boat bumped against the dock.

He didn't manipulate the cards, but he suspected his high rate of wins wasn't pure luck. A natural, St. Vrain had called him. By natural, St. Vrain meant a man who watched his opponents' hands and eyes and predicted the outcome partly on the watching and partly on how many cards had been dealt and what they'd been. He learned that quickly, but he wondered if he had some hidden gift that also helped.

With the constant danger of men turning against him if they discovered what he was, he needed every advantage he could find. St. Vrain had been a big advantage. He'd miss him.

Sherman took a deep breath and turned his attention to the city spread out before him, bright and shining in the April sun.

"Ready or not, New Orleans, I'm here," he said under his breath, and grinned at his bravado. The crowds and the noise and the city's size scared him half to death.

In Galveston, listening to the talk around him about the easy money to be made gambling in New Orleans, the notion had appealed to him because it seemed so simple. The times he'd played monte with Juan, he'd always won until Juan had refused to take him on anymore. There wasn't much to gambling, that's what he'd thought. St. Vrain had taught him otherwise.

He'd had to sell all his horses but Rawhide to pay the steamboat fare and have a bit left over for a stake. Rawhide he'd brought with him, below deck, and he was glad. The swaybacked dun would be one familiar thing in this strange and frightening city.

Country, St. Vrain had called him, and the gambler had been right. Well, the country lad would try his luck in New Orleans. He had no other choice.

Once Sherman collected his few belongings and retrieved Rawhide, he found he didn't have to look far to find a gambling establishment. They were all over—by the docks and along every street. St. Vrain had recommended an inexpensive hotel, the Chartes, but since it was already late afternoon, Sherman decided he'd look in on a few of the gambling houses first and visit the Chartes later. Rawhide had been fed aboard the boat, so he'd be comfortable enough tethered outside while Sherman gambled.

Walking along the narrow bricked streets, he did his best not to gawk at the handsome buildings with their latticed ironwork along the balconies. Vines with red and purple flowers grew over the walls that hid what he suspected were courtyards. The passersby all seemed to be talking to one another, mostly in French.

He'd never seen so many Negroes, the women wearing red or blue scarves—*tignons*—covering their hair. Many of the women were very attractive. St. Vrain had said the Negroes weren't all slaves, like the blacks he'd seen in Galveston. New Orleans, he'd insisted, prided itself on accommodating free people of color.

He tried the Royal first, finding it anything but—most of the men were dressed as roughly as he was. Sherman watched for a bit and decided not to sit down at the vingt-et-un table after he spotted the dealer sliding cards off the bottom of the deck. He didn't plan to try any other game.

"You might as well dump your money in the gutter as play faro," St. Vrain had warned. "And poker's got too many variations for me to teach you in so short a time. The Creoles, including me, enjoy craps, but there's too much of a chance of loaded dice. Stick to what you have a chance to win."

Sherman drifted in and out of three other gambling houses, two on St. Charles Street and one on Bourbon, before he found a vingt-et-un dealer he thought was honest in the Palace on Canal Street. By this time dusk had settled over the city. Sherman decided to try his luck for an hour or two, then go to the hotel and eat. When a player left, he sat down in the man's place.

At first he concentrated on the dealer and the cards, winning modestly. After a time he glanced at the gentleman to his right at the end of the table, white-haired, in a rusty black coat, playing a cautious game, keeping about even. The three men to his left were young, well dressed, and seemed to be friends. All had been drinking. The two next to him were plainly bored and kept urging their companion at the end to leave. As Sherman looked at him, the man, dark and curly haired, raised his hand from the study of his cards and smiled at his friends.

Sherman's breath caught. He knew him! After an instant

he realized he was wrong, that he'd never seen the man before, but he was so shaken that he carelessly lost the next hand when he failed to ask for another card.

Suspecting something from his past had surfaced, that the man reminded him of someone he'd once known, Sherman kept an eye on him, hoping other memories would be triggered. He was disappointed.

The man's two friends left, weaving their way to the door. "Quitters," the dark-haired man mumbled, the word slurred.

As Sherman watched him, fascinated, the man won hand after hand while violating every precept of vingt-et-un, proving what St. Vrain had told him:

"There is such a thing as luck—good and bad. If yours is good—ride the tiger. If bad, cash in before you lose everything."

The young drunk was riding the tiger. Suddenly the man swept up his winnings and staggered over to the faro table. Another man sat in his place. Sherman continued to play vingt-et-un until he'd tripled his stake, then quit. It was time to find his hotel and something to eat.

On his way to the door, he passed the faro table and stopped to see how Tiger was doing. Others had gathered around to watch and he peered over their heads.

"Never saw such luck," the man in front of him said. "He can't lose."

"Drunk as a lord, he is," another commented. "Don't know what he's doing, and that's the truth."

Sherman couldn't take his eyes off Tiger. Something about the way the man smiled, even though his smile was drunken and foolish, plucked at a chord inside Sherman's heart.

Tiger's winning big, Sherman noted, feeling a tinge of envy. St. Vrain's warning about big wins echoed in his head. Tiger was in no condition to look out for himself.

It's no concern of mine, he thought. Time I left. He didn't move. A thread from the past connected him to the man, making it impossible to walk away. As he continued to watch, getting a feel for faro, he took stock of Tiger. About nineteen or twenty, dark hair, brown eyes. Medium height and slender build. Expensive clothes.

"Tha's it," Tiger said as a game ended. "Gotta go." His words were barely intelligible. He stood and crammed gold coins carelessly into his pockets, some falling to the floor.

Pushing through the crowd, Sherman picked up the money and handed it to Tiger.

The man waved the coins aside. "Keep 'em."

Sherman dropped the twenty- and fifty-dollar gold pieces into Tiger's pocket. When the man staggered toward the door, he followed.

Outside, night cloaked the city and a cool wind blew from the river. Sherman unhitched Rawhide, waiting for Tiger to do the same with his horse. Instead, the man lurched off along the plank sidewalk—*banquettes,* they called them in New Orleans. Mounting Rawhide, Sherman walked the horse along the street beside Tiger.

Tiger staggered along block after block until Sherman wondered if he'd ever reach a destination. Finally Tiger turned down a street more dimly lit that the others. Sherman hesitated, pulling up on the reins when he read the street sign. Gallatin. At last he continued on, disturbed and apprehensive. The poor lighting cast ominous shadows and the disreputable men emerging from the ramshackle buildings exuded a sense of menace.

The hair on Sherman's neck rose with an increasing sense of danger. What the hell was he doing? Hadn't St. Vrain warned him to stay off Gallatin Street? Nothing but trouble could come from trailing a drunk with his pockets full of money, a drunk heading into what St. Vrain had called the hellpit of New Orleans.

Chapter 8

Sherman pulled Rawhide even with the staggering, weaving man he'd dubbed Tiger, wondering what in God's name Tiger could want in this run-down part of New Orleans, a section that was definitely not *la belle.* Instead of brick and stucco buildings with delicate iron traceries, the wooden dwellings on dimly lit Gallatin Street were little more than shacks. Filth heaped high in the gutters, making Sherman grimace at the stink.

A gaudily dressed woman emerged from a shadowed doorway to accost Tiger; Sherman reined in Rawhide, watching. He knew what she was; he'd learned about whores in Galveston, though he hadn't patronized any. Even if he hadn't worried about fathering a child, the idea of bedding a woman used by many men was distasteful to him.

She whispered something in Tiger's ear. He shook his head, fumbled in his pocket, handed her a gold coin, patted her on the rump, and, to Sherman's relief, weaved away from her. Sherman urged the dun forward before the woman could decide he was fair game.

Noticing an alley ahead, Sherman focused on it, trying to sense whether the danger lurked in its dark entrance. His sensing of life energies was all but useless in a city, he'd discovered, because too many people were crowded together for him to easily separate one energy from another.

He thought there were men in the alley, but he couldn't be sure. Damn this city, damn this filthy street whose shadows hid danger. Every instinct warned him to wheel Rawhide and gallop away. But he couldn't abandon Tiger. He'd have to haul him aboard Rawhide before getting the hell out of here.

He halted the dun and swung off just as Tiger turned into the dark alley, obviously intent on relieving himself. Cursing under his breath, Sherman sprang to Tiger's side. Before he could do more than thrust Tiger against the wall of a building and leap in front of him, four men lunged at them.

Sherman wore a knife sheathed in his boot, but the first man jumped at him too fast for him to draw it. The attacker was big and burly and a dirty fighter. As Sherman struggled with the brute, trying to fend off the others at the same time, from behind him he heard Tiger laugh, then the clink of metal hitting the bricks of the street.

The drunken fool was throwing money!

Burly tried a kidney punch; Sherman blocked it, at the same time smashing the edge of his hand against the bridge of Burly's nose. Bone crunched and Burly gave a hoarse cry and fell back. From the way the second man crouched, Sherman was sure he held a knife, blade up, ready to rip into Sherman's gut. Sherman kicked hard, felt fiery pain slash along his leg as the toe of the boot caught the knife wielder under the chin. His assailant crumpled to the ground and lay motionless.

Gold coins jingled on the bricks as though Tiger threw them by the handfuls. Intent on the recovering Burly, Sherman didn't dare look. Evidently hearing the jingling, Burly turned from Sherman and lumbered into the street, where the other two men were scrambling for the gold.

Sherman grabbed Tiger by one arm, dragged him from the alley, and flung him across Rawhide's rump. He swung onto the dun, wheeled him sharply, and urged him into a trot, keeping a firm grip on Tiger's belt. A glance over his shoulder showed Burly and the two others fighting among themselves.

He didn't draw a full breath until they turned off Gallatin Street onto St. Ann and passed St. Louis Cathedral. Reining in under a streetlamp, he turned to look back at Tiger and saw the blood. His blood. His pants were slit down the right leg and blood oozed from a deep cut along his calf.

Swearing, he tried to yank Tiger into a sitting position, but it was like attempting to mold soft butter. He shook him. "What's your name?" he demanded.

"Guy."

"Where do you live?"

"La Belle." Guy smiled at him and slumped in his grasp, out cold.

Damn. La Belle could mean anything, even *la belle* New Orleans, St. Vrain's beautiful city. At the moment Sherman didn't think much of the place.

What was he to do now? Further shaking had no effect; Guy slept on, oblivious. Checking Guy's pockets, he discovered most of the money was gone. Counting the remainder, he transferred the coins into his own pockets for safekeeping. There was nothing else on Guy to give Sherman a clue to his last name or where he lived.

It occurred to him Guy might have had a horse tethered outside the Palace and was, perhaps, known there. Gripping Guy's belt again, he set off for Canal Street.

When he reached the gambling house, he left Guy draped across Rawhide's back while he limped inside. Certain the man who'd won so much would be remembered, Sherman first asked the faro dealer, who recalled the winner but didn't know who he was. The name Guy meant nothing to him.

The vingt-et-un dealer shook his head. "We get scores of young Creoles coming in here. You can't expect me to keep track of who's who."

"Have you ever heard of a place called La Belle?" Sherman asked.

The dealer shook his head. "Sounds like a plantation is all I can tell you."

"Yeah," a player agreed. "One of them by the lake, I reckon."

Discovering "lake" meant Lake Pontchartrain, Sherman asked for directions before he returned to Guy, who was still draped over the dun's rump, snoring. When Sherman couldn't rouse him, he decided carrying two men any farther was expecting too much from Rawhide. Guy couldn't so much as sit up, much less stand, and though Sherman's leg had stopped bleeding, the cut ached like the devil. He wouldn't get far afoot.

Not knowing what else to do, he untied the dun and led him along the plank walk in front of the tethered horses, with Guy's head nearest the animals, and paused in front of every horse. The first two ignored him. The next stomped, pulling back on his tether. The fourth showed interest in Rawhide. By the time he reached the last horse, at the end of the block, Sherman was ready to give up—until the animal nuzzled Guy's head and whuffled.

"That's good enough for me," he muttered to the black horse with the white blaze on his forehead. "You're elected."

He transferred Guy's limp body from Rawhide to the black and tied him on. If the horse belonged to someone else, after all, then that would be Guy's problem to solve when he came to.

Riding Rawhide, he led the black through the maze of narrow streets, taking a deep breath of relief when the houses thinned. St. Vrain might love New Orleans, but he never could. Not so much because of tonight but because it was so crowded. Cities, he decided, were not for him.

At last trees replaced buildings and, finally, following a trail along Bayou St. John toward the lake, Sherman began to feel himself again, one with the night. He was at home only where people were few. Any love he felt was for trees and hills, for the land and what grew upon it, not for towns and cities. He belonged in the wilderness.

Glancing up at the half-moon shining bright and serene in the western sky, he whispered, "How can anything so beautiful be so cruel?"

"Whosh cruel?" Guy's slurred voice asked from behind him. " 'M hogtied," he complained.

Sherman dismounted and untied the ropes, helping Guy to slide onto the saddle, where he swayed but stayed upright, staring owlishly at Sherman.

"Your horse?" Sherman asked before remounting Rawhide.

"Good ole Starfall," Guy mumbled, trying to pat the black's neck and almost slipping from the saddle.

Deciding he'd have to continue on with him to make certain Guy didn't fall into the bayou, Sherman said, "You'll have to show me where La Belle is."

" 'S all gone. Smashed to smithereens years ago. Thirty-seven years ago."

Taken aback for a moment, Sherman shook his head. Drunks rarely made sense. "Where you live, I mean. Your plantation."

Guy smiled and again something twisted in Sherman's chest. Even three sheets to the wind Guy had a singularly sweet smile. "Lac Belle's where I live," he said. "Gonna take you home to Papa; he'll make you all better."

Since he didn't expect Guy to make sense, Sherman didn't bother to ask what that was supposed to mean.

It was well past midnight by the time they reached the gates of Lac Belle. Guy, now somewhat soberer, led the way to the stables.

"Ponce!" he called.

A half-grown black boy hurried up, yawning.

"See to the horses." Guy spoke in French. He slid off Starfall and glanced toward Sherman, who also dismounted.

Sherman had discovered when he met St. Vrain that somewhere in his past he'd learned French, because he recognized the French words the gambler mixed in with his English. He understood enough to know what Guy said to the boy.

He realized many New Orleanians spoke no other tongue, but up until now Guy had spoken American. No, English. He kept forgetting there was no such thing as an American language.

"We'll get Papa to tend to your leg," Guy said, switching back to English.

Sherman stared at him in surprise. He hadn't realized Guy was aware enough to notice his bloodstained pants leg.

"You'd best tell me your name," Guy added. "Papa'll never forgive me if I don't introduce you."

"Sherman Oso. All I know of yours is Guy."

Guy struck a dramatic pose, throwing his arms wide. "The single surviving scion of the Kelloggs and the La Branches stands before you. Tanguy La Branche Kellogg, at your service." He bowed, linked his arm with Sherman's, and led him between giant trees toward a large house, its white paint gleaming in the darkness.

They climbed several brick steps onto a brick terrace and entered through what Sherman thought must be a side door. The room was dark, but the glow of lamps beyond shed enough light that Sherman could avoid the furniture as he followed Guy through the room. A short corridor gave way to a large foyer lit by lamps in gilt wall sconces. Sherman tried not to goggle at the large gilt and crystal chandelier at the foot of a curving staircase.

"Is that you, Guy?" a deep voice called from a room on the other side of the foyer.

"I'm afraid so, Papa. I've brought you a patient."

A tall white-haired man emerged from an open doorway and stared across the foyer at Sherman, looking him up and down. His gaze focused on the bloodstained trousers leg. "So you have," he said.

"This is Monsieur Oso," Guy said. "Sherman Oso." He turned to Sherman. "My father, Dr. Kellogg."

"Come along, both of you," the doctor ordered. Without waiting to see if they obeyed, he strode across to another corridor.

Guy grimaced. "I was hoping to slip off to bed. No such luck." He followed his father, with Sherman bringing up the rear.

Dr. Kellogg led them to what looked to Sherman to be a well-equipped surgery, where he made Sherman sit down and put his right leg on a stool. Guy stood by, fidgeting, plainly unhappy at being in the room.

"I think the cut's closed over by now," Sherman said uneasily, as the doctor pushed the slit in the pants leg apart to look at his calf. "I heal fast."

Without comment, Dr. Kellogg cut the pants leg all the way open. "Bring me a basin of water," he told Guy.

After he'd washed the crusted blood from Sherman's calf, he examined the wound. "Knife?" he asked.

Sherman cleared his throat. "Yes."

"Clean cut," the doctor said at last. "All but healed. When did it happen?"

"I think we were in a fight," Guy said reluctantly.

Sherman nodded.

"When?" Dr. Kellogg persisted.

Guy shrugged. "This evening sometime."

The doctor's eyebrows rose. "No one heals that fast."

Alarmed, Sherman's mind raced. Should he concoct a story about an earlier injury? The last thing he wanted was to call attention to any oddity in himself. Before he came to a decision, the doctor spoke again.

"I'll amend that. In my experience I've never seen anyone heal that fast." His blue eyes met Sherman's. "You did warn me you healed rapidly."

Sherman swallowed. "Yes, sir."

"Then I'll let nature continue its work and do nothing but offer you a clean pair of trousers." He focused on his son. "Mr. Oso hasn't been drinking. You have. Exactly what happened tonight, Guy?"

Guy glanced at Sherman. "I think he rescued me, Papa."

"Think?" the doctor echoed. "That drunk, were you?"

Guy bit his lip. "I know I promised, but—"

Dr. Kellogg held up his hand, cutting off his son's explanation. "Suppose you tell us the events of the evening, Mr. Oso."

"We were in the Palace," Sherman began. "That is, I came in and happened to sit at a vingt-et-un table where Guy and his friends were playing." He went on to give a condensed story of Guy winning and being attacked by thieves. Reaching in his pocket, he pulled out the remainder of the gold coins and dropped them on the table beside his chair. "These are all that was left—the thieves got the rest."

Guy had been as intent on the tale as his father. Now he took a deep breath and looked the doctor in the eyes.

"I'm sure that's the truth, sir, but I can't say I recall any of it. I came to somewhere along Bayou St. John tied onto Starfall's back. You don't need to tell me I'd probably be dead in a gutter somewhere if Sherman hadn't rescued me."

Dr. Kellogg told him anyway while Sherman shifted uncomfortably on the chair. Underneath the scathing words, he heard the concern the doctor felt for his son. He couldn't help but envy Guy—he had a father who cared very much about what happened to him.

When he finished chastising his son, Dr. Kellogg turned to Sherman. "You'll stay with us at Lac Belle this night, Mr. Oso, and you're welcome to remain as long as you wish. Gratitude and hospitality aren't enough to repay you; but then, nothing is."

"I appreciate the offer for tonight," Sherman said, not willing to commit himself.

The doctor's shrewd blue eyes studied him. "You are, perhaps, a man who cherishes his privacy?" he asked finally.

Sherman was too surprised by the question to think before answering. "Yes, sir, I do."

"I thought so. Therefore I'll offer you the *garçonnière,* our bachelor quarters, separate from the main house, in the hope you'll remain with us for more than one night."

There was nothing left for Sherman to say but "Thank you."

"Feel free to regard Lac Belle as your own home," the doctor said. "You've only to ask and the servants will bring you anything you want."

Feeling overwhelmed, Sherman thanked him again.

An elderly Negro named Francois showed him to the *garçonnière*, a small eight-sided building on the opposite side of the house from the stables. Once inside, Sherman climbed the spiral staircase to the second floor and eased down on the four-poster bed with a sigh.

Damn but he wanted to stay at Lac Belle. Stay and see if he could unravel the fascination Guy held for him. Stay and get to know Guy's father, a man who'd understood his need to be alone. He shook his head. Dr. Kellogg saw too much too quickly. And whatever had attracted him to Guy came from his past—he might never fathom the reason.

He slept better than he had in months but woke the moment a door opened below. Morning. He rose quietly, peered down the stairs, and saw old Francois setting a covered tray on a table. The Negro laid a pair of trousers and a shirt carefully over the back of a chair.

"I'm awake," Sherman called to him in French, sure that a servant in a Creole household spoke no English.

Francois immediately lifted the clothes and started for the stairs. Sherman, unused to being waited on, met him halfway.

"*Merci*," he said.

"I hope you enjoy the food, sir. Does monsieur need anything more?"

Sherman shook his head, thinking if he stayed on here he'd have to improve his French—but he didn't intend to pass more than this one night, *garçonnière* or not.

He was finishing an excellent meal of mush, sausages, and fried bread with plum jelly when Guy opened the door and stuck his head in.

"Any coffee left?" he asked.

Sherman picked up the covered pitcher and shook it. "A cup or two, I'd say."

Guy plucked a cup from a cupboard, sat down opposite Sherman, and poured the strong, bitter coffee. "Creoles have a saying about coffee," he told Sherman.

"Noir comme le Diable
Fort comme la mort

Doux comme l'amour
Chaud comme l'enfer."
["Black as the devil
Strong as death
Sweet as love
Hot as hell."]

Before Sherman could respond, Guy pushed his coffee aside, rested his head on his hands, and groaned. "I don't dare swallow even one sip. My head's pounding, my stomach's rebelling, and every bone in my body aches. Why didn't you let them finish me off last night?"

"It occurred to me," Sherman said.

Guy raised his head, his dark eyes holding Sherman's. Slouched lower in his chair, he said, "I listened to you tell the story to Papa last night. What did you leave out?"

"What makes you think I omitted anything?"

"You had no reason to bother with me. Yet you followed me from the Palace into that Gallatin hellhole. Why?"

Sherman chose his words with care. "You were too drunk to know what you were doing and you'd won big. That can be a fatal combination anywhere."

Guy raised an eyebrow. Still watching Sherman, he pulled paper from one pocket, a dark crayon of some kind from another, and began drawing lines on the paper. A frisson of unease ran along Sherman's spine.

"What are you doing?" he asked.

"Sketching. You've got an interesting face. Different. Not French, not Spanish."

Harmless enough, Sherman decided, though he mistrusted attention being called to anything odd about himself. "You're an artist?"

"Not if Papa can help it." Guy continued to sketch as he spoke. "He believes my drawings are a waste of time." He scrawled a few more lines on the paper and shoved it toward Sherman.

The sketch was no mirror likeness. There was a suggestion of feralness in the slightly slanted eyes and a hint of the predator in the curve of his lip. Yet anyone looking at the drawing would know the face was Sherman's.

"You're good." With effort, Sherman kept his voice even. Guy was too damn good for his peace of mind. How could he see underneath the skin to what lay buried there? Both father and son, each in his own way, were too acute for Sherman's comfort. It was dangerous to remain here.

Someone knocked on the door.

"Entrez," Guy said without bothering to turn to see who might come in. He picked up the drawing and thrust it in his pocket.

It was the boy, Ponce.

"Master Guy, the doctor, he say come quick," Ponce said.

Sherman understood the simple French but wasn't prepared for Guy's anguished groan. Nor to see him grab the cup of cooling coffee and drain it.

Almost immediately Guy began to retch. Staggering to the open door, he vomited into the bushes beside the steps. "Can't help Papa," he gasped before a new convulsion of retching gripped him. "Too sick. Sherman, you go."

Not knowing what else to do, Sherman hurried after Ponce toward the stables, passing giant oaks hung with dangling gray moss. He knew Guy had deliberately downed the coffee to make himself sick, but if the doctor needed help, someone had to respond.

Dr. Kellogg was already mounted on a gray gelding. Starfall, saddled, waited beside him. "Where's Guy?" he demanded.

"Sick," Sherman said. "I volunteered. What can I do to help?"

"Let's hope your stomach's stronger than his," the doctor said, kicking the gray into a lope.

Sherman vaulted onto Starfall and followed, wondering just what he'd let himself in for.

When he pulled even with Dr. Kellogg, the older man shook his head. "I swear that boy will be the death of me. Take my advice, Sherman, and have your children when you're young."

"I don't mean to have any at all," Sherman said grimly.

The doctor slanted him a look but rode in silence. While he waited for Dr. Kellogg to tell him where they were going, Sherman glanced at the tall green stalks to either side of the road, so tall they closed off a view of anything else.

On the boat, St. Vrain had pointed out similar fields on the plantations along the river. "Sugar cane," he'd said. "Sugar's the main crop hereabouts, though we grow some cotton and some tobacco."

Negroes with hoes worked between the rows of cane, some looking up to wave at Dr. Kellogg as he passed. He waved back.

"How's that new baby of yours doing, Luke?" he asked one of the men.

"Tres bon enfant," the man called back, grinning broadly.

"The boy very nearly died," Dr. Kellogg said to Sherman. "Born with the cord wrapped around his neck. Thought I'd never start him breathing. I'm happy to hear he's a very good baby."

Sherman wasn't sure he'd ever get used to the idea of men owning men. No matter what color a man's skin, he was a human, not an animal.

"You're very quiet," the doctor observed.

"I've never been on a plantation before, sir," Sherman said. "Are all these cane fields part of Lac Belle?"

"Ours adjoin the neighboring plantation, Le Noir, with no fences marking the boundaries. That's where we're headed. The owner's Monsieur Gauthier and one of his slaves sliced into a leg with an ax. If Gauthier bothered to send for me, the injury must be damn near fatal and the slave valuable."

The inflection of Dr. Kellogg's voice as well as his words convinced Sherman the doctor didn't care for Gauthier.

"You're along to help me with the injured man," the doctor added. "I hope to hell I can save the leg. God knows what'll happen to the poor devil if I have to amputate."

Amputate? Sherman swallowed. No wonder Guy had forced himself to vomit rather than be conscripted to assist his father.

A black man, riding bareback, waited on the road between the cane fields to lead them to the injured slave. From his answers to the doctor's questions, both speaking in French, Sherman understood that a slave named Jacob had been chopping firewood when the ax broke and the blade buried itself in his thigh. Sherman grimaced.

Behind a pile of uncut logs, they found Jacob, a black man of about thirty, lying on the ground near an outbuilding, surrounded by wood chips and tended by two women, one young, one old. Two large oaks shaded the area. Even before dismounting, the doctor sent the younger off to fetch soap, water, and clean cloths. Kneeling beside Jacob, he slashed the blood-soaked left pants leg off, revealing a deep cut along the outer side of the thigh. Blood trickled from the wound.

"Not spurting," the doctor muttered. "Good. Didn't sever an artery."

Jacob's normally dark face was grayish, his eyes terrified as he watched Dr. Kellogg. Without thinking about what he was doing, Sherman knelt next to him, opposite the doctor. He took one of Jacob's hands in his, gripping it firmly. "Courage," he said.

The man raised his head to stare at him. Sherman soothed him as he would a frightened horse, using his own unknown tongue, hoping that, like the horses, Jacob would know what he meant without understanding the words. He kept speaking softly until the doctor said his name.

"Sherman. I need you here."

As he rose, Sherman motioned to the older woman to take his place.

He didn't recall ever threading a needle in his life, but the skill came easily enough. He watched, fascinated, as the doctor sewed the gaping edges of the wound together with black cotton thread, muttering to himself all the time he worked.

"I washed it clean, should keep down suppuration. Thank God he's healthy; he'll heal quickly. Lost a lot of blood. He ought to rest for a couple of days. Fat chance of that. I'll try to get him one." He tied off the thread and glanced at Sherman. "You'd better be listening, son. You have a lot to learn."

"Yes, sir." Sherman tried to ignore the warmth in his heart when the doctor called him son. It meant nothing. Nothing. But it was a hell of a lot friendlier than Mr. Oso.

Even if he couldn't afford to have friends.

Sensing someone approaching, Sherman glanced over his shoulder. A man. The women saw him, too, and immediately eased away from Jacob.

The master of Le Noir, Sherman decided. Unlike the doctor's practical dark frock coat and trousers, Gauthier wore clothes more suitable for the city—fawn trousers with a dark green waistcoat under his tan coat. He carried himself with the arrogance of a man used to having his orders carried out without question. His dark eyes flicked over the two female slaves, dismissed them, focused on Jacob momentarily, passed over Sherman, and fastened on the doctor.

"Well?" Gauthier demanded. "Will he be of any further use to me?" He spoke in heavily accented English.

Dr. Kellogg straightened. He and Gauthier were of a height, Sherman half a head taller.

"If you force Jacob to go back to work tomorrow," the doctor said slowly, "I can promise you he won't ever be much use to you again. If you give him three days rest, you'll likely find him as capable as ever."

Gauthier scowled. "On your feet, Jacob," he ordered in French. Seeing that Jacob meant to obey or die trying, Sherman leaned down, grasped his arm, helped the black man to his feet, and steadied him.

Gauthier glanced at the bloodstained ax blade, lying apart from the helve. "His carelessness has already ruined my ax. Are you telling me I should let this bastard lay around doing nothing as a reward?"

Sherman tensed. It was obvious the blade and helve had parted company through no fault of Jacob's. The loose blade had come damned close to killing Jacob, besides.

Dr. Kellogg shrugged. "It's up to you. Either he gets three days rest or you lose your investment in him."

Gauthier glared at the doctor for a long moment before turning abruptly to the women. "Take him to his quarters," he ordered. "Then get back to work, both of you." Again he spoke in French.

Sherman knew that Dr. Kellogg spoke perfectly good French, yet he used English with Gauthier, who was a Creole. Why?

As the slaves started away, Dr. Kellogg grasped Sherman's arm. "I'd like you to meet my assistant, Mr. Oso. Sherman, this is Monsieur Gauthier."

Gauthier hesitated, then offered his hand. As Sherman reached to grip it, the ground seemed to quiver beneath his feet. A reddish star disfigured the Creole's palm for an instant before vanishing.

Chapter 9

Sherman hid his shock as best he could, shaking Gauthier's hand and stepping back. The one other time he'd seen the red pentacle—on Don Alfonso's palm—he'd known the sign was to be feared. Now he knew why. Don Alfonso was dead, his throat torn out by the beast.

Was Gauthier to be the beast's next victim?

Sherman clenched his fists. Not if I leave Lac Belle before the next full moon, he assured himself.

"I'll concede one day of rest for Jacob," Gauthier said to Dr. Kellogg. "And that's more than he deserves."

The doctor shrugged. "You're paying for my advice."

"That doesn't mean I have to take it. Good day to you, Doctor." He nodded at Sherman without looking at him, swung on his heel, and strode away.

Dr. Kellogg packed his instruments into his bag, fixed the bag to the gray's saddle, and swung onto the horse.

Sherman, still shaken, mounted Starfall, and they rode back toward Lac Belle in silence.

"So you didn't care much for my neighbor," the doctor said finally. "Shows you've got good sense."

Sherman gathered himself together. Brooding over the pentacle solved nothing. He said the first thing that came into his head. "I noticed you spoke English to Monsieur Gauthier."

Dr. Kellogg chuckled. "We all have our devious conceits. It amuses me to speak English to Creoles I don't take to and French to Americans who offend me. So far I haven't been challenged."

Making an effort to be agreeable, Sherman said, "A man I met on the boat from Galveston explained Creoles to me—

those of French or Spanish extraction born in New Orleans. Are you a Creole, sir?''

The doctor shook his head. ''American, born and bred. Though I've lived among Creoles so long I sometimes feel I am one, as my wife was. And as my son is.'' He sighed. ''I suppose I'll find Guy snoring in bed when we return.''

Sherman did what he could to support Guy. ''He couldn't keep anything down, sir, not even a cup of coffee.''

Dr. Kellogg fixed his shrewd gaze on Sherman. ''Do you drink?''

''I can't say I've never had a drink of liquor,'' Sherman replied cautiously.

''Ever been blind drunk like Guy was last night?''

''No, sir.'' He could hardly admit he didn't dare lose control.

''Didn't think so. Yet you're his age—about twenty, aren't you?'' At Sherman's nod, he went on. ''Do you think it's unreasonable for me to want my son to follow in my footsteps, to become a doctor?''

How the hell was he supposed to answer that question? Sherman wondered unhappily. ''I don't know either of you well, sir, but I'd say it depends on what Guy wants.''

Dr. Kellogg waved an impatient hand. ''He doesn't know what he wants. Few twenty-year-olds do. How about you—what do you want?''

Sherman told him the truth. ''I want to make enough money to buy land in the wilderness and build myself a house where I can be alone.''

The doctor blinked. ''No bride to offer the comforts of home?''

Sherman shook his head emphatically.

''You don't care for women?'' the doctor persisted.

Feeling trapped, Sherman blurted, ''I don't want children!''

''There are devices a man may use to enjoy women without creating a child.''

''Foolproof devices?''

The doctor frowned. ''Nothing's foolproof in this imperfect world. But close to it, if a man remembers to use what's available. Unfortunately, a stiff prick makes an idiot out of the most intelligent of men and can turn an otherwise gentle man into a ravening beast.''

Sherman started at the word beast, glancing nervously at

him. The doctor reined in the gray, giving Sherman no choice but to bring Starfall to a halt there between the long rows of sugar cane. Surrounded by green, it was almost like being in a strange woods.

Dr. Kellogg smiled ruefully. "You're looking at me like a schoolboy expecting a whipping. Son, I don't whip anyone, including the Lac Belle Negroes. I was an Army doctor for much of my life and I saw enough brutality to last for an eternity. I wouldn't deliberately hurt you, but one thing a doctor learns early is that a festering boil needs lancing. You're a troubled man, young as you are. If ever you can bring yourself to trust me, I promise I'll try to help you, no matter what your trouble is."

Sherman couldn't meet his gaze. The doctor meant well, but if he knew what happened when the moon rose full, he'd change his mind in a hurry.

"You think about what I've said," Dr. Kellogg urged. "In the meantime I'd like to hire you as my assistant."

Sherman couldn't believe his ears. "Your assistant?" he echoed.

"Wasn't that how I introduced you to Gauthier? You're a natural healer, son. Whatever you said to poor Jacob calmed him and, I swear, even helped stop the bleeding. Such a talent mustn't go to waste. I need an assistant and I promise to teach you what I know. Are you willing to learn?"

With dismay Sherman felt the sting of tears in his eyes and blinked them back. My God, what a generous offer! To be paid to work with this white-haired doctor he admired, to enjoy the comforts of Lac Belle—how he longed to say yes. But it was impossible. He opened his mouth to say so.

"Wait!" Dr. Kellogg commanded. "Don't give me an answer immediately. Mull it over, talk to Guy, let the three of us get to know one another better."

Before Sherman could reply, the doctor kicked the gray into a trot. As he followed him, Sherman thought that Dr. Kellogg knew very well he had meant to refuse and wouldn't give him the chance, hoping he'd change his mind.

Did he dare stay at Lac Belle? He sighed, knowing very well he couldn't. Not only to protect those who wanted to be his friends—Guy and his father—but also to protect the one he believed he was destined to kill. Whatever kind of a man Gauthier was, he didn't deserve to have his throat torn out by the beast.

As they left the cane fields, Dr. Kellogg took a more roundabout route that brought them to the front drive. Sherman drew in his breath at his first real sight of the mansion. Six gleaming white columns rose two stories from the ground to brace the roof; a porch and a second-floor balcony were recessed under the overhang. Sunlight glinted from the panes of three dormer windows, two chimneys rose to either side of the roof, and from the middle of a square tower flew the Stars and Stripes of the United States.

As they rode up the drive, he wondered if the doctor had deliberately chosen this route to dazzle him with the beauty of the house, for dazzled he surely was.

"Your home is magnificent, sir."

"I'm pleased you like it. I'm told the house is a fine example of Greek Revival architecture. Lac Belle was built by my brother-in-law, Guy La Branche, after the cannons from British ships in the river ruined their original plantation, La Belle, in 1812. General Jackson led us to victory over the British—a fine officer, a good man to fight under. But of course that war was before your time. I'm getting on; not too many of us old veterans left."

Sherman could hardly admit he'd never heard of any 1812 war. "You don't seem old to me, sir," he said finally. It was the truth. Despite his white hair, the doctor's ruddy face bespoke good health and he moved as easily as a young man.

"Ah, but you're looking at me from the outside. From my point of view, on the inside looking out, I've come to realize seventy-six is a long, long way from twenty."

They continued on past green sweeps of lawn dotted with flower beds and flowering shrubs to the stables,

"You'll dine with me at noon," Dr. Kellogg said as they dismounted. "I'll have Francois ring the bell."

At the *garçonnière*, Sherman found Guy sprawled asleep on a settee in the downstairs sitting room. Before Sherman could ease away, Guy opened his eyes and saw him. He sat up, groaning.

"The way I feel, I'll never take another drink," Guy said. "I owe you thanks for rescuing me again. What bloody mess was it this time?"

"One of the Le Noir Negroes cut himself with an ax."

Guy winced. "Thank God I didn't have to be there. I can

hardly bear the sight of blood at the best of times—and this isn't one of them."

"Your father hopes you'll be a doctor one day."

Guy shuddered. "Never! I can't. If only he would understand. But he pretends to believe I'll get over what he calls my squeamishness." Guy pounded his clenched fist against his chest. "My horror of blood and disease is embedded deep in my heart, I swear it is. I'll never change." He eyed Sherman. "How about you? I take it you didn't disgrace yourself by fainting, as I did once."

"I was uneasy at first," Sherman admitted, "but when I tried to help the injured man I forgot about how I felt."

"Better you than me, then. What a blessing it would be for me if you'd stay on here and take my place as Papa's assistant."

"Uh—your father did ask me. But—"

Guy sprang to his feet, threw his arms around Sherman, hugged him, and, letting him go, cried, "You've saved my life, I swear it! And my head and stomach, too. I vow I'll never get drunk again if you agree."

"Your father didn't actually say I was to take your place."

Guy waved a dismissive hand. "A mere formality. Papa hates to give up on anything—especially me. He's no fool, though. Far from it. Now that he's found a replacement, the light will dawn. Ah, Sherman, you've almost made me believe in good angels. With you here, Papa's sure to give in eventually and let me sail to France. I correspond with La Branche cousins in Paris and they tell me I can learn more about painting and sketching in Europe in a few years than I could ever learn in America in a lifetime. You've no idea how I long to go, to be free to do what I wish to do with all my heart and soul." He smiled. "You must think me mad to ramble on like this."

Guy's smile triggered an almost-memory in Sherman. Sometime, somewhere, the other had smiled at him like that. The smile and the evocation of the past weakened his resolve to pack up and leave immediately. After all, the moon wouldn't be full for two weeks. As long as he made it clear to both Guy and his father that he couldn't remain permanently, he could stay on for at least a week without endangering anyone.

It was clear to him that Dr. Kellogg was wrong about Guy not knowing what he wanted to do with his life.

Whether or not Sherman became the doctor's assistant, obviously Guy never could be. If he stayed on for a while he might find words to help convince the doctor to let Guy choose his own calling.

"I can't promise how long I'll be here," he told Guy.

"But you'll try working with Papa?"

"For a week or so anyway. I need the money."

Guy raised an eyebrow but didn't comment directly. "Lac Belle, like a beautiful woman, is seductive," he warned. "The place gets a hold on you. I yearn to leave and yet it'll be difficult for me to give up Lac Belle. You'll discover what I mean soon enough—but then, perhaps you already have."

Beautiful as the mansion and the grounds were, Sherman thought, it wouldn't be Lac Belle but the people who lived there—Guy and his father—who'd be hard for him to leave.

Immediately after the noon meal, Dr. Kellogg gave Sherman his first lesson in the anatomy of the human body, using an articulated skeleton and illustrated textbooks. As he concentrated on memorizing the bones, Sherman couldn't help but wonder what *his* skeleton looked like. Completely human? And how about the organs that fitted so neatly within the human abdomen and chest—did he have something extra, an organ activated by the moon?

As his studies progressed, he longed even more to remain and learn all the doctor could teach him. If he knew everything there was to know about humans, maybe he'd find a clue to how he differed and how to control his difference.

The doctor saw private patients in the morning and treated the ills of Lac Belle Negroes in the afternoon. He refused to work at night unless an emergency arose. By the end of the week Sherman was so fascinated with what he was learning and the work he was doing that he dreaded the thought of leaving.

"There are plenty of doctors in New Orleans," Dr. Kellogg told Sherman after their Saturday evening dinner as the three men lingered over coffee laced with brandy. "At seventy-six I should retire."

Francois slipped into the dining room and walked quickly to the doctor's side, bending to whisper in his ear. As he did, Guy hurriedly excused himself and, to Sherman's surprise, all but bolted from the room.

"Another?" the doctor said when Francois finished.

"Damn the man!" He rose, not seeming to notice Guy's absence. "I'll need your assistance, Sherman."

In the surgery, a shivering black boy of about eleven huddled in a chair, a plump Negro woman standing beside him. A tattered and bloody sheet covered the boy's shoulders.

"Take the sheet off and get him on the table on his stomach," Dr. Kellogg ordered.

Sherman lifted off the bloody cloth as gently as he could, but it stuck in spots and the boy moaned when he pulled it free. Sucking in his breath at the sight of the lacerated back, the skin hanging in ribbons, Sherman lifted the boy onto the padded wooden table. What monster would beat a boy so viciously?

"Courage," Sherman murmured, as he had to Jacob. Knowing Dr. Kellogg would tell him what to do if he needed help, Sherman gripped the boy's hands in his and soothed him through the pain as the doctor washed the whip wounds with soap and water.

"You see what I'm doing?" Dr. Kellogg asked the woman.

"Oui, docteur." Her voice was faint and frightened.

"You must wash his back with clean water every day. Clean water, mind you. I'll give you a decoction of aloes to rub on—gently, gently, like I'm doing—for the pain. He's going to be badly scarred, I'm afraid. Remember, keep his wounds clean."

"Oui." Her voice was barely audible.

When Dr. Kellogg finished, Sherman lifted the boy's slight body from the table. "Where does he come from?" he asked the doctor in English.

The doctor scowled. "Le Noir. Where else? She risked her life as well as the boy's to slip away to bring him to me. They must return before they're missed."

"He's too weak to walk. I'll carry him on horseback." Sherman's voice was grim.

"Don't go beyond the edge of our property. If Gauthier catches you on Le Noir ground with one of his slaves, he'll have an excuse to shoot you. And no, I'm not exaggerating. The man has no conscience."

After Ponce saddled Rawhide, Sherman rode through the night with the boy lying across his knees and the woman holding on behind him. The closer he came to Le Noir, the hotter his fury blazed. Gauthier's plantation was well named—it must seem like perpetual night to the slaves who lived there. No one deserved to be beaten until the skin of his back was in shreds—and certainly not a boy.

"Stop here, monsieur." He barely heard the woman's whisper.

"I'll take you all the way."

Her voice rose. "No! He'll shoot you and he'll beat us for sure. Louis will die then. Please, monsieur, stop."

The thought of Gauthier beating the boy again made Sherman pause. He'd been warned twice—by the doctor and by the woman. They knew local customs better than he did. He reined in Rawhide and the woman slipped off.

"Set Louis on my back, please, monsieur."

Carrying the boy piggyback, she vanished into the darkness between the rows of cane. Still angry, Sherman rode back to Lac Belle.

"Can't Gauthier be stopped?" he asked the doctor.

Dr. Kellogg sighed. "In New Orleans, in all of Louisiana, slaves are property. Gauthier owns his in exactly the same way as he owns his plantation. If he chooses to burn down his house, I have no right by law to stop him, and neither does any other man. If he whips a slave into raw meat, the same holds true."

Sherman clenched his fists. "But he's worse than a beast."

"I can't deny that. But if I should try to interfere, he'd very likely kill me and get off scot-free by claiming I was inciting his slaves to rebel against him. New Orleanians are fearful of a slave rebellion—after all, the Negroes outnumber us."

The doctor ran a hand through his hair. "I once thought I could never bear to be a slave owner. Strictly speaking, I'm not, yet I profit from our Lac Belle slaves. If I could, I'd free every Negro here, but they're not mine to free. They, as well as Lac Belle, belong to my son Guy. We couldn't run the plantation without slaves. For us, it's free the Negroes and give up Lac Belle, or keep them slaves. I alleviate my guilt by treating them humanely and teaching the children to read and write and do sums."

Sherman remained silent, tamping down his still simmering anger. It was Gauthier he despised, not Dr. Kellogg. He had no right to vent his rage on the doctor.

"By the way," the doctor said, "I heard you speaking to

little Louis in the same tongue as you did to Jacob. It's a language I'm not familiar with."

Sherman thought quickly. He knew very well what he'd said to both Jacob and Louis in his own tongue, but it was impossible to admit he had no idea what language it was. He licked dry lips. "Uh—they're just nonsense words I use to soothe my horses. In California I broke and trained horses."

"Your words seem to work on humans, too. Or perhaps it's your touch. Or a combination of the two. You have a definite soothing effect on those in pain, son—it's a great gift you shouldn't limit to horses. And you're bright. I don't believe I've ever seen anyone master anatomy quite so quickly. You'll make an excellent doctor."

Not when the moon is full, Sherman thought grimly. "Thank you, sir," he managed to say.

Later, alone in the *garçonnière,* he tried desperately to come up with a way to remain at Lac Belle. He wanted with all his heart and soul to stay with Dr. Kellogg and learn more about medicine, wanted to spend his life healing others. He longed to become a doctor as badly as Guy wished to be an artist. And more, he felt at home with both Guy and his father. Almost as though they were kin.

At last he decided on a plan. He'd explain to Dr. Kellogg that he had to be away for three to five days each month, then he'd find a safe place away from humans and hope to God he'd survive the shifting without hurting anyone.

There were swamps near the lake where no one ventured. He'd heard tales of twenty-foot man-eating alligators, poisonous snakes, and vicious catamounts prowling the swamps—but what had his beast self to fear from animals?

Sherman rose in the gray light of predawn and left the bachelor quarters. Tentacles of mist from the lake wavered among the giant oaks, much like the gray moss draping their branches. Before the doctor roused, Sherman meant to walk the boundaries of the plantation fields. He must choose swampland far enough away to keep from discovery and yet not so far he couldn't get there on foot within an hour or two, since he didn't dare ride Rawhide when the moon was full.

He was prowling through overgrown brush far from the house, slave quarters, and other outbuildings when he discovered a tumbledown shack all but hidden by vines, near the edge of a vegetation-choked swamp. Poking around, he found two other decaying huts. Abandoned slave quarters? he wondered. Whatever they'd been, they were of no use for him.

As he turned away, he caught a glimpse of what looked like iron bars embedded in the side of a mound covered with wild grape vines. Clearing away even a part of the thick growth took some time, but at last he recognized what he'd found. A cage.

He shuddered and stepped back, momentarily transported back to the horror of being trapped in the grizzly cage.

Controlling his irrational spurt of panic, he forced himself to examine his find. The rusted iron bars were set solidly in unpainted gray cypress wood. The remnants of a chain barred the door. He yanked the rusted links apart and the door creaked open on rusty hinges. The cage was large enough for a man to sit but not to lie down in. A slave cage? He had no way of knowing.

Despite his brush slashing, the contraption was still half hidden by the luxuriant growth. If live grape vines were pulled across the front, the cage would be hidden completely. The rust hadn't seriously damaged the iron, and cypress wood, he'd learned, never rotted. If the cage were fitted with a heavy bar on the inside and a stout chain and padlock to replace the old one . . .

Sherman swallowed. God, no. He couldn't stand to think of being locked in a cage again, couldn't bear to lock himself in a cage.

Yet he could see it would work. Hands could use a key where a beast's paws could not. Hands could slide a bar into place that paws couldn't release. He'd be safe. They'd be safe—Guy and his father. And the slaves. And even that bastard Gauthier.

The alternative was the swamp, with its unknown perils. While the beast might survive there, what about before the change? Sherman didn't think he'd be any match for a twenty-foot alligator.

He stared at the iron bars for long moments. Finally, grimacing, he yanked grape vines into position until they covered the cage completely. He'd buy the chain and the padlock. He'd attach a heavy bar. And if he couldn't stand being caged, he'd try the swamp, alligators, snakes, and all.

Two days before the moon would be full, the unwelcome restlessness settled into his bones. "I must leave by noon," he told Dr. Kellogg at breakfast.

The doctor frowned. "Francois tells me there's a bad storm blowing in from the gulf," he warned. "You'd do well to delay your departure until the storm subsides."

Sherman glanced toward the window, where sunlight streamed past wine-colored velvet draperies into the dining room.

The doctor followed his gaze. "I've never known Francois to be wrong. He seems to have a sixth sense about the weather. If you'll delay leaving until later this afternoon you'll see that he's right. You haven't lived through one of our three-day blows, son. They must be experienced to be believed."

Guy wandered into the room, yawning. "Sorry, Papa, I overslept."

"I'm trying to convince Sherman a gulf storm is on the way," the doctor said.

"So Francois told me." Guy looked at Sherman. "You're not thinking of traveling in the midst of a hurricane?"

Sherman didn't relish the thought of being locked in a cage under any circumstance, and getting rain-soaked didn't make it more appealing. There'd be little point in enduring the discomfort if storm clouds cloaked the moon for a night or two and prevented the change. He could safely wait until late afternoon to see if Francois's prediction was right.

By noon, clouds drifted across the sun, the wind died, and a sense of oppression hung over the plantation. The doctor told Sherman he was free to spend the afternoon as he liked.

"I trust you're now convinced the storm is imminent and are prudent enough to remain with us until it's over," he added as he left Sherman and Guy alone.

"I'd like you to see my studio," Guy said as soon as the doctor was out of earshot.

Still uneasy about the weather, Sherman nodded a bit distractedly. He followed Guy up the wide, curving staircase, admiring the intricate carvings on the banister rail as well as the gilded ceiling medallions. The gleaming furniture and rich fabrics of the house awed him, while at the same time they evoked a nagging sense of familiarity.

Guy opened a door off the second-floor landing, revealing

a spiral staircase winding up into the tower. Sherman climbed the steps behind him. Eight windows sent light streaming into the square tower; even with the sky overcast the small room was bright. An easel, a painter's table, and a stool were the only furniture. Since the canvas on the easel faced away from the stairs, Sherman's attention went to the windows.

Below them outside, Negroes busied themselves tying up shrubbery and closing house shutters. Not a twig on any of the oaks or magnolias moved. Lake Pontchartrain's waters, dulled to gray by the overcast, lay smooth as glass. In the distance, the Mississippi River snaked silver among the trees. Otherwise, except for splashes of vivid color where flowers bloomed, the entire countryside was green with exuberant growth. Remembering the browns and golds of California, Sherman understood Cump's complaint of California's barrenness, a lack of greenery *he* hadn't minded. He'd felt at home there. Yet he enjoyed the wild growth here, too. It was cities he hated.

"What do you think?" Guy asked.

Sherman turned and found Guy had turned the easel so the painted canvas faced him. He drew in his breath in mixed wonder and dismay.

A cloud-plagued full moon barely illuminated the night. In the center, the octagon of the *garçonnière* gleamed a faint ghostlike white, menaced by the shadows of trees. The dark figure at the far left of the painting was scarcely noticeable at first, but, once seen, it drew the eye. On first glance the figure was a man's. A second look convinced the viewer the hulking darkness wasn't human, not human at all. Guy had painted a monster stalking through the grounds of Lac Belle.

"Good God!" Sherman stared from the canvas to Guy.

Guy smiled. "I thought you'd be startled."

Sherman swallowed. Forcing words past his dry throat, he asked, "What the hell is it?"

"*Loup-garou,* we call such creatures here."

Man-wolf. Werewolf.

Had his secret been discovered?

Chapter 10

"I've always been drawn to the macabre," Guy told Sherman as they stared at his somber and sinister painting in the tower studio. "No matter what I intend when I begin, once the brush is in my hand I find myself painting the dark side of life. This one was inspired when by chance I looked from my window the night you returned from Le Noir and saw you walking to the *garçonnière*."

Sherman swallowed. Guy's artist's vision could prove dangerous.

Guy smiled disarmingly. "Not that I see you as a monster. Something about the night suggested the theme."

"The moon wasn't full that night." The words were out before Sherman thought.

"Wasn't it?" Guy shrugged. "I must have recalled that a *loup-garou* needs a full moon to change from a man to a wolf. Tell me frankly, what do you think of the painting?"

"I find it frightening."

Guy looked pleased. "If you're moved, I've succeeded in what I tried to do."

"Do you really believe in werewolves?" Sherman asked.

"Why not? Just because I've never seen one doesn't mean *loup-garous* don't exist. Actually, I'm intrigued by the possibility they might. Aren't you?"

An impossible question. With no ready answer, Sherman shrugged. Never mind Guy's disclaimer, it disturbed him that he'd been the inspiration for the painting. Also upsetting was that the French tongue, like the Spanish and the English, had a word for shapeshifters. Were there others like him? God help them if there were. If shapeshifters had a God.

Guy crossed to a window, peering down at the workers below. "Hurricane weather makes me restless, makes me long to meet a mysterious, dangerous woman, one a man can never be sure of. Perhaps that's why I ventured into Gallatin Street the night I was drunk—to find my unattainable woman."

"The women on Gallatin seemed all too attainable," Sherman said dryly.

Without turning to look at him, Guy waved a hand. "I don't mean whores or any woman who's for sale. I dream of a beauty who walks the dark side of life, a mystery woman whose offer of love carries the threat of death. Creole belles are pretty but dull—any serious involvement with them leads to an all too predictable marriage. That's not for me. I'll never find what I want here, but perhaps in Paris . . ." His words trailed off.

Guy's words sent a thrill along Sherman's spine. In spite of himself he imagined a woman who understood and forgave his terrible aberration. He pictured her, fair and lovely, dressed in white. . . .

Guy turned to look at him. "Do you know my mother and father loved each other for years? Yet they were forced by circumstance to wait until they were over forty to marry. I'm like my father in that way—if I can't have the woman I want, I'll marry no other."

"I'll never marry."

Guy raised his eyebrows but didn't contradict the statement, saying mildly, "Every man to his own choice."

I have no choice, Sherman thought bitterly. Any fair maid I desire, understanding or not, will be safe only in my dreams.

"In the meantime, *mon ami*, New Orleans is full of beautiful and willing women," Guy added, crossing to the stairs. "I must introduce you to a few."

Sherman followed him down to the second floor. Just because he'd vowed never to marry didn't mean he wasn't as susceptible as any man to a pretty and willing woman's charms. Dr. Kellogg had insisted the devices a man could use to keep from fathering a child were close to foolproof. Did he dare take a chance?

"While we're upstairs, why don't you look at the bedrooms?" Guy said over his shoulder. "You'll be sleeping in one tonight, so you may as well take your pick."

Sherman frowned. "But I'm perfectly comfortable in the *garçonnière*."

"That building's not safe in a hurricane. You'll have to move in with us until the storm's over. No doubt Papa's had one of the servants fetch your belongings. I've already made a bet with myself about the room you'll choose."

Realizing he couldn't insist on remaining in the bachelor quarters, Sherman didn't protest further. Being in the house won't endanger anyone, he told himself firmly. The storm will prevent the beast from emerging.

But he wasn't happy about making the change. At Guy's behest, he peered into one second-floor bedroom after another, barely taking in the furnishings as he tried to quell his unease.

"This one will do," he said finally, pausing at the door of a room where a pale green paper with twining ivy covered the walls.

"The green room," Guy said. "I knew this would suit you. I'd have been surprised if you'd chosen another."

He *did* feel comfortable in the room, Sherman decided. Perhaps because of the green color, repeated in the carpet, the window draperies, and the bedspread. Unlike some of the other bedrooms he'd seen, the furniture was of light wood with a graceful design.

"My mother," Guy said, "claimed this was the most soothing room in the house. She insisted that, no matter how troubled a guest, after a night's sleep here he or she always woke refreshed. Not that I'm implying *you're* troubled—even if the way you pace at times does remind me of some great caged beast." He smiled at Sherman. "Perhaps that's why I changed you into a monster in my painting."

Beguiled by the open, trusting smile, Sherman couldn't believe Guy had fathomed his secret. Guy might paint what he saw with his artist's eyes, but he didn't understand what he saw was the literal truth.

"Lilette will bring you anything you need," Guy said. "You've only to ask." He winked.

A bit taken aback, Sherman stared at him, wondering if Guy really meant it. Lilette was one of the upstairs servants, pretty, her skin the color of café au lait, her curvaceous body inviting a man's embrace. She'd smiled at him more than once in passing.

"I *know* you've noticed Lilette," Guy went on. "A man

would have to be blind not to. I starting watching her when I was twelve. But, as Papa explained when I was thirteen, a man doesn't force himself on his female slaves unless he's a bastard like Gauthier. *You* don't own her, though. If she's willing—why not?''

Since he couldn't explain why not to Guy, Sherman merely nodded in acknowledgment.

Rain began before the evening meal, but the full fury of the storm didn't hit until close to midnight. In bed, Sherman listened to the wind whip around the corner of the house, shrieking like Baba-Yaga in pursuit of her victims. He could all but picture the old, ugly witch with her sharp nose and teeth, picture her flying through the fury of the night in her strange chariot. Baba-Yaga, the evil eater of human flesh.

Since he remembered her so clearly, Baba-Yaga must come from the same country as he. What country? Did she really exist? With what he'd learned about his own shape-shifting, he could hardly dismiss her as a myth, though he didn't believe that, real or not, she prowled through the storm here in New Orleans. This wasn't her country, any more than it was his. Besides, he'd sense anyone or anything as unusual as Baba-Yaga.

The United States had its own witches—or at least California did. He'd sensed that *Tía* Dolores was a *bruja* from the moment they'd met. He hadn't yet sensed another during his travels, but if he encountered any, he'd know early enough to be able to avoid them.

Thinking of *Tía* Dolores reminded him of Esperanza and his heart twisted with pain and jealousy. Esperanza was Don Rafael's wife now and he resented it, much as he tried to wish her well. He'd put her through such misery that the poor girl deserved to be happy.

If he closed his eyes he could imagine her in his arms under the live oak in the courtyard. He could almost feel her softness, how she'd responded when—

No! Esperanza was gone forever as far as he was concerned. Recalling their moments together only made it worse. Thinking about her reminded him of what Guy had said about Lilette's availability. Damn it, much as he'd like to bed her, he couldn't take the risk.

Forget women, he ordered himself. Remember instead what you are. Remember that the moon, almost full, is high in the sky at this very moment and only the storm clouds keep the beast from emerging. Who knows what might happen if you bed Lilette during a full moon, storm clouds or not?

True to the doctor's prediction, the storm lasted three days and the sky remained overcast for still another day and night. Sherman, by himself once more in the *garçonnière,* fought his restlessness successfully on the following night and then the temptation to change was over for another month. As the days passed, he grew more and more attached to the Kelloggs.

When the time of the full moon neared in June, he reminded the doctor after they'd finished seeing the morning patients that tomorrow he had to leave for five days.

Dr. Kellogg paused with his hand on the surgery door. "It's none of my business, but curiosity has always been my bane. You weren't able to leave last month for those five days. Yet you sent no messages to anyone, nor did you go anywhere after the storm was over. I've wracked my brain to understand what it is you must do that's so important you must leave for five days every month but still so unimportant that missing last month's five days apparently made no difference."

Sherman, unable to think of a reasonable excuse, blurted "I can't tell you."

The doctor waved his hand. "As I said, I had no business asking. Please forgive me for being a nosy old man and by all means take your five days."

Aware the nearly full moon rose near sunset, Sherman set off the next day in the late afternoon heat. As he tramped through the brush with sweat dripping from his face, he decided that New Orleans in June felt hotter than the California desert in midsummer.

Clouds of mosquitoes rose as he neared the swamps, and he wondered if the beast was immune to the pesky bugs. He wasn't, though the bites healed quickly enough—a fact that hadn't escaped the doctor's eagle eye. It frustrated Dr. Kellogg that he'd found no reason for Sherman's ability to heal rapidly.

Though Dr. Kellogg had no right to question him about the five days after he'd agreed to let Sherman take them, it was hard to resent the doctor's curiosity. Dr. Kellogg was equally curious about every unusual occurrence, be it odd symptoms in a patient, wilting sugar cane, a pink rosebush that suddenly produced one red bloom, or the mysteries of voodoo. Very little escaped his notice.

Arriving at the vine-covered cage, Sherman carefully pulled away the growth. With his mouth set in a grim line, he opened the barred door and plucked the chain from inside. Holding the chain, he watched the sun dip behind the trees to the west. Since he didn't intend to spend a moment longer than necessary locked inside the cage, he waited, brushing away the mosquitoes buzzing about his face. Until the restlessness began inside him, he could safely remain unfettered.

A small brown bird, a scissortail, perched on a cypress limb and stared at him with one beady eye. Frogs chorused in the swamp. A damp scent of mixed rot and new growth permeated the air. Green plants surrounded him. Wherever he came from he knew he'd never before seen such riotous growth as sprouted everywhere in New Orleans.

Slowly, insidiously, blue shadows crept across the greenery. The sun was down, the moon not yet visible. He waited apprehensively. Was that quiver in his stomach the first twinge of warning?

The quiver grew into a fluttering. Still he delayed. Just as he began to grow restless, Sherman sensed something more than the small animals close by. Something, someone, approached. An animal and a man. Tensing, he stared at the tangle of vines, small trees, and shrubs that prevented him from seeing more than two feet away.

A dog bayed. Too close for comfort. A deer or rabbit hunter with his dog? Sherman shook his head. Not with night coming on. Unless they hunted him.

Impossible. Wasn't it?

He glanced around uneasily, seeing the telltale glow of the rising moon above the trees. His restlessness increased; the inner twinges grew sharper, more urgent. If he tried to run, he risked changing where he wasn't safe. What if the beast doubled back and killed the man? On the other hand, if he locked himself in the cage and the dog tracked him there, he'd be exposed.

And if the man had a gun, he'd be dead.

But that presumed the dog was tracking him—and why should that be? Damn it, what should he do?

The edge of the moon rose pale and mocking over the

trees and he felt the first twist of the change wrench his guts. At the same time, the dog howled, an eerie cry of terror. Though the imminent change blurred his sensing, he thought the dog had turned tail, fleeing. Not the man. To his horror, he heard the man plunging through the brush, coming closer and closer. To doom.

Making up his mind, he crouched to enter the cage, struggling for control.

"Sherman!" Dr. Kellogg cried. "My God, son, what's wrong?"

Sherman turned, fighting against the redness clouding his mind as he stared at the doctor's horrified face. It was too late. For them both.

Moonlight beamed down on him, filling his veins with silver fire, stirring a lust for the hunt, the kill. Dr. Kellogg would be his prey. As he tore off his clothes, with his last vestige of humanness he forced words past a throat already changing.

"Get in the cage," he growled hoarsely. "Set the bar. Hurry, Doctor. Or you'll die."

Free! With the moon shining above, the beast savored the night sounds and smells. His hackles rose with the sense and smell of man. Where?

There. He recognized the cage for what it was—a trap. This time a man huddled inside and not him. Knowing he couldn't get at the man, he loped away toward the more promising smells drifting on the wind, the scent of red-blooded prey. The moon and the night were his. He meant to make the most of his freedom.

He ran through the darkness, avoiding the dangers of the swamp—the sucking sand, the snake with fangs of poison, the bull alligator bellowing for a mate. He'd survive the poison and could best the alligator but, held fast in the red talons of bloodlust, he chose to run down his quarry and feast.

But even as he pursued his prey, anticipating the hot and salty tang of blood, he felt the pulsing pull of another need. Like the bull gator, he lusted for a mate.

Sherman roused to the disquieting hum of mosquitoes. He brushed at his ears, then groggily opened his eyes to grayness. The sun hadn't yet risen and tendrils of mist curled among the cypresses. Frogs sang, birds twittered. In the distance a fox barked sharply once, twice, and fell silent. Something large splashed nearby, bringing him fully awake.

He sat up abruptly and looked around, blinking in confusion when he saw water, green with scum, on two sides of him. What the hell was he doing in the swamp? He stared at his hands, dark with crusted blood, and at his nakedness.

"Oh, God," he muttered.

The beast had hunted in the night. Hunted . . . what? Sherman swallowed, recognizing the taste in his mouth as blood. The last he remembered was standing by the cage with the moon rising and a dog braying. No, there was more. Dr. Kellogg. And then—and then what?

Alarmed, he leaped to his feet. Gobbets of gore and flesh led him to mangled remains. Heart pounding in panic, he finally realized he was looking at what was left of a deer. The beast had killed a deer. Not the doctor. Relief coursed through him until he began to wonder what had happened to Dr. Kellogg. The doctor had been there when the change began, he was sure. A faint recollection stirred. The cage. Had the doctor locked himself inside the cage? If so, the beast couldn't have gotten to him; he'd have survived.

But in that case, Dr. Kellogg knew what he was. Eventually the doctor would have let himself out of the cage and returned to Lac Belle. Sherman couldn't believe he'd keep it a secret that a beast was loose.

Like an echo of the night before, a dog bayed in the distance. Sherman forced himself to concentrate on sensing, his ability sluggish as always after a shifting.

An animal, yes, and a man. A hunter. Hunting him. Sherman nodded grimly. Dr. Kellogg, without a doubt. With a gun this time.

He scanned for other men, other hunters, but located only the one with the tracking dog. It was like the doctor to hunt alone. One man with a gun was enough to kill him.

Time to run. Sherman looked around desperately, seeking the best route. Nothing was familiar. He was deep in a swamp with treacherous terrain on all sides. The water might be shallow enough to wade through, but remembering the splash he'd heard, he feared gators lurked beneath its scummy surface. Turning away from the water, he plunged into the tangled growth.

He'd gone no more than a few paces before his feet sank

into ooze, into mud that sucked at his ankles as he tried to slog through it to reach solid ground. When the mud reached his calves, he realized the danger and struggled to turn back. The mud wouldn't let loose. The harder he fought, the deeper he sank.

Quicksand.

He wasn't near any vegetation that he might grasp to pull himself free. When the mud reached his thighs, Sherman stopped struggling, stopped moving at all, and listened as the triumphant bay of the hound trailing him came closer and closer. Or was it the track of the beast the dog followed?

When it seemed the hound would burst through the brush any second, the animal abruptly fell silent and Sherman had his answer. The dog tracked the beast and had come to the end of the trail. The scent of the beast and the man Sherman differed.

"Sherman!" Dr. Kellogg cried from beyond the concealing vegetation. "Sherman, where are you?"

Sherman, the mud slowly climbing toward his waist, wondered if the doctor seriously believed he'd answer. Yet one way or another he was doomed. Wasn't a quick death from bullets preferable to being slowly smothered in mud?

Making up his mind, he called, "I'm here, Doctor. In quicksand."

The tangle of vines and plants separating them parted and Dr. Kellogg's face peered through. He stared at Sherman for a long moment. Then, without a word, he vanished, the greenery closing over the opening he'd made.

Sherman cried out in pain and fear. How could the doctor leave him to such an agonizing death when a bullet would be so much more merciful? Unable to help himself, he began to flail in wild panic, sinking faster.

"Stop that!" Dr. Kellogg ordered.

Sherman gaped at the doctor, unable at first to take in that he'd come back, much less that Dr. Kellogg was thrusting a long pole toward him.

"Grab the pole and lay yourself on the mud as though you're swimming," the doctor ordered. "I'll pull you out."

With an effort, Sherman gathered his wits and obeyed. Surprisingly, once he levered himself into as much of a horizontal position as possible, he felt the clutch of the mud on his legs ease. Dr. Kellogg, hand over hand on the pole, slowly pulled him from the mire.

Finally Sherman felt solid earth under him, released his death grip on the pole, and lay gasping, face pressed to the moss beneath him.

After a time the doctor spoke. "Son, you're a god-awful mess of mud. I've got your clothes with me, but you'll have to wash first."

Sherman sat up, glancing warily at Dr. Kellogg. "Why do you still call me 'son'?" he asked hoarsely. "I know you saw what happened to me last night."

The doctor nodded. "I don't mind admitting you scared the shit out of me. But you also saved my life by telling me to lock myself in the cage. Why?"

"I didn't want you hurt. The beast—" Sherman shuddered, unable to go on.

"You can't control the beast you change into—am I right?"

Sherman nodded glumly.

"I'd say if any man ever needed help, you're that man. God knows I've never encountered anyone like you before, but I'm willing to lend a hand. I'll do my best for you, son, though I can't guarantee a cure."

Speechless, Sherman could only stare. Help him? Was he hearing right?

"First of all," the doctor said briskly, "how often does this change occur? From what I already know, I assume it happens near or during the full moon."

"Every full moon," Sherman said slowly, "except in bad weather. But why would you want to help me?"

"I'm a doctor, aren't I? I took an oath to help the afflicted. Besides, it'd take a damn rotten bastard to turn his back on a friend in need." He held out his hand to Sherman. "On your feet. We've got to get you washed and dressed and back to Lac Belle. Then I expect you to make a clean breast of everything you know about yourself. Everything, mind you. I can't work blind."

Once back at the house, the doctor explained to the worried Guy that Sherman had become lost in the swamps and narrowly escaped being sucked to his death in quicksand. "I need to give him a thorough examination," he added, and whisked Sherman into the surgery, leaving Guy behind.

"Sit down and begin at the beginning," Dr. Kellogg ordered.

Sherman took a deep breath. At last he'd found someone to tell the complete truth to, someone who knew what he was and didn't turn away in fear and disgust. He began with the beach in California, admitting he didn't know who he was, where he came from, or how he came to be on the beach. He told of the Californios and what had happened to him because of the *bruja* and how he came to New Orleans. The doctor listened, obviously spellbound.

"Now you know why I can never father a child," Sherman finished.

"I understand why you're afraid to, certainly. Yours is a fascinating case. Fascinating."

"Not to me."

The doctor shrugged. "I suppose not. You say the moon causes this shapeshifting. Have you ever changed otherwise?"

"Once, in a fight to the death—but the moon was near full at the time."

"I've thought of a plan to cage the beast when he emerges—assuming that's what you wish."

"God, yes!" Sherman exclaimed fervently.

"There's a small brick-lined wine cellar under part of this house. I'll have the wine removed, the door strengthened, and a sturdier lock put on. You'll spend tonight and the following three nights there." He smiled at Sherman. "One problem solved, at least temporarily."

"If any of your slaves learn I'm in the cellar, what will they think? Especially if the beast howls."

"We'll take care no one sees you enter or leave the cellar. As for any howling, I'll blame it on a dog I'm experimenting with. Don't worry. No one will discover your secret."

"I'm not so sure. Did you see the picture Guy painted of a *loup-garou* outside the *garçonnière* at night? He claims I inspired the painting. He also did a sketch of my face that hints at the beast inside."

Dr. Kellogg frowned, sitting for a time in thought. Finally he sighed. "Guy dreams of sailing to France and becoming a great artist. Perhaps it's time I let him try his wings. Much as I hate to admit the truth, it's clear to me that he's not suited to be a doctor. The La Branche cousins in Paris will keep an eye on him."

"I wouldn't want Guy sent away on my account," Sherman said. "But I know he longs to go."

"Then he will. It may be he has the ability to be an artist. I'm no judge. Speaking of *loup-garous*, though, what you changed into was no wolf."

Do I dare ask what the beast looks like? Sherman wondered. Or is the beast too repulsive to be described?

As if reading his mind, Dr. Kellogg said, "You've told me you have no memory of what the beast does—that implies you've never seen him." At Sherman's nod, the doctor went on. "He's larger than you, more massive, though I don't understand why. But then, I've never come up against a shapeshifter before.

"He has taloned paws instead of hands but is able, like a bear, to walk on his hind legs as well as all fours. But he doesn't look like a bear any more than he does a wolf. The face is a predator's muzzle with fanged teeth. The short, curly fur is black. Only the eyes remain the same as yours—golden yellow. He didn't come near the cage, you know. He looked at me and I swear he knew he couldn't reach me, so he didn't bother to try. That marks him as an extremely intelligent beast."

Listening to the doctor's description, Sherman suddenly wondered if the beast within him also heard and understood what was said. "Do you suppose he knows what I know?" he asked.

"That's one of the things we'll try to discover. Along with probing for the various ways in which you differ from a normal human. Don't take offense—I'm sure you realize you're not normal. It doesn't make you less of a man, never believe that. Think of yourself as having unusual abilities that a normal man lacks." Dr. Kellogg rubbed his hands together. "I can't wait to get started. Because I already know how rapidly you heal, I think we'll begin with an attempt to ascertain what might be lethal to you. I have a feeling you'll survive what would kill an ordinary man."

It was at that moment, grateful as he was, that Sherman began to wonder exactly what he was letting himself in for.

Chapter 11

Sherman woke in darkness, wearing only his trousers. For a moment he couldn't recall where he was. Sensing a man approaching, he leaped to his feat. Feeling the cool brick under the soles of his feet, he remembered he'd been locked in the cellar shortly after sundown.

"Sherman?" Dr. Kellogg called. "It's morning. Are you all right?"

"Yes, sir."

"Who is the President of the United States?" the doctor asked.

"General Zachary Taylor," Sherman replied. Since Dr. Kellogg was all but positive the beast couldn't master words, to be certain it was safe they'd agreed that Sherman would have to answer a different question each morning before the doctor would unlock the door.

The door swung open. Aided by the dim light slanting down the wooden steps from the outside entrance, Sherman found his scattered clothes and slipped them on.

"I didn't change," he told the doctor in a low tone. "I felt the urge and started to undress. But it didn't happen."

The doctor clapped him on the shoulder. "Good, good. It's too early to be sure, but maybe all we'll have to do is keep you from the moonlight on your susceptible days."

Even while he hoped they had the answer, Sherman doubted it was that easy.

"I found a surprising amount of information about shape-shifters in the La Branche library," the doctor confided as he shepherded Sherman up the steps. "I imagine much of it is superstitious nonsense, but we can't afford to dismiss anything without a fair test. After all, I still wouldn't believe a man could change his shape if you hadn't done so right before my eyes. We'll begin our investigations after breakfast."

Guy was waiting in the dining room. "Has Papa told you?" he asked Sherman excitedly. Without waiting for an answer, he flung his arms wide. "I'm sailing to France! Think of it, Tanguy La Branche Kellogg on the boulevards of Paris."

"I'll think of Guy Kellogg working to learn his craft," his father said dryly. "That's why you're going, if I'm not mistaken."

"Not merely to learn art, Papa, but to experience life." His warm smile embraced both men. "In moderation, of course."

"Of course." The doctor's tone was even drier.

"Ah, but you don't know I promised Sherman I'd never get drunk again. I intend to honor that promise—even in Paris."

Sherman hadn't realized Dr. Kellogg would act so quickly. Guilt that he was at least partly the cause of the doctor losing his son's companionship mingled with happiness that Guy's dream of studying art in Europe would come true.

Guy struck a pose. "When I reach the pinnacle of success, when I'm acclaimed as the world's greatest artist, I'll insist I owe it all to my far-seeing and understanding father and my good angel, Sherman Oso."

Sherman grinned at him, knowing he'd miss Guy.

"Before I leave," Guy went on, "we must have a farewell party at Lac Belle. Don't you agree, Papa?"

His father nodded. "By all means. If we have time to organize one before your ship sails."

"Sherman needs to meet people," Guy persisted. "You can't keep him closeted with the sick and injured all the time. At the party, he'll have a chance to get acquainted with some of my friends—male and female."

"We'll see."

Guy raised his eyebrows at Sherman, who shrugged. Since Sherman didn't dare pursue any friendships, he'd as soon not meet Guy's friends, especially the women.

Guy rode off to town immediately after the meal, intent on visiting his tailor to be fitted for new clothes. His last words were, "I devoutly hope he's *au courant* with the latest Paris fashions."

Dr. Kellogg immediately swept Sherman off to the surgery, where he handed him a dozen or more cloves of garlic strung onto a cord. "Put this around your neck," he ordered.

Grimacing at the strong reek of the garlic, Sherman obeyed.

"Feel anything?" the doctor demanded.

Sherman shook his head.

"Wear it a while longer just to be sure. The books I found lump vampires with werewolves, both being shapeshifters—vampires, so they claim, turn into bats. In any case, we must test everything mentioned in the books as repellent to vampires and werewolves. I realize you're neither, but we can only work with what information I'm able to unearth."

"I don't think your patients are going to appreciate the smell of my necklace," Sherman said.

"I'm not seeing any patients this morning. With the many doctors available in the city, they won't suffer. It's not every day a medical man gets a challenging case—and yours is the most unusual I've ever seen, or ever will see. I intend to devote most of my time to it."

"I never believed anyone would want to help me. I can't begin to tell you how much I—"

Dr. Kellogg waved his hand. "Don't thank me. I'm glad to have the chance to work on your unusual problem. The older a man gets, the more bored he becomes. You and your shapeshifting, son, are the most exciting thing to come down the pike since I met my wife-to-be in '04." Dr. Kellogg leaned back in his chair and looked off into the distance.

"The night we met, Madelaine wore a green gown that set off her black curls and sparkling brown eyes. She was the most beautiful girl at the ball. Creole, of course, while I was American. The United States had just taken over Louisiana from the French and we Americans were not popular in New Orleans. It took me years to win her."

"Guy told me you had married his mother late in life," Sherman said after a short silence.

Dr. Kellogg straightened. "To get what you most desire, the secret is to never give up. Never. Keep that in mind, son."

After fifteen minutes, the doctor allowed Sherman to remove the garlic necklace, then made him strip and examined him from head to toe. As Sherman put on his clothes again, the doctor slipped a gold crucifix on a gold chain over his head.

"We'll see if this has any effect," he told Sherman. "You're as healthy a man as I've ever seen. If you're wondering, everything inside you is in the right place and I couldn't detect anything extra. I already know you're taller and stronger than the average man and that you heal extraordinarily fast.

"One oddity is that both your forefingers are as long as your middle fingers. That's a quirk mentioned in one of the books—werewolves have long forefingers. In most humans the middle finger's longer."

Sherman stared at his hands. He'd never noticed.

"That gold crucifix around your neck bothering you any?' the doctor asked.

Sherman touched the cross. "As far as the smell's concerned, I prefer it to the garlic. It doesn't bother me at all."

"Scratch off garlic and crucifixes, then," the doctor muttered, making notes. "Let's try the silver amulet next." He picked up a silver chain with a four-leaf clover fashioned in silver. "Take off the cross and put this on."

Sherman fastened the chain at his nape. A moment later he ran a finger under the chain where it touched his skin. "Itches a bit," he said, moving his shoulders uneasily.

Dr. Kellogg's gaze assessed him. "You seem edgy."

"I feel like ripping the chain off."

"Ah. The silver bothers you, does it?" The doctor leaned closer. "Red welts. The book was right."

"Can I take it off?" Sherman asked, scratching his neck.

As soon as the chain was removed, the welts faded and the itching subsided.

"Most interesting." Dr. Kellogg said. "The silver irritated your skin almost immediately as well as affecting your mood."

"I've handled silver knives and spoons when eating," Sherman said. "And silver coins."

"Did the palms of your hands itch afterward?"

"I've had itchy palms from time to time, but I never thought to connect it with handling silver."

"You will after today," the doctor predicted. "Are you willing to undergo a bit of pain?"

Sherman nodded and, at the doctor's request, laid his arm on the table. He watched apprehensively as Dr. Kellogg picked up a scalpel. How far did the doctor intend to go in the interests of science?

Clenching his teeth against the momentary stinging, he held his arm steady as the doctor sliced into his forearm with the sharp blade, making two small parallel incisions. Blood ran down his arm and dripped onto the table. Holding the edges of the first incision apart, Dr. Kellogg eased the silver chain into the wound.

The first cut immediately began to throb and Sherman grunted as fiery pain shot up his arm. The bleeding, which had begun to ease, increased in the first cut but not the second.

Dr. Kellogg counted off a minute, then removed the chain. It took five minutes more for the painful throbbing to ease. At the end of a half hour the second cut was all but healed while the first still gaped open, oozing a few drops of blood.

"Silver definitely slows down your ability to heal," Dr. Kellogg observed, scribbling in his notebook. "And I'd wager my last dollar that whatever's harmful to you is also harmful to the beast. Didn't you say you thought the beast had been shot at and wounded?"

"Yes, when it escaped from the Californios' pit. Its bullet wounds were still healing when I came to myself."

"He, Sherman, not it. The beast is a male, just as you are. Remember, I saw him."

Sherman grimaced. He'd feared the truth, so avoided thinking about it. He hadn't wanted to face the fact that the beast might mate at some time. But, God, with what? He shuddered.

"You're worrying that he might find a female someday?" Dr. Kellogg shook his head. "I can't say it's impossible, but I do believe it's unlikely. True, you're one of them, but I'm not convinced shapeshifters abound.

"Let's get back to the bullets. I'm convinced the beast survived them because they were lead. If the bullets had been silver, as the books recommend for killing werewolves, you might not be sitting here now."

Sherman stared down at the two incisions. The second had closed but the first was still open, its edges an angry red. Because of the silver. If Don Rafael had known about silver bullets, he undoubtedly would have used them against the beast. And killed him.

"Do you think what's in these books is common knowledge?" Sherman asked apprehensively.

"The books are little more than a compilation of old wives' tales. Folklore. The writers of the books heard the stories somewhere. I suspect that among the ignorant and superstitious, tales of werewolves and vampires persist—as well as the remedies to use against them.

"Here in New Orleans, we have voodoo, practiced mainly by the Negroes but believed in to some extent by many Creoles. There's a tradition of shapeshifting in voodoo where the affected person changes into a snake. Is it true? Two days ago I'd have laughed at the question, but now—who knows? I have no idea how one could kill a man-snake, but a *voodooienne* would be able to tell me. That's what I mean about folklore."

Distracted for a moment from the realization of his vulnerability to silver, Sherman asked, "What's a *voodooienne*?"

"A voodoo queen. Here in New Orleans she's usually a free woman of color, not a slave. She's exactly what the title implies, a queen to her followers, their conjurer of magic spells, mixer of powerful potions, and seeress who looks into the future. She's respected, admired, and feared."

Dr. Kellogg peered at the inflamed incision. "Looks nasty, doesn't it? Let's give the arm a good cleaning with soap and water."

The cut took two days to heal and left Sherman with a healthy respect for the dangers of silver in an open wound. Plus the understanding the beast was more vulnerable than he'd thought—if a hunter knew about silver bullets.

Whether it was the inflammation or being shut in the cellar away from the moon's rays or a combination of the two, he passed through the full of the moon without shifting.

Guy booked passage on *Le Halbran,* a ship sailing on the first of July, and organized his farewell party for the last day of June. Since there was no way for Sherman to avoid attending, he patronized Guy's tailor, spending what seemed to him an inordinate amount of money for what Guy termed a *frac*—a frock coat—and trousers, both in sober black. When he wanted to choose a waistcoat as colorful as St. Vrains', Guy persuaded him to change to fawn.

"The frivolous doesn't suit you, *mon ami,*" Guy insisted.

"Always dress soberly to contrast with your immense vitality—you'll intrigue the women, if nothing else."

The night of the party, Sherman had no trouble finding a place on the dance card of any Creole belle he approached. When the lines formed for the quadrille, he maneuvered adequately, thanks to Guy's coaching, and also did well waltzing. He enjoyed holding one pretty, perfumed coquette after another in his arms—what man wouldn't? But it made him ache for more than a dance. Damn it, how could he stand being a monk all his life?

It was well after midnight when the party finally ended. The three men retired to the library for a nightcap.

"It was quite remarkable how everyone took to you," Dr. Kellogg told Sherman as he handed him a snifter of brandy. "Men and women alike."

"I noticed," Guy said. "When I saw the Ice Princess flutter her eyelashes at him I decided Sherman has some sort of secret allure."

Dr. Kellogg nodded. "I wouldn't be surprised."

Guy raised his eyebrows, causing Sherman to ask hastily, "Who's the Ice Princess?" He didn't care, but he also didn't want Guy to question the doctor's remark.

He listened with half an ear as Guy went on about how aloof the woman was. Finally Guy yawned, set down his glass, rose, said his good nights, and left the room.

"It affects animals as well," Dr. Kellogg said.

Sherman blinked. "What?"

"This fatal allure of yours. The books on shapeshifting mention the phenomenon and I've seen it happen. Look how fond my dogs are of you—even my favorite, Jefferson, prefers you to me. The horses will do anything you ask. That swayback dun of yours all but reads your mind. Even Madelaine's caged canary sings every time you enter the morning room."

"Yet the stable cats won't come near me," Sherman said, going on to tell about the *bruja*'s cat. "I think they sense what I am."

"Perhaps. Cats are said to be sensitive to ghosts—why not to shapeshifters? But I'll wager all animals fear the beast. Jefferson fawns on you when you're a man, but when he was tracking you, your changing certainly sent him howling for home." The doctor set down his glass. "I've located some aconite. During the next full moon we'll see what happens if I put some sprays of the plant in the cellar with you."

"I'm not familiar with aconite."

"*Aconitum napellus*. Some call it monk's head or wolf's bane."

Sherman stared at him. "What effect is it supposed to have on me?"

The doctor shrugged. "Maybe none. We'll wait and see. In medicine the tincture is occasionally used in treating fevers. I may even have some in my drug cabinet, though I rarely use aconite—it's too poisonous. But the books specify that wolf's bane must not only be fresh, it must be in bloom. Since it's grown in many gardens for the beautiful blue flowers, I inquired around and found an acquaintance willing to dig up a plant or two for me. Luckily aconite blooms in June."

Wolf's bane, Sherman repeated silently, hoping it wouldn't affect him as noxiously as the silver. The name of the plant was vaguely sinister, but, after all, he wasn't a wolf—or a werewolf, either. At least, not exactly. In any case, he trusted Dr. Kellogg and was willing to let him try anything and everything in a search for a remedy against the shifting.

Guy's ship sailed on schedule and the following week, due to numerous entreaties, the doctor began to see patients in the mornings again. Despite the many doctors in the city, Dr. Kellogg's patients preferred him, though many of them were satisfied to be examined by his assistant.

"Fine young man you've got there," an elderly gentlemen told Dr. Kellogg near the middle of the month. "You and me, we're not getting any younger. Glad to see you're training someone to take your place."

Sherman didn't believe anyone could take the doctor's place—he certainly didn't aspire to. How could he? He'd happily go on working with Dr. Kellogg for as long as he could. It would take years to learn all the doctor knew, and even then he wouldn't be the man Dr. Kellogg was; he'd still be a shapeshifter. No patient would be safe with him when the moon was full—as it would be two nights from now.

That same afternoon the doctor had Andre, a burly, very dark-skinned Negro, dig holes in the back garden for the three aconite plants sent by his friend. Sherman, watching the transplanting, noticed Lilette hovering near the back door and was aware Andre noticed her, too. When the doctor called Sherman closer to smell the blue flowers of the plants, Andre unobtrusively drifted toward the back door.

The flowers had a faint, sweet odor, nothing special. Nor did the smell affect him in any obvious way. He doubted that putting a stalk of the flowers in the cellar tonight would make any difference.

Near the end of the evening meal, Sherman, increasingly restless, flung down his fork. "This chicken has no taste," he complained.

Dr. Kellogg sprang to his feet, hurried to Sherman, and urged him from the chair. "Clear the table," he ordered the maid as he shepherded Sherman outside.

At the entrance to the cellar, Sherman balked. "It's too early." His voice rasped in his throat.

"Get down those stairs!" the doctor demanded.

Though he didn't want to obey, Sherman couldn't make himself ignore a direct order from Dr. Kellogg. The doctor clattered down the steps behind him and, without warning, shoved him through the open inner door so hard Sherman staggered halfway into the room. Even as he turned, surprised and resentful, the door slammed, leaving him in darkness. He heard the rasp of the iron bar. Then the lock clicked into place.

"You tricked me!" he protested hoarsely.

"No." The doctor's voice came faintly through the thick door. "We almost didn't make it in time."

The agonizing wrench in Sherman's gut prevented him from speaking. He was faintly aware of a subtle perfume in the air as he tore off his clothes, and then—nothing.

Free! But not outside, where he should be. Where was he? In the absolute darkness he tested his surroundings and gnashed his teeth in rage. He was trapped. Somehow he'd been tricked into a cage. Not the same cage as before—a larger one.

The brick walls offered no chance for escape, so he tried the wooden door. He flung himself at the door, again and again. It shuddered slightly but refused to give. Angered, he clawed at the wood, ripping off long splinters. He lifted his muzzle to howl his rage into the darkness but suddenly held, sensing the man.

A man waited on the other side of the door. Men carried guns. He could survive the ordinary kind of bullet, but the man outside this door knew his weakness. The bullets in the man's gun might be of silver.

He was safe inside the cage, but if he escaped, the man could kill him with the silver bullets. Frustrated, he dropped to all fours. He desperately longed to run under the moon in the sweetness of the night, but all he could do was pad from one side of the cage to the other, back and forth, back and forth.

Somewhere in the night dogs howled in fear, sensing him. He was no dog; he wouldn't howl. If he didn't make any noise at all, maybe the man would open the door to see what was wrong. He'd be ready; he'd strike him down before the man used the gun. Once he was free, he'd never be tricked into a cage again.

Sherman woke naked, stiff from sleeping on a hard floor. He knew someone had called his name and he stared into the pitch darkness.

"I'm here," he muttered, climbing to his feet and wondering where in hell he was.

"What is the day, the month, and the year?" Dr. Kellogg's voice was faint, Sherman thought confusedly, as though he spoke through a door.

He tried to collect his thoughts to answer. The day? He didn't know. The month? May? No, wasn't it June? July? The only date he was certain of was the year.

"1850," he mumbled.

"Day and month," the doctor insisted.

"July."

"Day?"

"Goddamn it, I can't remember!" Sherman cried.

Metal clinked, the door opened, sending dim light shafting into the room. The cellar. He was in the cellar.

"Come out, Sherman," the doctor ordered. "Hurry."

He shambled through the door. Dr. Kellogg slammed it shut, draped a blanket over Sherman's shoulders, and pushed at him, urging him up the stairs and into daylight. He was hurried into the house and thrust ahead of the doctor into the surgery.

"Thank God you changed back," Dr. Kellogg said.

Changed. Sherman's head began to clear. The beast had gotten free despite the darkness of the cellar.

"The wolf's bane," Dr. Kellogg said. "Never again. I pulled out those three aconite plants last night with my own hands and burned them. I'll destroy the flower stalk in the cellar as well."

"Wolf's bane," Sherman echoed, his thoughts still sluggish.

"It precipitated the shift. I wasn't even sure I'd get you locked in the cellar before the beast took over. My fault—I'll be more careful with the next thing I try."

"I remember smelling something sweet," Sherman said slowly.

"As if making you sniff the flower in the garden earlier wasn't enough, I had to put another in the cellar, trapping you inside with it." The doctor shook his head. "With that overdose of wolf's bane I feared you might not change back, even with daylight."

"So wolf's bane causes a change rather than preventing one. Is that what the book said?"

Dr. Kellogg shrugged. "I'm afraid so. I had to be convinced. At your expense. I'm sorry, son. It won't happen again."

In the cellar that night, Sherman managed to resist the urge to shift, but the next night, when the moon was completely full, he shifted again. In the morning they found great gouges in the wood of the door.

"Before the next full moon, I'll line the door with metal," the doctor said.

To Sherman's great relief, he didn't shift during his final two nights in the cellar, though his need to kept him from sleeping.

"We'll wait until the next full moon to analyze whether or not this is an aftereffect of the wolf's bane," Dr. Kellogg told him. "If you don't shift next month, we'll be more sure the aconite was to blame this time."

As the days passed, Sherman continued to assist the doctor with patients. During their free hours, he submitted to one test after another. Holy wafers, consecrated for communion in the Catholic church, didn't have any effect on him, nor did rowan branches or sprigs from ash trees. As one busy day followed another, he could forget for hours at a time that he faced another five tormented nights when the moon next grew full.

By the end of July, the Lac Belle slaves sought him out for medical advice, not Dr. Kellogg.

"*Docteur,* he be too busy," they'd say to Sherman.

He was pleased and flattered, though he always discussed each case and the treatment he'd given with the doctor afterward.

"The slaves prefer you," Dr. Kellogg told him. "They feel you're on their side."

Sherman wondered if this was true. He was sympathetic to the Negroes, equating their hopeless situation with his own. Neither the Negroes nor he had any choice about what had happened to them. He was as much a slave to his shifting as they were to those who owned them.

The very idea of slavery repelled Sherman, but at least the Negroes at Lac Belle were treated decently. Dr. Kellogg cared about them, cared for them, thought of them as humans, not animals. Sherman heard stores about Le Noir that filled him with sickened anger.

Busy or not, the time of the full moon rolled inexorably around again. On the evening Sherman was to spend the first of his five nights in the cellar, he and the doctor were taking a last stroll around the garden when Andre came running from the slave quarters.

"*Docteur, docteur,*" Andre cried as he neared them. "Come quick. She be bad hurt."

"You've got time yet," the doctor said to Sherman. "Go with him while I fetch my bag."

Sherman trotted behind Andre to the slave quarters. Andre stopped before one of the cabins and motioned for Sherman to go inside. As he ducked through the low doorway, a sizzle of blue energy stopped him in his tracks. His gaze flicked over the Negroes in the dimly lighted interior. Two women, a young girl on a cot . . . He drew in his breath. The child was covered with blood. He plunged into the room and knelt beside the bed.

The girl, thin and small, looked to be about nine. Her brown skin was ash-gray from loss of blood; her eyes were rolled up into her head. Blood was everywhere, coming, as nearly as he could tell, from either the child's vagina or her rectum.

"What happened?" he demanded as he put his hand on her tiny chest to feel for a heartbeat.

"From Le Noir," the woman at the head of the cot said. "Her twin carry her here." She nodded toward another child crouched at the foot of the cot.

Sherman's glance focused for a moment on the girl, sensing she was the source of the blue energy. He had no time to wonder about her. The other girl needed his full attention.

"She say her sister come crawling all bloody from the master's room," the woman went on.

"Master mean to take me next," the child at the foot of the cot whispered.

Horrified, Sherman realized what had happened. Gauthier had raped this child. He called for water and sponged away the blood as best he could to see how badly she was torn. He swallowed his anguished rage when he found the perineum, the space between the vagina and the anus, torn in two. He suspected the violence of such a rape must have ripped her insides as well, and his heart sank. How could he save her?

Dr. Kellogg spoke from behind him. "What's the problem?"

Sherman's voice shook as he told him.

"I'll take a look," the doctor said.

Sherman moved aside. Calming himself, he gently covered the girl's forehead with his hand and closed his eyes, willing his energy into her. There was nothing else he could do.

"I don't dare examine her internally," Dr. Kellogg said in English. "I'd just cause more trauma. The poor little thing's about bled out."

As he spoke, the child gave a sigh and Sherman felt her life go. Slowly he took his hand away, his stomach churning with renewed fury.

"I'm afraid she's gone." Dr. Kellogg spoke in French this time and the two women began to keen.

Sherman glanced at the dead girl's twin and saw her big black eyes fixed on him. There were no tears in those eyes, nor did she utter a sound. Blue energy crackled around her. He recalled what she'd said about Gauthier.

"We can't send her back to Le Noir," he said to Dr.

Kellogg, gesturing toward the girl, "or Gauthier will kill her, too."

"I'll take her to the house," the doctor agreed. He turned to the girl. "What's your name?" he asked.

"Mima."

Dr. Kellogg held out his hand. "You'll spend tonight in the big house."

She pointed at Sherman. "Does he live there?"

"Yes, he does."

Without another word she put her hand in the doctor's. He eased her off the bed to the floor.

"Get her to safety," Sherman said. "I'll see to the rest."

"You'd best hurry," the doctor reminded him.

"I know." His rage urged him to ride to Le Noir and confront Gauthier with the child's abused body, but the moon was close to rising and he dare not take the time.

After the doctor led Mima from the cabin, Sherman bent over the dead twin and wrapped her body in the bloody blanket it rested on. He picked her up. Outside, a group of Negroes stood silently watching. Sherman's gaze found Andre.

"Will you dig her grave?" he asked.

"Yes, sir. Me, I dig, do you tell me where."

"Can you find a box to put her in?"

"Find or make one, sir."

"I'm taking her to the doctor's surgery. Bring the box to the house first thing in the morning. We'll bury her then."

A murmur ran through the gathered Negroes. Finally Andre said, "Do you be saying the prayer over her grave, sir?"

Sherman's eyes burned with tears he was too angry to shed. "I will," he murmured.

He set off for the house with his sad little burden, striding rapidly, anger simmering in every vein. The sight of the nearly full moon inching over the trees made him increase his pace, but he was too wrought up to worry about what might happen to him. One way or another, he'd see to it that Gauthier paid for this.

He'd almost reached the stables when he sensed, then heard, a man on horseback pounding toward him. Moments later, the horse and rider appeared, silvered by moonlight.

"Gauthier!" Sherman's challenging cry rang through the night.

Chapter 12

Sherman, still carrying the dead girl, sprang in front of Gauthier's horse. Gauthier reined in his black so abruptly the animal reared.

"Where's the doctor?" Gauthier demanded angrily. "Tell him I've come for my property."

"Here's your property!" Sherman laid the dead child on the ground and flung open the blanket. Moonlight illuminated the girl's torn and bloody body. "Here she is, you murdering bastard."

Gauthier yanked a whip from its holder and slashed at Sherman's face. As the lash stung his cheek and temple, Sherman exploded. Red clouded his vision so he saw Gauthier through a crimson mist as he flung himself toward the man, ignoring the gut-wrenching shift inside him.

The whip slashed Sherman again, the horse screamed and reared in panic, fighting Gauthier's attempts at control. Dogs howled, Gauthier toppled to the ground, and the horse bolted. Gauthier scrambled to his feet and faced Sherman, his hand reaching for his holstered gun. He froze, his mouth dropping open.

"Loup-garou!" he cried—the last words Sherman heard.

Free! The beast snarled at the man confronting him, a man with a gun.

The beast sprang at his enemy. Blood gushed hot into his mouth as his teeth sunk into the flesh of the man's throat, slashing and tearing. When he was certain the man was dead, he backed off, spat out the ill-tasting blood, skirted another body, and loped into the moonlit night.

By the lake he ran down a deer, killed it, and feasted.

His bloodlust satisfied, he heeded the other need throbbing through him. Where was he to find a mate? He threw back his head and howled, a pulsating ululation that momentarily silenced every sound near him.

He'd called her. Would she answer?

The beast waited, called once more, received no reply. Finally he slipped away from the lakeshore, knowing it wasn't safe to stay in one place too long. He spent the rest of the night alternately calling and searching—to no avail. Near dawn, tired and frustrated, he sought a safe spot to sleep.

Sherman woke, naked, hearing Jefferson baying. He sensed a man with the dog. Jumping to his feet, he stared panic-stricken at the greenery surrounding him. He'd shifted again and the beast had run free. The last he recalled was Gauthier slashing at him with a whip and screaming, *"Loup-garou!"*

Oh, God, Gauthier must have seen him change. What had the beast done? Remembering the pentacle he'd seen on Gauthier's palm when first they met, Sherman grimaced. He didn't need to be told.

He couldn't regret the death. If ever anyone had deserved to die, it was Gauthier. But he was as responsible as if he'd killed the man before he'd shifted.

Who was using Jefferson to trail him? Dr. Kellogg? Or a hunter on the track of the beast? Could he escape?

Sherman scanned his surroundings. He seemed to be on the edge of a swamp—where, he had no idea. Trying to run could very well land him in quicksand again. He'd make a stand here. If another besides the doctor sought him, he'd claim he pursued the beast only to be attacked himself. Which might explain the blood that stained his hands and, no doubt, his face.

"Sherman!" Recognizing Dr. Kellogg's voice made him relax slightly.

"Here," he called.

Jefferson reached him first, tail wagging, coming to be petted as the doctor panted up, hanging on to the end of the long leash and carrying Sherman's clothes.

"The beast killed Gauthier." Sherman's voice was flat, making a statement rather than asking a question.

"You might at least say you're glad to see me," the doctor muttered.

"You know I am. After last night, I don't deserve your kindness."

Dr. Kellogg shrugged and handed him a wet cloth. "Wipe off the blood and get dressed."

Jefferson, nose down, was circling the area, obviously searching for the beast's trail that he'd been following, a trail that had ended here. Thank God, Sherman thought, dogs couldn't reason enough to understand he and the beast were one and the same.

"Did anyone besides Gauthier watch me shift?" he asked as he pulled on his clothes.

"I'm afraid so. Ponce, for one. Francois. They came to tell me. I can't be sure how many other servants also saw you but are afraid to say so. I've told them all to keep quiet about what happened last night, but—" The doctor paused, shaking his head. "Word will leak out. Slaves are great gossips. A rumor spreads from one plantation to another like wildfire. And God knows how many heard you during the night. I did myself. Those were bloodcurdling howls, son. No animal I know sounds like that."

Even though it had been the beast who'd done the howling, Sherman winced. "I might have made the cellar in time if Gauthier hadn't ridden up while I was carrying the dead child."

"Unfortunate. For both you and Gauthier. He got what he's long deserved. On the other hand, we can't have you punished for his death. I told the authorities a mad dog mauled him and I'd hunt the animal down and kill it today. They accepted the explanation, but once stories of you being a *loup-garou* surface, they'll ask more questions. While they might not believe in shapeshifters, we can't afford to have them suspicious of you."

Sherman could well imagine being clapped in a jail cell while those in authority waited for the full moon to see if he changed.

"What it amounts to, son, is that you'll have to leave New Orleans until all this blows over."

Sherman nodded, his heart heavy. He'd been happy at Lac Belle; he'd felt safe. How could he bear to leave the only man who accepted him for what he was?

"We've got a long walk back. Best to get started." Dr.

Kellogg unhooked the leash, called to Jefferson, and led the way toward Lac Belle, with Sherman walking disconsolately behind him.

"I've already made plans," the doctor said, waiting for him to catch up. "First, we'll find another name for you just to be on the safe side, should anyone start looking for Sherman Oso. After all, that isn't your true name anyway. Any preferences?"

Sherman glanced at the doctor. Always practical, always a step ahead of others.

"You choose for me," he said. "For luck."

The doctor smiled at him. "How about turning you into a Creole and calling you Nicholas Deplacer?"

Sherman's lips twitched into a reluctant grin. *Deplacer* was a French word for shift. "It's appropriate," he admitted.

"Nicholas shortens nicely to Nick, and I imagine that's what they'll call you in Michigan."

"In Michigan?" Sherman visualized the map of the United States in the Lac Belle library. Michigan was near Ohio, Cump's home state.

"I have a friend there from my Army days. I'll send a letter along with you asking him to help you get settled. Of course, I won't mention the shapeshifting—you'll have to cope with that on your own. I wish we'd had more time to experiment. I'm sure I could have found a solution eventually. Perhaps when this all blows over, you can return for a visit. I'd welcome the chance to do further studies."

"I'll miss you." The words couldn't begin to convey Sherman's sense of loss.

"And I, you. But you've learned enough to be on your own as a physician. You're headed for a frontier community where your skills will be valued."

Sherman stared at him. Practice medicine on his own?

"Don't look so alarmed, son. You're a natural healer. You'll do just fine. Now, about traveling. Obviously you can't leave until the moon starts to wane—four more days, to be safe. The trouble is, rumors will be flying by then. Since we don't wish to draw attention to your leaving, it's best not to be seen in the city. If you ride Rawhide north for a few miles, you can catch an upriver boat at one of the landings. The boat'll take you up the Mississippi to the Ohio

River and on to one of the canals that feed into Lake Erie. You'll only have a short trip overland after the canal."

Sherman had learned enough about the geography of the United States to have a fair idea of the route he'd be traveling to Michigan. He was quite certain he'd get there all right. What would happen then was another story.

When they arrived at the house, Dr. Kellogg insisted he try to sleep for the rest of the morning. "The Negroes are a superstitious lot and the less they see of you, the better," he added bluntly.

"What about the twin of the dead girl?" Sherman asked before going to the *garçonnière*. "Did you send her back to Le Noir?"

The doctor shook his head. "Not yet. Mima's staying in the servant's quarters at the back of the house and doesn't want to leave. Apparently she's an orphan. Her twin sister was the only relative she had. She'll have to return eventually, since she's Le Noir property."

No one was in sight as Sherman walked across the grounds to his quarters, but he felt watched by hidden eyes. The feeling grew stronger as he neared the *garçonnière*. With his hand on the door, he held, sensing the crackle of blue energy nearby. Inside?

He flung open the door. Mima sat on the floor, her dark eyes fixed on him.

"I be waiting for you a long time," she said solemnly as she rose to her feet.

She was a skinny little thing, her thin legs and sharp features reminding him of a bird. Her black hair, he noted, was clipped almost as short as a boy's.

"You can't stay here, Mima," he said.

"I *be* staying."

While her sparkling energy intrigued him, he had no time to investigate its meaning. Besides, she might be dangerous to him—how could he tell? She was the first person he'd sensed with the blue crackle since he'd left *Tía* Dolores. And *Tía* Dolores had been a *bruja*.

"My grandmama, she be a *voodooienne*," Mima said, as though he'd asked her. "My mama tell me before she die I be like grandmama. I got voodoo; I *see*. Meta, my sister, she don't. Just me. Grandpapa, he be Bras Coupe."

Sherman had heard of the infamous one-armed escaped slave who'd roamed the swamps for years and was never caught. Even today people claimed to see him now and then, though he'd be nearly one hundred years old.

"I *see* Meta, she going to die," Mima went on. "Don't want her to die, I bring her to doctor. You come and I *see* if I stay with you I don't die. So I be staying."

"Your master is dead," Sherman said gently. "He can't harm you like he did your sister. You'll be safe at Le Noir now."

Mima shook her head. "I be safe with you, not at Le Noir. Don't send me back. I die if you do."

"How old are you, Mima?"

"Old Polly at Le Noir, she say Meta and me, we pass nine summers."

"Then you're old enough to understand that you belong to Le Noir. Even if I wanted to keep you here, I couldn't."

"I could stay do you buy me."

Sherman sighed. "I can't do that. I won't be here long enough."

"When you go, I go." Her dark eyes pleaded with him. "Me, I be helping you."

Impressed despite himself by her earnest conviction that she belonged with him, he knelt on one knee, bringing himself to her level. "I must travel alone, Mima. But I'll ask Dr. Kellogg to buy you from Le Noir. The Negroes at Lac Belle are treated well. You'll be much safer here than you will with me."

She shook her head. "You never going to hurt me."

He stared at her, startled, until he realized she couldn't know what he was—she must mean he wouldn't hurt her in the way Gauthier had brutalized her sister. God knows that was true.

"I'll speak to the doctor," he repeated. "Right now, you must return to the house. You can't stay in the *garçonnière*."

He thought she'd argue, but she walked past him without a word. By the time he rose to his feet, she'd slipped through the door and was gone.

The encounter had shaken him. If the blue energy meant anything, her mama might well have been right in saying Mima had inherited some kind of power from her grandmother. He'd felt no uneasiness with her as he had when *Tía* Dolores was near—he couldn't believe the child was a witch.

Mima said she *saw*—foresaw was what she meant. She'd

known her sister would die, but was that before or after Gauthier raped the poor child? Once Gauthier was through with Meta, it wouldn't take a voodoo seeress to realize the girl was doomed. What ability did Mima have? He'd like to know—those with blue energy were rare.

He passed that night and the following three in the cellar without changing. By then, aware every servant he met was terrified of him, Sherman was ready to leave.

The doctor saw him off at dawn after Sherman saddled his own horse, not wanting to upset Ponce by making him handle the *loup-garou*'s belongings.

"You must write and tell me how you're getting along," the doctor said. "I'm sure you'll manage to let me know about the shifting without your words being obvious to another. It's damned frustrating not to be able to follow the most exciting case I ever came across and, of course, I'll miss your assistance and companionship, too."

"You'll see to buying Mima?" Sherman asked. "She may prove to have unusual abilities."

Dr. Kellogg nodded. "So you told me. Don't worry, I'll take care of the child." He gripped Sherman's hand. "Remember—think of yourself as Nick Deplacer because Sherman Oso no longer exists."

Nick let go of the doctor's hand reluctantly, feeling he was losing everything, even his identity. He swung onto Rawhide and set off, not looking back. Once again the beast had destroyed his life. Dr. Kellogg had suggested that with time he might return, but Nick knew he never could.

It was a long, hot ride around the lake to the river, skirting swamps, passing several plantations, where he saw fieldworkers but no white men. No one approached him. Near noon he rode through a more settled area, where he encountered more people and grew increasingly uneasy as well as warmer under the hot August sun.

Once he thought he caught a flicker of blue energy mixed with the many red glows around him, but he couldn't be certain. When no one he passed paid him any more than idle attention, he decided he wasn't yet being hunted and his tension eased.

After he reached the wide and swift-flowing Mississippi, he rode north along the levee, remembering how Bony Tail had spoken of the father of rivers as if its existence might be a myth. He'd already traveled farther than the Havasupai had ever gone in his life.

Nick sighed. He doubted if Michigan would be the end of his journeying. A man with his affliction had to lead a nomad's life, so he might as well give up his idea of building himself a haven in the wilderness. Sooner or later the beast would jeopardize his safety wherever he went.

He passed a sugar cane plantation with its own river landing and, between a long alley lined with oaks, caught a glimpse of a white-columned mansion that reminded him of Lac Belle. Shortly after, he noticed a change in Rawhide's gait, reined him in, dismounted to check his hoofs, and prised a fair-sized rock from the right front. Hoping the pastern wasn't badly bruised, Nick remounted.

The dun trotted on but favored the leg. Knowing it wouldn't help the injury if the horse continued to carry his weight, Nick got off again and walked alongside Rawhide, leading him. It wasn't a great calamity, since once they boarded a boat the horse's foot would have time to heal. He was tempted to turn back to the landing and wait for an upriver boat, but fearing they were still too close to New Orleans, he walked on.

He'd gone less than a mile when, among the various energy glows from field-workers and other riders, he sensed the blue flicker again. Scanning to find the energy, Nick decided it came from behind him and its possessor was on horseback, not on foot.

Was he being trailed? He mistrusted anyone whose energy glowed blue. A grove of great oaks just off the road ahead caught his eye. He'd stop under the trees and see what kind of threat followed him. At least there was only one.

A man on a black horse passed, then a drover on an empty cart. Two Negroes walked by, casting sidelong glances at him. Had they already heard about Lac Bell's *loup-garou*?

The crackle of blue grew stronger, more insistent. Finally he spotted its source—a boy on a pony, a black boy, plodding slowly toward him. Nick eased out pent-up breath only to tense again when he realized it wasn't a boy at all, despite the ragged trousers and oversized man's hat shadowing the face.

He stepped from the concealment of the trees into the road and faced the approaching rider, arms akimbo.

"What in God's name are you doing here, Mima?" he demanded.

"Me, I already tell you," she said calmly. "I go with you."

He scowled. "No!"

"I *see* you and me, we be together."

Nick took off his hat and wiped the sweat from his face. "That doesn't matter. You can't come with me." All the reasons flashed through his mind and he jerked his head toward the shade of the oaks. "Come over here and I'll explain."

Mima didn't argue. Once under the trees she slid off the pony's back, walked over to Rawhide, and reached up to stroke his neck. "I be sorry," she said softly.

"Sorry?" Nick snapped, watching the dun nuzzle her shoulder. "Sorry for what?"

"I don't mean to hurt your horse."

"What the devil are you talking about?"

"Pony, he slow. Your horse, he go fast."

Nick raised his eyebrows. Was this little black girl implying she'd arranged for Rawhide's laming? He couldn't quite disbelieve her—not with the blue energy crackling about her.

"Mima," he said as patiently as he could, "you have to return to Lac Belle."

She shook her head. "Can't."

"Even if you belonged to me I wouldn't take you along," he said. "As it is, I don't own you. Le Noir does."

Her chin came up. "Me, I don't belong to nobody. Not after Meta die. I go with you."

He gazed down at her in frustration. Reason obviously wouldn't work. "Mima, do you know what happened after Meta died?"

She nodded. "Other part of you, he killed Master. I be glad."

Nick, taken aback, stared at her.

"Me, I watch," she added.

My God, she'd seen him change! "Then you know why you can't come with me. It's not safe for you."

She compressed her lips. "I tell you—you don't hurt me. Other part of you, he don't either. Not *me*. I got voodoo."

"Mima—" Nick broke off. If seeing the beast didn't frighten her, no argument was going to shake her.

"You don't let me come, I run away and look for you." Her voice was determined. "Keep looking. Me, I *see* the truth—I die if you and me, we don't be together."

As if he wasn't in enough trouble, this child expected him to endanger himself further by helping a runaway slave escape. "Likely we'll both be caught," he muttered.

"No." Mima spoke positively. "You and me, we go up the river a long, long way in boats. Nobody catch us."

He looked from her to the fat pony that had been Guy's mount when he was a child. "Did anyone see you leave Lac Belle?"

"Old pony, he be in field, I take him. Nobody know."

Nick sighed. With Rawhide lame, he had no way to get away from her. In any case, he wasn't so coldhearted as to ride off and leave her here alone. Yet he couldn't take her back to Lac Belle—that would be too dangerous. And if he did, he believed she'd do exactly what she said—run away and look for him.

He tried one final time. "Mima, I would never hurt you. But the beast—I don't control him. He's a vicious monster."

She gazed up at him, a glimmer of impatience in her dark eyes. "He and me, we voodoo. He don't bother me. I don't bother him."

He wasn't convinced that was true, but what was he to do? A frisson ran along his spin as it occurred to him it was possible Mima *had* foreseen their future together. What did he really know about her abilities? Taking her along seemed the best solution to the immediate problem she presented, as well as giving him a chance to probe deeper into the mysteries of someone whose energy crackled blue.

As if she understood his capitulation, she said, "What I be calling you?"

"Nick," he said resignedly.

"Master Nick," she corrected.

He realized she'd thought further ahead than he had. If they traveled together, a little black girl and a white man, she'd have to pass as his slave. And since she dressed like a boy, it was probably best to let her remain one. He told her so.

"I'll call you Moses," he added.

"You teach me to say other words, like you and the doctor do?" she asked.

He gazed at her in amazement. Good God, a runaway

slave, in peril of her life, in the company of a man who changed into a beast when the moon was full, and she wanted to learn English. Mima was the most unusual child he'd ever run across.

The deep-throated whistle of a sidewheeler alerted him to a boat steaming upriver. "I'll teach you," he promised. "At the moment we've got a boat to catch."

Once aboard the *River Lady,* Nick was lucky enough to rent a stateroom with two bunks. He assigned the lower to Mima—he'd use the upper. Cautioning her to remain in the cabin, he strolled the decks. Encouraged when he didn't run across a single familiar face, he ventured into the saloon and, finding no one he recognized there either, sat down at a vingt-et-un table.

Though he had a modest sum left from his earnings as Dr. Kellogg's assistant, he needed more of a stake by the time he reached Michigan. He had no idea how much help, if any, the doctor's old army friend would be, and he wouldn't know anyone else in the small town of Monroe. While a man couldn't buy friendship, money could be counted on to smooth his path.

Using St. Vrain's gambling tips and his own ability to remember what cards had been played, he won slowly but steadily. Not wishing to call undue attention to himself, he left the table after he'd acquired a modest stake. There was always tomorrow.

When he brought a plate of food to Mima, she ate as though she were famished, even sucking the bones when she finished the chicken. She then climbed onto the bunk, curled up, and fell asleep.

He couldn't help but admire her determination. The trousers she wore were too big for her—they were Ponce's, he'd learned. Whether the stable boy had given them to her or she'd appropriated them, he hadn't asked. The trousers, held up by a length of rope, covered the lower half of her faded dress so that it passed as a shirt. She'd found the greasy and battered old hat hanging on a nail in the stable.

He woke in the night to hear her sobbing, eased himself to the floor, and sat on the lower bunk. He knew she wept for her dead sister and his impulse was to hold her in his arms to comfort her. Considering what Gauthier had done to her twin, though, he hesitated to touch her, lest she take fright. Finally he began to murmur to her in his own tongue, letting his hand come gently to rest on her head. He found his murmurs turning into a song:

> *"Spi mladenyets moy prekrasny*
> *Baiyoushki bayou*
> *Tikho smotrit mlsyats yhsni*
> *V kolibel tuoyou. . . ."*
> ["Sleep my little one, my pretty one
> bye-bye lullaby
> Quietly watches over your little crib
> the bright moon. . . ."]

A lullaby. From where and when? A picture grew in his mind of two identical dark-haired little boys nodding before a dying fire, and a soft-voiced woman seated in a rocker crooning the same words he sang. Before he could understand the memory, it slipped away and was gone.

Did the woman know the significance of "the bright moon"? he wondered. Is she my mother? And who are the boys? Is it possible I'm a twin like Mima?

He had no answers. As he continued to hum the lullaby, Mima's sobs gradually eased, and when she settled into sleep, he returned to the upper bunk, where he lay awake.

Guy had reminded him of someone in his past, an other he'd loved. Was the other his twin? If so, where was he now? Was the other a shapeshifter, too?

If only he could remember.

The next morning he told Mima she must remain in the room. He hated to keep her cooped up, but he knew it was safest for them both for her to stay out of sight. She didn't object, seeming content to do nothing but eat and sleep. Thinking about it, he realized she'd probably never had enough of either in her entire life.

But when he brought her food that evening, she stared up at him, her eyes big and round.

"Me, I *see* a bad man on this boat," she said. "He bring you trouble."

Nick couldn't ignore a foreseeing by Mima—not with that crackle of blue energy surrounding her. "What kind of trouble?"

"The man, he got a gun."

"What's he look like? Does he know me?"

Mima bit her lip. "Me, I don't be seeing all that." She reached for his hand. "You stay here where you be safe."

Gently he tugged his hand loose. "I'll be careful, I promise." He had no intention of remaining in the cabin when there was money to be had for the taking at the vingt-et-un games in the saloon, money he badly needed.

She scowled. "Going to be bad trouble do you go out there."

If there was trouble coming, he'd rather confront it than huddle in this cabin waiting. Besides, though he didn't go so far as to doubt her foreseeing, what she saw was so vague that it could mean anything.

"Don't worry," he told her as he left.

He chose his table with even more care than usual, mindful of St. Vrain's admonitions as well as Mima's warning. No brocaded-vest gamblers, no drunks, no men who peered suspiciously at the other players. He waited for a shuffle before sitting down.

After a time, winning, caught up in the rhythm of the game, his mind fixed on recalling the cards that had already been dealt, Nick forgot Mima's foreseeing. Eventually the man next to him got up and left. Though he was startled when a woman took the man's place, her presence didn't alert him to danger.

He'd never before seen a woman gamble on a riverboat. The other players seemed to find it equally unusual, but no one objected. Blond, somewhere in her mid-thirties, she was plumply attractive in her low-cut black dress. Though the musky scent of her perfume distracted him, he did his best to ignore her and concentrate on the game.

Until he felt her hand on his knee.

Chapter 13

As the blond woman's hand slid up Nick's thigh, he couldn't help his body's avid response. Her perfume filled his nostrils, which also aroused him. He retained barely enough sanity to realize he had to leave in a hurry or he might not be able to resist her enticement.

He'd started to scoop up his winnings when the woman removed her hand from his leg, squealed, and shied away from him, all but landing in the lap of the man with sandy hair and beard on the other side of her.

She pointed at Nick and said in a trembling voice, "That awful man put his hand on my—" Her voice broke and she covered her face with her hands.

Sandy glared over her head at Nick. "You bastard!"

She'd trapped him so neatly Nick knew it was no use to protest that he hadn't been the one to do the touching. He still didn't understand exactly what her game was until he glimpsed her hand inching toward his stacked winnings.

Quickly he pocketed the gold coins and rose. Every eye in the room seemed to be focused on him. Could he get away?

"No, you don't!" Sandy challenged, rising.

"What's going on?" a man's voice called.

Not daring to take his gaze from the belligerent Sandy, Nick saw from the corner of his eye a tall man in black striding across the room toward them.

"My dear Alicia, has something happened to you?" the man in black demanded.

Her only reply was a loud sob.

"This bastard insulted her," Sandy told Blacky.

Still several paces away from the table, Blacky stopped

abruptly and confronted Nick. "You scoundrel!" he exclaimed. "How dare you insult my wife?" He reached for his coat pocket.

A man with a gun. Mima's words rang in Nick's ears.

He tensed. Even if he could jump Blacky in time to avoid being shot, every man in the room was against him. He didn't stand a chance.

A shrill scream from the door of the saloon startled everyone. All action ceased. The screaming rose into a crescendo of terror and broke off.

"Fire!" a high-panicked voice cried into the sudden silence. "The boat be burning up!"

"Fire!" a man's voice echoed.

Seizing his chance, Nick leaped toward Blacky, ramming him hard with his shoulder. As Blacky staggered sideways, falling onto one knee, Nick sprang into the crowd stampeding toward the doors, pushing through until he was surrounded, shielded by the people intent on fleeing the saloon.

Once on deck, Nick neither saw nor smelled smoke. As he looked around, small fingers fastened on his hand. He looked down at Mima, hatless and barefoot, and suddenly he knew who'd first screamed "Fire." He grabbed her up, tucked her under one arm, and forced his way through the confused and milling mob until he was able to reach their cabin.

"No fire?" he asked once they were inside.

She shook her head. "One night old Polly take Meta and me to watch a lake boat burn up. Fire be all yellow in the dark. Meta and me, we think fire be pretty. Old Polly, she say fire scare people bad on boats. She say she on a riverboat that catch fire and most everyone, they jump in the river and drown. Old Polly, her skin be white where she get burned."

"So you decided if you yelled 'Fire!' you'd scare the man with the gun."

"Scare everybody," she corrected.

Old Polly's story aside, he was amazed at how quickly Mima had thought of a way to stampede the crowd in her effort to rescue him.

"You saved my neck," he told her.

Mima nodded. "Me, I know you be in trouble, I got to help."

"Help you certainly did. But thanks to what happened in

the saloon, our fellow passengers think the worst of me. We'd best get off this boat at the next stop." He began gathering their belongings.

"Me, I take off Ponce's pants," she said. "If I be a girl, they don't know me."

Once again she'd proved her quickness of mind. "Good idea," he said. "Those who saw the boy give the false alarm won't be looking for a girl."

St. Vrain had warned him of various scams but not this particular one. Would the man in black actually have killed him? he wondered. Blacky and the woman were obviously accomplices, and perhaps Sandy as well. She distracted her victims, then accused them of insulting her, hoping they'd be too confused to pocket their winnings. Was the man in black merely a backup, rushing to her rescue only if she failed to steal the money from the table?

The passengers would have little sympathy for a man who'd try to take advantage of another man's wife—who'd care if the husband shot him? It would be simple enough for the woman or Sandy to kneel beside the dead man and rob him under the guise of trying to help.

Of course he might not have died. As Dr. Kellogg had said, "With your healing powers, unless they used silver knives or bullets, I wouldn't be surprised if they'd have to hack off your head to kill you."

Decapitated. A cheerful thought. God knows if the doctor was correct. Thanks to Mima, he could postpone the day when he might have to put Dr. Kellogg's supposition to the test.

When they were ready to leave the cabin, he saw Mima had even tied a bit of red ribbon in her hair.

Noticing his smile, she touched the ribbon. "Andre, he going to marry Lilette," she said. "He bring her a pretty red ribbon and she cut off a bit for me."

Mima obviously liked colorful things. Perhaps the bit of ribbon was the first she'd ever owned, which seemed a shame. As soon as he could, he'd see she had everything she needed, everything she wanted.

As soon as they reached Michigan. *If* they did.

With Mima in tow, he descended to the cargo deck, skirting groups of still apprehensive passengers who weren't entirely convinced they were safe despite the crew's reassurances. Nobody paid particular attention to either him or Mima. He didn't see any of the scam trio.

A half hour later they stood with Rawhide and the pony on the dock in the hamlet of Cypress Green watching *River Lady* churn upstream. The town was no different than others they passed: a few houses, a store, and a wharf with a warehouse, the clearing surrounded by the ever-present, seemingly endless greenery of Louisiana.

Ignoring the curious stares of the few townspeople at the landing, Nick ambled over to an ancient white-haired Negro who sat fishing from the end of the dock

The old man glanced sideways at him, taking in Mima, who trailed behind. "Howdy, massah," he said.

English, not French.

"Any more upriver boats stopping here today?" Nick asked in the same language.

The old Negro shrugged. "They stops sometimes. You got to ask the man to run up the flag do you want to make sure." He looked beyond Nick. "Howdy there, l'il gal."

Mima smiled at him shyly.

"She only understands French," Nick said.

"Ya'll must be from New Orleans." The old man studied Mima as he spoke, ignoring the tugging on his line until Nick pointed out that he had a bite. Then he hauled in a large fish—the ugliest Nick had ever seen.

Eyes wide, Mima stepped back from the flopping monster.

"Only be a catfish; ain't gonna hurt you, l'il gal," the Negro said as he took a knife and deftly severed the fish's spine at the back of its head. Standing up, he lifted the still quivering fish. "Looks like I gonna eat good tonight."

Nick translated for Mima and again she smiled at the old man.

The Negro started to walk away, paused, and said haltingly, "Massah, I done feel the good in you." He touched his own chest. "In here. So I tells you that li'l gal, she don't be no common nigger."

"I realize she's special," Nick said, "but how did you know?"

The old man touched his chest once more. "I feels it in here." He appraised Nick from watery brown eyes and nodded. "I's glad we met. Brought me a catfish, it did. Good luck to you and the li'l gal, massah."

"Thank you." Nick watched the old man touch Mima's head gently in passing and hoped the luck the old man wished them came their way—beginning with the flag to stop the next paddlewheeler headed upstream.

He was loath to attract any more attention to himself and Mima than necessary. The dockmaster must have seen them debark from the last boat and asking him to raise the flag so they could board the next would make the man wonder why they'd left one boat only to get on another. If anyone stopped by later asking questions, the dockmaster would remember them.

You're being too careful, Nick told himself. Why would anyone come searching for you or for Mima in this tiny village? Get moving!

Telling Mima to stay with the horses, he strode to the unpainted shanty beside the dock. A roughly dressed white man lounged in the doorway.

"I thought this was Cypress Levee," Nick said, improvising. "It appears I got off at the wrong place."

The man pointed to the wooden sign beside the shanty. "That there says Cypress Green."

Nick shrugged. "I misread it."

"Ain't no Cypress Levee in Louisiana I ever heard tell of."

"I was told the town's in Mississippi. Would you flag the next upriver boat, please?"

"Don't see no reason why not." The man reached inside the shack and jerked on a rope. A white flag sprang erect above the shanty.

Noticing the man looking at him expectantly, Nick pulled a silver coin from his pocket and offered it, and the man took the silver with a nod of thanks. His fingers tingling slightly from contact with the coin, Nick joined Mima by the horses.

They waited over an hour before a paddlewheeler churned upstream, altering her course when the pilot noticed the white flag.

"She's the *Flying Catfish,*" Nick told Mima as the boat maneuvered toward the dock. "Maybe she's part of the old man's luck."

The *Catfish* was bound for St. Louis so they disembarked days later in Cairo, Illinois, and boarded an Ohio River sternwheeler which took them to Evansville, Indiana. There they got on a smaller boat that sailed the newly completed Wabash and Erie Canal to Toledo, Ohio.

By that time, Rawhide's stone bruise had healed. Nick stopped in Toledo only long enough to buy additional boy's clothes for Mima because she'd be more comfortable riding with pants on. She was still barefoot, insisting she'd never worn shoes. Mima would have to learn to wear them, but that could wait until they got settled and colder weather set in.

He rode Rawhide north along the lake road toward Monroe, Michigan, trailed by Mima on the pony. Because of the pony, he set a slow pace.

"That lake be big as Pontchartrain," Mima said, staring at the sunlit waters of Lake Erie.

"Bigger," Nick corrected, remembering the size of the Great Lakes on the United States map. He watched a schooner tack eastward, sails plumped by the wind, passing a sternwheeler nosing in toward Toledo.

The road wound along the shore for twenty-some miles, with sand dunes and the lake to the right and mostly saplings and underbrush to the left. Except for one stand of tall pines, most of the big trees had been cut, their stumps still visible through the greenery. They passed occasional farms carved from the surrounding woods.

They also went by more than one loaded wagon rumbling over the rutted road, and edged out of the way of other wagons heading south. Now and then riders on faster horses trotted past. As they neared Monroe, the woods grew thicker, the trees taller.

"Mon-roe, it smells good," Mima observed.

Nick, breathing in the lake-fresh air tinged with the scent of pine, nodded. The sight and scent of the deep woods went a long way toward easing his tension. Maybe their catfish luck would hold in this new community.

By late afternoon, farms again pushed back the trees. Very shortly they came in sight of the town—a few steepled churches and well-built houses, mostly two-story with neat gardens. As they entered the village, an occasional dog rushed up to bark at the horses' heels, upsetting Mima, who feared they'd bite the pony.

A large river, the Raisin, flowed through the town to the lake.

Three boys grouped under a tall maple gawked as Nick and Mima rode toward them. Just as they reached the maple, a cat squalled and someone yelled from high in the tree. Everyone looked up.

With a crash of branches and a shower of leaves, a boy fell from the maple, a kitten clutched in his arms. He slammed onto the road directly in front of Rawhide. The horse reared, twisting to avoid him. Quickly quieting the dun and bringing him to a halt, Nick slid from his back and ran to the boy. He dodged the escaping calico kitten, who spat at him and streaked through fence palings into the yard of a large white house.

Nick reached the downed boy and dropped to one knee. Blue eyes stared up at him from behind disheveled reddish blond hair. Nick pushed strands of hair off the boy's forehead, noting the pale face was twisted in pain. He looked about ten.

"Where does it hurt?" Nick asked.

"My shoulder." The boy gasped the words, reaching for his left shoulder with his right hand.

"Is Autie okay, mister?" one of the other boys asked.

Nick didn't answer, his fingers gently probing Autie's arms and legs. In the boy's left armpit he found an abnormal protuberance. The end of the humerus, the large arm bone, was clearly out of its socket. The sooner he reduced the dislocation, the less swelling and pain the boy would have.

Looking into the boy's blue eyes, he said, "Your shoulder's dislocated. I can put the bone back into place, but it'll hurt."

Autie firmed his jaw. "I can take it. Go ahead."

Nick asked one of the boys to take off his shirt and give it to him. He wrapped the shirt tightly around Autie's left arm and tied it, leaving the sleeves free. He then stood, eased the boot off his right foot, and sat next to Autie on the boy's left side, placing his bootless foot firmly into the boy's armpit. Holding the sleeves of the shirt he'd wrapped about the left arm, he pushed on the head of the humerus with his foot, at the same time pulling firmly and steadily on the sleeves of the shirt, as Dr. Kellogg had taught him.

A few seconds later he felt the end of the humerus snap back into place. He'd expected the boy to scream in pain, but Autie never uttered a sound. The sweat on the boy's brow showed he'd suffered.

"That does it," Nick told him, helping the boy to sit up. "You've got a lot of courage."

Autie took a deep breath and let it out slowly. "Thanks, sir." Glancing around, he added, "Where's the kitten?"

Nick jerked his head toward the yard. "Safe and sound."

Autie smiled faintly. "It's Libbie's. Libbie Bacon, I mean. She's Judge Bacon's daughter."

The way he said the judge's name spoke volumes. Judge Bacon was evidently one of Monroe's leading citizens.

"Can you move your left arm without pain?" Nick asked.

With only a bit of wincing, Autie was able to go through the full range of motion with the arm. Nick grinned at him. "You'll do. Think you can stand?"

Autie nodded and, with Nick's aid, got to his feet. The three boys closed in around him.

"Jeez, Autie," one said, "you could've been killed trying to rescue that dumb cat."

"Not me," Autie boasted. "I was born lucky."

Nick saw a small crowd had gathered. "The boy's fine," he said, walking to where Rawhide waited. "And so is Libbie Bacon's kitten."

Mounting the dun, he rode on with the pony close behind, aware people stared after them. He certainly hadn't slipped into town unnoticed.

Dr. Kellogg had described his friend Phillip Jenkins's house as being on the north side of town. "Phil runs a dairy farm," he'd added. "Claims he's got the biggest and reddest barn around. Toughest sergeant I ever knew. Hard as old boot leather. I can't picture him milking cows."

The Jenkins farm was a ways past the town. Barking dogs greeted them when they turned in the drive but quieted when Nick spoke to them, and escorted the horse and pony up to the house without snapping at their feet.

A gray-haired woman came onto the front porch and Nick swept off his hat. "Hello," he said. "I'm Nicholas Deplacer, a friend of Dr. Kellogg's. I have a letter from him to Mr. Jenkins."

"Dr. Kellogg, you say?" Without waiting for his nod, she smiled. "A grand person, the doctor. Why, our youngest is named for him. If you're his friend, you're welcome in our house. I'm Mrs. Jenkins." Her glance traveled to Mima and back to Nick. "You and—?"

"Mima is a gift to me from the doctor," Nick said. "He

decided I'd need help with housework since I've never done any."

Mrs. Jenkins appraised Mima in her boy's clothes. "A girl, is she? Looks kind of puny for working. Well, never mind, bring her on in with you."

As Nick dismounted, Mima slid off the pony before Nick could help her.

"Don't she speak English?" Mrs. Jenkins asked.

"She's learning. But she understands French better."

"Imagine that! Do they all speak French down in New Orleans? We got a lot of French around Detroit, but they talk almost as good English as me." Mrs. Jenkins chattered on as she led the way into the house, insisting on bringing them into the front parlor. "You wait right here while I get Mr. Jenkins from the barn."

Nick sat on a red plush settee and told Mima to sit next to him. She shook her head.

"Me, I don't be sitting with white folks." Easing down onto the carpet at his feet, she glanced around uneasily at the dark furniture and the green velvet drapes, everything prim and neat.

"I told Mrs. Jenkins you were a gift from the doctor," he said, "to help me in the house—when we find one. She seemed to think you were too little."

"Me, I be strong! I be keeping your house clean like this."

"Our house, Mima. You're not my slave. I don't own you. What I intend to tell people is that you're a free woman of color—or girl, rather."

She nodded, as though she'd expected no less. "I *see* that boy you help, he bring good luck to you," she told him.

After what happened on *River Lady*, he'd vowed to never again disregard Mima's predictions. "No danger coming up?" he asked.

She shook her head.

Phil Jenkins came in, stout, red-faced, and smelling of cows. Even before he read Dr. Kellogg's letter, he invited Nick and Mima to take the evening meal with them and spend the night.

"This says you're good enough to doctor people yourself," Jenkins said when he finished the letter. "You gonna set up in Monroe?"

"I don't know," Nick said, uneasy about passing as a

physician when we was nothing of the sort. "I imagine Monroe has enough doctors already."

"I'll tell you the place as needs a doctor bad," Jenkins said. "Nogadata. It's a village maybe eight, nine miles inland. Nary a doctor in the place. Man was complaining to me just the other day how far they got to travel if anyone gets sick or hurt. His wife started in to bleeding real bad one night and she like to've died afore he got help for her."

"I may take a look at Nogadata," Nick said.

Jenkins eyed Mima. "This un's scrawny as a baby bird fresh from the shell. If Doc was gonna give you a nigger to do your work, he could've picked a grown woman."

Thinking fast, Nick said, "I believe the doctor thought if I set up housekeeping with a black woman there might be talk. But with a child—"

Mrs. Jenkins bustled in, talking before she entered the room. "Penny Peters stopped by with the thread she bought in town for me and you'll never guess what she said. Do you know what Mr. Deplacer here did?" She plowed on, not waiting for answers. "That Custer boy—he's the one who lives with the Reeds, her brother or some such—fell out of a tree by Judge Bacon's house and dislocated his shoulder. Mr. Deplacer stopped his horse, got off, and in no time fixed that boy up as good as new." She fixed Nick with a frowning gaze. "And to think you never even told us!"

Nick shrugged, unable to think of a good response.

"Well, now, that'll set you off on the right foot," Jenkins said. "Folks in Nogadata'll know all about you afore you ever get there. You're right welcome to stay here with us till you make up your mind what you mean to do—any friend of Doc's is a friend of mine—but my advice is to set out your shingle where you're needed. Mind you, Nogadata ain't Monroe by a long shot, but a heap of good folks live there."

"Nogadata's an odd name," Nick said.

"Injun. Huron, maybe. Or Shawnee. Some claim it means some kind of fish and others say it's Injun for wildcat. Take your pick."

Wildcat fish? A prickle ran along Nick's spine. An omen? Was he meant to go to Nogadata?

Late the next morning, Phil Jenkins insisted on riding with Nick to, as Jenkins said, "introduce you around" in

Nogadata. "You can leave the little nigger gal here with Ma," he added.

But Mima trembled in terror at the idea of being parted from Nick. In order not to be slowed by the pony, Nick sat her behind him on Rawhide.

They rode inland through tall maples and oaks along a road that was little more than two ruts. Though a lake breeze diluted the July heat in Monroe, it didn't penetrate into the woods and the air soon grew stifling. Swarming black flies bit both people and horses, making the trip even more unpleasant and causing Nick to wonder what he was doing there.

When at last they reached the wide clearing of the town site, Nick's mind was about made up. Omen or not, this wasn't the place for him. But as they rode into the village, bisected by a stream, the flies disappeared. When they forded the shallow creek rather than crossing by the narrow wooden bridge, the gurgle of the water brought a smile to Nick's face. He couldn't help but be charmed by a community where a stream flowed through the center of town.

"Mostly Pennsylvania Dutch live here—Germans, you know," Jenkins said. "They grow potatoes, trap for fur, and make furniture." He pointed to a long, low shedlike building. "You'd be surprised how many folks buy their chairs and tables. Even clear down to Cincinnati."

He reined in his dappled gray and dismounted. Nick followed suit. In the next half hour he met what seemed like the entire population of the place.

"Yah, we hear about Dr. Deplacer," a stocky blond man named Zweig said, and Jenkins winked at Nick, who was startled to be addressed as doctor.

He started to correct Zweig when his attention was caught by a woman in a high-waisted white dress that fell in folds to her shoes, quite unlike the current fashion, which featured a long vee waist and a wide skirt thrust out by crinolines. She stood on a stoop, her unbound hair so blond it appeared silver in the sunlight. Nick knew he was staring, but he couldn't take his eyes from her. She was the most beautiful woman he'd ever seen. All else faded from his senses. Feeling drawn to her by invisible threads, he took a step forward.

As though from a great distance, he heard Jenkins say to Zweig, "Never saw that gal before. She a stranger here?"

"She's visiting the Lindenblatts." A tinge of disapproval showed in Zweig's voice. "Waisenen, her name is—a Finlander. Young Mrs. Lindenblatt's a Finn, you know."

Mima, who'd stuck as close to Nick as his shadow, grasped his hand and tugged hard, breaking the spell. He tore his gaze away from the woman to look down at her.

"That lady in white," Mima whispered, "I *see* she bad, bad trouble for you."

He knew better than to discount Mima's foreseeing. He only hoped he'd be able to stay away from the lovely and dangerous Miss Waisenen. He turned and walked away quickly—too quickly to see the crackling halo of blue energy over the woman.

Chapter 14

A week later, on a hot and muggy Saturday, Nick and Mima moved into a vacant house in Nogadata, furnishing it with cast-offs from the Jenkinses and a new table and chairs, courtesy of Henry Zweig, who owned and operated the small furniture-making business. Nick had decided on the house after finding a backyard shielded by a dense cedar hedge that contained an outdoor entrance to a root cellar.

Phil Jenkins's wagon had scarcely driven away when someone knocked on the still open door.

"Doctor, be you in?" a man called.

Nick hastily pulled a shirt over his bare torso and hurried to the front of the house. To his surprise, Kurt Lindenblatt stood on the porch with Miss Waisenen in his arms, her white gown stained and soiled, her long blond hair draped over his arm.

"Liisi's hurt," Kurt said gruffly.

Nick did his best not to stare at her. "Bring her in," he said.

"She twisted her ankle in the woods," Kurt added as he followed Nick to what had been the front parlor but was to be his office. At the moment its furnishings were a cot and an old desk and chair.

Nick motioned to the cot and Kurt eased Liisi onto it before standing back.

"I'll go get the missus," Kurt said over his shoulder as he left the room, closing the office door behind him.

Alone with Liisi Waisenen, Nick took a deep breath, trying to control his inner trembling. He'd have to touch her, examine her, and he couldn't allow his attraction to her to show. He had to calm himself, to think of her as a patient, not a troublesomely beautiful woman. Somehow, he must ignore her beauty . . . as well as the blue energy he now saw surrounding her.

Behave like the doctor you're pretending to be, he admonished himself.

"I've seen you before, but we haven't met," he said as evenly as he could, pulling over the chair so he was sitting beside the cot. "I'm Nicholas Deplacer."

"My name is Liisi. Liisi Waisenen." Her words were delightfully accented and she lifted her hand toward him as Creole ladies did.

Though he'd learned to bring a woman's hand to his lips in the approved fashion, he didn't dare kiss hers. God knows what would happen to him if he did. Since he couldn't avoid doing something, he took her hand in his, turning it over as though to examine the palm.

He froze. Time seemed to stop for a long moment as he stared at the red pentacle etched into the flesh of her palm until it faded and disappeared.

"It is not my hand I have hurt, Doctor." Liisi's voice jarred him out of his shock. "It is my ankle."

Nick swallowed, trying to gather his wits. Not *her*! He couldn't permit the beast to kill her. Never!

Liisi tugged gently at the hand he still held and, numbly, he released it.

"My left ankle, Doctor," she said firmly.

"Yes, yes, of course." He leaned over and reached for her foot, noting that her white kid boot was unbuttoned almost all the way down.

With shaking hands, he eased it from her foot. A white stocking covered the foot and ankle, then disappeared under the hem of her gown, its silk soft and slick under his lingering fingers. The stocking would have to come off. Despite the shock of seeing the star on her palm, arousal tingled through him as he imagined reaching under her skirt to her thigh and easing the top of the stocking from under the garter that held it against her soft skin.

With an effort, he drew his hand away and said formally, "Miss Waisenen, your stocking must be removed before I can examine your ankle." He turned his back.

What was he doing here? he asked himself bitterly as he tried not to listen to the suggestive rustle of her clothing.

How could he set himself up as a doctor, knowing what must happen when the moon was full?

Worse than the rustle of clothes was her energy. He could feel it tugging at his mind, exciting him further. What *was* Liisi? A witch? He sensed no evil, despite Mima's warning.

"I am ready, Doctor." Liisi's voice, soft yet clear, was as lovely as the rest of her.

He turned to her, determined to concentrate solely on her injury. He touched her swelling ankle with gentle fingers, feeling for broken bones and finding none.

"You have a sprain," he told her at last, keeping his gaze on her ankle. "That means you've wrenched and twisted your ankle joint. I'll wrap it for you, but healing takes time. It'll heal faster if you stay off your foot."

She sat up. "*You* could make it heal faster."

Startled, he looked at her. Her slightly slanted eyes, more gray than blue, held his.

"I can feel your healing power," she said, her voice barely above a whisper.

He couldn't look away. Her gaze seemed to penetrate his very soul. "You have power, too," he said, feeling the words drawn from him against his will.

"I cannot heal myself without your help." She reached for his hands and placed them around her swollen ankle. "Please," she whispered.

Nick closed his eyes, willing a flow of energy through his hands to her. Attempting to transfer his energy to another wasn't new to him, he'd tried it with some of Dr. Kellogg's patients. Sometimes he'd helped, sometimes not.

"Mmm." Her murmur was almost a purr and he felt, like a mind caress, the surge of her energy meeting his.

He was bound to this woman in ways completely beyond his control. She had only to beckon—

A tap on the office door made his eyes snap open. He removed his hands from Liisi's ankle, unsure how long he'd kept them there.

He cleared his throat. "Who is it?"

"Toivi Lindenblatt."

"Please come in." He rose as a very pregnant dark-haired woman waddled through the door.

"Oh, my poor Liisi," she said, stopping at the side of the cot. "Are you badly hurt?"

"I do believe Dr. Deplacer has healed my sprained ankle," Liisi said, smiling at her friend. "We are fortunate he came here to take care of us."

Mrs. Lindenblatt laid a hand on her distended abdomen. "Yes, I know."

Nick wondered if there was a midwife available or if he'd be expected to deliver her baby when the time came. Though he'd helped several of the Lac Belle slave women through childbirth, he was by no means accomplished.

"See, Doctor, the swelling is gone," Liisi said, drawing his attention to her ankle.

His fingers confirmed what his eyes had trouble believing. The ankle appeared entirely normal.

"And it no longer pains me," she added.

"You ought to stay off that foot for a day or two," he cautioned. Realizing she needed to put her stocking back on, he smiled at both the women and went to the door. "I'll wait in the hall," he said.

A few minutes later Liisi emerged from the office, walking easily, using her left leg without any apparent pain. "What is your fee, Dr. Deplacer?" she asked.

He wanted to say there was no fee, not for her, ever; but, mindful of Mrs. Lindenblatt behind her, he did not. Recalling Dr. Kellogg's modest charges, he named a low amount. "One dollar."

"Oh, but you cured my sprained ankle," she protested. "I owe you much more."

"Perhaps it wasn't a true sprain," he said. "I really did very little except examine your ankle."

Her gray eyes met his, telling him without words that he'd done much, much more. "I will see that you are paid," she murmured, and he knew she meant more than the dollar he'd set as his fee.

He watched her leave through the open front door. She walked with her head held high, like a princess. Even her soiled gown didn't detract from her graceful bearing. He could hardly wait until their next meeting.

"You in trouble," Mima said from behind him. "She done voodoo you."

Her words brought him back to reality. What Liisi might or might not have done wasn't the trouble. *He* was the problem. Or, rather, the beast was. He'd seen the pentacle on Liisi's palm and the full moon was but a few days away. He had to make damn sure the beast would have no chance to get at Liisi.

The only one who could help him was Mima. Though it was a terrible burden to place on her child's shoulders, he had no choice.

"Mima," he said, "come with me."

In the backyard, she followed him through a slanted outside door down into the root cellar dug under part of the house. The only light in the cool and dank enclosure came from the open door.

"You know what I am," he said. "You saw me change at Lac Belle."

She nodded.

"I'm counting on you to help prevent me from changing during this coming full moon."

Mima waited to hear what he wanted done, her dark eyes steady, not showing a trace of fear.

He told her how he meant to reinforce the door and how she was to lock him inside for five nights, not letting him out, no matter what, until daylight, and even then not before he answered a question.

"Your questions can be about our trip up the river," he said. "Anything we both know. Make certain I answer correctly, that my voice sounds like a man's. If anyone comes to the house at night and wants to know where I am, tell them I've gone into Monroe and won't be back until noon. Do you understand?"

"I be doing what you tell me."

"No one must see you let me out. No one."

"Me, I don't let them. I say I be helping you and that's what I be doing. Only—" She paused.

"Only what?" he said finally.

"Lady in white, she shine like you. Maybe she know."

He raised his eyebrows. "Shine? What do you mean?"

"Most people, they don't shine. You be shiny all over like when the sun, he shine on the lake. Lady in white, she shine just like you."

He lifted Mima into his arms and hugged her. "You shine, too, did you know that?"

She stared at him. "Me?"

"When I look at you I see a blue sparkle all around you. As you said, most people don't have it. And you're right, Liisi Waisenen sparkles, too."

"Lady, do *she* see me shine?" Mima asked, her voice fearful.

Nick set her back on her feet and looked down at her thoughtfully. "I suspect she does. And me, too. But that doesn't mean she knows about my changing or your foreseeing."

Mima caught his hand. "She bring trouble."

Remembering the pentacle, Nick nodded. "I'm afraid so. But it's not her fault."

Mima's doubtful face told him she didn't agree.

"I'll start working on the cellar door before I do anything else," he said grimly.

But he had to wait. Between the merely curious and those with genuine ailments, it seemed to Nick that most of the population of Nogadata came by the house before sunset. He didn't dare be caught reinforcing the door, lest he set someone to wondering why, so he had little chance to work on it.

Not all the townsfolk dropped by empty-handed. Mrs. Zweig, heading a delegation of four matrons, arrived in the late afternoon. "We bring food to welcome you," she announced, smiling archly.

She directed the placing of a cake, a platter of cold ham, a plate of fried rabbit, a bowl of succotash, and a loaf of freshly baked bread on the new dining room table, all the while eyeing Mima dubiously. "Your slave girl don't look too strong," she added.

"Mima's free; she's not a slave," Nick said. "And she's quite capable."

"It's a shame she's dressed like a boy," Mrs. Zweig went on. "I'll bring over one or two of my daughter's outgrown dresses."

Since he was renting the house from her husband, Nick took care not to show his urgent wish that she and her friends would leave so he could get on with the door.

"Thank you," he told her. "I haven't had time to buy Mima proper clothes."

The arrival of a bearded old man with a swollen, abscessed, and very smelly leg routed the women. Nick treated the man, Zeke McMasters, as best he could in his underequipped office.

"You have to keep your leg clean," Nick told Zeke. "Wash it every morning."

Zeke fingered his tobacco-stained white beard as he stared at Nick. "Wash me leg every day?" he asked incredulously.

"Every day," Nick repeated. "And make sure you use clean water each time."

"Hell, I don't wash meself more'n once a month."

"The rest of you doesn't matter. The leg does. If you don't keep it clean, the leg will get worse. And don't put on dirty pants over the clean leg."

"Wash me pants, too? Man, for a doctor you sure got some quare idees." Zeke left, shaking his head.

He was followed by a woman bringing in her young son with a felon at the tip of his right forefinger. The boy screamed when Nick lanced the pus-filled sore but his sobs subsided as Nick coaxed him to watch the yellow matter drain from the open wound.

"It won't hurt so much now," Nick assured him. "But you have to soak your hand in warm water with a pinch of salt in it for a half hour every morning and every night for a week or the felon might come back. You wouldn't want to go through this again, would you?"

The boy shook his head, fascinated with the oozing pus. "Yuck," he said, grimacing.

Turning to the mother, Nick tried to impress on her to throw out the used water after each soaking. "Warm fresh water every time," he finished.

Dr. Kellogg had taught him about the soaking. "All you're trying to do is keep the part clean," the doctor had said. "But unless you mystify it a bit, they don't listen. A pinch of salt doesn't do any harm; neither does the soaking. Make the soak twice as long and twice as many times as is really needed so at least they'll do it once in a while."

Nick thought now he probably should have insisted Zeke soak his leg, though he suspected the old man might find that treatment just as "quare."

There was a respite after the boy and his mother left. Nick grabbed several pieces of rabbit to eat as he hurried out back to work on reinforcing the cellar door. The ladies of the town, he found, were good cooks.

During the next few days he was kept so busy he didn't finish putting the heavy wooden bar and the chained lock on the door until late in the afternoon of the first of the five dangerous nights of the moon cycle.

Sunset, he'd discovered, came later in Michigan than in

New Orleans and twilight lingered longer. Since he feared the rising of the moon, he didn't dare wait until true darkness before Mima locked him in.

"It's time," he told her. He removed the soiled piece of canvas he'd placed over the cellar door to hide the chain and lock and to shut out any glimmer of moonlight. "Remember to put this back," he cautioned.

"Me, I don't forget what you say," she assured him solemnly.

Nick descended the few steps carved into the earth and eased the door closed after him. "Lock it," he called to Mima.

The thud of the bar settling into its slot, the rattle of the chain, and the click of the key told him she'd obeyed. He sat Indian fashion on the blanket he'd laid over the dirt floor and stared into the darkness. God help him and the townsfolk if he changed and the cellar failed to hold him.

He couldn't bring himself to think about what Liisi's fate would be.

He'd once thought of poor Esperanza as a fairy-tale princess in her white nightgown. But Liisi was a truer image of those golden-haired beauties in the tales he remembered. Regal, lovely, and unattainable. He hadn't seen her since she'd walked from his office, but Lindenblatt had told him the ankle didn't bother her at all.

He'd healed it, but not alone. The combining of his energy with Liisi's had healed her sprain. He'd never forget the thrill of how her energy had caressed him in a way he'd never dreamed possible. Yet he was half afraid to meet her again. Was she afraid, too? What did she see when she looked at him? Merely the shine Mima saw or the dark and dangerous beast within?

Restlessness overtook him, driving him to his feet. He rolled up the blanket, set it to one side, and began to pace the small confines of the root cellar, the dank scent of mold filling his nostrils.

I will not change, he vowed. I must not. Each time I've seen a pentacle, that person has died. Killed by the beast. Liisi must not die. She *will not* die!

A sound from above startled Nick awake. He sat up in darkness, hard ground underneath him.

"We get on a boat in New Orleans." Mima's voice came came faintly to him. "What be the name?"

"The boat was called *River Lady,*" he said, raising his voice.

He heard a scuffling sound and narrow strips of daylight filtered into the cellar. Mima had removed the canvas. The lock clicked, the chain rattled. The bar thumped open.

"Stand clear," Nick said. He climbed onto the lowest step and reached overhead, pushing against the door, opening it as he climbed from the root cellar into the bright morning sun.

He smiled at Mima and she smiled back, reaching for his hand. "You be you," she said happily.

The next three nights passed in much the same way and, as on the first night, no one came looking for the doctor, so Mima wasn't forced to lie about his whereabouts.

When Nick came up into the muggy dawn of the fifth day, he was relieved to think he had only one more night of this moon cycle to spend locked in the damn root cellar. He hated being caged. The cellar at Lac Belle had been bad enough, but this one was even smaller and much dirtier.

Already he dreaded next month's imprisonment, but how else could he keep the beast from harming others? Just as the locks kept him caged, the darkness had kept the beast caged inside him.

The late August sun beat down mercilessly and by noon the heat was so oppressive that Nick, standing with Mima on the front porch, found it an effort to move. There was no hint of a breeze; not a leaf stirred, not a pine needle quivered. He looked longingly at the nearby woods, where shadows under the trees teased him with their promise of coolness.

So far today no one had needed his services. Too hot to be sick, he thought. His gaze was drawn, as always, to the brown-shingled Lindenblatt house across and down the street from his. He hadn't caught so much as a glimpse of Liisi since he'd treated her ankle and the more time that passed, the stronger his need to see her again became.

If he dropped by the Lindenblatts' now, would she welcome his visit?

"You be thinking about *her,*" Mima said from beside him.

''What makes you say that?'' he demanded, annoyed because she'd guessed correctly.

''You look like Andre when he see Lilette, like you be a hungry man.''

He slid a glance her way. Still barefoot, Mima wore a calico print dress in blues and greens, a gift from Mrs. Zweig, somewhat faded but in much better condition than the rag of a dress she'd brought from Le Noir.

Hot as it was, he envied her bare feet, but his conscience smote him. Why hadn't he gotten around to buying her the clothes she needed? Instead of mooning over a woman he didn't dare approach, he ought to be thinking of Mima, the only person in the world besides Dr. Kellogg he could trust. God knows he couldn't survive without her.

''We'll ride into Monroe tomorrow,'' he said, determined to make up for his negligence.

Somewhere in the woods a jay called and his gaze searched the trees as if the bird summoned him. Like the jay, he belonged among the trees, not in a stifling house.

''I'm going for a walk in the woods,'' he told Mima.

Her eyes widened and her lips pressed together, but she nodded, saying nothing.

''You needn't worry,'' he added in a low tone. ''I'll be all right as long as it's daylight.''

She didn't reply, continuing to watch him. Did he only imagine she looked uneasy?

Damn it, she was the child, not him!

Without another word, he descended the steps and strode along the path leading into the woods. As soon as the trees closed around him, he could feel himself relax. The high branches shut away the sun and he slowed, savoring the shadowy spaces between the large trunks of the pines and the scent of the evergreens mingling with the dusty, every-changing smell of decay from the forest floor. Brown needles crunched under his boots. Knowing how those same needles would feel cool and prickly on the soles of his bare feet, Nick yielded to an irresistible urge.

Yanking off his boots and socks, he dug his toes beneath the needles to the cool earth below and smiled. How good it felt!

He wandered on, coming to a stand of oaks, where gray squirrels chattered to him from overhead and he stopped to watch them flick their tails indignantly at his intrusion. A rustling of the forest duff warned he wasn't the only intruder and he waited to see what made the noise. Not human, he knew, but an animal.

A porcupine, armored with quills, waddled purposefully toward him, not the slightest alarmed by his presence. Nick stepped aside, prudently granting the porcupine the right of way. It climbed a cedar and disappeared into the greenery.

He passed beyond the oaks, once more under giant pines. Though he couldn't feel a breeze where he walked, the boughs overhead whispered to one another in an ancient soothing rhythm that made him sigh, acknowledging his need to rest. Though he hadn't changed during his nights in the cellar, his restlessness had kept him awake most of the time.

Here among the trees where he belonged, here he could rest.

Liisi knew the moment he stepped into the woods and immediately she shielded herself from him. Was he looking for her? If so, he wouldn't find her. And yet, at the same time, she half wanted to be found.

For a time she stayed away, but finally, as if drawn by a force beyond herself, she tracked him, finding it easy because he hadn't shielded himself. He never did. Perhaps he didn't know how. He intrigued her, especially since she couldn't fathom his inner power. Healing, yes, but something darker lurked there, too. The little Negro girl had power as well but none of his dangerous darkness.

Until he revealed what he was, she was much better off keeping clear of him, as she'd been doing. And yet she followed him. Why?

She had to admit he was outwardly attractive. Already every unmarried girl in the village daydreamed about him. And, if the truth be told, some of the wives as well. What charmed them wasn't only his handsome features or his tall, well-built body. Though he did nothing overt, he exuded allure, drawing women as a flower draws bees.

Men took to him as well. So did dogs. The meanest cur in the village wagged its tail for Nick Deplacer.

But she wasn't a dog. Nor was she a foolish girl to be trapped by this man's strange allure, no matter how compelling. She trailed him not because she couldn't help herself but because she needed to observe him when he wasn't aware of her, to discover his secret. She knew he had one—any man with such a vital energy aura had power. He couldn't keep his concealed forever.

Not from a *noita*.

Chapter 15

Liisi didn't need her *noita* power to sense the approaching storm. Tiny rays of sunlight no longer slanted through fissures in the dense canopy of leaves and needles, and the patches of sky she glimpsed through the fissures were no longer blue but an ominous coppery gray. Overhead the boughs danced faster to the wind's increasing rhythm.

She paused, knowing she still had time to turn back and reach shelter before the storm broke. But she was close to Nick Deplacer and he hadn't moved for some time, leading her to suspect he slept. If she retreated, she might never find a chance to creep up on him again. Liisi decided to go on.

The intensity of his energy flow reminded her of her father's during the times he'd failed to shield himself. Her shields were in place, for she dare not take a chance with unknown powers—as her father had done in Finland one too many times. Arno Waisenen had been a broken man, the spirit gone from him, when they arrived in the United States seven years ago. He'd survived the trip because she kept him infused with her own energy, but after they landed, she'd been too depleted to be able to keep him alive for more than a few months.

Until now she'd never met anyone remotely like her father. If this man she tracked *was* like him. She mustn't waste this opportunity to learn more about Dr. Deplacer.

The gloom under the trees darkened, but his starshine glow of energy drew her like a beacon. There! She could see him now as well as sense him—he lay sprawled under a pine no more than twenty paces away. She stopped, traced a protection rune in the air between them, and then slowly, cautiously eased closer.

Her art should keep him from waking and, since she knew his name, with luck she'd be able to enter his mind.

Nick never slept deeply; some part of him—the beast?—always remained alert. He woke abruptly, aware someone—something—watched him. Opening his eyes to slits, he looked for the watcher without moving, but failed to find it.

He knew he was in the woods; he'd fallen asleep on a bed of pine needles. Whatever watched him was close but hidden. Since he had his back against the bole of the pine, the watcher was either to one side or in front of him.

Why couldn't he sense its energy more clearly? It called, but in a manner he couldn't define. He thought the call was meant for him but didn't understand either the meaning or the reason.

Though every muscle in his body tensed for action, he forced himself to remain still, afraid sudden movement would scare off the watcher before he could discover its whereabouts. What could it be? He sensed no ordinary human glow nor any blue crackle, either. And he'd never before encountered any animal like this.

Thunder rumbled far off and he realized for the first time how dark the day had grown. The calling grew more urgent, buzzing in his head like a persistent mosquito. Unsure whether he had the ability, Nick concentrated on tracing the call to its source. He'd about decided the watcher was to his left when suddenly the call stopped.

In one fluid motion, he rose and leaped to the left, glimpsing a flash of white beyond the thick trunk of a pine.

Human!

Liisi Waisenen stepped from behind the trunk, her slightly tilted eyes quicksilver in the storm light, the familiar crackle of blue surrounding her. Stunned, Nick aborted his charge, stopping in front of her. He didn't understand why he hadn't sensed her sooner, but he knew she was the watcher.

''Why?'' he demanded, all too aware of the invisible current of power between them.

She raised her chin. ''If you mean why was I hiding behind the tree, the answer is simple. I didn't want you to see me.''

"Why were you watching me?" As he spoke, thunder rumbled, closer now.

She shrugged. "Why does any woman watch a man?"

Annoyed at her evasion, he resisted the impulse to fasten his hands on her shoulders and insist she explain exactly what she'd been doing. The peculiar intrusive calling could have come from no one else—what had she meant by it? He wanted to know, he needed to know, but he didn't dare touch her. God only knew what might happen if he did.

Wind lashed the boughs overhead. Though it was so dark under the trees he couldn't clearly see her expression, he was certain she didn't fear him. He wished he could be as sure he had no reason to fear her.

"You called me," he accused, bringing his resentment into the open. "Not aloud. Don't lie to me. I know you did."

"It's beginning to rain," she said. "You may not mind getting wet, but I do." She started to turn from him.

He grasped her arm. She tried to wrench away. Then, somehow, she was in his arms, his mouth hungrily seeking hers. For a long, heart-stopping moment, she responded to his kiss, pressing her soft, uncorseted body against his.

Lightning flashed, sizzling around them. Wood shrieked, ripping apart as a tree to his right split in two and crashed to the forest floor, accompanied by a deafening roll of thunder. Liisi pulled free of him and fled, leaving him as riven and devastated as if the bolt had struck him rather than the pine.

He'd known from the moment he first saw her that he couldn't have her, but now that he'd had a taste of the forbidden, he refused to accept his loss.

He stood amid the wind and rain, the stench of electricity and burned wood in his nostrils, his face raised to the lightning-bright sky, and shook his fist at the heavens.

"Damn You!" he shouted through the thunder's boom. "Why was I born? Why?"

He didn't know how long he wandered in the woods, but the storm had long since passed over and the sky was a deep twilight blue when he heard Mima calling his name.

He didn't want to answer. The woods were his home. He belonged here, and here he'd stay. But her voice, childish and frightened, touched his heart. Slowly, reluctantly, he turned.

"I'm coming," he called to her.

Mima ran to meet him, caught his hand, pulling him toward the village with an urgency he didn't try to resist. Once they reached their house, she led him into the backyard.

"Moon, she be rising. You got to get down there." Mima pointed to the cellar door.

He shook his head, feeling he couldn't bear to be caged ever again.

"You *got* to!" Mima insisted. "Maybe *she* die if you don't."

He stared at the child, her words chilling him with their truth. Fighting the restlessness welling within him, he lifted the door and descended into the dank cage of the cellar, letting the door slam shut behind him. He growled when he heard Mima locking him in.

He couldn't stand the feel of his damp clothes against his skin. He wanted them off. Needed them off. Needed to be free. . . .

Frantically, Nick fought against the pounding inner urge. He'd resisted changing the other four nights; he wouldn't let go now. He clenched his fists to prevent his hands from tearing at his clothes and began to pace the too-small cellar. Rainwater had seeped in; he could feel muck under his bare feet. Where were his boots? He couldn't remember.

He paced back and forth, back and forth. One more night, he told himself over and over. Only one more night. The rhythm of the pacing and the repetition of the words seemed to ease the gnawing inside.

The night was endless. He'd been in this cage forever; he'd be here forever. Morning would never come. He was in hell without the chance of redemption.

Abruptly he paused in his pacing, all senses alert. Someone was on the other side of the cellar door. *She* was there. Nick's control snapped. He tore off his shirt. His gut twisted in the dreaded, familiar shift, and he was powerless to stop it.

The child was in the house, Liisi knew, and probably sleeping. But he was not. He was nearby but not inside. She'd taken great care to creep out of the Lindenblatt home without rousing anyone and she was determined not to return until she'd solved the mystery of what he was. It had been a terrible mistake to try to probe his mind. She wouldn't do that again. But there were other, more subtle ways to learn what she must.

Your father died because of his curiosity, a voice in her head reminded her. *Take care you don't follow in his footsteps.*

Liisi huddled into her black cloak. It wasn't mere curiosity driving her. She fought for her very life! He and she were bound by bonds she couldn't sever, a binding that would last a lifetime. But, if she must face that dangerous darkness inside him without knowing beforehand what it was, how long would her life last?

True, she was afraid to go near him, especially at night, despite all her protective amulets and spells. At the same time, she had little choice. If she fled from him, leaving the only friend she had, Toivi Lindenblatt, sooner or later, because of the binding, he'd find her. If she stayed, she must discover his secret or die.

Without moving, Liisi traced his brilliant energy aura to the backyard. She crept cautiously around the corner of the house and found herself confronted by a thick cedar hedge. Using her sharp Finnish blade, she sliced off the branches until she'd cut a hole large enough to crawl through.

The moon, just past full, dusted the night with silver, its light strong enough to see him if he was in sight. There was no sign of him. Yet she knew he was there. Somewhere. She focused all her attention on his energy.

Underground!

She inched closer to where the energy level was strongest. An old piece of canvas covered the spot and she eased it aside, finding the door to a root cellar underneath. She stared in disbelief at the padlocked chain and the heavy wooden bar. Why was he locked inside the cellar?

A burst of energy flung her backward, sending her sprawling. Deep in the cellar something snarled, a vicious animal sound that could not have come from a human throat. Liisi stifled a scream.

As she climbed hastily to her feet, whatever was inside the cellar attacked the door. It knew she was there and meant to reach her!

No, not it. Worse. He. The raging beast was as thoroughly male as Nick Deplacer. She shuddered, all too aware of what would happen if she didn't escape.

Terrified, she gathered the cloak around her, raced for the hole in the hedge, wriggled through, and ran faster than ever before in her life. If she didn't reach the Lindenblatt house before he escaped, she would die.

Free! Yet not free. He was caged. Caged, while his mate ran free. He sensed her presence. With a snarl of rage, he flung himself up at the door of the cage. Wood bulged and creaked. Slivers of moonlight penetrated the darkness and he shivered with pleasure as they caressed his fur.

Gathering himself, he assaulted the door again and again, hearing the wood strain until at last it splintered under the fury of his attack. He forced his way through into the moonlight, truly free.

His mate was gone, though her scent lingered, mingling with other exciting odors of the night.

He'd find her; she couldn't escape him. But before he tracked her to her lair, he must satisfy his more urgent lust. For blood. Raising his muzzle, he sniffed carefully, untangled the deer scent from all the others, plunged through a hedge, and loped into the woods, hunting under the moon.

At sunrise, Nick found a folded blanket beside the path leading into the village. He wrapped it around his nakedness, hesitated, then stepped onto the path and strode boldly toward the village.

He sensed the man approaching before he saw him but didn't break his stride. No matter who it was, he was desperate to get to Mima and discover what had happened during the night. She must be alive—who else would have left the blanket where it was?

He had a confused memory of Liisi being outside the root cellar, a memory he prayed was false. Because if she'd been there when the beast broke loose, he couldn't go on. Let them kill him. He'd be better off dead.

Nick gritted his teeth, grimacing. He'd washed the deer's blood from his body and rinsed his mouth in the stream, but the metallic aftertaste remained. God grant it was only deer's blood.

He recognized Zeke McMasters's white beard before the old man reached him.

"I see ye abide by your own advice, Doctor," Zeke said,

his gaze on the blanket. "Had an early bath in the creek, did ye?"

Nick gathered his wits. "How's the leg?" he managed to ask.

" 'Tis true me leg's better, but I'll be damned if I mean to wash the rest of me every blooming day. If'n the good Lord meant me to be that fond of water he'd've made me a fish 'stead of a man." Zeke chuckled at his own wit.

Forcing a smile, Nick nodded at him and strode on. The old man's words stuck in his mind. Zeke would never be anything else but a man, that much was sure. Unlike Nick Deplacer.

He reached his house without encountering anyone else. The village folk were early risers—how many had caught a glimpse of him from a window, he couldn't be sure. At least no one was waiting with a gun.

Taking a deep breath, he mounted the steps. The front door opened before he reached it.

"You found the blanket," Mima said.

He stepped past her, closing the door behind him. "What happened?"

"Something wake me up," she said. "Me, I go look out the window. Moon, she be shining bright on *her.*"

Nick swallowed before he could push the name past his dry throat. "Liisi Waisenen."

Mima nodded. "She pull off the canvas. Down in the cellar, you change—me, I feel it here." She laid a hand over her heart. "Beast, he smash the door."

Nick gripped her shoulder. "What happened to Liisi?"

"She run off before the beast got free. Beast, he come out, he look around, he sniff the air. He leap over the hedge and me, I can't see him no more. I run to front window and *she* be climbing her steps. She go in her house. The beast, he don't come near that house."

Nick eased out the breath he'd been holding. Liisi was safe; she was alive.

"You tell me never go out when the beast, he be loose," Mima went on. "Me, I stay in. When moon, she go down, I take your blanket and leave it under the trees because you say the beast, he likes the woods."

Nick hugged Mima to him. "Thank God I have you."

Liisi might have been frightened by the noises from the cellar last night, but she hadn't actually seen the beast, she couldn't know he was a shifter. And what she didn't know she couldn't tell. He'd been given a reprieve and so had she. But neither of them could count on another. He'd make damn sure to be nowhere near this town during the next full moon.

When, on the following day, he discovered that Liisi Waisenen had left Nogadata, Nick wasn't surprised, though the news left him despondent. It didn't change his mind about what he must do. He knew he had to get away from people completely during his dangerous days.

Through Phil Jenkins, he found a tiny, uninhabited island for sale in Lake Erie and bought it with some of his riverboat winnings.

"I like to fish alone," Phil told him, shaking his head, "but buying an island to make sure no one bothers you really takes the cake."

Latching on to the excuse Phil unwittingly provided, Nick let it be known in Nogadata that he was an avid fisherman and intended to go off by himself from time to time to indulge his passion.

A month later, Liisi still hadn't returned. Nick successfully delivered Toivi Lindenblatt's son, discovering from the new mother that she had no idea when or if Liisi meant to come back.

"I haven't heard from her," Toivi complained. "I can't think what got into her, rushing off like she did. She promised to be here when the baby came. At least she could let me know where she is."

When he left for his five days on the island, Nick tried to convince Mima to come into Monroe and stay with the Jenkins family, but she refused.

"Me, I take care of this house while you be gone," she insisted stubbornly. "I be here waiting."

After leaving Rawhide at the Jenkins farm, Nick paddled to his island in the canoe he'd bought, the afternoon sun so warm on his shoulders that halfway across he stopped paddling and removed his shirt. A breeze ruffled Lake Erie's blue waters, waves nudging against the boat as though to drive it back to the mainland.

The rocky isle was over a mile from shore with no hospitable landing site—one of the reasons he'd chosen it. He reached the high bluff on the shore side, circled halfway around to the one small break in the cliffs, too narrow to bring even his small canoe through. Nick bundled his shirt into his canvas pack and strapped it onto his back. He slipped over the side into the water—only waist deep due to rocks beneath the surface. Holding the mooring rope, he eased through the fissure and climbed to the top of the bluff. From there he hauled the canoe up hand over hand.

Now he was safe and could explore at his leisure. There was a wide cleft in the middle of the island where a small grove of tall pines flourished. Maple, birch, and poplar grew around the edges of the grove. Though he saw squirrels and birds, he knew without searching there'd be no big game on the island—it wasn't large enough to sustain a deer herd.

He'd brought bread, ham, and cheese and planned to fish in the lake for the rest of his meals. Nick smiled wryly—wasn't fishing his reason for being here?

He supposed the beast wouldn't be pleased to find itself marooned on an island too small for good hunting. Since he could swim, he supposed it could. The mainland was a long way off, though, farther than he'd attempt.

Nick shifted his shoulders uneasily, uncomfortable as always when he thought about that other part of himself. If only he had some control over the beast after it emerged. Unfortunately, he couldn't even recall what the damn thing did when it was free.

He knew the beast wasn't an it, but he preferred not to call it a he. Bad enough to know it tore animals apart and ate them raw—he couldn't bring himself to speculate what it might mate with.

After a light meal of ham and bread washed down by lake water, Nick walked the perimeter of the island, judging it to be almost a mile around. From the top of a bluff he watched the sun disappear, setting the clouds and the sky afire and painting a Toledo-bound schooner's sails red. Black smoke drifted across the tinted sky from a paddle wheeler churning east.

The sky gradually darkened. Larger islands to the southeast became smudges on the deep blue of the water as the long evening settled in. The moon, near full and already above the horizon, glowed as yellow as a wolf's eye. In the woods behind him, an owl hooted four times.

Hearing the owl made Nick understand what kept the squirrels from taking over the island. In its way an owl was as voracious a predator as the beast. But an owl killed and ate to live. The beast didn't have that excuse.

Turning away from the lake, Nick strode toward the pine grove, where he'd left his supplies. If and when the change came, he didn't want to be on the bluff.

"They ain't no accounting for women," the grizzled owner of the rowboat complained to Liisi as he pulled away from shore.

"That may or may not be true," she said tartly. "But as long as you're being paid to row me, it makes little difference."

He shrugged. "Where we're going, they ain't no decent place to land. 'Specially when it gets dark."

"You've told me that. And it's not yet dark."

He scowled but said no more, bending to his rowing.

Liisi tried to put her disquiet from her mind but failed. She wasn't at all certain she should be in this boat, heading into danger she didn't fully understand. The alternative, though, was unacceptable. For this entire month she'd been angry with herself because she feared to let her dear friend Toivi know where she was. How could she continue to live like that?

Her father had taught her to study one's opponent and discover his weaknesses before confronting him. In the brief time she'd had, she'd tried to find a weakness—and failed. But at least she was no longer cowering in some hidey-hole waiting to be discovered—she was choosing the time and place for the inevitable confrontation.

She was a *noita,* not some timid girl who ran away and hid from peril. Her fingers tightened around the amulet resting between her breasts. Would it work?

She clenched her jaw. What she brought with her *had* to work. If not—the word for what would happen in her own tongue was *kamala.* Terrible, hideous beyond description.

Why was she cursed with this binding? Why must she be bound to a monster? She'd done nothing to deserve such a fate.

Ah, but she was forgetting how little control humans had over their fate. Even *noitas.* Or, perhaps, especially *noitas,* who dabbled in the forbidden.

How quiet it was on the lake in the evening. No gulls flew overhead squawking. There was only the lap of the waves against the wooden hull of the boat and the rhythmic plash of the oars. The lights of Monroe were behind her; the darkness of the island loomed ahead. She was leaving the familiar for the unknown.

The yellow September moon was two days from full. She hadn't dared wait until the night of the full moon when his power would be the strongest.

"Going to get your pretty dress soaked, that you are." The boatman's voice, though not loud, startled her. "No way onto the island without you get in the water."

"You explained that before," she said. "If you don't mind, I'd rather we didn't talk anymore. At all."

For whatever use it would be, she'd shielded herself, but sensing the boatman, he'd know someone approached.

"Suit yourself," the boatman grumbled and fell silent as he maneuvered the boat close to the rocks.

Liisi watched the moon rise and hugged herself, shivering.

Free! The beast loped from the shelter of the trees into a clearing where the caressing moonlight fell directly on him. He raised his muzzle and sniffed the night air.

Small animals and birds. No deer. Somehow he'd known there wouldn't be. Squirrels and such held no interest for him, so he trotted up the incline to the top of a bluff. Water below, water as far as he could see. He could swim if he had to, but he wasn't fond of water.

Leaving the bluff, he reentered the woods, ran through the trees until they thinned and gave way to another bluff. At its top he gazed down again at water and lights twinkling on the dark bulk of land some distance across the water. Something splashed between him and the lights. A man in a boat, going away from him—no danger there.

Island. He blinked as the word came to him. He remembered what it meant. Land surrounded by water. Like a cage without bars. Unless he swam. He preferred to avoid the water.

A faint scent came to him and he raised his muzzle to identify what it was and the location.

Human! On the island. His hackles rose. Was he being hunted?

He'd do the hunting!

Fixing on the scent, he trotted into the woods once more, where pine scent mingled with the human, and circled to approach from behind. Between one step and the next, he identified who he hunted. He halted abruptly.

Her! His mate!

Lust rose in him, driving him forward, all thought of stalking forgotten as he raced to find her. She was here. She could no more escape from the island than he could.

This time nothing would stop their mating.

Chapter 16

Moonlight bathed the island, leaching all color, turning everything to silver. There were no night sounds except the waves breaking on the rock face.

The island animals knew, Liisi thought. They hid and remained silent through fear. But it wasn't the animals he hunted. He hunted her. Though she was shielded, she felt him stalking her, and the hair on her nape rose. She increased her pace. Resisting the impulse to run, she hurried to the closest large tree and, her back to it, stared into the moonlight, waiting.

Her right hand clutched the amulet she wore on a leather thong around her neck as she did her best to quiet the frantic pounding of her heart.

Between one rapid heartbeat and the next, he suddenly appeared in front of her, leaping, it seemed, from nowhere.

Monster! Beast! She'd never seen anything so horrible. Not man, not animal, he stood on his hind legs, looming over her, his yellow eyes gleaming with lust, his furred muzzle concealing the sharp fangs of a killer.

Liisi swallowed her scream. The awful sight momentarily robbed her of her wits, making her forget the words she must say, but her left hand rose into the air between them, automatically tracing the runes to ward him off for a few precious moments.

She slipped the thong over her head and kissed the amulet. Holding the figure in both her hands, she raised her arms as though offering it to him. Moonlight glinted on the steel.

He stared at her hungrily, paying no attention to the amulet.

Her mind steadied and she started to chant in her own tongue. *"Luonotar, oi Ilman Neiti,"* she began. Her voice quivered at first, gradually strengthening with her belief in herself:

"Luonotar, Lady of Creation,
You, who formed the iron in the earth
Plucked forth by Ilmarinen,
Mighty smith who forged the steel
And fashioned the sword;
Vainomoinen, great hero,
You, who blooded the blade;
Dark Louhi, whose magic
Shattered the sword
And fashioned the charm—
Grant me use of the power
That lies in the charm.
Luonotar, Lady of Creation,
Make me strong as the steel
Of Ilmarinen's crafting,
Brave as mighty Vainomoinen,
Wise as dark Louhi.
Lady, grant me power."

The monster hadn't moved. With bated breath, Liisi stepped forward, holding out the amulet. She raised on her tiptoes, touched the steel briefly to the beast's head between his ears, and then flung the thong around his neck before backing away.

An arrow of light blazed into his brain, blinding him, transfixing him. He couldn't make a sound, couldn't move. Pain wrenched his gut.

Nick stood in the moonlight, staring in disbelief at a vision in white. He must be dreaming. God knows he'd dreamed of Liisi often enough this past month. She couldn't actually be here, that was impossible. As he gaped at her, he was dimly aware of something unfamiliar around his neck and his hand rose to his chest. He started when he felt metal under his fingers.

"No!" Liisi cried. "Don't take the amulet off. Not yet."

He took a step toward her and stopped, suddenly remembering he'd shifted, letting the beast free. He glanced at the moon, riding high. How had he changed back to himself? Impossible!

"I'm dreaming," he said hoarsely.

"You're awake." Her voice was flat and positive.

He took two more steps and gripped her shoulders to test her reality. He smelled her enticing lavender scent as he touched her. Then he felt their energy mingle and everything else faded. He pulled her to him and lowered his mouth to hers.

If she protested, her words were lost in his kiss. Their kiss. She was warm and soft and eager in his arms. Her response and the electric intermingling of energies under the moon's caress aroused him beyond reason.

He tore off her clothes, needing her as naked as he was, needing flesh against flesh. The moonlight turned her to silver in his embrace and, as he possessed her, for an instant he remembered the deadliness of silver. But when a man rode high as the moon itself, it was far too late for second thoughts.

When he could think again, he reached between them to touch what she'd called the amulet, still on its leather thong around his neck. With a shock, he realized she must have put it over the beast's head. Raising on one elbow, he looked down at her, meaning to ask her what the amulet was.

She lay curled next to him, her moonlight-fair hair spread around her, so beautiful it took his breath away. As he bent to kiss her, a dreadful thought slithered into his mind.

"God grant you're not with child," he blurted.

Liisi smiled a secret smile. "A *noita* has children only if she wills it. I do not wish for a child, so I will have none. Believe me, for I speak the truth."

"What's a *noita*?"

"A Finnish wizard. I'm one, as my father was. We have certain powers."

That explained the blue energy.

She reached for him and drew him down to her. "Whatever binds us one to the other is more powerful than I," she murmured in his ear. "Or than you."

Bound. To her. To a Finnish witch. He'd resent such a binding if his desire for her would let him. But all he could think of was possessing her again. And again and again.

Much later she explained how she'd slipped the thong over the beast's head.

"It was to save my life. Otherwise he would have killed me trying to mate." She shuddered in his arms. "The beast is bound to me just as you are—I had to find a way to shift you back to human and to prevent any more changing or I was doomed. Thank God and the Lady what I did succeeded."

"What *is* this amulet?"

"It's crafted from steel taken from a magic sword. It is said Ilmarinen himself forged the blade. He was the first smith and the greatest. Iron makes the most powerful of charms and steel is, of course, basically iron."

Nick squinted at the charm. "I can't see well enough to understand what this represents."

"A man's body, a wolf's head. Half man, half beast. It was my father's. In Finland he wore it to protect him against strange creatures of the forest."

A thrill ran through Nick. "Do you mean there are others like me?"

"I don't know. Perhaps. My father spoke of shapeshifters, but I never expected to come face-to-face with one." Again she shivered. "You are really very terrible when you shift, very frightening. A killer."

Nick thought about what she'd said. Others like him! Would he ever meet one? Despite hating his shapeshifting, it excited him to imagine meeting one of his own kind.

He said nothing of this to her. Holding her hand in his, he kissed her palm. "Did you know I read your fate in your palm the day we met? I feared you'd be my next victim and I knew I'd rather die than harm you. Even if you are a witch, you're a brave woman, coming to this island when you knew what waited here. You understand what I am—how do you have the courage to lie here with me without fearing I'll change once more into the beast?"

"You won't change again," she said, stroking his cheek.

He stared at her. "How can you be sure?"

"To be safe you must wear the amulet when the moon is full. But I will teach you a spell to keep the monster inside where he belongs and once you master the spell it will work even without the amulet."

Nick raised his eyebrows. "You seem so positive."

She shrugged. "After all, I am a *noita*."

"The last witch I met tried to kill me. She damn near succeeded."

Liisi stiffened in his arms. "Are you saying you don't trust me?"

His grip tightened. "Bound to you as I am, I have little choice. We must be together, you and I, so I choose to trust you. Besides, the other witch was old and ugly, while you're the most beautiful woman I've ever seen."

She relaxed slightly. "You realize we must marry."

Her words jarred him, but he immediately grasped their truth. He needed to have her near him, living in his house, sleeping in his bed. Marriage was the only possible answer if he intended to go on living in Nogadata.

"Must I offer for your hand?" he asked.

"I would like a formal declaration, yes." Liisi eased away from him. "You must understand I always believed I would love the man I married."

He looked into her eyes, silver as the moonlight, witch eyes he could lose himself in. Love. What was it? Had he loved Esperanza, or had that been merely the desire of a man for a woman? He couldn't be sure. The only person he was certain he truly loved was Dr. Kellogg. And, perhaps, Mima.

"I won't lie to you and claim love, Liisi. What's between us is too powerful to deny, but I can't call it love. Will you marry me anyway, knowing we don't love one another?"

She sighed. "As you say, I have little choice." She ran her fingertip lightly over his lips. "The village folk will think it very romantic—how you searched for me, found me, and convinced me we must marry. For that's the story I plan to tell. My reason for leaving Nogadata so abruptly will be that I feared my feelings for you were not reciprocated."

Her touch aroused him, making him aware how much he was going to resent any separation from her. "The wedding must be as soon as possible."

Liisi smiled her maddening, secret smile. "Every woman in town will hate me because I'm the one you chose."

With the help of the Jenkinses, two days later Nick and Liisi became man and wife. Nick, uncertain about the amulet's protective powers at first, discovered the steel figurine not only prevented his shifting but also removed the desire to shift. By the time they returned to Nogadata, he was as happy as he could ever remember being.

Before they arrived at the house, he told Liisi all he knew about himself.

"Speak in what you believe is your true tongue," she asked when he finished.

"Su da vol's't'v'i im," he said. "With pleasure."

Liisi frowned. "I don't understand the language, but that sounds like Russian to me. Say some more words."

Excited by the sudden hope he'd learn more about his past, Nick told her in the same language how beautiful she was.

"Yes, I'm certain that's Russian," Liisi confirmed with a grimace. "I don't like Russians—no true Finn does."

Elated by her identification, he grinned at her. "What does it matter? We're both Americans now." He kept his pleasure hidden, not wanting to provoke her by admitting how happy he was to learn the name of the country he might have come from.

Russia. A huge territory on the maps. If he was Russian, where in that vast country had he lived? Even if he sailed across the ocean to Russia, without knowing his true name he'd have no idea where to begin looking. Simply knowing Russian was his native tongue wasn't enough.

"It is true we are Americans," Liisi said. "I have no more desire to return to Finland than your little Mima would have to return to the land of her ancestors, Africa."

"I'm fond of Mima," he said. "She'll always have a home with me."

"Don't worry, she and I will get along," Liisi told him. "Once Mima understands I'm as much concerned for your safety as she is, she'll accept me. I've never met anyone who could foresee the future. Perhaps Mima can help me try to do it and I'll teach her what I can."

"She's a bit afraid of you."

Liisi shook her head. "That will pass. Mima has nothing to fear from me. As for your missing past—what a burden not to know your origins. No wonder I couldn't learn more about you that stormy day in the woods. A *noita* must know a person's *real* name and, since you've forgotten yours, perhaps I never will discover all your secrets."

"I have no secrets I'm aware of; I've told you everything."

"Every man, woman, and child has secrets, Nick. We can't help ourselves."

"Come to think of it, I omitted one thing," he admitted. "I have land in California. It's not valuable, since my acreage is in the foothills of the mountains away from all settlements and no gold has been found there. I once dreamed of building a house for myself there and living all my days alone. But now—" He smiled at her.

"I have never been to California," she said. "Is it so very different from here?"

He tried to explain what it was about the state that fascinated him but wasn't sure he succeeded. "But I can't go back," he finished. "The Californios have long memories."

"Nevertheless, you must keep the land."

He shrugged, secretly pleased at her words. Even if he never set foot on it, the fact he owned California land satisfied some yearning deep within him.

Nick and Liisi's hasty wedding was the talk of Nogadata.

"Me and the missus hope she settles down and don't go wandering off in the woods no more," Lindenblatt told Nick. " 'Tweren't fit for a grown woman."

"I'm so glad you brought her back," Toivi Lindenblatt said. "But you could have told me what you both were up to."

Mima didn't say anything, just watched Liisi from the corners of her eyes and hardly spoke to her except to answer a direct question. Nick finally took Mima aside, showed her the amulet, and explained that, thanks to Liisi, he now had control over his shifting.

"You're my friend, Mima. You always will be. Your home is with me and always will be." He smiled at her. "Unless when you grow up you decide to get married and go off to live with your husband."

Mima shook her head. "Me, I don't get married. I stay with you."

"With me and Liisi," Nick said. "Don't be afraid of her. She can teach you how to use your energy."

Mima thought this over. "Me, I want to heal sick folk like you do," she said finally.

Nick nodded. "I can teach you about the human body,

but I don't know how to show you the way to use your energy to heal. Ask Liisi for help."

Somewhat to his surprise, Mima did just that.

Months passed. Unused to peace and happiness, Nick worried at first that something would happen to destroy both. He learned the Finnish chant and found Liisi's prediction correct—he didn't shift, even without wearing the amulet.

Mima gradually acquired a small menagerie of animals—ones she'd healed herself, with Liisi's help. Besides the horses and the pony, the barn housed an ornery nanny goat, a half-grown lamb, three hens, and a rabbit. The two dogs were allowed limited use of the spacious new house Nick had built for the three of them.

Months turned into years. Eleven years. Mima grew. She spoke a more educated English and had learned to read, write, and do sums. Though she remained slender, her body changed into a woman's. Some of the young townsmen eyed her with interest, but Mima never gave them a second glance. Nick wondered if she might act differently if a man of her own race wooed her, but there were no Negro men in Nogadata.

Even though two other doctors settled in the community, Nick's practice thrived, along with the town. A sawmill was built and, because trees were cut to feed the insatiable saws, the woods receded.

Liisi stayed the same and yet not quite. After many sessions with Mima, she began casting stones to foretell the future. Some of her stones were gathered or purchased locally, and others came from the trunks she'd brought from Finland. And every year she mingled less with the townspeople.

Sometimes the urge to try to trace his origins in Russia took hold of Nick, making him restless, but whenever he discussed the matter with Liisi she convinced him such a search would be futile without more information than he possessed. He knew she was right and yet a nagging sense of dissatisfaction, a vague feeling he should be doing more than he was, kept him from being truly happy.

In March 1861, in Washington, D.C., Abraham Lincoln was inaugurated as President. Not exactly of the United States, since seven states had seceded from the Union. And in March the first of the monsters were born in Nogadata—a two-headed calf to one of the Zweig cows. The poor creature lived for a week. By the time it died, most of the Zweig chickens were producing double-yolked eggs.

"Mrs. Zweig says they've been hexed," Mima reported.

"She'll eventually blame me," Liisi said. "Mrs. Zweig has never approved of me."

"Not liking you has nothing to do with blaming you for double-yolked eggs," Nick said.

"Wait," Liisi insisted. "You'll see that I'm right."

He didn't take her words seriously.

In April, soon after South Carolinians fired on Fort Sumter, Phil Jenkins, though now an old man crippled with rheumatism, answered President Lincoln's call for militiamen by helping to form a Monroe cavalry unit.

"It's hell to get old," he confided to Nick. "But if I can't sit a horse and fight like I used to, I can damn well train others to do it." He looked Nick up and down. "Men like you."

"But I'm a doctor," Nick protested.

"The Army's sure as hell gonna need doctors, too."

Nick shook his head. This wasn't his fight.

"An old man don't forget the past, son," Phil went on. "The first time I met you and your little black gal, I recall how you told Ma and me that in your opinion slavery was evil." Phil smiled grimly. "Still think so? Mima's free enough, but what about them that ain't? The South's chockfull of slaves and likely to stay that way less'n we raise ourselves up an army and show them Confederates who's boss."

Phil's words echoed in Nick's mind as he rode back to Nogadata. For the first time in years he thought about Gauthier and how horribly he'd treated his Le Noir slaves. While all slave owners couldn't be as twisted as Gauthier, owning human beings was wrong. Was evil.

He'd rescued Mima. One out of how many? Though he'd heard accounts of the Underground Railroad and knew Detroit had an active branch, he hadn't offered to help escaped slaves. For eleven years he'd done nothing about their plight. He'd enjoyed his life and forgotten their misery. He, who knew how terrible slavery could be. Hadn't he been a slave himself to the beast within him until his wonderful Liisi set him free?

Who would set the southern slaves free?

An army, Phil had said. An army made up of men. Men like Nick Deplacer. Here was a chance to resolve his dissatisfaction with his life.

How could he justify staying home?

Chapter 17

Nick found Liisi and Mima in the kitchen making soup.

"The Army?" Liisi cried, after he explained about Phil Jenkins's Monroe cavalry unit. "Are you telling me you mean to go to war? Mima, do you hear what he's saying? He wishes to leave us and ride off to get himself shot and killed by the Confederates."

Two sets of eyes, one pair gray, the other sable brown, stared accusingly at him.

"I don't plan on being killed," he muttered. They both knew he'd be hard to kill—why were they so upset? Mima, at least, should understand his reason for wanting to take arms against the South.

Mima touched Liisi's arm. "Might be we can try a foreseeing?"

Liisi flipped the long, sharp knife she'd been using to cut up rutabaga so its point stuck into the pine top of the worktable. Her father had taught her as a child to toss knives at targets and she'd never lost her skill.

"Come," she ordered Nick. "I'll cast the stones. If you won't listen to me, perhaps you'll heed the stones."

Nick followed the women upstairs to the room Liisi had set aside for her *noita* belongings. He didn't like this room, with its faded tapestries of ancient Finnish heroes performing obscure deeds, and never entered unless Liisi asked him to.

When the house was first built, the room was no different from the other bedrooms, but once Liisi hung the tapestries and scattered other *noita* paraphernalia about, it became her room, taking on an ambience that made the hair rise on his nape.

Liisi lifted the fur bag of stones from a small chest and sat Indian fashion in the exact center of the room on a round blue silk rug. After Nick and Mima sat facing her, she undid the fastening on the bag and took out eight stones, roughly equal in size, each about as large as a quail's egg.

Nick knew them by heart: granite, for eliminating errant energy; crystal, to focus the summoned energy; agate, to stabilize; amethyst, to promote foreseeing; coral, for wisdom; obsidian, for strength of purpose; turquoise, to protect; and malachite, for strength of will.

The ninth stone was a ruby, for luck, set into a gold ring. Liisi opened the velvet-lined ring case and passed it to Mima. Mima breathed on the ring and handed the case to Nick, who also breathed on the ruby before returning the case to Liisi. Liisi slipped the ring onto her left forefinger and set the case aside.

One by one Liisi passed the stones for them to breathe on. When she had them all gathered again in her lap, she closed her eyes and held out her hands. Nick took one and Mima the other, then they joined their hands to form a circle. Liisi chanted under her breath in Finnish, slowly at first, then faster and faster, the words not quite comprehensible.

Nick concentrated on linking his energy with both Mima and Liisi. Suddenly, without any movement on Liisi's part, the stones flew from her lap and fell onto the blue carpet. He didn't always participate when Liisi cast the stones, but when he did, it always startled him when the stones flung themselves from her lap.

Liisi opened her eyes and released their hands, bending over the stones to read their pattern. He didn't pretend to understand how she did it.

"Turquoise has chosen to protect you," she said to Nick. "You are fortunate. But granite blocks crystal, so there will be danger. Coral touches amethyst, warning of change for the worse. Malachite and agate are separated by obsidian—" Liisi paused, her brow furrowing. "Strife," she whispered at last. She glanced at Mima. "Gather the stones," she ordered.

Mima picked them up in the order Liisi had named them, cupping the stones in her hands and closing her eyes. Long moments passed. Though the day was warm for March, a cold wind seemed to slither into the room and coil hazy tendrils around Mima.

"I *see* a man with hair as red as flame," Mima intoned. "I *see* fire, burning, burning. Blood. Death."

A chill ran along Nick's spine. A dreadful foreseeing. Nevertheless, his mind was made up—he'd go to war.

Before he had the chance to enlist, Liisi took to her bed—Liisi, who was never sick. Despite all the remedies he tried, she not only failed to get well, she grew weaker. As the months passed, he became desperate.

"Since nothing works, this must be an ill-wishing," Mima told him in late October. "Some enemy wished Liisi ill and found a way to send his evil past her guards. Did you notice the mountain ash she planted in the front?"

He nodded. "Dying."

Nick hadn't before associated the dying tree with Liisi's illness, but now he wondered. Liisi called the mountain ash a rowan tree and had planted it, she'd claimed, to protect the house and all within.

"To cure her, we first find out who her enemy is," Mima went on. "Then we find a way to turn the ill-wish back on him."

Nick recalled Liisi complaining about Mrs. Zweig disliking her and saying the woman would blame her for the two-headed calf. He hadn't paid much attention at the time and there'd been no more animal monsters born. Six months ago, though, in Monroe, one of the married Zweig daughters, Greta, had been delivered of an anencephalic baby, an infant born without most of its brain. The poor deformed creature was still alive.

"The baby," he muttered. "Can it be because of Greta's baby?" He thought of stout, red-faced Mrs. Zweig, the most respectable of matrons, and shook his head. It was equally impossible to imagine her husband involved in any witchcraft—hexing, as the Germans called it.

No, not the elder Zweigs. And not placid Greta, either. But what about the man she'd married?

"Do you know Greta Zweig's husband?" he asked Mima.

She scowled. "Him! Guntar Rilke caught me in the woods when I was twelve, meant to take me just like Monsieur Gauthier took my sister. He didn't know Liisi was with me. She came running, pointed her finger, and that man, he couldn't move.'' Mima smiled grimly. ''Liisi, she told him if he ever came near me again she'd turn him into the fat pig he looked like.''

Shocked, Nick stared at her. ''Why didn't you tell me at the time?''

Mima shrugged. ''Liisi, she said better not, you'd beat him and have all the Zweigs on your back. Besides, she scared him off for good.''

Liisi was right, as usual, Nick thought. If he'd known, he might very well have killed the bastard. He drew his lips back from his teeth. He damn well *would* kill Rilke if he turned out to be responsible for Liisi's illness.

''You look like the beast when you do that,'' Mima said.

''I feel like him.'' He spoke through his teeth.

She frowned. ''Don't go to thinking you'll let the beast hunt down Guntar Rilke. You risk your own life and, even if Guntar dies, Liisi will still be sick. If he hexed her, we have to undo the hexing to make her better.''

Calming himself with an effort, Nick tried to order his thoughts. Guntar had a reason to hate Liisi, but did he have the ability to hex? That was witchcraft and he'd never noticed any blue crackle around the man.

''I think I'll have a talk with Lindenblatt,'' he said.

''First, you and me, we must try to heal the mountain ash,'' Mima said.

Just under the soil line they found knife gashes through the bark of the small tree, the slashes girdling the trunk and cutting off its lifeline of sap. Mima placed her hands on the gashes and Nick covered her hands with his, willing healing energy into the tree, hoping they'd succeed.

''Gonna dig her up, are you?'' Lindenblatt's voice jarred Nick from his near-trance. ''She sure don't look like she'll make it.''

Nick took away his hands and stood, leaving Mima with the tree. ''She won't die!'' He spoke so vehemently that Lindenblatt blinked.

Nick tried to force a smile and failed. ''I need to ask you a few questions,'' he said. ''Mind coming inside?''

He didn't mention Liisi's name or her illness, but he could tell from Lindenblatt's uneasiness that the man had a fair idea of why he was being questioned about hexing.

After insisting he didn't believe in such nonsense as sticking pins in wax dolls, Lindenblatt finally admitted there was a hex witch in Monroe. "They call her Sister Wenda and she lives on Grindstone Lane down by the river," he finished. "I stay away from her—it ain't safe to mix with witches."

Though tempted to ride into Monroe immediately and confront the woman, Nick held back. He couldn't afford to make a mistake. Since he couldn't shield his energy—Liisi had tried unsuccessfully to teach him—he was unable to prevent the witch from recognizing his power before he reached her door. But what good was his healing power against her evil? How could he outwit her?

He had but one possibility.

Four nights later, Nick rode into Monroe on his black stallion, Ombre. He left the horse at Jenkins's and walked to Grindstone Lane. Nick remembered the lane from when he'd first come to Monroe. Jenkins had taken him down it to the River Raisin to show him the site of the massacre in January of 1813, during America's war with the British.

"Where we was, Doc and me, down in New Orleans," Jenkins told him, "weren't no Injuns allied with them redcoats. But up along the frontier in Michigan, the British had the Shawnees, Ottawa, and Potawatomi tribes on their side on account of Tecumseh convincing them to trust the redcoats."

Tecumseh. The Indian leader Cump had been named for.

"What happened here at River Raisin was the fault of an American general," Jenkins went on. "Old Winchester weren't half the man Andy Jackson was—General Jackson wouldn't've stood for no massacre, no sirree. How it happened, first there was a fight and the redcoats won. The redcoat officer marched off with his prisoners and left the wounded behind at Frenchtown—what this was called in the old days afore it got named after President Monroe.

"Them Injun redcoat allies, they stays on, camping in the woods by the river whooping 'er up in celebration and drinking rotgot. Well, now, rotgut curdles the brain of any man, but if he's an Injun, he goes stark raving mad—two hundred or so drunken Injuns, without Tecumseh or the redcoats around to stop 'em. They swoops down on Frenchtown and all them poor wounded soldiers and whatever settlers was left, murdering and scalping. Just to make sure nothing's left alive, they burns the houses."

Jenkins had shaken his head. "Ain't no man in Michigan ever gonna forget that day."

Nick could only hope his encounter with the hex witch along this same river wouldn't prove to be as much of a disaster for him as that long-ago battle had been for the Americans.

A waning not-yet-gibbous moon rose over the trees as he came in sight of Sister Wenda's cottage, the small house all but concealed among dark evergreens. Sensing the blue flicker of energy inside, he knew she was home. Striding boldly up the path, he knocked on the door.

As though expecting him, she opened the door immediately, her sea-green eyes flicking over him. She smiled slowly, languorously, and stepped aside to allow him to enter.

Lindenblatt had told him he heard she was about forty years old. Nick didn't know exactly what he'd thought she'd be like, but what he saw sure as hell wasn't it. Red hair curled about her face and fell in waving, flaming clouds over her shoulders. She wore no fashionable hoops, and her green gown was low-cut and bound with a wide jet-beaded belt under her full breasts, the gown skimming her voluptuous body as it fell in soft silken folds to her ankles.

A man would have to be a eunuch not to respond to such an attractive woman.

"How can I help you, Doctor?" she asked in a husky, amused voice as she closed the door.

Nick fought the spell she cast. "If you know who I am, you know why I'm here," he said. "And what I want."

"Everything has its price," she murmured. "I'm sure we can reach an agreement. In here." She gestured toward a cozy sitting room off the entry hall where a fire blazed on the hearth.

She touched his arm with the pointed nail of her forefinger, her musky perfume enticing him, filling his mind with images of her naked in his arms. Damn, but he wanted this woman. He could think of nothing but having her. He took a step toward her.

A yowl startled him and he held. A gray cat, fur on end, dashed between him and Wenda, disappearing into the depths of the house.

The witch's cat. Nick came abruptly to himself. His hand

closed over what he carried in his pocket and he stepped back, grimly hanging on to the shreds of his control.

"Your cat's afraid of me." His voice challenged her. "Can you guess why?"

Wenda smiled mockingly. "*I* don't fear you."

"I want what you concocted for Guntar Rilke. You will give it to me."

"For a price, yes."

Should he bargain with a witch? "The price?" he asked cautiously.

"Can't *you* guess?" Her hands skimmed the air close to her body, tracing her curves.

Nick's eyes widened. He was momentarily speechless.

"It's useless to pretend you don't desire me." Her voice was a purr, caressing his ears.

He had to swallow before he could ease words past his dry throat. "I can't pay your price."

Her smile fled. "You *will* pay it, Doctor, willingly or otherwise." Her hand began a gesture in the air between them.

Terror gripped Nick as he felt what remained of his control dissolving. If the witch spelled him into bedding her, what might happen? In his heart he feared such a union would doom Liisi and, eventually, him. Plus the horrible danger of fathering a monster like himself.

Never! He pulled the steel amulet from his pocket and flung it at Wenda.

An almost-forgotten wrenching twisted his guts and, as he tore at his clothes, he heard her laugh.

If she thought he stripped in eagerness to join with her, she was badly mistaken.

"I'm a shapeshifter," he warned, his voice already half a growl. "I have no control over the beast I become—he'll kill you."

He saw the pupils of her green eyes dilate in fear and knew she saw the beast emerging. As she backed away, he leaped at her, grabbing both her wrists in one of his taloned hands. He threw her to the floor and scooped up the steel amulet in his free hand.

"The change is temporarily halted," he told her, hoping it was true. He'd never tried anything like this before. "Give me what I need and the beast stays trapped within me. Refuse and he runs free. And you die."

"In the back room," she whispered.

He hauled her to her feet and, holding her wrists, pushed her ahead of him along the hall, snarling in his struggle against the increasingly demanding urge to shift all the way, to free the beast.

Thirteen wax mannikens nestled in red boxes arrayed on a black table in a room that raised Nick's hackles with its wrongness. After a moment's thought, he eased the leather thong holding the amulet over his wrist to free his hand and carefully placed all thirteen of the boxes with their hideous contents into a larger, empty wooden box. Carrying the box, he thrust the witch ahead of him to the front door.

"Open it!" he ordered, realizing with dismay his voice was scarcely intelligible. His control was all but gone. "Leave this town," he told her. "Go back to where you came from. Or face the beast."

As she threw the door open, she hissed, "We'll meet again one day. In Pennsylvania."

He burst from the witch's house, running, flinging the amulet's thong around his neck in midflight, searching his mind for the right words to chant before it was too late.

When he reached Jenkins's, Ombre snorted at his approach, dancing away from his touch, sensing the beast's continuing fight to emerge. It was some minutes before he calmed the stallion enough to mount him. Between his struggle with the horse and with himself, the ride home was a nightmare.

Mima took the box from his shaking hands when he staggered into the house and disappeared into the *noita* room with the thirteen wax mannikens.

Nick, who'd taken the precaution of having a basement dug under the house, hurried down the steps and into the room without windows he'd had built into the basement. Shut inside, he bowed his head and, one hand closed around the amulet, chanted Liisi's charm against shapeshifting over and over for the rest of the night, fighting the beast's ravening need to burst free.

The next morning, Liisi was conscious for the first time in weeks, though still very weak. Nick sat on the bed spooning broth into her mouth while Mima told them both what she'd done with the mannikens.

"All those little dolls, they got pins stuck in them or strings knotted tight around parts of them. Some, they were partly melted from being burned. I took out the pins and took off the strings and then, one at a time, I held them in my hands and tried to heal their sickness." She smiled at Liisi. "And you woke up."

"Thank you." Liisi's voice was faint, her smile a bare twitch of her lips. She reached one hand to Nick, one to Mima.

Nick didn't tell Liisi what had happened with Sister Wenda until she'd regained some of her strength—and then he didn't tell her everything. Some things were better kept secret from a wife.

When after several months Liisi recovered completely, Nick found her travail seemed to have turned her against the town.

"Why don't we leave here and travel to your California land?" she asked Nick in April. "They don't like me in Nogadata. You ought to see that by now."

"Guntar Rilke was your enemy, not the townspeople," Nick said soothingly. "He had a grudge against you."

"Mima was twelve when I threatened Guntar," Liisi responded. "He might have been upset eight years ago, but not enough to try to get even. He was pushed into what he did. First, by hearing his mother-in-law complain about the two-headed calf and the double-yolked eggs and saying she'd been hexed. She pointed the finger at me, I'm sure. Then that poor little baby was born to Greta and he decided I was to blame, no doubt encouraged in his belief by his mother-in-law. In my opinion, Mrs. Zweig drove him into visiting the hex witch. She hates me. She'll turn the entire town against me, given time."

Seeing it was useless, Nick didn't argue with her, but he thought she was exaggerating. No wonder she was disturbed, after what she'd been through.

"Besides," Liisi said, "I fear war will destroy you. Do you wish to die without ever knowing where you came from or why you were born?"

Nick stared at her. "I'm more likely to be destroyed if I return to California. I've explained why." He put a soothing hand on her shoulder. "Everything will look better by summer. You'll be feeling as good as new by then. We'll take a trip to Detroit—they've opened a new museum there."

"You don't understand," she said with a sigh, shrugging off his hand. "Why are men so blind?"

* * *

The Detroit trip didn't raise Liisi's spirits. Nor Nick's. Seeing so many men dressed in Union blue, he felt ashamed not to be doing his part. In September of '62, when the Confederates crossed the Potomac River into Maryland and threatened the nation's capital, he decided he had to enlist. There'd be no further threat from the hex witch, she'd long since gone from Monroe—back to Pennsylvania, he supposed.

Liisi was completely well now and even the mountain ash in the front yard was thriving. And he had plenty of money in the bank for Liisi and Mima to live on.

They could manage very well without him. After all, how much longer could the war last? Six months? A year at the most. In any case, he was determined to be part of it. What was a man's life without a cause? He'd found a worthy one—fighting for what he believed was right.

One thing and another, including Phil Jenkins's death, delayed him, but in late November he headed into Monroe, determined to enlist in the cavalry. But when he tried, he encountered an obstacle—since he was a doctor the Army expected him to treat the wounded rather than ride against the Rebels.

"I'll think it over and let you know tomorrow," Nick said.

He stopped by to see Mrs. Jenkins, whose daughter and two children had moved into her house after the daughter's husband was killed in September in the fighting at Antietam. The two widows insisted he stay for supper and spend the night at the farm.

Nick took a stroll around town before the meal and was nearing Judge Bacon's house on Monroe Street when he saw a young man in uniform weaving along the sidewalk toward him, obviously drunk. Just as the soldier—a captain, if rather gaudily dressed—reached the Bacon house, he fell onto his hands and knees and vomited into the street.

Nick strode to him, conscious of faces in the windows of the Bacon house staring at the spectacle the young soldier was making of himself.

Helping the man to his feet, Nick asked, "Where do you live? I'll take you home."

"Can't go home," the captain said mournfully. "Lydie'll

fuss." His words were so badly slurred Nick could hardly understand him.

"Is Lydie your wife?"

"M' sister. She'll fuss."

God knows the captain probably had cause to drink. Sympathizing with his plight, Nick said, "Come along with me. We'll walk until you feel better."

Nick steadied him as they passed by the Bacon house and turned onto Front Street, walking along the river toward the docks. He thought the captain was oddly dressed for a Union officer. Though he wore regulation blue, his broad-brimmed hat was Confederate gray and a bright red kerchief was tied around his neck. With his reddish blond hair, worn longer than customary, and his shaggy mustache, he verged on the flamboyant.

Evening shadows were gathering by the time they reached the end of a pier and stood, huddled against the cold, staring at the icy water of Brest Bay.

"I might's well jump in," the soldier said morosely. "He's sure to hear about me."

"Who?"

"Judge Bacon."

Nick's eyebrows raised. "I think he saw you. Why are you worried about the judge?"

The soldier sighed. "Libbie. Miss Elizabeth Bacon. After this her father will never let her speak to me again." He shook his head. "They call me lucky, but seems I can't do anything right when it comes to Libbie. When I was ten I fell out of a tree trying to rescue her kitten and now I—"

"Autie?" Nick said, surprised. "You're little Autie?"

"Captain George Armstrong Custer, at your service, sir," he said, coming to wavering attention and staring at Nick with his bloodshot blue eyes.

"I fixed your arm when you fell from that tree."

Autie clapped him on the shoulder. "Damned if you aren't the doctor!"

"Nick Deplacer. I'm afraid I didn't recognize you as Monroe's hero, Captain Custer. Everyone's heard of your remarkable exploits in battle; we're all proud of you."

The captain's face flushed and he ducked his head, obviously embarrassed. "I lead brave men," he mumbled.

"I'm trying to enlist in the cavalry myself," Nick went on, "but the army wants me to serve as a doctor. Maybe you *can* be of service. Do you think you can help me get on a horse instead of stuck permanently in a field hospital?''

''Hell, yes, I can. It may take time, but I'm General McClellan's aide. I'll speak to him personally.''

''Thanks.'' Nick smiled. ''I'll remind you again tomorrow, when your head's clearer. Where are you staying?''

''With my sister, Mrs. Reed.''

''I believe you've sobered up enough to face her now.''

Autie rolled his eyes. 'You don't know Lydie.''

In June of '83, Captain Deplacer was finally transferred from his medical unit to the 1st Michigan Cavalry. He cheered along with the other Wolverines when they learned the new commander of the Second or Michigan Brigade their regiment belonged to was to be Brigadier General Custer. In July, the brigade, including the 1st Michigan and Nick, rode behind their commander into Pennsylvania.

General or not, Autie Custer still tied a red kerchief around his neck, though he'd exchanged the gray hat for a black one with a gold star pinning up the wide brim on the right side. Gold spurs decorated his high-topped boots. Nick hadn't yet ridden into battle under him, but he'd listened to those who had.

''He's got guts, the general,'' a veteran sergeant named Ulrich had told him. ''No doubt about that. Always rides way the hell out in front. Seems like he figures ain't no bullet got his name writ on it.''

Recalling the ten-year-old who'd suffered without a whimper through the pain of having a dislocated shoulder pulled back into place, Nick nodded. Autie was courageous as well as lucky.

God knows there were enough unlucky soldiers. He'd treated bullet and shrapnel wounds after the defeat at Chancellorsville in May and had lost his own battle to save many of the injured men. Though he was a healer, he wasn't a miracle worker. Nor did he have the heart for surgery, for sawing off maimed arms and legs as though they were so many pieces of wood. He'd welcomed the long-awaited transfer to the Michigan 1st.

Riding along the dusty Pennsylvania road with his unit, Nick grimaced as he noted the brilliantly colored paintings on some of the barns. Hex signs. He couldn't help remembering Sister Wenda's threat to meet him in Pennsylvania.

Try as he might, he'd never completely forgotten her. He'd never expected to be in her territory—yet here he was.

Nick shrugged. He was here to fight the Rebs, not rendezvous with a witch. Like other civilians, Wenda would stay as far as she could from any shooting. Ability to hex didn't mean an immunity to bullets.

That night, bivouacked with the others near Heidlersburg, Nick lay on his back in the warm, breathless night staring up at the full moon as it climbed the sky, and chanting Liisi's charm under his breath. He hadn't come close to changing since the night with the hex witch, but he dared not let down his guard.

He'd come to love Liisi with all his heart and soul and yet it wasn't her image that haunted his dreams in the Pennsylvania night. Wenda, with her red hair and witch-green eyes, beckoned to him, offering her lush curves, and he responded, wanting her despite the danger. He'd have her whatever the consequences.

He woke abruptly, heart hammering against his ribs, to the milky half-light of dawn. The moon was setting behind a woods and the other men of his unit surrounded him, most still sleeping. There was no witch lying with him, no crackle of blue energy nearby. But as he pulled on his boots, Nick sensed she'd somehow deliberately invaded his dreams.

The Second Brigade stood to horse shortly after sunrise. Hours passed with no order to ride. It was getting close to noon before a courier arrived with orders and the brigade, the 1st among them, rode down the Harrisburg road toward Gettysburg, nine miles away.

Around two o'clock they halted at Rock Creek. Nick listened to the nerve-shattering bombardment ahead, but the fighting was hidden by a ridge. All he could see were the clouds of white smoke billowing above the hill. In the hours that followed, General Custer moved the brigade time and again across the fields, but it wasn't until five that they moved out along a dirt road toward Gettysburg.

They'd gone several miles before Reb cavalry confronted them. General Custer, leading the Michigan 6th, charged, shouting, "Come on, you Wolverines!"

Nick, left behind with the rest of the 1st, listened to the clash of sabers and the crack of pistols up ahead, expecting to be called into action at any moment. When the remnants of the 6th began straggling back, he started to wonder if the

Rebs were winning. After Custer returned, riding with a private because his own horse had been shot out from under him, Nick understood how bad the defeat was.

Under a full moon, they rode behind the Union line to find a safe night camp. Refugees—wounded men and stragglers—blocked the road, whimpering tales of defeat to all who passed by.

Custer rallied his men. "We lost a skirmish, but the battle's yet to be fought. Tomorrow we'll send the Rebs hightailing it back to Charleston, damned if we don't."

But it was near twilight of that day before Nick's unit faced the enemy.

" 'Tis Jeb Stuart and his men," Sergeant Ulrich muttered as the 1st fell into formation. "We'll give 'em hell."

Nick tensed. Jeb Stuart's cavalry was formidable indeed—equal to or surpassing any Union cavalry. Custer took his place at the head of his columns. He raised his saber, shouted "Come on, you Wolverines!" and pounded toward the solid ranks of advancing gray.

Wild yells burst from the throats of the men around Nick as they spurred their horses after their general. He yelled along with them, caught up in the fever of battle induced by Custer's reckless courage.

A red mist clouded his vision as lust for the kill captured his mind.

Death to all Rebs!

Chapter 18

In the shadowy evening light Nick spurred his rangy sorrel, concentrating on the galloping figure four lengths ahead of the regiment, hearing Custer's defiant battle cry mingle with Rebel yells. Artillery roared in the distance, accompanied by the pop-pop-pop of rifle fire, but like the Michigan 1st, the oncoming Rebs held to their sabers.

With a ringing clash, the two lines met. Nick swept through the Rebels shouting, saber slashing. Steel clanged against steel, men swore, and horses reared, squealing. In the near darkness it grew difficult to tell enemy from fellow soldier and impossible to keep in rank.

To his horror, he caught sight of the general's distinctive figure surrounded by Rebs. With a howl of rage, Nick forced his sorrel between two Reb horses, swinging his saber furiously from left to right as he bored through the encirclement.

Using the diversion, Custer cut his way free. Nick was pounding after him when suddenly the rising moon, just beyond full, slid from behind a cloud, piercing him with a shaft of silver light. His horse reared, pawing the air. Feeling his insides twist, Nick screamed, "No!"

Between struggling against the urge to shift and trying to manage his spooked sorrel, he didn't see the Reb to his left in time to parry the saber thrust. The blade caught him above the hip, slicing through until it grated on bone. Shocked by the pain, Nick lost control of the sorrel, and the horse threw him. He thudded to the ground, rolling desperately to avoid churning hooves as the battle raged around him.

He smacked hard against rock. Head swimming, his uniform blood-soaked, he dragged himself around the huge rock into a narrow passageway between giant boulders, where he collapsed. Even in his confusion he knew the saber wound must be already closing, but he was also aware he'd lost so much blood that his body needed time to recover from the loss.

Too weak to move, Nick lay on the ground between the boulders, listening to the cries of men and horses and the clash of sabers. It seemed to him the sounds came from another world, one he'd left behind. He glanced at the dark sky. The moon had disappeared behind clouds, but in any case, the urge to change had left him.

As full darkness shrouded the field; the sounds of battle gradually diminished. When the cicadas began their shrill courting he knew the soldiers—Union and Reb—had abandoned the field for the night, leaving nothing behind but the dead and the wounded. He had no idea who'd won the skirmish or the battle. At the moment he didn't care.

Since he had no choice but to stay where he was until he grew stronger, Nick eased himself into a more comfortable position and closed his eyes. To his distress, instead of a reassuring darkness, he saw Wenda, her green eyes gleaming with triumph, her white arms reaching for him. He cursed under his breath and opened his eyes.

From the moment he'd marched into Pennsylvania her unwelcome presence had slipped into his head every time he let down his guard. He wondered if she knew he'd entered her territory and deliberately plagued him or if his images of her were only a residue of the spell she'd cast over him in Monroe.

To shut her from his mind he began silently counting, first in Russian, then in Finnish, French, Spanish, English and, finally, Havasupai.

Flickers of light startled him until he realized they had nothing to do with him but were fireflies searching for one another to mate.

As the hours passed he regained enough strength to rise to his feet, the healing saber wound giving him only a twinge of pain. When he eased from his lair between the boulders, he noticed flickering lights over the field—not fireflies this time but men with lanterns searching for the wounded.

Because of his almost infallible sense of direction and his excellent night vision, Nick was certain he could reach camp on his own. He left the safety of the boulders, walking slowly through the darkness toward where he was sure the Union line lay.

After a time he began to feel the walk was interminable and the way far too long. Where was the low stone wall, the apple orchard? Where were the woods? Why couldn't he hear the night sounds of a camp? Where were the intermingled odors of men and horses? Most unsettling of all, why couldn't he sense the presence of other men? Or even animals?

Alarmed, Nick halted, peering into the darkness, all his senses searching, searching—and finding nothing but a faint scent of musk. He tensed. A low, husky laugh echoed in his head.

"Come to me," she whispered in his mind, over and over again. His attempts to resist her allure were futile. Slowly, inexorably, his feet began moving against his will, carrying him where he dreaded to go. Blue energy crackled around him, hurrying him along.

Eventually he was allowed to stop and he knew he'd arrived. Somewhere. In the darkness he heard no natural sounds, smelled no normal night odors, sensed nothing but her. Where in God's name was he?

A woman's long, pointed nails raked gently along his cheek. Her fingers. The hex witch was here with him, the musk of her perfume arousing him even as he fought his own desire. Laughing low in her throat, she touched him more intimately and he was powerless to resist. She fondled him, making him forget everything else so that he reached for her, no longer able to remember why he must not.

She was naked under his hands, soft and inviting. He couldn't see her, but he remembered those lush curves very well. The nipples of her full breasts hardened under his caress and when he touched the warm dampness between her legs his need grew frenzied.

"I kept my part of our bargain. I brought you here to keep yours," she whispered as he flung off his clothes and bore her to the ground.

Her words registered without him understanding their meaning. Nothing had meaning except her eager body under his. He plunged inside her, excited into madness by her scent, her feel, the spicy, forbidden taste of her mouth.

Their joining sent him racing along a dark tunnel into a

noxious cavern where flames danced and leaped, reaching for him, entwining him in their deadly, unforgettable hell-heat. He moaned with the exquisite agony, wanting it never to end even as he struggled toward release.

The fire embraced him, consumed him, burned him to ashes that swirled away into nothingness.

Nick roused soon after the rain began. It wasn't quite dawn. He was naked; he lay in the tramped grass of a meadow.

My God, the beast ran loose! he thought in horror. He sprang to his feet and glanced quickly around. The first thing he saw were clothes strewn haphazardly onto the grass near him. His clothes, the uniform pants stiff with blood from the now-healed saber wound. Hurriedly, he pulled them on.

Never before had the beast come back to where the change had occurred. Why was there no taste of blood in his mouth? He raised his hands closer to his eyes to check for blood-stains in the dim light. No stains, but he caught a faint whiff of musk.

Musk. Wenda. He'd dreamed of her, dreamed he'd taken her, dreamed of hell. Or had it been a dream? Casting about, he sensed more than one normal glow of energy in the distance but no witch crackle. Looking with his eyes as well as his special sense, he saw two dead bodies all but hidden in the tall grass some twenty paces away, one dressed in blue, one in gray.

He tried to imagine Wenda luring him to this meadow of death in the darkness. Would she come onto a battlefield? He shook his head in confusion. The only thing he felt sure of was that he hadn't shifted shape last night. He'd remained a man.

Either he'd gotten lost and wandered to this meadow or Wenda had spelled him to her here. But if so, had she been here in body or in spirit? The dream, if that's what it was, had been very real—he could almost feel the soft warmth of her now. He recalled the searing flames all too clearly.

He couldn't hold to the illusion she'd been a dream. Either in person or in spirit, she'd gotten what she wanted from him. Never mind that he hadn't acceded to the bargain; the hex witch had taken her payment for Liisi's cure.

He couldn't bear to think Wenda had actually lain with

him, for if that was true, he might have fathered another like himself. Nick groaned. Even if he wasn't in the middle of a war, he doubted if he'd ever be able to track her down and discover the truth.

The scent of smoke drifted to him on the damp dawn breeze, reminding Nick his present position was precarious. Union or Reb campfire? He'd best reconnoiter before it grew any lighter.

Setting all thought of Wenda aside, he slipped cautiously through the grass of the meadow, searching for a familiar landmark and getting wetter by the minute. After a time a weak, flickering aura to his right made him hesitate. He knew what he sensed must be a wounded soldier. Friend or enemy?

What the hell difference did it make when a man needed healing? Nick swerved to the right. Moments later he saw a slumped figure in the grass, one leg twisted at an impossible angle. Blue uniform. Sergeant's stripes.

He knelt beside the man, looking for injuries other than the obviously broken right leg. He grimaced at the sight of the soldier's maimed face. The right eye was gone and the scalp and cheek were slashed open to the bone. The rain streaked the blood oozing from the wound.

After removing the red kerchief from his own neck, Nick grasped a still attached flap of skin and hair, laid it back across the gaping wound as gently as possible, and bound the injury with his kerchief. The man groaned but didn't regain consciousness.

Nick cut reins from a dead horse and retrieved empty saber sheaths from three dead Rebs. He twisted the injured man's leg into alignment, gritting his teeth against the sound of the grating bones, and, using the saber sheaths as splints, he bound them to the broken leg with the reins. As Nick finished, the sergeant opened his remaining eye.

"Damn, m' head hurts like hell," he mumbled.

Nick stared down at him. "Ulrich!" he exclaimed. He hadn't recognized the man until he spoke.

"Captain?" Sergeant Ulrich sounded as surprised as Nick. He raised a hand toward his bandaged head.

"Don't touch that," Nick said sharply. "You've got a broken leg as well as a head injury. I'll find transport to take you back to camp. Lie still and keep your hands away from your head until I return. That's an order, Sergeant."

As Ulrich mumbled what may have been an assent, his eye drooped shut.

In an adjoining orchard Nick found an empty supply cart under a tree loaded with tiny green apples. He cut the harness and yanked the cart free of the dead horse. Grasping a shaft in either hand, he pulled the cart back to Sergeant Ulrich and lifted the stocky man into its soggy bed, taking care to keep the right leg straight.

As he trudged through the rain pulling the cart, Nick finally saw the low stone wall he'd ridden past when the 1st charged the enemy. Sure now of his bearings, he quickened his pace, swerving to avoid dead men and horses, at last sensing the presence of the living. If the Union had won the skirmish, he was near Union lines. If not . . .

Nick shrugged and plodded on. He was weaving from exhaustion when a sentry challenged him. By then he was past caring whether the man wore blue or gray.

When he saw the blue of the sentry's uniform, Nick knew the Union had been victorious. The knowledge failed to thrill him as much as it would have a day earlier.

The bloodlust of battle had tempted the beast inside him. It had almost broken loose last night, would have if the Reb's saber slash hadn't reversed the beginning change. He couldn't afford to take another chance. Though he still believed in the rightness of the Union cause, now he understood that, because of what he was, his part in the war must be a healer's, not a fighting man's. As Liisi had warned, war could destroy him.

As soon as he'd rested, Nick made his way to the field hospital, where he located Sergeant Ulrich and treated him first. After sending a message to General Custer by way of a wounded cavalryman who, after treatment, was able to rejoin his regiment, Nick continued to care for the men injured at Gettsyburg.

Two days later Custer found Nick riding beside the long line of ambulances carrying the wounded back to Washington.

"Sergeant Ulrich says you saved his life," Custer said as his horse fell into step alongside Nick's.

"And I've been told your charge turned the tide in our favor at Gettysburg," Nick said.

"The Michigan 1st, not me," Custer corrected. "I challenge the annals of warfare to produce a more brilliant or successful charge of cavalry.'' He glanced at Nick. ''You were part of that charge. Yet here you are doctoring again.''

''Some men, like you, General, were born to lead. Some were born to fight. My talent lies in healing. I was foolish to try to turn away from what I do best.''

Custer frowned, finally nodding. ''I'll arrange for your transfer,'' he said, touching his hat in a final salute as he spurred his horse.

As the months passed, the war became for Nick a nightmare of severed limbs, disembowelments, and dying men. In April '64 he and Hank Ulrich, who was now attached to the medical unit as an orderly, were assigned to Nashville to be a part of the western armies.

''Hear tell we're gonna push south this month,'' Ulrich confided to Nick as they left the barracks hospital. ''Gonna be a big battle.'' He shook his head. ''When I rode with the 1st, I never figured what happened to them Rebs I shot. Never cared. Since Gettysburg I sure as hell've seen the other side of war.''

Nick glanced at Ulrich's disfigured face, his missing eye covered by a black patch. ''You're as needed now as—'' He broke off, his attention caught by the red-bearded man striding toward them.

''Cump!'' Nick exclaimed before noticing the general's stars on the uniformed shoulders. He saluted hastily.

Sherman stopped and stared at Nick. ''Damn it, I know you,'' he said after a moment. ''California. You're my namesake. Sherman Oso.''

Nick shifted his shoulders. ''I'm Nick Deplacer now, sir,'' he said.

Sherman's eyebrows rose, his gaze sharpening. ''A doctor, are you?''

''Yes, sir.''

''Assigned to my army. Good. I won't ask why the name change. We'll talk sometime.'' He strode on.

''Jesus,'' Ulrich breathed. ''Damned if that wasn't Uncle Billy Sherman himself. A friend of his, are you?''

''Not exactly. He helped me a long time ago. In California.''

''Good kinda friend to have, a general. Specially Sherman. He runs the whole western shebang. Military Division of the Mississippi, they call it.''

In May the western army marched toward Atlanta. In the night camps, Nick, restless, often came upon General Sherman, who seemed attracted to darkness. In time Nick came to look forward to these brief encounters, though he found only traces of the young lieutenant he'd known in California.

"This country swarms with thousands who'd shoot me on sight," Sherman said to him one night in June, on the outskirts of Atlanta. "They'd shoot me and thank their God they'd killed a monster."

In the darkness Nick's smile was grim. What would Sherman say if he knew the truth about Oso/Deplacer? Wouldn't he also shoot on sight?

"I don't hate southerners," Sherman went on. "I lived among them. I know them. All in all, I'm more kindly disposed to the southern people than any general army officer. But war is war."

"I treat the bloody results every day," Nick reminded him.

Sherman sighed. "You can't qualify war in harsher terms than I do. War is cruelty and you can't refine it. War is hell. But I'm committed to this fight and I'll push forward until we have a permanent peace. No matter what I'm called by the people of the South." He glanced at Nick. "They'd hate you as much as they do me if they knew you saved my life in California." He put a hand on Nick's shoulder. "There've been times I wondered why my life was spared, but on the whole, I'm glad you were at that night camp."

On the evening of November 15, Nick, standing on a hill overlooking Atlanta, watched as flames flared, spreading through the center of the city, rising like red and yellow beacons announcing Sherman's victory.

Nick remembered Liisi casting the stones and Mima's foreseeing of blood and flames. God knows he'd seen enough of both. As smoke billowed over the stricken city, he wondered, as he had so many times since his enlistment, if Liisi had written him.

Difficult as it sometimes was to get mail delivered to the troops, other men received letters from home. But not Nick. Though he'd sent letters to Liisi, none had been answered. Was she all right?

He wasn't quite all right himself. Being in the midst of so many men kept him continually uneasy—his special sense was useless in such crowds. If he couldn't get away alone like this at night, he thought he might go crazy. He knew that Sergeant Ulrich worried over his solitary night excursions and he suspected the energy glow on the nearby hill to his left was Ulrich, keeping an eye on him. He sensed no other men near.

The sudden click of a rifle bolt directly behind him startled Nick. As he started to turn, a shot rang out. He whirled in time to see the man behind him slump to the ground, a rifle slipping from his grasp.

But he'd sensed no one behind him! Was he losing his ability? As Nick knelt beside the motionless figure, he heard Ulrich shout his name.

"Are you okay, Doc?" Ulrich demanded, pounding up the hill. "Did I get the bastard in time?"

Nick looked up at Ulrich. "He's dead. A Union private. One of our men."

"It don't matter what color uniform he wears," Ulrich said. "He had the damned rifle aimed at your head. Christ, he wasn't no more'n six feet from you—would've killed you for certain. I saw him clear as anything, outlined against the fire, so I got off a good clean shot afore he could pull the trigger. He meant to kill you, Doc, sure as God made little green apples."

Nick stared down at the young soldier. Why in God's name would one of their own men want to kill him? Kill Nick Deplacer? It wasn't as though he were General Sherman.

A Californio? Nick touched the dead man's blond hair and shook his head. He couldn't understand why he hadn't known the soldier was behind him, hadn't sensed any energy glow.

"Poor bastard must've gone berserk, like," Ulrich said. "Sometimes they do, go to killing everything in sight."

Nick rose to his feet and put a hand on the sergeant's shoulder. "You saved my life."

"I owed you, Doc, damned if I didn't. Now maybe you'll listen to me and stay in camp, nights."

Nick squeezed his shoulder and dropped his hand. "You know, Hank, before I enlisted two years ago, I thought the war would be over in six months—a year at the most. Now I wonder if it will ever end."

* * *

Seven months later, on a bright June morning, Nick jumped down from the train at the Monroe station and hurried to the Jenkins farm. To his surprise, houses dotted the acreage. The farmhouse and the barn remained, surrounded by perhaps a half acre of ground where vegetables sprouted in neat rows.

After her startled but enthusiastic welcome and her telling him how glad she was the war was over, Mrs. Jenkins admitted she'd sold off most of the land.

"The town's growing by leaps and bounds," she said. "I asked myself, what did I need a farm for? For no good reason, that's what. Peggy and me can't do the work by ourselves and the two girls aren't much help. Young John's no farmer, never was; he plans to stay in the Army. Besides, the money comes in mighty handy. We kept two cows, the horses, and a few chickens, that's all."

"I was hoping you'd lend me a horse," Nick said, glad enough to see her but eager to get to Nogadata.

" 'Course I will, you know that." Her smile faded. "I suppose you let your wife know you're coming home?"

"No, I thought I'd surprise her."

Mrs. Jenkins glanced at her daughter and then away, refusing to meet Nick's eyes. Peggy looked down at the floor.

Nick stared from one to the other, unease flaring. "Is something wrong with Liisi? Mima?"

Mrs. Jenkins folded her arms across her ample bosom. "So far's we know, your wife's all right. Mima, too. That's all I mean to say, so don't bother to ask any more questions. My advice is to saddle up and ride home."

Peggy, never much of a talker, nodded solemnly.

Nick, alarmed by now, hurried to the barn. A few minutes later he trotted down the drive on a dappled gray gelding, waved to the women watching from the front porch, and struck out for the Nogadata road.

As he urged the gray into a lope, he was vaguely aware the road had been widened and also corduroyed over the low spots. There was considerable traffic, too. Carts, wagons, and carriages rumbled over the horizontally laid logs, some going into Monroe, some toward Nogadata.

By the time he reached the town, he had no eye for any changes and little for the people he passed who, recognizing him, called greetings. His entire attention was fixed on getting home. He breathed a sigh of relief when he came in sight of the house and saw the place was intact, looking much as it had when he left.

Mima was leaning on the front porch rail, staring down the street as though expecting him. He waved, but when she didn't respond he kicked the gray into a last burst of speed, then reined in at the front and dismounted.

"Mima!" he cried, running up the stairs, his arms held out to her.

She burst into tears and turned away. Conscious of passersby stopping to gawk, Nick grasped her wrist and led her into the house.

"What in God's name is the matter?" he demanded as soon as the door closed behind them. "Where's Liisi? Is she all right?"

"Don't know," Mima wailed.

Nick's heart stood still. He gripped Mima's shoulders. "You don't know where she is?"

"Don't know *how* she is." Tears ran down Mima's cheeks. "I been real scared."

"Is Liisi in the house?"

Mima shook her head, beyond speech.

He took a deep breath, controlling his urge to shake her into making sense. Instead, he pulled her against his shoulder and patted her back. "Calm yourself," he soothed as best he could, apprehensive as he was. "I'm here. There's no need to be frightened. Stop crying and tell me what's happened."

"You be mad," Mima mumbled between sobs, sounding like the nine-year-old he'd first befriended.

"I won't be angry with you." He held her away from him. "Wipe your eyes—that's a good girl."

Mima pulled a handkerchief from her pocket and mopped her wet face. "Liisi, she told me I had to stay here till you came home, said the house needed to be taken care of, said somebody had to be here when you came."

"Where the hell is *she*?"

Mima bit her lip. "In California."

"California?" Nick's voice rose to a shout. "What in damnation is she doing there?"

Mima sniffled. "I knew you'd be mad."

Nick tried to calm himself. "Look, I know this wasn't your fault. Here, sit down." He motioned her into the parlor, where she perched on the edge of a chair. He leaned against the fireplace mantel. "Start at the beginning and tell me everything."

"You remember how Liisi, she told you they don't like her in this town? She was right, they don't. They don't care much for me, neither, but they mostly leave me alone."

Nick straightened, his hands clenching. "What did they do to her?"

"It seemed like she lost her only friends when the Lindenblatts moved to Detroit. None of the other ladies would talk to Liisi. Then some of the stores, they wouldn't sell her what she tried to buy. After while they began leaving notes on the door about her being a witch and she'd better get out of town. She decided to go after they killed one of the dogs. Her favorite." Mima looked at him, her eyes brimming.

"Don't start crying again," he said firmly. "What happened next?"

She swallowed. "Liisi, she showed me these papers about land in California. She said she'd been paying taxes on the land with her own money and she was going there to wait for you. Going to build a house. She said I had to stay here till you came, then you'd bring me with you to California and we'd all be together again. Only it took you so *long*. I knew you weren't killed 'cause I'd feel it if you died, and I didn't. But I thought maybe you forgot about us."

Nick closed his eyes for an instant. "I'd never forget about you, Mima. And certainly not about Liisi. Didn't she get my letters?"

Mima nodded. "Some letters came after she left. I saved them, didn't open them 'cause they were to her."

"Why in hell didn't she write and let me know what she meant to do?"

Mima hunched her shoulders. "She said I had to tell you."

"*You* should have written me, then."

"She made me promise not to."

Nick threw up his hands. "What's the use of talking? I suppose there's no choice but to go after her. To California, of all places. She knew I didn't want to go back there. I told her why."

"Liisi, she said she won't ever set foot in this town again."

Nick shook his head. Knowing Liisi, she'd never change her mind. Might as well sell the house before he and Mima left. He'd grown a beard on Sherman's final march from Atlanta to the sea but shaved it off before coming home. Best to grow one again; maybe the Californios wouldn't recognize a bearded Nick Deplacer as the shapeshifter they sought to kill. After all, it had been over fifteen years ago.

But he sure as hell didn't mean to stay in California any more than Liisi meant to return here. And he wouldn't soon forgive her for the secretive way she'd left.

Anger burned in his gut. He felt betrayed—by Liisi, by Mima, and by the townspeople of Nogadata who'd professed eternal gratitude when he'd healed them. He should have learned by now to trust no one but himself.

The knock on the door startled Nick. As he strode to answer it, he scowled. Under the circumstances it could hardly be one of the townspeople welcoming him. No doubt someone needed his services. Damned if he'd provide any!

He grasped the knob and flung open the door.

Hank Ulrich's one good eye stared at him from the marred face. " 'Tis me, Doc. Thought you might could use my services again."

Chapter 19

Shortly before sundown on a late October afternoon in '67, three riders crested an oak-dotted hill and paused at the top to gaze at the valley below.

" 'Tis a goddamned castle!" Hank Ulrich exclaimed.

Nick stared in disbelief at the gray stone mansion, complete with a three-story tower, turrets, dormers, balconies, and seven chimneys. Had they come to the wrong place? He knew Liisi had money of her own—but this much?

"Liisi *said* she meant to build a big house." Mima's voice held awe.

Nick remained silent as he brought binoculars to his eyes. He swept over the valley—the castle and its outbuildings, a few cultivated fields, grassland, and a large pine grove. No other houses. No neighbors.

Far off, beyond the low hills hemming in the valley, rose snow-capped Sierra peaks. This was definitely the land he'd bought—the surveyor's map he carried pinpointed the location. According to the map, he owned this hill and those hills on the other side of the valley. He owned the entire valley except for a portion that curved to the east behind the southern hills.

Something white fluttered from the tower balcony and Nick zeroed in. Through the magnifying lenses he saw a woman waving a white scarf. At him. He caught a faint crackle of blue energy.

Liisi!

For an instant something deep within him rebelled, resenting her witch's ability to foresee, to know in advance he was coming. For a second or two he had difficulty separating Liisi's welcome of him from Wenda's entrapment of him in Pennsylvania.

Damn it, Liisi was his wife, not a conniving hexer!

"She's waving at us from the tower," he told the others, and urged his black into motion, suddenly unable to control his eagerness to hold Liisi again, despite his fury at what she'd done.

When she met him outside in the drive, he enfolded her in his arms, the sharp edge of his anger blunted. Nothing, he vowed, would ever separate him and Liisi again.

Later that night, softened by their lovemaking, he lay beside her in the new and large mahogany four-poster, with no anger at all left inside him.

"Why a twenty-room castle?" he asked, idly twisting a strand of her pale hair between his fingers. "You've only furnished seven of the rooms."

"When I cast the stones they told me to think of the future."

Nick didn't see how the future would affect the size of the house they'd need, since Liisi well knew there'd never be children. But at the moment he was too content to argue. "You might have written me," he said.

"What was the use? You would never have agreed to come to California even if I'd told you the stones and Mima's foreseeing said we must. Do you know Mima saw this very valley in her vision?"

"How could I know? The two of you conspire to keep secrets from me."

Liisi touched his lips with her fingers. "Will you swear you've never kept a secret from me?"

Instead of replying, he leaned over and kissed her, ending the conversation.

Because he'd had to travel to the valley from San Francisco, where their ship docked, Nick had seen for himself that the day of the Californios was over. The vast ranchos were gone, broken up into American-owned farms. He hadn't spotted even one don or vaquero on his journey and so he'd assured himself it was safe, after all, to remain in California.

As the days passed, Nick felt happy and at peace in his valley, more so outdoors than in the elaborate stone mansion with its peaked roofs and unfurnished rooms. Liisi had insisted all the rooms be paneled in walnut, oak, or mahogany, so despite the many windows, he found the vast castle a bit gloomy. She'd chosen the site well. Though in the valley, the house sat on a rise with a fine view of their property. Tramping the golden hills with their scattering of trees in the clefts where rainwater collected, he realized he never wanted to leave these lands. Was it possible he'd at last found his home?

He even liked their nearest neighbor, separated from them by about five miles. Paul McQuade had built a two-story adobe house in the part of the valley that curved out of sight behind the hills. McQuade raised cattle on the hills and vegetables and fruit on his valley acreage.

"He and his wife, Adele, have been kind to me," Liisi said. "Unlike others I could mention in Michigan. She's going to have a baby soon—I assured her you'd be here in time to help."

Though Nick had no desire to take up the practice of medicine again—he'd seen enough injured men for a lifetime—one week after his arrival, Paul McQuade rode in to ask for Dr. Deplacer's services. Just after midnight Nick delivered Adele of a healthy son, sandy-haired and square-shouldered like his father.

By the following spring, because Paul's fields produced a surplus of vegetables and fruit and Nick had money for financing, the two of them decided to set up a canning business in the closest community, a hamlet called Thompsonville some thirty miles to the east. Hank Ulrich was hired as manager.

The business thrived from the first and one year later they were doing well enough to buy produce from other small ranchers in the area. By the third year they'd doubled the size of the plant. Early in '72 Nick made up his mind to travel to San Francisco to increase the market for their products.

To his surprise, both Liisi and Mima protested.

"I've ridden to Sacramento a dozen times," he said. "Not once did either of you worry. What's so different about a trip to San Francisco?"

"Water," Mima said.

He stared at her in surprise. "Sacramento's on the American River—that's water, isn't it?"

"Mima saw the ocean, not a river," Liisi put in.

Nick turned to Mima. "You didn't mention a foreseeing. What was it?"

"Water and death," Mima said slowly. "A big ship, bigger than the one we sailed on. And drowning."

Nick smiled. "I promise I'll keep away from the bay and from ships. And I'm not a likely candidate for getting shanghaied."

"We warned you not to go to war," Liisi reminded him.

"I came back intact, didn't I?" he countered, beginning to feel testy.

Liisi's gray eyes held his. "Did you?" she asked.

He blinked. What did she mean? The saber slash had healed and he'd never admitted to her how close he'd come to shapeshifting during that battle. And it was true Hank Ulrich had saved him from that crazed private. His only other perilous encounter had been with the hex witch.

How could she know about that? Impossible.

Nick shook his head. "I'll be careful, but I'm riding to San Francisco."

He set off a week later on a soft April morning, riding his favorite black stallion, Nochi. He stopped in Thompsonville, spending the night at Ulrich's.

Hank, now in his fifties, had married a widow with grown children and was, he claimed, happier than he'd ever been in his life.

"I thought General Custer was the lucky one," he said to Nick as the two of them sat over coffee. "Yes, sir, I did. "But there's no doubt in my mind, Doc, as to how you were *my* piece of luck. Smartest thing I ever did was head for Michigan 'n find you 'stead of going home to Pennsylvania."

Hearing the state mentioned reminded Nick of Wenda. Ever since Liisi's implication that he hadn't come back from the war intact, the witch and her spells had been on his mind. He set down his coffee cup and leaned forward. "I think you told me once your folks were German."

"Pennsylvania Dutch, that's me."

"They're the ones with the hex signs on the barns."

Hank shook his head. "Not my folks. They wanted no truck with such foolishness. Didn't believe in hexing." He grinned. "Leastways, not out loud."

"Do you know anything about hex witches?"

Hank shrugged. "Some. People do talk."

"Is it true a hex witch can appear to someone without actually being there in person?"

"You mean sending a spirit like? Jesus, I don't know. Never heard one could. Mostly they stick pins in dolls and curse folks, all's I ever was told."

Damn it, Nick told himself, Wenda couldn't have really lain with me. Not in that meadow of the dead.

It was time to put her from his mind once and for all.

Two days later, at Sacramento, Nick boarded a riverboat for San Francisco. It wasn't until he reached his room at the Baldwin Hotel on the corner of Powell and Market that he realized he wasn't wearing his amulet. Not that it made any real difference—he often left it off when the moon wasn't full. The dark of the moon had just passed; he'd be home long before the next full moon. Besides, the chant was enough to keep him safe.

In the hotel dining room that evening he overheard talk of a ship in port.

"A big hulking three-master," the man said to his dining companion. "Painted and gilded like a parlor house madam. Those Russians don't do things by halves. Their officers wear as much braid as a Mexican general."

Russia. The word echoed in Nick's head. Where he'd come from, if Liisi was right about the language he spoke—and he had no reason to think she wasn't. He'd been a Russian before he became an American. Did he have family there? Would he ever find out?

The questions teased him through the meal, taking away his appetite. His increasing desire to have a look at the Russian ship finally made him push away from the table. He left the hotel, setting off for the docks through a twilight haze.

In his eagerness to reach the ship, Nick scarcely noticed the suffocating sensation of so many energies crowding about him. He'd suffered the feeling throughout the war years without ever really growing accustomed to it and he usually found cities even worse than army camps.

On the wharf, he stopped a passing roustabout to ask where the Russian ship was moored.

The man pointed. "Out there she be. Can't miss her."

When he spotted the three-master, Nick walked to the end of the pier and stared across the darkening water at the ship from his homeland. Sharp though his night vision was, he wasn't sure of the name on her bow. *Nachornaya,* he thought the first word was. Black.

Will I ever sail to Russia? he wondered. Is there any use? I don't even know my—

Belatedly, he sensed the rapid movement of energy behind him, someone rushing toward him. He whirled, throwing up his arm too late to deflect the blow. An iron bar caught him hard across the head, sending him to his knees, stunned.

"Diablo!" the man cried as he flung himself at Nick. *"Lobombre!* I knew you'd return one day."

Don Rafael! Dazedly, Nick struggled to throw off the Californio. He heard the unmistakable swish of metal against leather and realized Don Rafael had pulled a knife. Frantically he tried to twist free. Failed. Felt a burning pain along his side, unadulterated agony.

Silver, he thought dimly. Don Rafael's learned to use silver against me. He'll kill me with his silver knife. In desperation, Nick gripped the don's arm and threw himself over the edge of the pier, carrying the Californio with him. As they splashed into the chill water of the bay, Nick felt his guts wrench so violently he screamed. Then his head struck a piling and he knew no more.

Free! Hurt. Water. Swim. Hard to move legs, cloth binds them. Rip off. Dark. Need moon. Hurt, hurt, hurt. Danger. Man splashing nearby. Kill? Too weak. Swim away. He doesn't follow. Can't swim? Swim or drown. He drowns. Not me. Swim, not die. Never die. Live!

Weaker. Hurt. No shore, only water. Need moon. Can't swim any longer. Can't stay free.

Water poured from his mouth as he vomited, gasping for air. He lay on his stomach, naked, over a barrel, felt hands pummeling his back, forcing more water from him. His insides seemed filled with water.

When at last there was no more to be coughed up or vomited, the pummeling ceased. He was jerked upright, a man on each side. Sailors.

"All right now?" one asked.

"Yes." His voice was hoarse and he staggered with weakness.

"Got a nasty lump on your head, a knife slash over your ribs, and you damn near drowned. What happened?"

For a moment his mind was blank and then a torrent of memory flooded in, full of horrors he tried to shove from his head. He must say something, but he had to pick and choose, which was difficult in his dazed state.

"I need to sit down," he said.

A sailor ran up with a blanket. The man to his right—the first mate, judging by his uniform—wrapped it around him and eased him to the deck. He slumped against the bulkhead, hugging the blanket to him.

"I had gold," he said slowly. "My shipmates jumped me. Four of them. Robbed me, stripped me, beat me, and tossed me over the rail to drown."

"Not off this ship."

"No, not a Russian ship. American. I signed on in the islands."

"You got a name?"

"Sergei," he said. "Sergei Volek."

"We're the *Black Eagle*, out of Vladivostok, bound for home," the first mate said. "We're weighing anchor at dawn. If you want to be set ashore, tell me now."

Sergei shuddered, more from the images roiling in his mind than from what was said to him. Go ashore? He feared what was in his head, but he feared the unknown land ashore even more. He stared at the early night sky, noting the sliver of moon near the horizon. Setting. He'd be safe for a time.

"I need a berth," he said at last.

"We're short three seamen. We could use you. I'll ask the captain if he'll take you on. Where are you from?"

"St. Petersburg." It wasn't a lie. He'd been born there.

The mate nodded. "How old?"

"Nineteen."

The mate frowned. "Had a hard life, have you? You look at least ten years older." He turned to a sailor. "Volek needs a drink. Draw him a ration of vodka while I talk to Captain Gregorski. And slap a bandage on that knife slash."

Sergei swallowed the vodka thankfully, feeling his insides glow in response. His head had all but stopped aching, but his side still hurt. It puzzled him that the wound over his ribs was still open. He usually healed much faster.

The mate returned as the bandage was being wrapped around him. "The captain agreed we need another man,

Volek. Not superstitious, are you? You'll be inheriting a dead man's clothes."

Sergei glanced at the blanket wrapped around his nakedness and shrugged. "Beggars can't afford to be superstitious," he answered. "Thanks for the offer."

A few minutes later, the blanket still around him, he crawled into his appointed hammock and closed his eyes, exhausted.

A face formed behind his closed lids. His own face, down to the last detail, yet not his face. He bit his lip to keep from weeping as the memories he'd kept at bay exploded into his mind like an artillery shell, breaking his heart all over again. . . .

Chapter 20

Sergei Volek came to in pitch darkness, his heart hammering. He'd had the dream again, the nightmare of bloody death. He sat up, naked, shivering in the chill, and pulled on his reindeer-hide trousers. He reached over to touch Vladimir. His twin's pallet was empty.

"Vlad?" he called softly.

The exit ladder from their underground yurt leading up through the smoke hole creaked.

"Vlad?" he called, louder.

"No need to shout." Vladimir's voice.

Sergei heard him jump off the ladder onto the ground. A moment later red glowed as his twin blew on a smoldering coal to restart their fire in the pit below the ladder.

"I expected to be back before—" Vlad began. He broke off to look searchingly at Sergei, then glanced at the reindeer hide covering the woman's exit tunnel before turning back to face his brother.

"Are you all right?" Vlad demanded.

"I just woke up. Why wouldn't I be all right? Where were you?"

Vlad, crouching in front of the fire pit, didn't answer. "I had a bad dream," he said after a moment, "so I climbed the ladder to go out and get some air."

A tiny flame licked at the kindling, caught, and grew. Vladimir added more fuel. Sergei watched him, not believing a word his twin had said.

Shadows began to dance along the dirt walls of their yurt as the fire flared brighter. Vlad stood up, lean and rangy as a wolf. Sergei stared at him in confusion. This had happened before—two months ago. He'd roused from the same bloody nightmare to find himself alone. Vlad had crept in, then lied to him about where he'd been. Cold dread trickled along Sergei's spine.

What was wrong?

"You're sure you're all right?" Vlad repeated.

Sergei nodded.

"Gray Seal's been prowling around outside our yurt again," Vlad said.

Gray Seal, the Kamchadal tribe's shaman, had been unhappy ever since the two of them came to live in the native village after their guardian, the Cossack Peter Turgoff, had died. Twins, Gray Seal claimed, were bad luck and attracted evil spirits.

The Kamchadals had befriended the boys from the day they arrived from St. Petersburg, teaching the green-as-grass eleven-year-olds how to survive in Kamchatka. For six years Sergei and Vlad had hunted with the boys and men, gone fishing with them in the *bats* hollowed from poplar logs, and been made welcome in their underground dwellings.

Gray Seal had never been friendly, but he'd never spoken against them until they settled into this yurt after Turgoff was killed by a wolf in March. That March night two months ago was the first time Sergei had roused from a nightmare to find Vlad gone.

"What was it *you* dreamed tonight?" he asked Vlad.

His twin came to sit on the pallet next to him. "Like before. Running on all fours. Rending and tearing living flesh. The taste of blood. And—and enjoying it."

Sergei swallowed, imagining the salty taste of blood in his mouth. "I dreamed the same. Again. When I woke, you weren't here."

Vlad stared at him, then nodded to himself. "Serg, it's time to tell you the truth about why I was gone tonight. Past time. You'll have trouble believing me, but I swear it's true. Will you listen?" Vlad gazed into his eyes.

"Something's wrong," Sergei whispered. "I knew it was."

Vlad nodded.

The soft brush of hide boots against dirt startled both of them into leaping to their feet. A hand pushed aside the reindeer skin covering the woman's tunnel and a slim figure appeared in the opening.

"Deer Woman!" Sergei crossed to her.

She put her finger to her lips, shot a furtive glance at Vlad, then flung herself into Sergei's arms. He held her close. She was Gray Seal's daughter, the prettiest young woman in the Kamchadal tribe, and he was flattered she'd chosen him for her lover. Surprisingly, though he and Vlad were identical, she never confused them.

Deer Woman pulled away to look at him again, her black eyes, set slightly aslant in her round face, glazed with fear. Taking his arm, she led him to the wall of the yurt as far away from Vlad as possible. There she pulled his head down, but instead of kissing him she whispered into his ear.

"I was outside and saw your brother go down the smoke hole ladder. My father saw him, too. Even now he harangues the men to come after you both. To kill you."

Sergei looked toward Vlad, who'd turned his back to them.

"Why?" he asked her.

"Moss Belly lies dead, with his throat torn," she whispered. "Like the Russian who was your guardian. You must come with me through the woman's tunnel. Quickly. Let Gray Seal find only the guilty one here."

"Guilty? He can't think that Vlad—"

Deer Woman covered his lips with her hand. "Don't speak of it. We must hurry."

He shook his head, resisting her pull toward the tunnel. "Vlad comes with us."

"No!" Terror widened her eyes and shrilled her voice.

"Gray Seal is wrong. Vlad never killed a man. He wouldn't, not like that." Sergei spoke low, urgently. "He and I are as one person. I'd know."

She clamped her lips stubbornly together.

"Where I go, he goes," Sergei repeated, turning away from her and motioning to his brother. "Vlad, Gray Seal means to kill us. We've got to slip through the woman's exit and make a run for it."

As Vlad hastily pulled on his boots, Sergei crammed their hoard of gold coins into a wide leather belt he buckled around his waist next to his skin before donning his reindeer jacket with the sable-trimmed hood.

Deer Woman, standing by the tunnel, shifted from one foot to the other. "Hurry," she urged.

She crept ahead of them through the tunnel, never used by a Kamchadal man, lest he be defiled. Sergei came next, though Vlad usually led, for Sable Woman wouldn't let his twin near her. They eased into the frosty May night, where the north wind clutched at them with icy fingers. Clouds covered the stars and the moon.

"The *Alchovnik,*" Deer Woman said into Sergei's ear. "Hide there, it's your only chance to escape to Petropavlovsk."

There was no place of safety other than the port city where they might catch an outbound ship.

"Will you come with me?" he asked.

"With *you,* yes. With both of you, no."

But she left the village with them, hurrying along beside Sergei until they reached the wilderness of alder brush that grew so densely it was all but impenetrable—the *Alchovnik.*

"There's a bear trail here," she told Sergei. She raised herself to touch her lips to his. Before he could hold her close, she backed away from him and fled toward the village, disappearing into the darkness.

Sergei started to call after her, then shook his head. She was too afraid of Vlad to listen to any pleas. And she'd be safer in the village than with them.

Vlad crouched and entered the opening made in the tangle of alders by the Kamchatka bears, the only paths through the *Alchovnik.* Sergei plunged after him, grateful when the bite of the wind eased. For some reason he felt unusually tired and the cold cut to the bone.

In the blackness they crept along slowly, feeling their way, their fur mitts catching on the sharp alder twigs. Sergei looked back, seeing nothing but the dark.

"Do you think Gray Seal can convince the men to follow us?" he asked.

"We're all right if they don't set the dogs on our trail. But at best we won't make Petropavlovsk before late tomorrow."

They groped on and on in the darkness until Sergei's legs trembled with fatigue. He couldn't recall ever feeling so exhausted. By the time Vlad stopped to rest, Sergei slumped against his brother, too tired to speak.

Morning lightened the bear tunnel to a gray gloom before they went on. Overhead the sky was hidden by matted alders that also pressed in at them from both sides. They were forced to trot along at a crouch, since the pathway was barely wide and high enough to accommodate a full-grown bear traveling on all fours.

"Let's hope there's a ship waiting when we reach Petropavlovsk," Sergei said. "That's if we ever find our way through this tangle."

"Cheer up, Serg." Vlad glanced back at him as he spoke, his face no more than a blur of white in the gloom.

Sergei had no need to see Vlad's face. It was identical to his—high cheekboned with golden eyes and a curly black beard. Quite different from the Kamchadal men, with their broad flat faces, slanted eyes, and scanty facial hair.

"I'll cheer up when we're aboard an outbound ship," Sergei said.

"Maybe I should call on old *Kut* to have one ready and waiting for us at the wharf in Petropavlovsk."

Sergei snorted. *Kut* was Raven, the Kamchadal version of their creator. It was wise to beware of any gift from that old trickster.

"You'd do better praying to God," he said.

"I've already tried that." Vlad's voice lost its lightness. "I'm afraid God's abandoned us, like Father did."

In the six years they'd been here, neither of the twins had discovered a reason for their exile to cold and gloomy Kamchatka. Did what happened last night have anything to do with Father's decision to send them here? Sergei wondered. At the same time he realized he didn't want to know exactly what had happened—not if it involved Vlad, the person dearest to him in all the world. He'd die for Vlad.

Not once had Vlad asked him why Gray Seal had decided to kill them, although Sergei was certain his twin hadn't overheard Deer Woman's whispers. Was it because he already knew?

As if in answer, Vlad increased his speed. Sergei hurried to catch up, the heaviness of the gold coins in his waist belt matching the heaviness of his heart.

The gold had come from their father—all that was left of home, gold coins and a few hazy memories of their parents and their sister in St. Petersburg.

Sounds were muffled in the wild tangle surrounding them, but Sergei knew if dogs were tracking them he'd hear them howl. The Kamchadals were excellent hunters even without their dogs, though. He looked over his shoulder to check their back trail and found no sign of pursuit, but the trail twisted and turned so crazily it was impossible to see farther than a few yards.

Vlad shouted an alarm. Quickly Sergei turned, but too late to stop from slamming into his twin. Vladimir sprawled headlong. Sergei stumbled sideways, the sharp alder twigs stabbing at his shoulder.

In the gloom ahead, a Kamchatka bear snorted, swinging its head from side to side to pick up their scent.

Before Vlad could scramble to his feet, the bear charged. Sergei yanked his knife from its belt scabbard, leaped free of the clinging brush, and flung himself into the bear's path, shouting in defiance.

The bear was huge, all but filling the tunnel. Sergei knew the overhanging alders would keep it from rising onto its hind legs, but it could as easily kill them on all fours. The bear opened a yellow-fanged mouth, roaring a challenge. Its rank odor filled his nostrils.

He had one chance. A native trick. Sergei turned the knife, a small Kamchadal dagger, point upward. He tried to step aside as he rammed the knife into the bear's open mouth. Sharp teeth raked his forearm as he thrust the dagger point as hard as he could into the roof of the bear's mouth and left it there.

The bear's shoulder hit Sergei, knocking him flat. He rolled away, then sprang to his feet. Vlad, knife in hand, stood beside him.

The bear howled in pain, rearing up, head crunching into the alder branches. Blood dripped from its muzzle, mouth held open by the dagger in its throat. It was a male, brown fur grizzled with age.

Vlad jerked his head, pointing forward. Sergei hesitated. Shouldn't they try to finish off the animal? Vlad grabbed his arm, pulling him along. The bear groaned and pawed at its mouth, paying no heed to them as they dodged past. Sergei knew the bear was doomed. Eventually the dagger point would penetrate its brain and kill the animal, but he wished it were already dead and out of agony.

"He'll last long enough to scare off any pursuers," Vlad said when they'd put several twists of the trail between themselves and the bear. He grinned at Sergei. "You spiked him as neatly as any Kamchadal."

Maybe so, but he'd lost his knife and now was unarmed. Sergei tried to tell himself it didn't matter, that no one was in pursuit, that there'd be a ship waiting when they reached the town. His arm throbbed where the bear's teeth had penetrated the reindeer-hide sleeve, and he clenched his jaw against the pain as he ran behind Vlad. Just as well the bear's teeth got him instead of Vlad—he healed faster.

If the Kamchadals overtook them, they'd be forced to fight. Sergei pictured old Gray Seal in his shaman's bear headdress exhorting the men to track them down, believing them to be evil spirits in the form of humans. Kill them and throw the severed pieces of their bodies to the scavengers.

"You saved my neck," Vlad said. "That damned bear meant to turn me into dog meat."

"You'd have done the same for me."

Vlad's smile faded. "Always. No matter what. Remember that, Serg."

"We're running because Moss Belly was murdered last night," Sergei said, hoping to rid himself of his dark suspicions about his brother.

"I know."

"His throat was torn out. Like Turgoff's in March."

"Yes."

A question hovered on Sergei's lips. Did you do it, Vlad? He couldn't ask it. What difference would it make if he knew for sure? Vlad was his twin, his other. No matter what, just as Vlad had said.

"Moss Belly was Deer Woman's suitor," Vlad commented.

"She didn't want him."

"No, she preferred you. Moss Belly meant to kill you."

Sergei thought this highly likely. The man had been glowering at him for weeks. Is that why Vlad— No, he refused to think about it.

They ran on in silence. Rested. Ran again. The tunnel grew gloomier and Sergei knew it must be getting close to evening.

"Do you think we're lost in here?" he asked.

"No, the brush is thinning," Vlad called over his shoulder.

Moments later, Sergei stood with his brother in the open on the side of a hill above Petropavlovsk. Dusk shadowed circular Avacha Bay and, beyond, the cold sweep of Bering Sea lay past its narrow mouth. Lights flickered from ships anchored in the harbor and glowed from windows of the houses ashore.

To their left loomed the three volcanos. Kamchatka Peak belched smoke and flame above the snow covering its cone. The ground trembled.

"The mountain spirits are loose tonight," Vlad said. "It ought to make the Kamchadals forget about us."

"Maybe." Sergei glanced at the sky. Cloud-covered, as usual. "Let's not take any chances, just the same."

Vlad looked up at the clouds, wet his forefinger, then held the finger into the air. "The wind's from the northwest. A seagoing wind to blow ships through the bay mouth into the ocean. Come on, Serg, we'll find ourselves one of those ships."

They threaded their way downhill through birch groves. By the time they approached the outskirts of the town, darkness surrounded them. As they hurried along the narrow streets, Sergei swiveled his head from side to side, checking each alleyway.

"Not so fast," he warned. "Make sure the way is clear."

"We've left them far behind," Vlad scoffed. "How could they get here ahead of us?"

"They couldn't. But Gray Seal could have sent some kind of message to the Kamchadals who live just south of town."

"Not unless old *Kut* flew with magic wings to deliver his message for him. Gray Seal has you spooked, Serg. Do you actually believe he can send his spirit traveling through the air?" Vlad grinned and punched Sergei's shoulder with his fist.

"I don't know what I believe anymore." He grabbed at Vlad's arm. "Slow down."

Vlad shook him off. "We're almost to the wharf." He quickened his pace to a trot.

The hair on the back of Sergei's neck bristled with unease even though he could find no reason. Lights from windows cast dim squares onto the mud of the road, enough light so he could tell the few men he passed were Russians, not natives, but he couldn't shake the feeling danger was close at hand.

He started to call a warning to Vlad when the moon broke through the clouds, flooding the street with its pale light. He drew in his breath as the rays touched him.

"Hurry!" Vlad shouted back at him.

Sergei began to run, seeing Vlad disappear around the corner of a warehouse. He could hear the lap of water against the dock pilings. The tall masts of a ship thrust above the roofs. They were in luck. He didn't care where the ship might be headed; anyplace was better than Kamchatka.

Sergei had almost reached the corner of the warehouse when he heard a man shout from somewhere ahead.

"Kitaii!"

The Kamchadal word for wolf.

Suddenly the night was hideous with noise. Over the snarls of dogs and the yells of angry and frightened men, Sergei heard Vlad's warning cry and flung himself around the corner of the building. Men and dogs surrounded Vlad. Shouting in rage, Sergei ran toward his brother.

A gut-wrenching twist in his middle staggered Sergei. He gasped as he felt himself turning inside out. An indescribable tingling shot from the base of his spine up his back and into his skull.

What was happening to him?

A malamute broke loose from the pack and flew at him, fangs gleaming white in the moonlight. Sergei tried to crouch to meet the dog's attack, but a desperate need to be naked overwhelmed him and he tore at his clothes, struggling to release the heaviness binding him around the middle.

The malamute stopped abruptly, turned tail, and fled, whining. Sergei groaned with the wrenching agony, at the same time realizing his senses had never been so keen. He smelled the fear of the dog. The terror of the Kamchadals penetrated through the fishy odor of seal oil smeared on their bodies. His ears hurt from Vlad's screams.

Though his body still felt as though it were being torn apart, he raced toward the men attacking his twin. A Kamchadal lifted a huge silver cross above his head, a cross whose end was filed to dagger sharpness. Three other men held Vlad spread-eagled on the ground. The cross slammed down, piercing his brother's beast. Vlad cried out once and was silent. At the same time a terrible pain struck Sergei's chest. He howled in anguish and rage. Then all went dark.

Free! He heard men's shouts of triumph change to terror as he launched himself at the throat of the man holding the cross. His teeth tore flesh and the taste of blood ran salty on his tongue. He spat, not liking human blood.

Turning on the others, he heard their cries of panic as he slashed right and left with his sharp fangs. Men and dogs ran from his murderous fury. Only one man stood his ground on the edge of the quay, an old man wearing the head of a bear atop his own. An eerie blue glow surrounded him.

He recognized Gray Seal.

"We meet, Wolf," the shaman said. "And you will die like your other half."

He growled deep in his throat. The red of bloodlust dimmed his vision, clouded his mind.

Gray Seal raised an ivory-handled dagger, the blade gleaming silver in the moonlight. "Come to me, Wolf," he crooned. "Come to your death."

Gray Seal shimmered in his sight and changed to a bear with a dagger in its throat, a bear thirsting for blood. Then the bear shimmered and changed back to a man.

He longed to taste the shaman's blood; the urge to kill ran molten in his reins. But he held, watching warily. What challenged him was not merely a man.

The shaman chuckled, a cold and fearful sound. "You are afraid, Wolf," he taunted. "You know who will win."

Wrongness sent the hackles bristling on his back. Why didn't he smell seal oil? The rank odor of bear? The shaman sent off no scent at all.

His lips pulled back from his fangs in a threatening snarl. Gray Seal's dark eyes flashed blue flame as he sprang at the shaman. Gray Seal shimmered again, losing substance. When his fangs sought the shaman's throat they found not flesh but air. He attacked no man; he attacked nothing at all.

Blue sparks crackled along his fur, burning like fire. Too late he realized where his leap would take him and tried to twist sideways to avoid plunging over the edge of the wharf.

Down he plummeted, splashing into the icy waters of Avacha Bay. Just before he went under, he thought he heard the shaman's triumphant laughter. The numbing chill of the water soaked through his fur until his bones were ice. As he rose to the surface, he felt a wrench. He was shifting, changing, his mind whirling dizzily as he fought to keep from sinking beneath the water. A heaviness at his waist threatened to drag him under.

* * *

Sergei came to himself, naked, paddling weakly beside the hull of an anchored ship. The moon was gone; he swam in darkness. With fingers so cold they could scarcely feel, he scrabbled at the slippery wood of the ship but found no handholds. Water washed over his face, choking him.

Vlad was dead. He was drowning. Dying. The Kamchadals had won. He'd soon join Vlad.

No!

Sergei struggled to the surface, driven by a force rising from deep within him, a life force he was unable to resist. Again he desperately explored for a handhold, finally touching something that moved under his fingers. He clutched it.

A rope ladder.

Painfully he pulled his chilled body up the side of the ship. As he dragged himself over the rail, Sergei looked back at the lights of Petropavlovsk. His lips formed his brother's name.

He looked down at his own nakedness. *"Oborot,"* he whispered. "Shapeshifter."

Not Vlad but Sergei.

He was the guilty one. The evil, vile one. No dreams, his nightmares of running in the night, of blood and torn flesh. Vlad had followed him and seen, had tried to watch over him, to keep him safe. Vlad had died in his place.

If he'd understood what he was before now, he might have been able to save his brother. But he hadn't remembered the earlier changes any more than he remembered what had happened after this last one. Would he have believed even if Vlad had told him? He could hardly believe it now.

The moon slid from behind a cloud. Sergei watched with growing alarm while its silver light traced a path leading east across the bay. His body began to tingle as though the light were warm.

The moon! Somehow the moon triggered his changing. He dived for the darkness of the hold, hearing a sailor shout at him, and fought frantically against the moon's power. He had to remain a man. If he changed shape aboard the ship, they'd discover what he was.

They'd kill him.

Sergei knew he deserved death, but the darkness dwelling within him commanded him to live and he was powerless to resist.

Chapter 21

Six months later, in September, Sergei Volek reined in his Mongolian pony in a spruce grove on a low hill outside St. Petersburg, looking down at a country lodge—a frame building of two stories with a one-story ell on the south side. The dacha was badly in need of paint. Weeds and alder and birch saplings thrived in the once meticulously landscaped grounds. Holes marred the roof of one outbuilding, and another leaned crazily.

Before their exile, he and Vlad had come every summer to this dacha. Then, everything from house to fields had been well-kept. His throat still tightened when he thought of his dead twin, the more so since he'd learned from the sailors on the *Black Eagle* during the crossing how many years had passed between that terrible night in Kamchatka and now.

He recalled the two years after leaving Petropavlovsk, but he could remember nothing that had happened to him after his Spanish shipmates on *Sea Maid* had beaten him and flung him overboard off the California coast. How he'd survived, where he'd lived, what he'd done in those twenty-four missing years was a blank. He could hardly believe he was forty-two, not nineteen.

Obviously he'd learned to control his shapeshifting—but who had taught him the charm to prevent it, the strange words he found himself chanting when the moon neared full? What enemy had attacked him and left him to drown in San Francisco Bay?

Sergei shook his head. He might never learn what had happened during the missing years, but he was determined to discover why he and his twin had been exiled to Kamchatka so ruthlessly, why they'd never been told of their dreadful heritage. Vlad had died because neither of them knew about the shapeshifting. The man who could answer his questions, the man responsible for Vlad's death, lived in the dacha.

Taking a deep breath, he urged the pony through the trees and down the hill.

At the front door, he stared a long moment at the knocker. Then he lifted the black iron wolf's head and slammed it hard onto the metal plate once, twice, three times.

"I'm here, damn you," he muttered. "I've come home."

A pretty young woman with brown hair opened the door and, before he thought, Sergei cried, "Sonya!"

She smiled wistfully. "I'm Natasha Gorski," she said. "You must have known my mother."

Sonya was her mother! His sister, Sonya. *Must have known,* Natasha had said, instead of *must know.* Was his sister dead? True, she'd been twenty when he and Vlad were born—but now dead?

Pulling himself together, he said, "I'm sorry if I distressed you. I've come to call on Alexis Volek."

Natasha frowned, her eyes flicking over him. At last her brow cleared and she stepped aside, her gesture inviting him in. "May I ask your name?" she said.

"Sergei Volek. He'll know who I am."

"A relative!" Nastasha's voice rose excitedly. "How wonderful! I thought you looked quite a bit like grandfather. He and I believed no one in the family was left alive except the two of us. Please come this way."

Sergei followed her, puzzled. Wouldn't Sonya's daughter have heard his name? Or had he and Vlad been expunged from all family records? Alexis Volek had a great deal to answer for.

Natasha led him into the small book-lined room he remembered from his summers here as a study. A white-haired man sat in a cracked leather chair, reading, an oil lamp on a table to his right, a pipe on an ash-stand to his left. The man looked up from his book and Sergei stopped, his throat closing over as his eyes met the sad, dark eyes of Alexis.

Where was the vigorous black-haired man he remembered so well? His father was old beyond belief.

"Grandfather, this is Sergei Volek," Natasha said into the silence. "Do you know, he mistook me for my mother?"

The book dropped from Alexis's hands, sliding onto the floor. "No," he whispered. "No, impossible."

Sergei swallowed. "My brother is dead, but I'm very much alive."

Alexis rose. Spreading his arms wide, he strode across the room. Before Sergei could move he found himself gripped in a bear hug.

"My son, my son," Alexis murmured, his voice cracking. "My dear, lost son Sergei. God has not forgotten me, after all."

Without warning, tears filled Sergei's eyes. His arms rose to hold his father close. At this moment there were no questions he needed answered.

Half an hour later Alexis and Sergei sat at a small pine table in the kitchen while Natasha served bread, butter, berry jam, and cheese. Tea bubbled in the samovar.

"We have little enough these days, my son," Alexis said. "Not so much as a cook or a maid. Do you recall the house in St. Petersburg?"

Sergei nodded. "I tried to find you there at first."

Alexis sighed. "Because I had been a guest lecturer at the university, my enemies found ways to link my name with the student Communists. After that young and crazy Communist fool Karakozov tried to assassinate Czar Alexander last April, I was lucky to escape with my life." He smiled wryly. "I'm fortunate they left me this dacha in addition to my life. Poor Natasha's father didn't fare as well; she's now an orphan." He glanced at his granddaughter. "Luckily, Natasha and I have each other."

"Communists?" Sergei asked, confused. What were they?

"I forget you've been sailing on ships all this time and missed the changes. But this is no time to talk of politics; this is a time of celebration. I'll just say that after the serfs were set free in '61, Russia went crazy. Voleks have always been loyal to their czars; I'm no exception. Alas, a man makes enemies who seek to undermine him. And often succeed."

After they ate, Alexis brought Sergei back into the study, shutting the door and waving him to a chair.

"I know you have questions," Alexis said when he'd seated himself, "but they must be asked in private and you must save them until you hear my story. What I have to tell you, son, is for your ears alone. You must never speak of this to anyone except your eldest son, should you have one."

Sergei shook his head. "No children. I'll never have children." He hoped he spoke the truth. God knows he wouldn't inflict shapeshifting on an innocent child. He could only pray he'd felt the same during those missing years.

Alexis took his pipe and turned it over in his hands without filling it with tobacco. "I'll begin," he said at length, "with a night in 1830, when you were but four months old."

At midnight Alexis Volek stood next to the nursery door in the upstairs hall of his city house. Outside, St. Petersburg was quiet after the week of festivities celebrating the completion of the paved highway to Moscow. In a few years there'd be a railroad. Times were changing in Russia, and for the better.

Unfortunately, there were some things that never changed. His jaw clenched as he fingered the hilt of the silver dagger he wore at his belt. His appointment to court meant he could delay no longer. What use would he be to Czar Nicholas if anyone found out?

He eased open the nursery door, hearing the snores of the fat peasant girl that Varda had imported from Finland as a nursemaid. Embers glowed in the fireplace like the red eyes of wolves. There was no sound at all from the wide double cradle that stood before the hearth. On its burnished hood the gold inlay of the Volek family crest shone dully in the gleam of the dying fire—two men standing, each with an arm about the shoulders of the other.

It was three generations since the double cradle had been in use. Why, after so many years of peace, were the Voleks again cursed with twin boys?

Alexis slipped silently across the room to the cradle and looked down at the sleeping babies. Which was Sergei, which Vladimir? Identical curls of dark hair lay on the forehead of each as they snuggled together. A father had a right to be proud of such healthy and handsome sons.

If he and they weren't Voleks.

His fingers traced the golden crest on the cradle's hood as he watched the babies. He felt the head of the figure on the right—round, a man's head. His fingers moved to the left, felt an identical head. There was no irregularity to show it had been altered by his great-grandfather, the pointed ears lopped off, the pointed muzzle removed. The original Volek crest with its fearful history no longer existed.

But his twins did.

Alexis sighed and crossed himself. He eased the slim dagger from its sheath. Slowly he raised the dagger above the cradle.

One of the babies opened his eyes, golden eyes. Outside the house a carriage clattered past. Alexis and his son stared at one another while the clop of hoofbeats and the rattle of wheels faded into silence. He wondered if the child somehow knew what he intended to do and his fingers trembled on the knife hilt.

The other boy opened his identical golden eyes and looked up at his father. His lips parted in a wide smile, whereupon his twin began to smile, too.

Alexis closed his eyes. His hand fell to his side. How could he be expected to plunge a knife into the hearts of these smiling innocents?

One of the boys *was* completely innocent. Why must he die because his brother bore a curse? If only there was a way to tell which was afflicted. There wasn't, Alexis knew. Not for many years to come—not until manhood, when the taint of the cursed one would burst into evil flower when the moon rose full.

I should have drowned them at birth like unwanted puppies, he told himself. Should have dropped them into a sack weighted with stones and tossed them into the Neva when they were still squalling red newborns fresh from Varda's womb.

Now it was too late. He'd grown fond of them, his two darling sons. Yet he couldn't let them live.

The evil was ancient, stretching back so far into family history it was hard to believe his ancestors had ever lived free of the sign of the *volka,* the wolf.

He remembered his father telling him the story when he was thirteen, saying he was entering into manhood and must bear the burden of bitter knowledge to pass on to future generations.

Hundreds of years before, there had lived a girl named Samara who'd been one of his forebears. Samara was beautiful but strange, given to wandering in the forest despite the danger of wolves. And of worse. The local wise woman warned Samara that the *lieshui,* the spirits of the forest, sooner or later would ensorcell her, but Samara refused to listen.

Though she paid no attention to the village youths who came to court her, one day Samara brought a stranger home with her, a man dressed in silver-gray who wore a cloak of wolfskins. Samara smiled at him and would look at no one else. She said his name was Volek.

Her family, along with the rest of the villagers, disliked and feared this man from the forest, but when it became clear Samara was with child, her father gave her to the stranger in marriage.

On the night after the wedding a full moon rose. It was then the wise woman crept into the bedroom of Samara's father and woke him.

"Death rides the moon," she hissed. "You have welcomed a beast into your house. You have wedded your daughter to a son of the forest spirits, an *oborot* who is both man and beast. Rise and stab him with a silver knife while he sleeps or he will kill you all and gobble your hearts before morning."

Samara's father roused his three sons and, armed with knives, they slipped into the bridal chamber and fell on the slumbering groom. The sons withdrew in terror when the stranger's flesh, penetrated by their steel knives, closed over immediately. But the father's silver knife rose and fell until blood stained the bedcovers and dripped onto the floor.

The bridegroom howled and fell back against the bed. Though they believed he must be dead, when he began to change into a horrible beast, the men took fright, gathered up the screaming Samara, and ran from the room, carrying her to the wise woman.

The woman forced infusions of herbs down the girl's throat to rid her of the child she carried. When her father and his sons returned to drag away the beast, he was gone. Neither he nor the stranger were ever seen again.

Samara didn't miscarry, despite all the potions she was fed. When she was finally brought to the birthing bed, she fell into a trance when the first child was born and died as the second child slipped from her womb. Her father meant to kill the babies, but when he saw how human they looked—identical twin boys who, except for their golden eyes, resembled his own sons when they had been babies—he hadn't the heart.

The old wise woman, who might have convinced him the twins must not live, was dead herself by this time, savaged by a wolf while she hunted for firewood in the forest. Or at least the villagers preferred to believe it was a wolf.

Samara's twins grew to manhood and the full moon rose and one of them . . . changed. The villagers hunted him and stabbed him through the heart with a silver dagger when he returned to human form. And so he died, but the other escaped, fleeing to a faraway city. There he took the name of Volek, which was his by right, and in due course luck brought him a wealthy wife who bore him nine children, none of them twins.

"But every time twin boys are born into the Volek family, if they are identical one will carry the curse of the *oborot*," Alexis's father had finished. "For many years we've been fortunate. You must never forget, though, that it can happen. It is your duty to tell this story to your eldest son when he comes of age so he may pass on the warning."

Alexis opened his eyes. It seemed to him that his sons had looked into his soul and knew what dwelt there. The dagger in his hand seemed heavier than silver, as heavy as lead.

"You must wield a silver knife," his father had warned. "Else an *oborot* will not die."

Somehow he must bring himself to use this knife of ancient silver.

The opening door of the nursery crashed into the wall. He whirled to see who dared disturb him. Varda rushed to his side, her eyes wide and frightened.

"Alexis, no!" she cried, seeing the dagger.

The Finnish nursemaid groaned and sat up on her cot, rubbing her eyes. Hastily Alexis sheathed his knife. Varda was bending over the cradle to look at her babies and he put his arm around her waist, urging her toward the nursery door. Behind them one of the boys began to cry, joined by his twin. Varda hesitated.

"Let the nursemaid care for them," Alexis said, drawing his unwilling wife through the door and down the hall, where he led her into their bedroom, closing the door.

He faced her, hands on her shoulders. "It's best not to grow too attached to the boys," he told her.

"They're my babies!" she cried, flinging away from him.

"One is. The other is something besides that, as I've warned you. Something evil."

"So you say."

"I speak the truth. On the brink of manhood either Sergei or Vladimir will become a ravening monster. Not only will we be in danger, but our lives will be ruined. We'll be ostracized. Forced to leave St. Petersburg, if not Russia. If our daughter Sonya marries young Gorski, he'll cast her into the street once he knows. Is this what you want for us, Varda?"

"I don't believe it has to happen, even if what you tell me is true."

"It will happen."

"The boys are still my babies. Until it does happen, you can't keep me from them."

Alexis looked down at her dark loveliness, feeling his insides twist. They were his babies, too.

"I saw you at the cradle with the knife," Varda whispered. "If you use it, if you commit such a terrible sin, I swear to you I will kill myself."

He sighed, defeated. "I give you my word I won't use the knife on our twins. I haven't the heart. We'll keep the boys with us as long as it's safe—until they're eleven or twelve. Then they'll have to be sent away. I have holdings in Kamchatka—that might be the best place for them."

"Kamchatka! Why, there's nothing in that wilderness except a few natives and their dogs."

"Exactly," Alexis said. "In such surroundings, when the evil surfaces, the *oborot* can do little harm to anyone. I'll send Turgoff with the boys. He'll have to know the truth so he'll be prepared to act when one . . . changes. There is no man I trust more than Turgoff; he would never betray me. When Turgoff returns with the normal boy the death of his twin will be called an accident."

"And if there is no change, what then?"

"If I'm wrong, I'll thank God and bring the twins home when they're twenty-one."

She bit her lip. "If you're right and the worst happens—what of the other? What if he kills his brother before Turgoff can stop him?"

"Nothing will happen to the unaffected twin. He's the only person in the world safe from his brother once the changing begins."

* * *

Sergei stared at his father after the old man finished the tale. He knew in his heart he couldn't have harmed Vlad, beast or not. But Vlad had died because of him, anyway.

He knew now it was no wolf who'd savaged Turgoff. The beast inside him had killed the Cossack to save its own life. Just as it had killed the Kamchadal man who sought Sergei's death. And Vlad knew how Turgoff and Moss Belly had died; he'd watched the shapeshift, followed the beast, and seen the killings.

If only Vlad had told me what I was, what I'd done, Sergei agonized.

Would I have believed him if he had?

"You must take care," Alexis warned. "Twin sons must be smothered at birth because there's no way to predict which twin will grown up to change under the moon. Voleks must not loose a beast on the world. I failed in my duty, yet if I had not, when I die Natasha would be left alone and helpless. God was good; the beast twin died, you lived."

Sergei couldn't bring himself to tell his father the truth.

"Your brother didn't by any chance father a child on some Kamchadal girl before his death, did he?" Alexis asked.

Sergei's heart leaped in sudden horror. As far as he knew, Vlad had not. But what about him? He'd lain with Deer Woman more than once. How did he knew she hadn't been with child when he and Vlad escaped from the village? The possibility had never once occurred to him. Until this moment. He cringed at the thought of a beast inadvertently left to run loose among the Kamchadals.

"Father," he said slowly, "I must go back to Kamchatka and make certain no Volek child lives."

Alexis started to protest, then stopped and nodded. "It is your duty," he agreed. "Natasha and I will wait for your return."

Chapter 22

Riding across Nevsky Prospeckt, the main street of St. Petersburg, on a cool and overcast June morning, Sergei turned to glance at the boy he'd shepherded from Kamchatka across thousands of miles of snow and biting cold. Wolf had learned to sit a horse correctly even if his table manners left much to be desired. He stood straight now instead of crouched over and had almost lost his feral look.

Sergei had entered the Kamchadal village posing as a trader. He'd never forget his first sight of nine-year-old Wolf, huddled naked inside a filthy pen as if he were an animal. The boy had given him one frightened sidelong glance and cringed away as if expecting a blow.

At the time, Sergei had had no idea who the boy was, but he had to quell his impulse to tear open the pen and free the child immediately. Instead, he concealed his sick horror and turned away to face Owl Wing, the tribal shaman now that Gray Seal was dead. So far none of the Kamchadals, including Owl Wing, had recognized Sergei—though any real shaman would quickly recognize power in another. But Owl Wing lacked the blue crackle that Gray Seal had possessed, making Sergei wonder just how effective a shaman he was.

Still, there was no question Owl Wing had tribal prestige. Best to move carefully.

"Are the boy's parents dead?" Sergei asked, moving on past the pen, hoping his question sounded idle.

"He is not a boy but a wolf cub," Owl Wing insisted. "That is why we pen him."

"Why not simply kill him and have done?"

"Too dangerous. Wolf's grandfather was a beast in human form. If we kill his spawn, who knows what havoc the freed animal spirit within the boy might wreak upon our village? Luckily the mother died bearing a second child. It, too, died, so we were spared another such as Wolf."

Sergei's heart leaped within him. Owl Wing meant him! *He* was the beast in human form. He gritted his teeth. His daughter by Deer Woman was dead, as Deer Woman herself was. How dare they pen his grandson? He couldn't sleep that night for thinking of the child, miserable and naked in his cage. In the morning, he made the shaman an offer.

"I collect curiosities," he said. "I will buy this wolf cub, take him from your village, and exhibit him in the Western cities."

Owl Wing glowered at him. "Never! We do not loose a beast on the world."

Sergei shrugged, trying to appear unconcerned. "Too bad. I would pay well. Does the boy have no living relatives I might talk to?"

"None. He is not for sale."

Two nights later, Owl Wing conducted a hunting ceremony, an involved and intricate performance of divination, using the innards of seals. As the drums pounded and the bells tinkled, Sergei crept to the pen and wrenched it open.

Wolf cowered away from him, whimpering.

"Hush!" Sergei commanded. "I am your grandfather, come to take you home with me."

Wolf went limp, allowing Sergei to toss him onto his shoulder and carry him off. Days later, as the two fled for their lives, Sergei discovered that the terrified Wolf had believed, like the other Kamchadals, that his grandfather was truly a beast and meant to kill and eat him.

They'd traveled for months across cold, barren Siberia to reach St. Petersburg, and every day Wolf had become less of an animal and more of a human—but Sergei kept wondering if the boy would ever completely trust him.

Now, at last in St. Petersburg, Wolf's expression was dazed as he stared uncomprehendingly at the ornate and beautiful buildings of the city. Sergei shook his head, thinking of what Alexis would say when he saw the boy and discovered he was the great-grandfather of this odd creature.

I never intended to be a father, he thought, but damned if I'm not already a grandfather.

Wolf had been a single birth, not a twin, so he was safe from the shapeshifting. When he was older Sergei meant to teach him about his dark heritage so the boy wouldn't pass on the Volek curse. His energy aura was peculiar—not a normal human red glow, nor the blue crackle of a witch or true shaman. It was a strange shade of violet, a color Sergei had never seen before—as though red and blue had somehow merged. As far as he could determine, the boy showed no unusual abilities.

Perhaps he never would—and be the happier for it.

Turning off on the road leading to the dacha, Sergei made certain Wolf followed on his shaggy Mongolian pony. At first the boy's sad plight had outraged and distressed him. He'd been determined to help the child, but he'd had no real feeling for Wolf himself. During their long and difficult journey together, though, the boy's courage, obvious intelligence, and eager curiosity had impressed Sergei. Gradually, fearfully, he'd grown fond of Wolf, despite his determination to remain aloof. The lesson he'd learned when Vlad had died was that it was dangerous to love anyone.

Wolf was an unusual-looking boy with the black slanted eyes and straight black hair of the Kamchadals. But instead of their round face and full features, Wolf's face was thin, his features sharp. He promised to be taller than most Kamchadal men as well. His skin was sallow, not as dark as a Kamchadal's or as light as a Russian's.

Whatever he looks like, he's mine, Sergei thought. My grandson. Will I ever get used to the idea?

When they reached the dacha he'd trim the boy's hair as well as his own. They were both as shaggy as their ponies after the long trek through the wilderness.

"We're almost to my father's house," he called to Wolf in Kamchadal, not yet able to think of the dacha as home.

Wolf nodded once. Though he spoke Kamchadal well enough and had learned considerable Russian on the journey, he seldom said anything that wasn't absolutely necessary.

"You will address my father as sir," Sergei reminded him, "and his granddaughter as Cousin Natasha."

Again the single nod.

They rode in silence until they came to the lane to the dacha. As they turned in, Wolf's head lifted and his nostrils dilated as he sniffed the air. "Ashes from fire," he said in Russian.

Now that it was called to his attention, Sergei noticed the same smell. No doubt peasants burning old stubble off a field.

"You'll be able to see the dacha when we reach the top of this next hill," he told Wolf.

As they climbed through the spruce grove to the crest of the hill, Wolf smiled. Spruce trees he knew, and he breathed in the familiar odor gratefully. The place his grandfather called St. Petersburg had frightened him with its clamor, crowds of strangely dressed people, and gigantic buildings. He was glad they were not to live there.

His life had changed so completely, he hadn't caught up yet to the changes. He wondered if he ever would. To him, his grandfather was a god. Grandfather didn't look or act like a beast. He never beat him or hurt him in any way; he gave him food, clothes, taught him skills and answered questions. Wolf wasn't certain how long these pleasures would last, but he meant to enjoy them while they did.

He kicked his pony into a faster pace to keep up with Grandfather and they reached the summit at the same time.

"Oh, my God!" Grandfather cried, looking down.

Wolf followed his gaze and drew in his breath. There was the fire he'd smelled. The blackened remains of a wooden house lay below, the ash stench strong.

Grandfather spurred his pony and raced down the hill. Wolf followed as best he could, fearing to let his grandfather out of his sight. All his good fortune came from the tall man with the curly black hair and beard who'd set him free from the horror of the pen. He'd begun to believe that Owl Wing had lied about Grandfather—how could such a godlike man be a beast?

Grandfather reined in sharply. A moment later a man appeared from behind a small unburned building with a gaping hole in its roof.

"Who are you?" Grandfather demanded of the man.

"Don't be angry, honored sir," the man said. "I am Gregor and I mean no harm. I have a small farm nearby." Wolf knew enough Russian words to understand the meaning.

"Where's my father?" Grandfather asked sharply.

"Dead, sir, in the fire the soldiers set. We buried him two days ago."

Wolf stared unhappily at the stricken expression on Grandfather's face.

"Natasha Gorski?" Grandfather asked.

"She was unhurt. The czar's men took her with them. A prisoner."

"Where?"

"To the czar's palace. We had no means to prevent them from taking her. Your father was a good man, betrayed by his enemies. We would have hidden him and his daughter if we'd had any warning the soldiers were coming. You must be on your guard against them." His glance shifted to Wolf, then back to Grandfather. "I can offer you and the boy shelter for the night."

Wolf and Grandfather spent the night in the man's barn. In the dark, Wolf heard weeping and huddled into the straw, frightened. Grandfather was his protector, strong and valiant, afraid of nothing. Why was he crying like a child?

Finally unable to bear the sound, Wolf uncurled and touched Grandfather timidly on the shoulder. Grandfather started, then pulled Wolf into his arms, holding him close.

"You're shivering," Grandfather said hoarsely. "Are you cold?"

"Scared."

"Don't be." Grandfather's voice grew stronger. "I won't let the soldiers capture you."

Wolf didn't know how to explain it wasn't soldiers he feared.

"I hoped we'd find a home here, you and me," Grandfather said. "How foolish I was to believe I might ever find a home. We can't stay in St. Petersburg or any place near the city." His tone grew grim. "But I'm not leaving without Natasha."

Wolf knew the czar was the headman of Russia and that he lived in a big house called a palace. He'd seen soldiers with long guns resting against their shoulders marching in St. Petersburg and understood a soldier's job was to kill the czar's enemies.

"No gun, you," he said to Grandfather.

"One gun against so many would be useless. I'll have to use my wits." Grandfather's laugh was harsh. "For whatever they're worth."

Wolf clutched his hand.

"Don't worry," Grandfather assured him, "I'll rescue

Natasha somehow. Didn't I rescue you? But you must stay here with the man who helped us while I go to the city. His name is Gregor. He'll be kind to you if—well, he's a good man.''

Wolf clutched harder. ''I go with you.''

Grandfather loosened Wolf's desperate hold. ''Listen to me. You're a strong and brave boy. You survived in the pen and you survived our journey here. If anything happens to me, you will survive with Gregor. Do you understand?''

Wolf didn't want to say yes, but he nodded once, reluctantly.

Dark as it was, Grandfather must have seen the nod. ''Good,'' he said. ''Now I must tell you a secret I hoped not to burden you with until you were older. Listen very carefully and try not to be afraid.''

Wolf didn't think he wanted to hear this secret, but Grandfather hadn't asked how he felt about it.

''I am a Volek,'' Grandfather went on, ''and because you are my grandson, *you* are a Volek. Though the Kamchadals treated you as a beast, you are not one, nor ever will be. I am different. Inside me a beast lives, a terrible ravening monster more dangerous than any wolf or bear. I've learned how to keep him inside so you and others are safe from him, but he is forever there, waiting to escape, to kill.

''You will grow into a man and desire a woman because that is the way of the world. Though you're not a beast yourself, you can pass on my inner beast to your children. This is the dark misfortune I've given to you, Wolf—the ability to father a beast. You must never have children! Never! Promise you will heed me.''

Wolf tried to digest what he'd been told, but his mind roiled in confusion. He'd been reviled by the people in his village as a beast. Grandfather had freed him and insisted he was a boy and must learn to behave like one. What was he, really?

Grandfather gave him a little shake. ''Promise me!''

''I promise,'' he said, not certain exactly what he was agreeing to but wanting to please Grandfather and frightened by the knowledge that there really was a beast inside Grandfather, after all.

In the morning Sergei spoke to Gregor, asking him to care for Wolf.

Gregor nodded. ''It happens I have no son, sir. Only

daughters. I will watch over the boy as though he were my own.''

As Sergei rode off on one of Gregor's rawboned mares, he was conscious of Wolf's dark eyes watching him. He knew the boy must be terrified, being left in a strange place with a strange man, but there was no help for it. If all went well, Sergei would be back. If not, Wolf at least had a home.

Natasha had been taken to the Winter Palace in St. Petersburg. Gregor, though, said that Czar Alexander and his family were not in residence there but were visiting their estate in the Crimea. Gregor suspected the killing of Sergei's father and abduction of Natasha had been by order of Count Antoshkin, an intimate of Czar Alexander, and known to be an enemy of the Voleks.

''It's said that some years ago your sister refused the count's suit in order to marry another,'' Gregor had added. ''After her wedding to Ivan Gorski, the count vowed to exterminate the Voleks, one and all. Antoshkin knows of your return to Russia. Beware the trap he's set for you.''

With Natasha as bait, Sergei thought as he neared the city on his swaybacked horse. He'd chosen the horse because she reminded him of another horse, one from his missing years. Where or when, he had no clue. But he felt that somewhere, sometime, a swaybacked horse had brought him luck. At the moment he needed all the luck he could get.

The Winter Palace would be well guarded. He must find a way to slip inside secretly, because otherwise he had no chance to rescue Natasha without being caught in the count's trap.

On the outskirts of St. Petersburg he found the road blocked by a throng of people crowding around a wildly gesturing man in a tattered deerskin tunic decorated with ribbons and iron crosses. Tiny bells hung from his sleeves, tinkling with the man's every movement. The garment reminded Sergei of those Kamchadal shamans wore.

''I see the future,'' the man shouted, his unkempt hair wild about his face. ''You are all doomed. Doomed.'' He repeated the word one more time with relish. ''Doomed!''

Noting a faint blue glow about him, Sergei tensed apprehensively.

''What do you see ahead for me, *iurodivye*?'' a woman cried.

An *iurodivye*! A fool-for-the-sake-of-Christ, a holy fool!

Sergei hadn't seen an *iurodivye Krista radi* since he'd been a child in this very city. Rich and poor, everyone flocked to consult these traveling holy men. Despite their dirty, torn clothes and eccentric behavior, they were invited everywhere, even into the finest homes.

Sergei studied the man carefully from his vantage point on the horse, above the crowd. Suddenly the holy fool glanced up and his mad, dark eyes met Sergei's.

"You on the horse!" he called. "What is it you hide from God and man?"

The holy fool saw inside him!

Conquering his impulse to turn and ride off, Sergei met the stare as calmly as he could. It was not wise to try to escape, for the *iurodivye,* if he chose to, could send the crowd stampeding after him. Sergei could escape, but he couldn't afford the undesirable attention the hue and cry would create.

"I conceal nothing from God," Sergei countered. "What I hide from man is best not to know."

The holy fool grinned, showing gaps among his teeth. "You can hide nothing from *me,*" he crowed triumphantly.

"Ah, but you are more than a man. Allow me my secret, if you will, Master of Fate."

After a long moment the *iurodivye* nodded. "Consider it my gift to you, unfortunate one." With a flick of his fingers he dismissed Sergei and returned his attention to those surrounding him.

Sergei sighed in relief and skirted the crowd, continuing into the city. He hadn't ridden far before his hand rose to finger a strand of the overlong hair he'd not yet cut. Neither had his beard been trimmed. He smiled.

In the late afternoon, the two guards stationed in front of the multiturreted baroque palace stopped a filthy barefooted wild-haired man in his tattered, bell-bedecked tunic as he attempted to shuffle past them.

"Holy one," the guard to the right said deferentially, "I regret that I cannot let you pass."

"God has called me to the czar's palace," the holy fool shouted. "Do you dare to defy God?"

The guards glanced uneasily at one another. "Honored one, don't accuse us of defying God," the right-hand guard begged. "We have orders to obey."

''Who dares counter God's order?'' the *iurodivye*'s loud voice caused passersby to stop. A crowd began to gather, attracted, as always, by a holy fool.

''The czar is away,'' the left-hand guard said placatingly.

The holy fool's eyes flashed angrily. ''I was ordered to the palace, not to the czar.'' He began to chant in a language that was not Russian nor French, spittle frothing at the corners of his mouth.

''He's cursing us,'' the left-hand guard whispered nervously.

''Let him in!'' a man cried from the crowd.

''Since when does the czar turn away holy men?'' another voice demanded.

''What goes on in the palace that must be kept hidden from a holy fool?'' a woman asked.

A window on the second floor of the great square palace was thrust open. ''What's going on down there?'' a man's voice demanded.

Everybody except the holy fool looked up.

''An *iurodivye* requests entrance, sir,'' the right-hand guard said.

''Well, then, have someone escort him in, you stupid peasants.'' The window slammed shut.

''I have said there is suffering here,'' the holy fool muttered as he stalked along a lamp-lit corridor on the palace's second floor, a guard at his side. ''It is God's will I tend to the suffering.''

''Honored one,'' the guard said, ''you have been through every room on the ground floor and those that are not private on the second. No one suffers here.''

The holy fool's amber eyes blazed. ''You lie!''

The guard's shoulders shifted uneasily.

The holy fool stopped, glaring at him. ''When you lie to me, you lie to God.''

The guard's prominent Adam's apple rose and fell as he swallowed nervously. ''I dare not speak further, holy one,'' he whispered.

''After God turns His face from you, do not expect me to help when you suffer the torments of hell.''

The guard's face blanched.

''I feel her suffering.'' The holy fool spoke softly, but his voice vibrated with passion. "In here." He clenched a fist over his heart.

The guard made a strangled noise. "You *do* know!"

"God knows all. I obey His orders. Where is she?"

The guard glanced over his shoulder, indecision and fear on his face. "On the top floor," he whispered finally. "The third door to the left from the top of the stairway." He pointed along the corridor. "But you must go without me."

The holy fool left the guard behind and hurried up the steps to the third floor. The third door to the left was locked, but the key had been left in the keyhole. He turned and then removed it and, carrying the key with him, entered the room, shutting the door behind him.

Natasha lay motionless and naked among soiled, blood-stained covers on a bed shaped like a sleigh. She was sprawled on her face, her legs and arms askew like a doll flung down in anger. For a long, terrible moment, he thought he was too late, that she was dead. Then he detected a faint life force.

He rushed to her side, aware he had no time to waste, no time to find out how badly she was injured—already he sensed someone approaching. She moaned when he wrapped a quilt around her, but she didn't rouse. To leave his hands free, he eased her over one shoulder. Quickly crossing the room, he reached for the doorknob, but before he touched it, the knob turned.

He stepped back barely in time to avoid being struck when the door was flung open.

A tall, white-bearded fat man of about sixty faced him. The man held up a hand. "You will remain where you are," he ordered.

Frozen in place by what he glimpsed on the man's palm, the holy fool said nothing at all. A red pentacle. On whose hand had he seen such a dreadful symbol before?

"You, I am sure," the man said, "are not an *iurodivye* for all your wretched garb and religious prattle. You are, I have no doubt, Sergei Volek. I congratulate you on your ingenuity, little use though it proved to be. No man outwits Count Antoshkin."

Though he realized the masquerade was over, Sergei admitted nothing. "I came for Natasha Gorski," he said. "I will leave with her."

The count smiled and gestured toward the corridor. Sergei had already sensed men gathering there. Guards. Armed. Six of them.

"Natasha is mine," Count Antoshkin said. "I have no intention of letting her go. My men have already enjoyed her. Before I finish with Sonya's daughter, the czar's entire army will have used her. As for you, Volek spawn—"

A growl rumbled deep in Sergei's throat. His sister's daughter violated? Treated like a common whore?

"I'll kill you," he howled.

The count laughed and motioned the guards forward. He pointed to one man. "You. Take the girl from him. She's yours for the moment." He gestured to the rest. "Hold him so he can watch how Voleks deserve to be treated."

Fury clouded Sergei's mind as the soldiers advanced toward him. He stepped back, his gut twisting agonizingly. He dropped Natasha on the bed. Bells tinkled wildly as he tore off the ragged tunic and snarled at the men.

"Jesus!" a man exclaimed, his voice raw with terror.

Free! He sprang at the first man, slashing with his fangs, rending with his talons, tasting blood, man-flesh, hearing hoarse screams, smelling the stench of fear as the others tried to run from him.

"Stupid peasants!" a man shouted. "Use your guns!"

His enemy! Slashing right and left, the beast forced his way through the fleeing men until he reached the enemy. His vision clouded by the red of bloodlust, he leaped for his enemy's throat, hearing the satisfying death gurgle as the man's hot blood ran into his mouth. Foul-tasting! He spat out the blood. A gun roared, but he felt no bullet's sting. He whirled, sprang. The man dropped the gun and ran. He overtook and killed him. Not one of the seven escaped death.

When no man was left to kill, he trotted back into the room and sniffed at the only live human remaining. A woman. She didn't move. He growled, hesitating, the bloodlust fading. She didn't threaten him. Why kill her?

He didn't belong inside. The forest was his home. Humans were not his proper prey. He must escape from this human dwelling. As he started for the door, bells tinkled under his feet, startling him, confusing him.

Where was the moon? He needed the moon to stay free. He must run free! He must. . . .

* * *

Sergei stood in the middle of the room, dazed and naked, his feet tangled in filthy rags. No, not rags, he realized as his mind cleared. A holy fool's tunic.

Natasha!

She lay across the bed, rolled into a blanket.

Two dead guards sprawled near the door, their throats torn and bloody.

The beast! Sergei took a deep breath. Thank God the beast had spared Natasha. He must flee with her. Now!

Not naked. Not as the holy fool. How? Sergei glanced around and nodded.

A few moments later, dressed in a dead guard's uniform, carrying Natasha, now completely hidden inside the rolled quilt, he stepped into the corridor. Four more dead guards lay between him and the stairs. On the stairs he stepped over the maimed body of Count Antoshkin and smiled grimly.

Death came to those who underestimated this particular Volek.

He strode through the palace without being stopped and finally reached a back entrance. Once he was free of the palace, finding his way to where he'd left the mare was simple enough. He held Natasha across his thighs as he rode from St. Petersburg under an overcast night sky.

Not until he left the city did he recall the pentacle he'd glimpsed on the count's palm. He'd first seen that symbol on Turgoff's hand, two days before the Cossack was killed. It had been Turgoff himself who'd told Sergei the name of what he'd seen, the five-pointed star within a circle. Red as blood. Red as death.

The beast had killed both men.

Why had they been so marked? The beast had also killed six soldiers. And at least one Kamchadal man. Sergei had seen no symbol on any of them.

If his father was alive, he might have known. Sergei sighed and shook his head. He'd come back too late to save his father. He could only pray Natasha wouldn't prove to be fatally injured by the count's depraved and diabolical revenge. And that he could somehow get the three of them—Natasha, Wolf, and himself—out of this country that murdered Voleks. Out of Russia.

To where? He had no idea.

Chapter 23

A week passed before Natasha was strong enough to travel. Even then, Gregor's wife protested.

"She doesn't yet have all her wits about her, poor girl." Arms akimbo, the stocky, graying woman glared at Sergei and Gregor. "Men are beasts, and that's the truth."

Gregor glanced at Sergei and shrugged.

Sergei nodded. "Beasts, yes, sometimes we are. But Natasha's in grave danger here and so are you for offering us your hospitality. The czar's soldiers may track us to your cottage. Each hour we stay puts us all at greater risk. We'll leave at dawn."

Just after midnight, Sergei and Wolf were roused by Natasha's screams. Wolf rose from the blankets on the floor by the hearth and hurried to her cot. Sergei remained where he was. When the nightmares came, Natasha feared the sight of any man and wasn't reassured even by the presence of Gregor's wife. For some reason, Wolf was the only person in the cottage she trusted completely.

After a few moments her screams subsided to weeping and, finally, murmurs, as Natasha babbled on to Wolf. When she at last fell asleep once more, Wolf returned to the hearth.

"Grandfather," he whispered.

"I'm awake," Sergei replied.

"Gold, Cousin Natasha says. Gold buried in shed. Shed with hole in roof."

Wild imaginings of a disturbed mind? Sergei wondered.

"Cousin Natasha says *her* grandfather buried gold," Wolf added. "In southwest corner."

Sergei sat up. His father had buried gold? If he had money, he could use it to pay passage on a ship for the three of them. Instead of a long journey by land, they'd quickly be free of Russia.

Provided they could board a ship without being arrested by the czar's men. And provided there was any gold in the first place. Still, given their desperate need for money, what choice did he have but to dig in the southwest corner of the dacha's shed? Now, before it grew light.

Sergei rose and pulled on his boots. At the door, he found Wolf at his heels. "You stay here," he ordered the boy. "Cousin Natasha may wake again."

"Watcher wait," Wolf protested. "Watcher catch you."

Sergei froze. He sensed no human presence outside the cottage. What did the boy mean? Was this watcher some Kamchadal superstition?

"No one's outside," he said.

"Watcher is." Wolf insisted. "Came at sundown."

Sergei closed his eyes, letting his extra sense roam free. Gregor and his wife, Natasha and Wolf, here in the cottage. Animals in the barn and their pens. Small wild animals of the night. No human glow near the cottage, none at all. He cast farther, with the same result. No humans.

"I don't sense a watcher," he told Wolf.

"I feel him."

The boy had never lied to him. Sergei didn't believe he was lying now. He knew Wolf couldn't sense energy glows because he'd tried, and failed, to teach him how. In any case, there *was* no energy glow outside. What in hell did the boy sense?

"Did your mother tell you tales of spirit watchers?" Sergei asked.

"Kut."

In the Kamchadal tales, Raven, old Kut the trickster, was master of the world. Maybe Wolf believed Kut had followed them from Kamchatka. "Is it Raven waiting for us, then?"

"No. Man. Killer."

The hair rose on Sergei's nape. He laid a hand on Wolf's shoulder. "How can you tell?"

"I feel him." Wolf touched his forehead. "First little. Now strong. Dark." Sergei felt a shudder run through the boy.

He thought of Wolf's unusual violet glow and took a deep breath. He may have uncovered the boy's talent. But if he had, who or what waited in the dark? Never had Sergei met any human—or even a witch—he couldn't sense.

Or had he? In the back of his mind doubt flickered. There'd been a night somewhere in those missing years, a night when someone stalked him, someone he hadn't sensed. Try as he might, he couldn't bring back the memory.

He eased the door open and peered into the night. The last quarter of the moon was rising above the spruce grove on the hill, casting a pale light. Gregor's dogs, chained beside the barn, made no sound. He couldn't believe whatever it was that waited didn't have a scent. That meant the watcher wasn't close enough to alert the dogs.

"We need the gold," he told Wolf. "If it's there. I can't risk going near the dacha during the day, when I might be seen. The digging must be done tonight."

"You dig. I watch."

Sergei conceded the point. Under the circumstances, he needed Wolf with him.

Sergei's Kamchadal dagger was sheathed in his boot and Wolf would assure he wasn't taken by surprise. He'd also borrow Gregor's spade from the barn.

"One watcher?" he asked Wolf.

Wolf nodded.

Damn it, Sergei Volek was more than a match for one!

On foot, they reached the shed on the dacha property with no interference. Its door was missing and Sergei stationed Wolf at the open entry while he wielded the spade. He'd dug about two feet down when the blade grated on metal. Probing carefully, Sergei uncovered a tin canister smelling faintly of tobacco. A mental image of Alexis with his pipe gave Sergei a pang. Inside was a bag of gold coins.

Thank you, Father, he said silently.

Without counting the coins, Sergei crammed the bag into his pocket. "Let's go," he told Wolf.

They were halfway back to the cottage when Wolf, trotting along beside Sergei, suddenly grasped his arm. "Ahead," he whispered urgently. "He hides behind trees."

To skirt the spruce grove would take them far out of their way. With no guarantee the watcher wouldn't stalk them.

"Whatever happens, you run to Gregor," he ordered Wolf, then shifted the spade to his left hand, eased the dagger from his boot, and strode on, all senses alert.

Wolf gave a strangled squeak of alarm. Sergei tensed.

From the corner of his eye he saw a dark figure leap from behind a spruce. Moonlight gleamed on the attacker's knife blade. Sergei twisted to meet him. Too late to swing the spade. Sergei flung it aside and threw up his left arm.

"Die, *oborot*!" the man shouted as his knife plunged down, missing Sergei's chest but slicing into Sergei's arm above the elbow. Agony ran red-hot along Sergei's nerves.

Silver!

He snarled in rage and pain, thrusting the sharp Kamchadal dagger into his attacker's chest once, twice. As the man staggered back, the dagger embedded in his flesh, Sergei saw the spade glance off his head. Wolf!

The attacker turned toward the boy who was still holding the spade. Sergei leaped, hooked his right arm around the man's neck and yanked, hard. Bones cracked.

"Dead," Wolf said moments later as they stood in the moonlight over the attacker's motionless body.

Sergei retrieved his dagger and plunged the blade into the earth to cleanse it of blood, wincing with the throbbing, burning pain in his left arm. He studied the dead man.

Bearded, dark hair and eyes. Maybe thirty. An ordinary-looking Russian dressed in ordinary clothes. With no more energy aura alive than dead, an extraordinary trait. A man who'd stalked him and tried to kill him with a silver knife. A man who called him a shapeshifter.

He was certain he'd never seen the stalker before; the man was a total stranger.

"Do you feel any other stalkers?" he asked Wolf.

"No."

"We must leave as soon as we reach the cottage."

Wolf nodded.

By the time they got to Gregor's, Sergei had his teeth clenched against the agony from the silver knife wound. Gregor's wife cleansed and bound his injury, but though the bleeding stopped, he could scarcely use his arm. He felt sickness spreading through him.

Urgency thrummed in him. After listening to his father's story, he'd dreamed of exploring what was left of the ancient forests that had sheltered his forebears, in an effort to trace what had created beings like himself. No more. Who knew what other perils lurked here in Russia? They must leave this dangerous, malevolent country without delay or they'd all perish.

"Natasha will ride with you on your pony," he told Wolf. "If I can't help her get aboard the ship, you must. Do you understand?"

Wolf, his eyes wide and solemn in the lamplight, nodded once.

The trip to St. Petersburg's port was a nightmare of pain. Somehow Sergei managed to buy passage for the three of them on the three-master *Silver Gull,* but he didn't recall boarding the ship, nor the first two days of the voyage.

When he came to himself, he was sprawled on a lower bunk in a tiny cabin, weak and parched. The first thing he saw was Natasha's concerned face hovering over him. Then he noticed Wolf crouched at the foot of the bunk.

"Thirsty," Sergei croaked.

"Thank God you've come back to us!" Natasha cried, reaching for the water carafe.

Wolf beamed at him.

After that, Sergei rapidly got well. His poisoning from the silver and his need for care had apparently sparked Natasha's recovery. Though she never smiled, she was once more in possession of her senses. They shared one cabin, she and Wolf in the upper bunk, he in the lower until he improved enough to insist on switching to the upper.

"You spoke of California when you were delirious," Natasha said. "Is that where we're going to live?"

"I don't know," he told her. The ship, he knew, was bound for Brazil. When he'd booked passage, he'd been too sick to care about its destination, as long as it was away from Russia.

Brazil was as good as anywhere, perhaps better than California.

The moon waxed. On the evening it was two nights away from full, Sergei, along on the aft deck, began his protective chant in the language unfamiliar to him.

"*Suomilaino?*" a voice called from above him.

Sergei stopped chanting and glanced up. He'd been aware sailors were in the rigging but hadn't realized he'd be overheard.

"Sorry," he said in Russian. "I don't understand you."

The sailor, a blond man about Sergei's age, climbed down to the deck. "I heard you speaking Finn," the sailor said in accented Russian. "I thought you might be one, like me."

Sergei shook his head.

"You don't understand Finnish at all?" the sailor persisted.

"Afraid not."

The sailor took off his cap and scratched his head. "You sure as hell sounded like some *noita* casting a spell."

The strange word hit Sergei like a hammer blow. "A what?" he managed to ask.

"*Noita.* You'd call them wizards. Sorry to bother you." The sailor gave him a salute, put on his hat, and sauntered off.

"*Noita.*" Sergei repeated the word to himself. "*Noita.*" A woman's face shimmered in the air before him, a beautiful woman with moonlit hair and silver eyes.

"Come home," she whispered. "Come home to me. To Liisi."

As her image dissolved, disappearing, an avalanche of memories crashed over Sergei, sending him staggering against the rail: Liisi—his beautiful *noita* wife. Mima. California—his home. Events from his twenty-five missing years rocked him. Love. Marriage. Death. The war. Californios. Dr. Kellogg.

How could he have forgotten?

When he recovered enough to move, he hurried to find Natasha and Wolf to tell them he was taking them home. To California.

Neither Natasha nor Wolf seemed either excited or pleased when he finished his explanation. Natasha began to cry.

"Your wife," she sobbed, "she'll turn me away."

"What are you talking about?" Sergei demanded. "Liisi would never do such a thing."

"The soldiers," Natasha wailed.

Sergei wrapped his arms around her. "It's not your fault," he soothed. "Liisi wont blame you any more than I do."

"But," she sobbed, "I fear I'm with child."

At her words, Sergei's joy deserted him. They'd never know who the child's father was, but that made no difference. Natasha's baby would be half Volek. With the dark Volek heritage. And, oh God, what if she carried male twins? He'd have to kill them.

"You might be wrong," he said hopefully.

Natasha drew away, wiping her eyes. "I pray I am wrong.

But God has turned His face from me and I feel in my heart prayers are useless."

"She pen me, your wife?" Wolf asked.

Sergei stared at him, not understanding what he meant.

"Like shaman did," Wolf added.

Sergei did his best to convince Wolf that Liisi wasn't that kind of a shaman and he tried to persuade Natasha she'd be welcomed, pregnant or not. But he couldn't share his fear with her, nor what the dreadful outcome must be if twin sons were born to her.

On a January afternoon seven months later, the three of them, on horses purchased in San Francisco, rode up a new road to the Volek stone castle. Sergei, impatient, eager to see Liisi, nevertheless noticed changes other than the new road. Granite columns flanked the entry to the drive and an evergreen hedge ran along either side. Green and orange globes of fruit hung on small trees—an orange grove!

He'd pictured his wife pining for him, weeping from the loss. Perhaps she had, yet she'd found time to make improvements. Sergei shook his head at his pique. God knows Liisi must have been shattered when he didn't return from San Francisco. She hadn't heard from him in three years. He should be glad she'd held things together. And even prospered, by the look of the place.

Did she know he was coming? He doubted it. He'd sent no word. And she hadn't been waving from the tower balcony this time.

Yet someone had seen them coming, for the front door opened before he reached it. A strange young woman wearing an apron over a dark blue dress smiled at him.

"Welcome home, sir," she said, stepping aside so he could enter. "I'm Belinda and I've been asked to tell you that your wife is waiting in the sitting room. José will tend to the horses."

Servants!

Sergei thanked her and ushered in Natasha and Wolf, shepherding them through the entry toward the sitting room. If he couldn't surprise Liisi by his homecoming, she'd certainly be amazed to discover he'd brought home a pregnant niece and a Kamchadal grandson.

He ushered Natasha, holding Wolf's hand, into the sitting room, his eager gaze searching for his wife.

He'd half expected her to come running to meet him as

she had before. She did not. Seated on an overstuffed couch, Liisi didn't even rise to greet him. He strode toward her, then stopped abruptly.

To either side of her sat a small boy of about two, each one with a thumb in his mouth. He gaped at them and they stared back at him from identical golden eyes. His eyes. In fact, the boys were completely identical.

They were twins. His twins.

Volek twins.

"No!" he shouted. His mind churning with agonized fury, he swung around and strode from the room, through the entry, and out the front door.

The horses were gone. He raced around the house and plunged into the pine grove, dodging trees, running, running until he could run no more. At last he collapsed on the brown needles, exhausted.

He lay there while evening shadows gathered and coalesced into darkness, his mind balking at what he'd seen, at what he must do.

The moon rose. When its first rays slipped between the pine boughs to caress him, Sergei sat up. The moon, a hairline from full, gleamed silver through the trees. He knew he must begin the chant, but the words wouldn't come. Yet he must. Sergei sighed and closed his eyes. He must.

A howl rose, quivering on the night air. His eyes flew open. He sprang to his feet. Wolf? Coyote? He shook his head, listening, searching through the darkness with his special sense.

The howl came again, a challenge ringing in the December night. Challenging prey? Or the night? Or . . . him?

Bathed in the moonlight, Sergei felt the first warning twist inside him. It was almost too late to begin to chant.

He caught a flickering sense of someone—something?—in the distance. Not human energy, not the blue crackle of a witch. More like starshine, faint and elusive.

What was this challenge from the unknown? The wrench inside him grew stronger, more urgent. Sergei raised his face to the moon, welcoming the silver light as it heated his blood. Soon it would be too late to resist what must happen.

In his heart he knew the challenge wasn't aimed at him, not at his human self. What called in the night challenged the beast trapped within him.

He was a responsible man. He had a fine home, a family.

Money. Many who depended on him. He was a husband, an uncle, a friend, a grandfather. And, God help them and him, he was the father of twins.

Because of a howling in the hills did he mean to turn away from everything he was? Everything human? Risk his own life and, for all he knew, the lives of those he loved?

He hesitated only a moment before ripping off his jacket and flinging it to the ground.

In the morning Sergei returned home wrapped in a blanket he'd found at the edge of the pine grove. It reminded him of that long-ago time in Nogadata when the beast had escaped from the root cellar and Mima had left a blanket in the woods to cover his nakedness after he shifted back to human. No doubt Mima had left this blanket as well. At least *someone* cared about his welfare.

He found Wolf and Natasha eating breakfast in the walnut-paneled dining room, sitting side by side at a long table meant to seat twelve. There was no sign of Mima or Liisi. Or the twin boys.

Wolf stared at him wide-eyed and Natasha, though she tried to be polite, sent frightened sidelong glances his way. She couldn't know what he'd done, but he feared Wolf might suspect that the beast Sergei had promised him never escaped had run free under the moon last night.

With . . . what? Only the beast knew.

Sergei winced at the memory of his bloodstained hands when he woke at dawn in the pine grove near the carcass of a half-eaten mule deer. The taste of blood still lingered in his mouth despite the many creekwater rinsings. With so much of the deer eaten, he had to have shared the kill with another, but he had no idea who or what the other was.

He might be better off not knowing, yet he'd never rest easy until he discovered what else hunted in the night when the moon was full.

Meanwhile, he had more urgent problems here at home.

"Where's my wife?" he asked Natasha.

"Upstairs, Uncle Sergei." Her voice quivered and she laid a protective hand on her distended abdomen.

Unable to reassure anyone in his present mood of mixed guilt and anger, he turned and strode toward the stairs. He was halfway up before he noticed Wolf trailing him.

"Stay with your cousin," Sergei snapped.

Wolf stopped, hunching his shoulders as though expecting a blow. The gesture made Sergei grit his teeth in anguish, but he continued on without another backward look.

Liisi wasn't in their bedroom. By following the happy sound of children laughing, he found Mima in the twins' nursery, where she was dressing them. The boys immediately grew silent. Mima glanced his way, neither smiling nor speaking.

"Thanks for the blanket," he said gruffly.

Her short nod showed him he'd thanked the right person.

The little boys eyed him with doubt. Sergei stood frozen under their golden stares.

"Hello," one twin said finally, his voice small but brave. The other boy echoed him. "Hello."

Sergei swallowed, memories of Vlad and their childhood closing his throat with grief. Like these two, they'd done everything together. Until . . . Sergei shook his head.

"Hello," he managed to croak. His gaze shifted to Mima. "Where's Liisi?"

"In her special room in the tower." Mima spoke flatly.

Damn it, did Liisi intend to hide from him among her casting stones and Finnish tapestries?

He left the nursery and stomped up to the tower. The door was locked. He pounded, ready to tear it down if she refused to let him in.

He heard the bolt drawn. The door opened. Liisi stood before him, the colored light streaming through the stained-glass windows turning her fair hair bloodred.

"Well?" she demanded, lifting her chin.

Ready for a fight, was she? Sergei pushed past her into the room and slammed the door shut. "Why?" he asked.

"One betrayal begets another." Her voice was as cold as the chill of her gray eyes.

"Betrayal?" His voice rose. "What in hell are you talking about?"

"You gave *her* a child. Why deny me?"

Sergei gaped at her. She couldn't mean Deer Woman. During his life with Liisi, because of his loss of memory, he wasn't even aware there'd been a Deer Woman in his past. And he'd fathered no other child. He started to say so and stopped abruptly.

Gettysburg. The hex witch.

"I thought she was a dream," he blurted, off balance.

"You don't make babies in dreams."

"But I—" He paused, trying to find a way to regain control of the situation. "How do you know there's a child."

"She sent word."

"You mean you got a letter?"

Liisi shook her head. "There are messages that have no need to be spoken or written or sent across telegraph wires. Oh, yes, she made very certain I knew. In case you're interested, your daughter is the same age as your grandson."

Ten. As if trying to smooth his disordered mind, Sergei ran a hand through his hair, then hastily clutched at the slipping blanket.

"Yet you run from the sight of *my* children," Liisi said angrily.

"They're twins." Sergei's voice was sad. "Wolf was a single birth. Like a daughter, he can only pass on the curse to his children. But identical twin sons—" He sighed. "I learned from my father that one will be like me."

"Is *that* all you're worried about?"

Sergei couldn't believe his ears. "All? All? God knows it—"

Liisi waved a dismissive hand. "Didn't I find a charm to control your changing?" She paused, giving him a level look. "When you choose to use it."

He glared at her, angry because of his own guilt. She had reason to be upset about his deliberate shifting last night but, damn it, to come home to unexpected twin sons would drive any Volek man past reason.

"I'll control our son's shifting as I did yours," Liisi assured him. "Which one is it—Ivan or Arno?"

It was the first time he'd heard their names. He smiled despite himself—one Russian name, one Finn. How like Liisi.

"I don't know," he admitted. "There's no way to tell until they reach manhood."

Her eyes grew bright and eager as she leaned toward him. "You must tell me everything your father said. Everything."

Her well-remembered enticing scent, woman and lavender, filled his head, banishing everything else. He'd been away from her so long. Too long. And, oh God, she was as beautiful and as desirable as on the day they'd met.

The blanket slid from his shoulders, falling to the floor as he reached for her. "Damn it, Liisi," he said hoarsely, "it's been three years. First things first."

Chapter 24

Sitting on the top rail of the horse corral fence, Wolf took a deep breath of October air, smelling the sweet scent of orange blossoms mixed with the earthy smell of horse. He thought California was a wonderful place to live, even though he wasn't sure Grandfather's wife liked him.

Mima had liked him right away and Wolf preferred her company to anyone else's—except for Grandfather's. He thought her smooth, dark skin was the most beautiful color he'd ever seen.

Ivan and Arno were fun to play with once he got over fearing he'd hurt them. Cousin Natasha's new baby might be fun, too, once she got bigger. All little Tanya did now was cry, sleep, smile, and eat.

Wolf himself enjoyed eating. He'd never seen so much food in his life as was piled on the dining room table at each mealtime. And everybody, even the women and children, could have all they wanted.

Mima was teaching him English, the language of California, and already he'd learned many words—far more than Cousin Natasha. She was only interested in her baby.

The great stone house still awed Wolf and he spent as much time outside as possible. He'd made friends with José, who tended the animals. José spoke yet another language, Spanish, and Wolf knew some Spanish words, too.

He was happy here, but he missed Grandfather. He wasn't sure why Grandfather had to go off and leave them. Grandfather's wife was still angry about him going. She'd argued with Grandfather the night before he left, the two of them making so much noise Wolf couldn't help but overhear.

"Damn it, Liisi," Grandfather had shouted, "General

Sherman's my friend. So is Custer, for that matter. Cump says he needs me, that it's vital I ride with Custer. God knows *you* don't need me; you've got a better head for business than I'll ever have. Hell, you tripled our income while I was in Russia."

"Business!" Grandmother's voice was as barbed as a harpoon. "Who's talking about business? I need you here beside me. The twins need you. And what about your niece and grandniece? Wolf? Mima?"

"I won't be gone forever. Six months at the most."

"That's what you said when you went off to war the first time. The second time you left you simply disappeared for three years—I didn't even know where you were. This time, how do I know you'll *ever* come back?"

"If I recall correctly, *you* left *me* while I was in the Union Army. How do you think it felt to come home and find you gone?"

Grandmother spat a string of words in Finnish.

"Damn the woman!" Grandfather exploded. "That hex witch affair was *not* my fault. She certainly won't turn up in the Dakota Territory. General Custer is fighting Indians, not witches."

"I thought you claimed to be a friend of the Indians," Grandmother said.

"In this country only the Havasupais are my friends. I have nothing against those Indians Custer is riding against—Sioux and Cheyenne—but a man must take sides. Cump and Autie are my friends. We've fought together. If Cump says I'm needed, I'll go."

"I saw that letter, don't forget. 'Like a thoroughbred horse, Custer needs the right man to handle him and you're the best handler of horses I've ever met.' That's what General Sherman wrote. Are you to travel halfway across the country and face hostile Indians merely to nursemaid Autie Custer?"

"Liisi, women don't understand these things."

"I understand more than you think. You've been home six months and you're bored. Now you've been handed an excuse to leave us again. Leave *me*."

Grandfather's voice softened, grew sad. "I don't want to leave you, Liisi—you're my life. But I do have an urgent reason to go away for a while."

After a long silence, Grandfather's wife had said, "The urge to shift has come back, hasn't it?"

Frightened, Wolf had put his hands over his ears and refused to hear the rest. He'd never forgotten what Grandfather had told him in Gregor's cottage, never forgotten about the beast that lived inside Grandfather.

Wolf had heard howling on the night they first arrived here and tried to hide, afraid the beast was loose. Mima had found him under his bed and held him close, murmuring soothingly. He was glad of her company, but without being told, he was aware that she knew, as he did, who the howling beast was.

If he didn't mean it, why had Grandfather promised him he'd never let the beast run free? And what was Wolf to make of the answering howl drifting on the cold night wind? Who was the second beast?

Here in the sunshine, the memory of that terrible night seemed faint and far away. Yet, if he turned his head, Wolf knew he'd see the darkness under the trees in the pine grove where the sun barely filtered through the boughs. The grove was always shadowed. Like Grandfather.

At least nothing had howled in the woods since he left.

Grandfather didn't return in six months. It was two years before he rode up one June afternoon on a big sorrel with a white blaze on its forehead. Warned by Grandmother of his coming, Wolf had watched all day for him. He sent Arno and Ivan running to tell everyone, then held them back when they would have rushed into the drive to be the first to greet their father.

It was fitting that Grandmother should be first. Wolf respected her; she awed him. He'd been relieved when she began to treat him as part of the family, insisting he call her Grandmother, but he never felt fully at ease with her. Like Owl Wing, she was a shaman, so never to be completely trusted.

He stared in surprise as she gathered up her skirts, flew down the front steps, and ran like a girl toward Grandfather. Astonished, he watched Grandfather rein in the sorrel, lean down, and lift Grandmother into the saddle, holding her in his arms while they kissed as enthusiastically as a courting couple.

He turned away, feeling heat stab through him, as it had

begun to do whenever he thought about women. He wished he had a girl to kiss like that.

Wolf didn't have a chance to do more than greet Grandfather until after the evening meal.

"Time for the men to retire to the study," Grandfather said as he rose from the table, beckoning to Wolf to join him.

Wolf followed proudly. He'd been pleased to find he'd grown enough so that his head was now level with Grandfather's shoulder. But his pride and pleasure abated when he remembered what he must reveal without delay.

"Liisi says you've been a big help to her," Grandfather said as he settled into his leather chair.

Wolf, standing next to the desk, smiled. "The twins mind me," he muttered shyly.

"Good. Come on, sit down."

Wolf perched on the edge of a straight-backed chair. He cleared his throat. Since he couldn't think how to begin, he blurted, "Something howls at night again."

"Again." It wasn't a question. Grandfather sighed. "Yes, Liisi told me."

"Mr. McQuade's lost some steers," Wolf went on. "He and the other ranchers think it's wolves. They mean to hunt them down."

Grandfather's golden gaze held his. "What do *you* think, Wolf?"

Wolf had never lied to Grandfather. He took a deep breath. "You know what howls. You once ran with it."

"It's not that simple." Sadness laced Grandfather's voice. "What I know and what the beast inside me knows are not one and the same. When he's loose I have no control, I'm not aware of what he does, and I can't remember afterward, when I return to myself. But yes, I suspect the one who howls is a shapeshifter like me."

Wolf nodded. He'd come to the same conclusion two and a half years ago. "They'll kill him."

"The ranchers, you mean." Grandfather clenched his fists. "What in hell can I do? After the last time, I swore I'd never shift again, swore I'd never come to myself with blood on my hands and its salt-sweet taste on my tongue. And yet I was forced to shift to live, there on that hill of death with Custer." He shuddered.

"I set the beast loose to kill men, Wolf. Kill the poor

damned Indians who were only trying to hold their lands. I had nothing against those men, but I doomed them to death. I'd rather die myself than allow it to happen again."

"Mr. McQuade will ask you to hunt with him," Wolf said after a long silence.

Grandfather dropped his head into his hands. "Oh, God, how can I track down one of my own kind?"

Wolf had no answer, but he did have more to say. "Some nights it prowls close by the house. Like it wants something."

Grandfather sat up abruptly. "You've seen the beast?"

Wolf nodded. "I didn't tell anyone. I was waiting for you."

"What did the beast look like?"

"Big. Sort of like a bear, sort of like a wolf. Claws. Fangs. Sometimes runs on all fours, sometimes walks upright."

Sergei recalled old Dr. Kellogg's description of the beast after seeing Sergei shift. "In other words, like me when I change," he muttered.

Wolf's dark eyes were solemn. "I've never seen you change."

"I hope to God you never do!"

"The other beast is a man, too, isn't he?" Wolf asked after a moment.

"He must be."

Wolf continued to stare at him, waiting.

What the hell does he expect of me? Sergei wondered. But he knew. I can't, he thought. I can't.

The only thing he could do was change the subject. "Have you ever sensed any more stalkers like that one who attacked me in Russia?"

Wolf shook his head.

"I've been meaning to tell you," Sergei continued, "that I think I came up against a stalker in this country once, fourteen years ago when I was in the Union Army. I couldn't sense him, just like at the dacha. He damn near killed me—would have, except Hank Ulrich saw him aim the gun at me and shot him dead before he could fire. I believe now he knew I was a shapeshifter and that he had a silver bullet in his rifle. He was one of our own men, a Union soldier. It makes me wonder. If there were two stalkers, there damn well might be more."

"I'll keep watch for them," Wolf said.

"Good. As for the beast, I don't see a way to help him. If I don't shift, I'd have to find him in human form. And where is he? Who is he? When he's a beast, even if I break my vow never to shift again, how do I know the beast within me could be of help?" Sergei stared at his hands. "All I'm sure of is that I can't hunt him with the ranchers. But I'll make damn certain he doesn't harm any of us."

"I'm glad you came home, Grandfather." Wolf spoke fervently.

Sergei's gaze assessed him. Growing, becoming a man, but still a boy. A boy who was too young to take on the responsibilities of a man.

Yet I rode off and left him here to do just that, Sergei thought with dismay, picturing Wolf sitting up on the nights when the moon was full, watching fearfully and wondering what to do while the beast prowled around the house.

"I won't leave again," he promised Wolf, knowing Liisi was right and that he shouldn't have gone away in the first place.

His efforts to help Custer had proved futile. No one could have saved Custer on that hill. Custer had been phenomenally lucky all his life, but there at Little Bighorn his luck had run out.

So much death. Soldiers. Sioux and Cheyenne. And the poor damned buffalo, slaughtered so the Indians would be forced onto the reservations or starve. It sickened Sergei.

Here at home, another child had been born, a child able to pass along the terrible unwanted trait of the Voleks. Little Tanya would have to be warned when she grew old enough. So would the twins. Sergei clenched his jaw. Damn Liisi for having them and himself for his inability to kill them when he first returned from Russia.

Unless Liisi worked another miracle with her charms and amulets, sooner or later he'd be forced to kill the twin who shifted.

Wolf's voice startled him; he'd forgotten the boy was in the room.

"Grandfather, there's something I have to tell you about the twins. Ivan's like Tanya and Natasha. Arno is different."

Sergei's eyebrows rose. "What do you mean, different?"

"I feel a shadow inside Arno. Like in you."

To Sergei, the twins' energy auras were as identical as

their appearances. Was it possible Wolf could sense the shifter before the boys grew to manhood?

"Arno," he said, musingly.

Wolf nodded.

Could he trust Wolf's perception? As he pondered, Sergei decided he couldn't bring himself to kill Arno even if he was one hundred percent certain Wolf was right. Not without giving Liisi a change to work her magic. They'd know if Wolf was right in a few more years. When Arno shifted.

"What we need is a wall around the property," Sergei said.

"To keep the beast out?"

Sergei shrugged. "Or in."

Two weeks later, Liisi persuaded Sergei to take her along when he made a trip to Sacramento to look over the new McDee Canning Factory. The small business he and Paul McQuade began was expanding so rapidly the company could hardly keep up with the demand for its products.

McQuade had been fascinated by Sergei's edited account of his memory loss and recovery and had offered to change the company name to McVee now that Sergei knew his real name. Liisi had advised against it, so Sergei had declined. She'd been right so often he couldn't ignore her advice.

They stabled their horses and carriage at Ulrich's in Thompsonville and took the stage into Sacramento, returning three days later laden with packages from Liisi's shopping. They were within a mile of home when Liisi, who'd grown increasingly uneasy since leaving Thompsonville, suddenly clutched Sergei's arm.

"Mima," she whispered. "She's in danger. Something's wrong, Sergei. Hurry!"

He whipped the horses. "Can you tell what's wrong?"

"She's sending danger signals, that's all I know." Liisi closed her eyes, concentrating.

What the hell could be wrong? Sergei asked himself. The beast? True, the moon was waxing, but it was still five days away from full. According to Wolf, the beast was never seen nor heard except during the peak of the cycle. But what other danger was there? Indians? Sergei shook his head. The scattered groups of Miwoks still living in the far hills hadn't bothered settlers for years.

Bandits robbed travelers on occasion, but bandits rarely

strayed from the main roads. None had ever been seen near the valley.

Sickness? Injury? A snakebite? There *were* rattlers in the valley and the hills. Mima knew how to treat snakebite, though. Was the danger only to Mima? Were Natasha and the children safe?

As soon as the carriage passed between the granite columns, Sergei shouted for José. What he got instead was Paul McQuade, running down the drive toward him. Sergei reined in the horses, the carriage rattled to a stop, and he leaped to the ground.

"That beast got Mima last night," McQuade said in lieu of greeting. "We've got a posse searching."

Dread left Sergei temporarily speechless.

Liisi joined the two men. "What happened?" she demanded.

McQuade took off his wide-brimmed hat and scratched his head. "As near as we can figure, Mima went out after dark without telling anyone. Natasha says that Wolf was amusing the children with games when suddenly he jumped to his feet, called Mima's name, and ran from the house. He came back an hour later. Without her."

"Did anyone see or hear the beast?" Sergei asked.

McQuade shook his head. "Stands to reason that's what got her. Night before last the beast killed the new cook the Haskins hired a couple of months ago. Didn't no one see or hear it that night, either. But they found footprints. Besides, she was mauled pretty bad. We mean to gun down that devil-beast once and for all."

"You go ahead and join the others," Sergei said grimly. "I'll be along as soon as I can."

Inside the house, Wolf confirmed what McQuade had said.

"I didn't see him, but it must have been the beast who took Mima. He didn't kill her; she's still alive. I feel it." Wolf's fists clenched. "I wanted to find her, but I had to come back. Natasha and the little ones were alone."

Sergei nodded his understanding and approval. "I'll find Mima," he promised, hoping against hope he'd find her alive. "You'll keep watch, Wolf, from inside. Everyone must stay in the house tonight."

"In my tower room," Liisi added. "I have spells to keep anyone and anything from entering that room. We might be a bit crowded, but we'll be safe for the night there."

Belinda was home in Thompsonville taking care of her sick mother. José didn't live at Volek House. His cabin was several miles away, not far from McQuade's spread. At the barn, Sergei found José eager to get home to his family before dark, and so let him go.

Did the shifter need the moon? Sergei wondered as he returned to the house. The moon wouldn't rise until nearly midnight, but that might not make any difference.

In the storage room he took down his rifle and checked it carefully. Turning to leave, he found Liisi waiting. She offered him a small leather pouch.

"You may need these," she said.

He loosened the drawstring and peered inside. Three silver bullets. The hair bristled on his nape.

"I had them made after I heard the howling for the first time," she told him. "They'll fit your rifle."

"I can't kill him."

"You may have to," she insisted.

"If I brought him here in human form, could you help him? Would you?"

"I don't know if I could. I'm afraid not. I was forced to help you because I was bound to you by forces beyond both of us. The twins are ours, so I understand how to help the one who will need it. But I'm not bound to this other. My lore does have limits and I fear he's beyond them."

"Would you try?"

Liisi considered. Finally she shook her head. "I'll do nothing that endangers my family. Remember, Sergei, how many we care for. They'd be helpless without us."

The twins. Natasha and Tanya. Wolf might survive on his own, but he wasn't yet a man. Reluctantly, Sergei conceded the point. Even if he found the other shifter in human form, he didn't dare bring him to the house.

Carrying his rifle, he set off in the early dusk, intensely aware of the pouch with the three silver bullets resting in his jacket pocket. His special sense surveyed the fields and woods, searching for energy auras. He had no intention of joining McQuade's posse because he'd hunt best alone.

God grant Mima was alive and unhurt.

True darkness was settling over the woods when he sensed someone following. He stopped, probing, rifle at the ready. Long, tense moments later he lowered the rifle with a muffled curse. A violet energy glow.

Why the hell was Wolf following him when he'd been ordered to stay behind to protect the women and children? And, come to think of it, how was the boy able to track him in the dark?

"I know you're there, Wolf," Sergei called.

He swore at Wolf as the boy trotted up to him.

"Liisi's spells keep those at home safe," Wolf insisted when the angry blast was done. "I had to come. I'm the only one who can find Mima."

"How did you trail me?"

"I always know where you are, Grandfather. You and Mima. In my head."

About to order him to return, Sergei paused. Why not use Wolf's self-proclaimed ability? The boy was already in danger simply by being in the woods at night with a beast loose. There was no guarantee he could protect Wolf, though he'd sure as hell do his best.

"All right, prove your ability," he muttered crossly. "Find Mima."

Wolf turned in a slow circle, pausing halfway around. He stood motionless for a time, then took a deep breath and started off. Sergei followed on his heels.

In the distance an owl called four times. Otherwise there was no sound in the forest except the soft sough of the wind overhead and the crackle of pine needles under their boots. Sergei fought his inner yearning to feel the needles under his bare feet. He longed to test the wind for scent and know exactly what animals shared the woods with him, longed to hear every night noise, no matter how faint, longed to run, hunting, his voice challenging all others.

You don't remember the running, the hunting, he told himself firmly. Only the beast remembers. The longing comes from him. When he runs free you're locked within him, you taste none of the pleasures, know nothing, feel nothing. Yet you're to blame for what he does because you allow him to go free. You have a choice; he has none. You are a man who knows right from wrong; he does not.

It's wrong to loose a beast on the world. Evil.

Wolf set a fast pace. As they climbed into the hills, the pines thinned. Sergei kept glancing up, fearing moonrise. If Mima still lived and the other beast remained a man, she had a chance.

They came out from under the trees and Wolf stopped.

Sergei caught up to him. Wordlessly, Wolf pointed to the jumble of rocks ahead of them, barely visible in the starshine. Somewhere among those rocks, mixed with human energy was a blue flicker. Mima! Alive!

But Sergei also sensed the white glow he'd noticed only one time before. In these very same hills. Before he'd shifted and hunted with the other. Now the other waited for them in his lair.

Sergei was certain the other could sense them, so there'd be no way to creep up and surprise him. A direct attack was the only feasible plan. Motioning Wolf to stay behind him, he strode rapidly toward the den he knew must be concealed among the rocks.

He heard a warning growl. Broke into a run. Reached the rocks. A wild-haired, heavily bearded man, naked except for a loincloth, leaped from an opening among them and faced Sergei.

"I'm here, Mima!" Sergei called as he halted.

"His wife's in here with me," Mima called back. "She's having a baby."

The other snarled and the hair rose along Sergei's spine as he saw the man begin to change. His response was immediate—the familiar wrench of his gut. Realizing he couldn't control what was happening to him, Sergei thrust the rifle at Wolf.

"I'm starting to shift," he told Wolf in Kamchadal as he tore off his clothes. "Barricade yourself in the den with Mima as soon as I lure him away." He hoped to God he could remember what his intentions were once he changed.

Free! And the other with him. He lifted his muzzle and howled. The other answered, the howls rising through the night, calling to the moon to shine on them. They needed the moonlight.

The other snarled at the human who scrambled among the rocks. He jumped between the other and the human. Men weren't prey. The other snapped at him, but he avoided the fangs. He was bigger, stronger. Older. He was the leader. The other must follow.

With a quick slash he tore a furrow along the other's shoulder. The other whimpered in surprised pain, giving ground. He growled, advancing, and the other snarled again but finally crouched, acknowledging him as the leader.

The moon rose and, with it, the bloodlust. Run! Run and hunt! He leaped forward and the other, his torn shoulder already healing, joined him. Together they raced down the hill and into the woods.

Two deer, drinking from the creek, sprang into flight when he and the other burst from between the trees. He chose the male, knowing the other would follow him. Together they'd run down the prey, taste the sweet hot blood at the kill, and then feast.

Caught up in the bloodlust, he was hardly aware of the men until he heard the crack of rifles. Behind him the other howled in pain and rage. He glanced over his shoulder. The other writhed on the ground. Wounded. The red suffusing his mind faded and disappeared. He turned to go back to the other.

Again the roar and stink of guns. A bullet stung his upper back leg, slowing him. The other struggled to rise, got to his feet, and wobbled toward the cover of the woods. Men followed him, firing their guns.

If he tried to reach the other, he risked being shot again. He wanted to help, but if too many bullets found him, he'd die. He turned away and, making a wide circle to avoid the men with guns, fled toward where he'd met the other, knowing there was a den among the rocks.

Through the woods, up the hill. To the rocks. He halted abruptly. Humans. One outside the den. No gun. He snarled warningly as the man started toward him. Not prey but enemy. The man advanced, crooning to him. He crouched to leap. To kill.

Froze. Too late he realized the man's words wove an unbreakable net around him. The man came on, still chanting. He touched the beast's head with something metal. Pain pierced through the beast's skull and he howled in agony.

Sergei found himself standing in the moonlight wearing nothing but his steel amulet. Which he hadn't had on when he left the house. His left thigh throbbed from a bleeding wound. Wolf stood beside him, rifle in hand. Sergei glanced from the rifle to his injured leg.

"I didn't do that," Wolf said hastily.

"But you did put the thong of the amulet around the beast's neck—and lived to tell about it. How in hell—"

"Grandmother taught me the right words." Wolf glanced

to the east. "I heard shooting—was it the posse? Did the other beast get hit?"

"If I was wounded, he must be." Sergei donned his discarded clothes as he spoke, ignoring the blood seeping through his pants leg.

He sensed Mima in the lair and another human. The other's wife. He had no idea where the other was now, even though he was sure his beast self must have run with him. Obviously they'd met up with the posse.

"If he's not too badly injured," Sergei said, "he'll return here to his den."

Using his special ability, Sergei scanned the area, sensing a weak starshine energy. The beast, wounded. He also sensed five humans. The posse. All approaching from the east.

What now?

As if reading his mind, Wolf handed him the rifle. "His wife can't have her baby," he said. "Something's wrong. Mima says that's why he brought her here—to help. But she needs medicine and it's at the house."

Sergei had forgotten the woman was about to deliver a child. Good God, another shifter?

Thinking quickly, he decided what must be done. "Can you find your way back to the house?" he asked Wolf.

Wolf nodded.

Sergei pointed. "The beast and the posse are coming from that direction. "Go the opposite way and take the woman and Mima with you to the house. Hurry!"

Moments later a young Indian woman crawled awkwardly from the den opening, with Mima behind her. "She's Morning Quail," Mima said to Sergei as Wolf helped the woman to her feet.

"You've got to get her to the house before the beast or the posse get her," Sergei said. "If you can make her understand, tell her she may die otherwise."

Terror distorted Morning Quail's pain-wracked features and he realized she knew what he'd said. Leaning on Wolf and Mima, she hurried away with them, walking surprisingly fast, considering her grossly distended abdomen and her labor pains.

Whatever happened, he'd done the best he could for her. Taking a deep breath, Sergei strode down the hill to the east, rifle in hand.

By the time he reached the beast, the posse was so close behind he expected to see them at any moment. The beast dragged himself along on three legs, the bones in the fourth leg shattered, with splinters poking through the blood-soaked fur.

He had no chance. Yet Sergei knew how difficult a time the shifter would have dying, no matter how many times the posse shot him. Sergei reached for the leather pouch in his pocket. Froze. The pouch was empty.

Belatedly, he realized that Wolf, aware of how silver poisoned him, must have loaded the rifle for him. He brought up the barrel. Aimed for the heart. At the last moment the beast looked up, fixing its golden eyes on him.

"Forgive me," Sergei whispered as he pulled the trigger.

His bullet pierced the beast's heart, dropping him in his tracks.

The posse arrived to find Sergei standing over the naked body of a young man with scabbed dirt- and blood-smeared skin and a tangled mass of uncut hair and beard.

"That him?" McQuade asked incredulously. "That's the beast?"

Sergei nodded. "He'd taken Mima to a den in the rocks—I sent her home with Wolf before I tracked him."

One of the other ranchers, a stocky red-faced man named Porter, slapped Sergei on the back. "Good shot. We winged him, but he got away." He squinted down at the body. "Some kind of wolf man, I guess. Could've sworn we was shooting at an animal."

"There was two of the damned things," a rancher named Renwick insisted. "I saw two with my own eyes."

"You and that rotgut you swill," McQuade told him. "It's a wonder you didn't see four." He bent over the body. "There was just one and here he is. Christ, the man's full of bullets. Look at that leg with the bones sticking out. Don't see how he got this far, shot up like he was."

Porter spat. "Hell, he don't hardly look human. Lived like an animal. He ain't gonna feel pain like a normal person."

"You hurt?" McQuade asked Sergei, his gaze on the bloodstained pants leg.

Sergei gestured toward the body. "His blood. Got it on me when I knelt to make sure he was dead."

"Anything else in that den of his?" Renwick asked.

Sergei shook his head.

"Mima all right?" McQuade asked.

"She was lucky," Sergei said. Fatigue from the shifting, the pain in his thigh, and the guilt in his heart made him wonder how much longer he could keep up his casual front. "He didn't hurt her, didn't even rape her."

Porter laughed. "Must be that black skin of hers put him off. Never fancied nigger gals, myself."

"We ought to bury him," Sergei said.

Renwick scowled. "Leave him for the animals to eat, that's what I say."

They finally decided to drag the dead man to his lair, shove him inside, and block the entrance with a rock. When they'd finished, Sergei bowed his head.

"May you rest in peace," he murmured.

Renwick frowned at him, but McQuade nodded.

No one heard Sergei's final, silent words to the dead shifter. I saved what I could, *compadre.*

I saved your child.

Chapter 25

"Thank God you're home," Liisi cried when Sergei, close to exhaustion after the shifting, reached the house. "Quick, in here." She all but dragged him into the kitchen.

Morning Quail lay on a blanket on the floor, her eyes closed, her dusky skin an ominous gray. Mima knelt beside her. "The baby lies wrong," she told Sergei. "Crosswise. The waters have already broken."

He peeled off his jacket, rolled up his shirtsleeves, and washed his hands in the basin of water on the floor beside the laboring woman.

"Bend her legs at the knee and hold them apart," he ordered.

When Liisi and Mima did as he told them, he knelt between Morning Quail's legs and eased his hand inside her. He found the neck of the womb open and, reaching farther, felt the baby's shoulder. He groped until he touched its feet and grasped them, turning the baby so the feet entered the womb's opening. He tugged gently.

As he pulled, Morning Quail's muscles contracted, shoving the baby into the birth canal and allowing Sergei to deliver it feet first. A boy, smaller than normal. Luckily. Otherwise he might not have been able to get the baby out. As it was, the child wasn't breathing.

He thrust the baby at Mima. "Do what you can," he snapped. Then he shouted for Wolf.

The boy came running.

"Hold Morning Quail's left leg the same way as Liisi's holding her right."

Wolf obeyed. Another strong contraction delivered the afterbirth. Sergei, looking at Morning Quail's still distended abdomen, frowned, a dark suspicion clouding his mind. He palpated her abdomen with gentle fingers between her continuing labor pains. What he felt confirmed his fears.

"There's another," he said, hoping his voice didn't show the horror he felt. Another set of male twins!

The second baby eased out headfirst. When he finally held it, squalling, in his hands, he stared down in pleased surprise. A girl. His father hadn't warned of any danger with fraternal twins, only identical males.

These babies would be carriers, not shifters. Although that was bad enough, at least he had them here, under his control.

As he rose to his feet, something clinked onto the floor. He looked down. The bullet from his thigh, thrust from him by his rapid healing. He picked it up and tossed the bullet into the kitchen slop bucket. He needed no extra reminder of tonight—the other's twins would be more than enough. Or at least the girl. He wasn't sure the boy would live despite Mima's efforts, and at the moment he was too tired to care. There were already too many children in this house carrying shifter traits.

In the morning he found Morning Quail in one of the upstairs bedrooms, sitting propped against the headboard of the bed, holding one of the babies. Mima sat on the side of the bed holding the other. Apparently the boy had survived.

Morning Quail had made a remarkable recovery. He hadn't realized she was so young, hardly more than a girl. An attractive girl with her sleek black braids, light brown skin, and dark eyes. After one quick glance, she didn't look at him again.

"Show him the cross," Mima said to her.

Morning Quail slipped her hand under a pillow and held up a metal cross about the length of his index finger. He took it from her gingerly, expecting the cross to be silver. When he found it was tin, he tensed, examining the cross closely.

Many years ago he'd bought a tin cross, not having enough money to afford silver or gold. He'd had initials engraved on the back. Holding his breath, he turned the cross over.

EMA/UK. Esperanza Marie Alvarado/Ulysses Koshka. Every hair on his body stood on end.

It wasn't possible! He looked from the cross to Morning Quail.

"Where did you get this?" he asked hoarsely.

"She tell you." Morning Quail spoke so softly he barely heard her. She nodded toward Mima.

"She's shy about speaking to men," Mima said. "The cross came from him. Her husband. It was his, brought with him to the tribe."

"My God," Sergei muttered.

The cross belonged to the shifter. Brought with him. Sergei swallowed. This was the same cross he'd given to Esperanza Alvarado, the best present he could afford at the time.

"Did Morning Quail tell you anything more about her husband?" he asked Mima.

"She said he was a gift from the gods, brought home to a Miwok village by the husband of a woman who'd lost her child. The cross came with him. The Miwok family raised him, but when he grew to be a man the tribe cast him out, then fled their village.

"Last year he stole Morning Quail from her people to be his wife. He confessed what happened to him during a full moon and gave her the cross. She was to hold it up to him if he tried to hurt her when he became a beast. Apparently the cross worked."

"Crosses never affected me," Sergei said.

Mima shrugged. "He believed this one to be a gift to him from the gods."

Sergei shifted the cross from hand to hand as he tried to piece together what must have happened. Don Rafael had told him that the son Sergei and Esperanza conceived had died. But what if, unknown to Don Rafael, she'd delivered twin sons and only one had died?

He wouldn't put it past *Tía* Dolores, devious as she was, to conceal the truth from everyone. But she'd be too afraid of compromising her mortal soul to kill a baby outright. It wouldn't be beyond her, though, to expose the living twin on a hillside to live or die as God willed. And there the bereaved Miwok father would find him. With the cross.

He thought he'd come close to the truth—the explanation of why another shifter existed. Tears pricked Sergei's eyes. *He'd* fathered him. And last night he'd shot a silver bullet into the heart of his son.

He stared from one baby to the other.

His granddaughter. And another grandson. Two more Voleks.

And he was the man who'd vowed never to father a child.

After a long silence, he glanced at Morning Quail and saw she slept. He hesitated, then took the baby Mima held into his arms.

"Which one do I have?" he asked.

"The girl."

"Has Morning Quail named them?"

Mima shook her head.

"Then I will. The boy's name is Stefan, after his great-grandfather, and the girl—" He paused. "Samara," he said finally.

The baby puckered up her tiny face and wailed.

Looking down at her, Sergei had the irrational thought she resented being burdened with the name of the ancestress who'd brought doom into the Volek line.

A surge of protectiveness flooded through him. He rocked Samara in his arms, crooning an old lullaby he remembered from his childhood.

"Sleep, my little one, my pretty one . . ."

Samara's sobs diminished and ceased.

"You sang that song to me once," Mima said softly. "On the riverboat."

He smiled at her, remembering. "A Russian poet, Lementev, wrote it. My mother sang the lullaby to us, to Vlad and me when we were little. Like you, Mima, I lost my twin. You and I, we share that loss."

"But we saved these twins," she reminded him.

Yes, Sergei thought, we did. Will I ever be sure if we were right or wrong?

Three years later, on a warm June evening, Wolf found his grandfather admiring the new iron gates built to shut the world away from Volek House and its inhabitants.

Grandfather didn't look fifty. Any stranger would guess that Mr. McQuade, two years younger, was ten years older than Sergei Volek. Wolf had to peer closely to find gray in the black hair and beard and Grandfather moved with the agility of a twenty-year-old.

Time hadn't mellowed him, either.

Might as well get it over with, Wolf told himself. Taking a deep breath, he strode up to him.

"Don't blame Mima," Wolf said. "It was my fault."

Grandfather turned to look at him. Wolf flinched inwardly from the sorrow in the golden eyes.

"I don't assign blame," he said. "How can I? If nothing else, my own past prevents me."

Wolf wondered what Grandfather blamed himself for. Wolf's mother's birth? Fathering the shifter he'd had to kill? Or was it something to do with the hex witch he and Grandmother had quarreled over before he rode off to the Dakota Territory?

"Now there are eight of the blood of my blood here at Volek House," Grandfather said, turning back to contemplate the gate. He paused, seemed about to add something, then shook his head, muttering under his breath.

Wolf thought he'd said "God help her; I can't," but he couldn't be sure.

"Of these eight," Grandfather continued in a normal tone, "Natasha is the only adult—though I suppose at sixteen you're close enough to be counted as one. The other five are infants and children. Innocent. Helpless. Their fate rests on my shoulders." He glanced at Wolf. "Did it ever occur to you that ultimately *you* will be responsible for the little ones?"

"No." He spoke the truth. Grandfather seemed indestructible. "I think of you as immortal."

Grandfather smiled wryly. "I'm sure shifters are no more immortal than true humans. I can testify that we age. Eventually I expect to die. When I do, you'll be the oldest male Volek. The patriarch."

Wolf tried to imagine himself as head of the family. He failed.

"Grandmother would never let me," he said.

Grandfather laughed. "You're right. But she won't live forever, either. I'm certain shamans and witches, like shifters, are mere mortals."

Wolf hadn't come to talk of death and dying—quite the opposite. He changed the subject. "We've always been close, Mima and me," he said. "This just sort of happened, with neither of us realizing it was going to. But if anyone's to blame, I am. You explained about the Voleks to me years ago at Gregor's house in Russia."

Grandfather sighed. "You were only a child. Still, you aren't one now and you should have known better. So should

Mima. My God, she's known what I am longer than any of you. Also, she's older than you and presumably wiser."

Wolf gnawed on his lip, looking at the ground rather than at Grandfather. "We couldn't help it."

"And Druse is the result. Another carrier of the Volek heritage."

"She's not male twins!" Wolf spoke hotly. He thought his newborn daughter was the most wonderful child in the world. "She'll never be a shifter. She's a perfectly normal little girl."

Grandfather put a hand on his shoulder. "Son, we don't yet know what Druse will be. She's a Volek, true, but Mima also carries unusual traits. Whatever Druse turns out to be, we'll love her, as we do all our children. But you must promise me you and Mima will never have another child."

Grandfather pounded a fist against the iron bars of the great, spiked gate. "I had this put here to keep us safe. The gate and the walls shut out intruders, even though the gate can be opened to let friends in. To visit us, not to live with us. Voleks can't afford outsiders living in the house. That's why Belinda and Rosa come in to work only during the day now and why José lives elsewhere.

"We have a terrible secret, Wolf. No one must ever discover what it is or every Volek, including the innocents, will be hunted and killed. By ordinary humans. Even those we once might have called friend. Never forget this truth. And never forget, either, that somewhere out there"—he waved a hand toward the road beyond the gate—"may be more stalkers, those who recognize shifters in their human forms and try to kill them."

Wolf stared at the gate. Thinking about his tiny baby daughter, he shivered.

"Our friends wouldn't hurt the babies," he protested.

"I saw innocent babies killed." Grandfather's voice was bleak. "I watched soldiers murder pregnant woman, babies, and children for the crime of being Indians in a white man's world. 'Nits make lice,' General Sheridan said to defend this atrocity. So don't tell *me* that Volek children wouldn't be slaughtered if our neighbors discovered what I am."

Wolf stared at his grandfather as shadows crept over the land. Spring peepers began to shrill, heralding the coming of the night.

"The safety of the clan comes first, Wolf. If you don't remember that, we'll all perish."

Wolf walked back to the house alone in the gathering dusk, leaving Grandfather by the gate. When he became aware of his slumped shoulders, he squared them with an effort.

Sergei watched the crescent moon sinking in the sky. Setting. The moon waxed; in two weeks it would be full, shedding beautiful, disturbing silver light over his world. Over him. Enticing the beast within. By luck it had been Renwick who'd seen him in beast form, seen two beasts on the night the other beast died. Since Renwick drank heavily, nobody took him seriously. But if McQuade had been the one . . .

He shook his head. A narrow escape. As Custer's death at Little Bighorn had proven, luck eventually runs out. He'd not take any more chances; he'd never shift again.

He'd begin this new decade by making this house the family's fortress, keeping them safe and outsiders at bay. All except Voleks—and Mima, of course—were outsiders.

He wondered what had possessed Mima to lay with Wolf without thought for the consequences. If she didn't know of herbs to prevent conception, surely Liisi did and would have given them to Mima for the asking. Wolf, he understood. The boy was at the age where his prick ruled his head. He'd been that age himself, once. Which was why Wolf existed.

Why the Voleks? he asked himself. What purpose, if any, was I created for? He thought of Ivan and Arno, his twin sons. When they're old enough, he decided, I'll tell them about the Russian forests and the mystery hidden there. Perhaps when they're grown it will be safe for a Volek to travel in Russia and they can search for our origins. For a reason. There has to be a reason.

He wished Dr. Kellogg was still alive—the only man who'd tried to understand the reason with him. But the doctor had died some years ago and now there was no normal man he dared trust with the truth.

Darkness settled around him. Peepers chorused, somewhere in the distant hills a coyote howled. God grant nothing but coyotes roamed the hills from now on. About to turn away from the gate, Sergei held, his special sense alerted.

Riders. Three horses, three men. He tensed, his hand

reaching for a pistol that wasn't there. He didn't go armed within his own walls.

Whoever they are, they're not enemies, he chided himself, but he didn't relax, his attention fixed on the road outside the gates. Whoever rode this way was coming to Volek House, for the road led nowhere else. He'd learned the hard way that night riders seldom brought good news.

He didn't have to let them in. He was damned if he would. He concentrated on their energy glows and frowned. One was different. Reddish, like a normal human, but shadowed.

Apprehension prickled Sergei's nape as he stood waiting, hearing the pound of hooves, then the creak of leather, finally a man's voice as the horses stopped. "Damn, there's a gate."

"Who are you?" Sergei called. "What do you want?"

A man slid from the lead horse and strode to the gate. "Sherman?" he said. "Sherman, is that you?"

Sergei, struck dumb, stared through the darkness at the dim outline of the man.

"Oh, hell, I know you've changed your name," the man went on, "but to me you're Sherman Oso."

Then Sergei recognized the voice. "My God," he said. "Guy Kellogg."

A lantern hung from a post beside the gate; matches were in an oilskin packet on a shelf below. Sergei struck a match and lit the lantern, holding it up. The man outside his gate was Guy, without a doubt. As he looked at him, Sergei understood why he'd befriended Guy long ago in New Orleans. Something about Guy reminded him of his lost twin. Of Vlad.

"I've searched the country for you," Guy said. "A man who changes his name is hard to find."

He turned, gesturing, and when two people walked out of the darkness into the circle of light Sergei realized he'd been wrong in believing all the riders were male. These two were women.

The elder, about forty, dark-haired and exotic-looking, had the odd energy glow. Concentrating on her, Sergei scarcely noticed the younger except to see she resembled Guy.

"I've come to you from Paris," Guy went on, "because I believe you're the only man in the world who can understand and cure her strange affliction." He put an arm around the older woman. "This is my wife, Annette." He gestured toward the younger. "My daughter, Cecilia."

Sergei nodded. "Sergei Volek." He gave no greeting, as much disturbed by Guy's words as by Annette Kellogg's abnormal aura. He wondered why Guy thought he could help. Was it because of Guy's damned artist's eye that had seen the underlying darkness in Sherman Oso? Or did Dr. Kellogg break his vow of silence before he died?

The clan comes first, Sergei reminded himself firmly. Whatever was wrong with Annette Kellogg could only mean trouble for the Voleks.

But how could he turn Guy away? Hadn't Guy's father saved Sherman Oso's life and his reason? Hadn't Dr. Kellogg proved to be a friend many times over?

Sergei took down the great iron key from its hook on the lantern post. He inserted the key into the lock and slowly turned it, then drew back the bar holding the gates closed.

Taking a deep breath, he said formally, "Guy La Branche Kellogg, I welcome you to Volek House. You, your wife, and your daughter will be my honored guests."

He tried his best to hide his dismay at his own violation of clan safety and his heart-deep fear of the consequences. Though he'd yet to exchange a word with her, Sergei knew by her energy aura that Annette Kellogg was not a normal human.

He'd invited her in.

Had he also invited danger and disaster into Volek House?